For Home and Hearth

The Tucker Clan Saga
Book One

Ethan Warrener

Copyright

For permission requests, contact ethanjwarrener@gmail..com.

Book Cover by Erin Parrot and Marcus Siebert

Illustrations by Marcus Siebert

Second edition ISBN: 979-8-9855309-0-2

For Helen Baker. I never knew you on this earth, but your compassion has continued to trickle down through the generations.

Contents

Characters

The Hollands

Mr. Phil Holland- Gunsmith

Mrs. Leah Holland- Phil's second wife, blood mother of Clive and Margaret

Ella Holland- The gunsmith's daughter, a couple years past marrying age with a shy disposition to account for it

Clive and Margaret Holland- Ella's younger half-siblings

Bill Puckett- The Powderman

The Taylor Boys

Amos Taylor- The clan's golden boy, a promising young man, Phil's apprentice guncrank

Harvey Taylor- The eldest of the boys, apprenticing at his father's smithy

Dale Taylor- The youngest of the boys, still shy of apprenticing age

The Drifter- Omar Walking

Mr. Elvin McDaniel- The Watchman

Ralph McDaniel- The Watchman's son and apprentice, a bookish kid

Mr. Sam Chambers- The clan Schoolmaster and Middlespeaker

The Brodys

Old Man Brody- The clan patriarch, few call him by his given name, "Salvador"

Mr. Job Brody- Local farmer and crack shot

Ricky Brody- Job's eldest son

Mr. Arnold Brody- The clan butcher

Mrs. Charlotte Brody- Arnold's wife

Becky Brody- Arnold and Charlotte's eldest daughter

Reverend Oliver Brody- The spiritual leader of the clan

The Fillmores

Mr. Rick Fillmore- Hunter and trapper

Victor Fillmore- Rick's son, of the same profession

Mrs. Sophie Fillmore- Victor's new bride, daughter to Bill Puckett and close friend to Ella and Becky

Dr. Jacob Bernhard- The clan physician

Mrs. Helen Bernhard- The doctor's wife and the clan nurse

Mr. Shane Bunton- The carpenter

Nigel Bunton- Shane's son

Mr. Alfred Bunton- Shane's brother

Bert Daly- The town good-for-nothing, a real ornery cuss

Melissa Daly- A young woman with an unsavory reputation before her marriage to Bert

The Grierson Settlement

Johnny Grierson- Head of the settlement, a mean, one-eyed son-of-a-gun

Edward Grierson- Johnny's cousin

The Coles- One of the prominent settlement families

<u>Families tending the outlying farms</u>
The Newells- To the south
The Hadleys- To the south-west
The Job Brodys- To the north
The Craines- To the west

<u>Other Clansmen of Note</u>
Deek Evans
Clyde McDaniel
Joe Garmen
The Finches

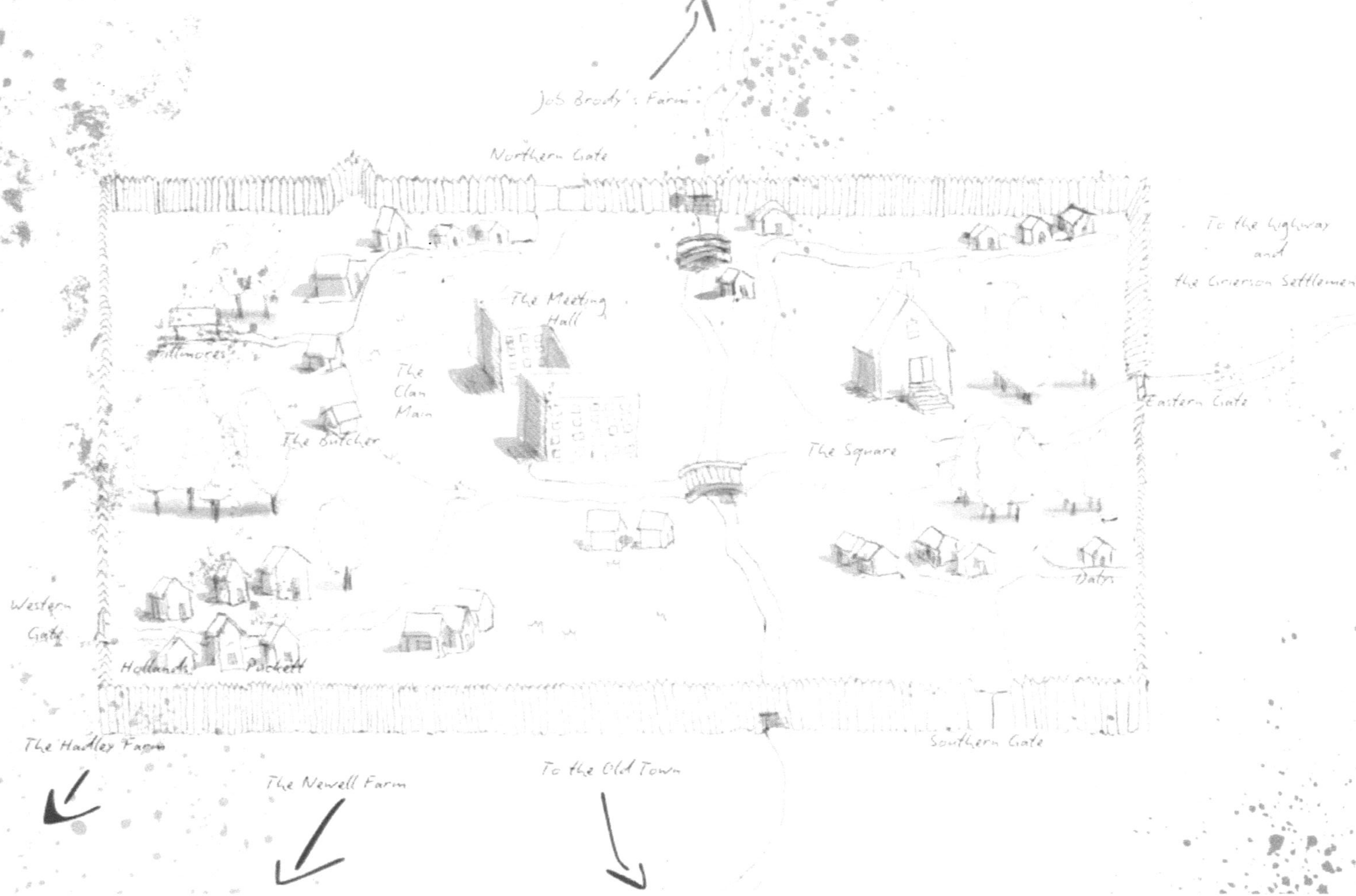
Job Brody's Farm
Northern Gate
To the Highway
and
the Grierson Settlement
The Meeting
Hall
Fillmores'
The
Clan
Main
Eastern Gate
The Butcher
The Square
Western
Gate
Hollands
Puckett
The Hadley Farm
Southern Gate
To the Old Town
The Newell Farm

Chapter 1

Strangers and Unbreds

Sparse snowflakes drifted down from an ashen sky to meet their brethren lying heaped on tree boughs and in shallow drifts. A haggard precipice jutted out from the tree line, facing the early winter morning that bloomed a pallid gray under a cloudy sky.

A lone figure stumbled out from the forest onto the cliff, a tattered cloak clutched around him. Hunched and shivering, he paused at the edge to scan the hill-rumpled horizon and gauge the distance to the ice-choked creek below. Something neither purely human nor animal bellowed deep in the forest, back the way he'd come. His hooded head snapped back around to face the call. Another howl echoed through the frosted woods to answer the first.

The man pulled the flintlock rifle from his shoulder with trembling hands and fumbled with a paper cartridge, only to drop the charge into the snow. He cast his rifle aside with a low curse and instead strung his bow. He waited with a nocked arrow, the shaft rattling against the yew, until the growing caterwaul in the forest banished all hope.

His hand went to the blade at his side as he sank to his knees. He ripped it free of its sheath and brought it up to his throat. He closed his eyes, took one last deep breath ... and stopped. He lowered the blade and turned to face the east, beyond the cliffside. He sniffed the air carried up to him by a teasing breeze.

The cloaked form struggled to his feet, returning the short sword to its sheath and unstringing his bow, leaving the fouled rifle behind. He swung a shaking boot over the edge, searching for a foothold on the flinty crag, crawling away from his stalkers and toward the scent of a human settlement.

The children of the Tucker clan gawped at the fresh blanket of snow so pure you kept from walking in it as much to keep from spoiling it as to keep your feet dry. Those Tucker boys old enough to heft a gun filtered out of homes and shops in buckskin leggings and padded coveralls, boots wrapped in plastic to keep out the damp, bows and rifles and muskets bristling as they gathered in little packs in the street. Their breath fogged the crisp morning air under the chilled, muffled glow of a gray sky.

The first snowfall of winter, lacking enough ice yet on the ponds or creeks to cut for root cellars, marked a new hunting season for the clan. Brown-furred rabbits stood out against their new white background, and the little critters were loath to run and soak their fur, even to escape a young man hankering for rabbit stew on a cold day.

Young Amos Taylor, though scarcely a month into his apprenticeship, found the same liberality with his master as the other boys. The kid was a quick learner, he'd put in good work for the gunsmith the week previous, and he promised to bring back enough rabbits to feed the master's family for a week. The gunsmith, likely craving some rest and solitude of his own, assented with the magnanimity of someone who wasn't coming out way ahead in this deal and waved Amos Taylor to the door.

At the back of the shop, the gunsmith's eldest daughter looked up from the yellow-leafed tome on medieval gunpowder corning and swept hair the color of wash-water from her eyes. She watched the handsome young man shoulder his rifle and lead his little brother out of the shop and into the snow to join the hunters waiting outside.

When Amos had gone, the daughter turned back to the book she'd borrowed from next door and pretended to read while her father lit up a pipe. He settled himself onto a wooden stool with a contented sigh and stared out the plexiglass garage window at the cotton-white neighborhood.

"Hey, Pa," she said, still fixed on the book in front of her, "seein' how all the fellers got the day off, and it *is* a Tuesday..."

The pipe popped out of Phil Holland's mouth and became a wand he jabbed at his daughter. "Oh, no, you don't, Ella. I don't mind you spending time with your friends, but we ain't got the rations to waste on any of your hare-brained cooking ideas. Everybody in the clan still remembers what you all poisoned us with last Harvest Eve."

That was a low blow. No one had *died*, after all.

Ella closed the gunpowder book and waved away the motes of decaying book-dust now churning in the lantern light as she turned a plaintive face to her father. "If it ain't good, I'll give up my rations and eat up whatever we make."

"Ain't you got the washin' to do?"

"Not in this cold snap. But I think Bill's makin' another go at the guncotton next door, and he might use the help if you need me busy."

That did the trick. "Uh uh. No way. It's bad enough he's got you grindin' powder over there, I won't have you spillin' acid on yourself or getting blowed to smithereens whenever Bill lets his mixin's get away from him. Go experiment with food if you want, but you stay away from Bill's experiments. Go on, go." Her father sighed and waved Ella toward the door. His voice held the resignation of a man who'd long since given in to the stubborn ruination of unified women, but who still feigned a fast standing out of principle.

Ella beamed as she only did for close kin. "Thanks, Pa."

The hunters had not left town by the time she stepped out into the snow, and Ella averted her gaze. She had a reputation for staring, despite her years-long effort to correct the notion. She'd always had a wide-eyed look about her, like she was either scared witless or over-awed by anything she laid eyes on. She snuck a glance back toward the gate to see some of the hunters, Amos Taylor among them, waving at her. She dared to wave back, and she straight away crossed the path of the oncoming oxcart they'd been trying to warn her about. When the oxen had settled and everyone else'd had their laugh, Ella tucked her blazing cheeks into the collar of her coat and trudged the rest of the way across town without exchanging a further "howdy" with a single clansman.

At the door to the butcher's home, she knocked as if afraid to break the door off its hinges. When no one answered, she ventured another knock. Sophie Fillmore—Ella still had not gotten used to Sophie's married name—answered the door, one hand on her swollen belly. "Ella! I thought it was you. Looks like the cold's got you apple-cheeked."

Ella could tell that her friends Sophie and Becky had started some time ago—amidst the ubiquitous wintertime tang of woodsmoke, she caught the sharp odor of whiskey vinegar. Ella stuck her head in the door and tried to unsnarl the other smells wafting aloft.

"I figured we'd gravy some turnips, Ella," Sophie said, foreguessing Miss Holland's question. "Come on in! Becky got pulled away to dress a couple chickens, but she'll be back to pickle some hogs' feet with us soon. We've been waitin'."

As if in answer, the cantankerous rumbling of Becky's mother thundered in through the open kitchen window from the slaughterhouse, followed by the daughter's gainsaid whinging. Mrs. Brody was the sort of woman always heard before seen. Young Becky Brody insisted she must have been adopted, and some Tucker clansmen were apt to agree when comparing the twain.

"How's Pappy getting along these days?" Sophie asked.

"I ain't seen him today. He's trying to cook up the smokeless powder again, and Pa don't want me near Bill when he tries that."

"He's been after me and Victor for our sow's dung, but I keep tellin' him our hog could flow like a river and it wouldn't be enough to suit him, as often as he comes over."

"I don't think it's the manure he's really after," Ella murmured. Bill's home had grown lonely and quiet in the year since Sophie had left.

Sophie leaned up against the sheet vinyl countertop, one fist on her waist. "Well doggone it, a girl's gotta grow up sometime. My Victor wasn't going to wait forever, and I was a-pushin' seventeen myself. I got a family of my own to take care of now." Her shoulders sagged a bit as she sighed. "But you get over there and make sure he uses the sulfuric acid fresh outta the 'still. He gets careless with that stuff unless someone gets after him."

Ella nodded. "It's okay if you miss him, too. We ain't more than a ten-minute hike across town..."

Becky entered the kitchen from the attached slaughterhouse clutching a bald, headless chicken by its legs. "Hey, Ella! Mighty good to see you again. What're you all jawin' about? Let's get the gravy started."

Ella motioned to the milk pail on the counter. "Only milk to add to it." She set a cast-iron skillet on the wood-fired stove to get some heat.

"Gravy oughta have more animal fat in it than that," Becky said, wrinkling her nose at the woeful lack of lard or tallow. "Did you hear my Pa's been takin' me shootin'? Says I could go on an unbred hunt sometime."

Sophie shook her head. "That's daddy-girl talk. You're liable to get your face carved up, lookin' for trouble like that."

"Eh," Becky waved Sophie's concerns away. "I already got me a man who won't care about a scar or two."

Ella and Sophie looked at each other. Though ludicrously unaware of it, Becky Brody was deemed the handsomest, sweetest creature ever to grace this earth by all the eligible boys in the clan—about thirty of them. Boys who hadn't seen her butcher a chicken.

Sophie crossed her arms over her belly. "Then why didn't you go out rabbit huntin' today, if you're so keen to spit lead?"

Becky wrestled with the dead bird to crack a joint free of its socket. "It's a *Tuesday*, Sophie. Gals before guys. The hammer on my gun's busted anyhow. I half thought Ella'd bring it with her today. Pa left some pigman teeth to pay for it when it's fixed." Becky gestured to the jar of misshapen molars resting on the sill.

"The sear's worn down. Amos is workin' on it." Ella answered. She flicked a droplet of water onto the cookstove, and, not seeing it sizzle, stoked the coals in the firebox and opened up the damper.

"Yeah?" Becky turned with renewed attention at the mention of young Mr. Taylor. "How's that new apprentice workin' out for your pa?"

"Fine." Ella looked down at the skillet. It wasn't hot enough yet to toast the flour, but she tossed some in anyway and stirred it into the trifling dollop of oil.

"Fiiiine?" Sophie asked, leaning forward to rest her chin on her hands, eyes wide.

"Pa's got a skip in his step again," Ella explained, still staring at the clumps of greasy flour in the skillet. "It's not like he's got his son back, but I haven't seen Pa so lively since ... you know. Amos has got the makin's of a fine guncrank."

"Uh huh." Becky said.

Ella bit her lip and turned away from her tormentors. She dumped a measure of milk into the hot skillet, and savory heat swelled up to warm her face and mask the blush in her cheeks. "You'll, uh, you'll be due soon, won't you, Sophie?"

"Don't try to weasel out of it, Ella," Sophie said, wagging a finger. "You're older than me and Becky both. If you don't start doing something soon, all the good men of the town'll be taken and you'll have to wait for a widower to show up. You won't get another shot like Amos." She sidled up to examine the gravy. "This is gonna thicken up too much. Hand me the milk."

Now that they had unavoidably brooked the subject, Ella rolled her eyes toward Sophie as she passed the milk. "He's been apprenticing for a *month*, and you're already plannin' my wedding."

"Ella's right," Becky said. "I think it's more romantic to wait longer." Becky clutched a bloody scrap of meat to her breast. The sight was enough to set Ella giggling.

"Don't encourage her, Becky. She's being too picky." Sophie stirred the gravy, tapped the wooden spoon against the side of the skillet, and left it to stew.

"I'm not picky; I figure most Tucker men would suit me fine." Ella returned to the turnips, plucked one from the basin, and cut it into chunks.

"What's the holdup, then?" Becky asked.

Ella shrugged. "It ain't as easy as you'd reckon it."

"Nonsense. You can get a man easy, but you've got to act like you enjoy the company. It's all about how you present yourself." Becky shook a severed wing at Ella for emphasis, bits of blood and fat flinging into the air. She ripped out the chicken's heart, crop, and gizzard with a sickening squelch and set them aside before washing her hands in a basin by the back kitchen door.

"I just ain't much at ease around young fellers."

"Neither was Sophie, and she got over that pretty quick. Amos is pretty near livin' in your house. You can put yourself at ease once you get used to a guy." Becky examined the gravy, made a scrunched-up face, and tossed in a bit of flour to thicken it.

Ella cut a bad spot from a turnip. "Amos Taylor don't seem like the kind of boy I could get used to."

"What's wrong with Amos?" Becky asked as if she'd been slapped.

"Nothing's wrong with him," Ella said, "except that he's just a little ... much for me. Like eating a whole pie by yourself."

Becky stared, blinking once. "I could think of worse problems."

Ella sighed. "We've ... We've got a bunch of turnips here. Reckon we could make another casserole?"

"Don't got any cream o' mushroom," Sophie said. She inspected the gravy and added some milk to thin it out. When she turned away, Becky added some flour.

"We can make some."

"Don't got mushrooms," Becky said. "Ella, I'm telling you, if you just fix yourself up a little—"

"Want to try mashed turnip candy again?"

"That was the biggest waste of sugar I ever did see," Sophie said, adding some milk to the gravy. "And I'd eat anything."

"Well, then I'm about out of ideas." With the back of her hand, Ella wiped away the damp collecting on her forehead. "We're not going to make a cattle trough of gravy for all these turnips, are we?"

"I dunno, looks like we're most of the way there," Becky said as she added more flour to the gravy.

Sophie fetched a couple jars to pickle the hogs' feet. "Ella," she said, "we don't mean to tease you so much about Amos. We just don't want you to miss a good thing when it... What the heck? Why is this gravy so thick?"

By mid-morning, out in the southwest woods, Amos and his eleven-year-old brother had split off from the rest of the hunters to chase down a rabbit trail. A mere ten minutes of fruitless wandering set Dale Taylor to whining. The kid had the irksome bent of wagering little and quitting early. "Harvey's already got enough rabbits to feed our whole family, Amos. Let's go back."

"What about the powdermaker and Master Holland, huh? They don't got no one hunting for them. Let's keep going." Amos was not about to give in to his younger brother's griping.

"Aw, come on, Amos," Dale moaned. "My feet are gettin' cold."

Amos crouched to peer through the thickets up ahead. "Shut up, Dale."

"Why couldn't we bring Burpy with us? Nigel Bunton brought his dogs."

Amos turned on one knee. "I said shut up, Dale! I swear, you want to scare off every rabbit between here and Gooseneck Run?"

"Yes. I want to go back."

Amos pushed his younger brother face-first into the snow in disgust.

"Hey!"

Amos pushed himself to his feet off his brother's back. "Keep belly-achin' about the cold, and I'll freeze your nose off, you lowdown wimp."

That shut Dale up long enough for them to make some headway. They crossed the wide spaces of old-growth forest unclogged with brush to examine patches of wild newer growth. Places that had once been a solitary driveway or trailer park were now, fifty years later, islands of viciously competing flora, shot through with thorny vines and poison ivy. The young trees sprouting up from them could not yet strangle out the riffraff and restore order to the forest floor. Nasty stuff to climb through, but perfect for finding small game, had game not been so scarce.

They came up over a crest in the woods and stopped at a steep embankment. Snow piled up in a round pillow, softening the landscape and hiding the edge of the drop-off, perfect for out-jacking an ankle if they weren't careful. They inched up to the edge when a movement in the mist between the naked trees caught their eye. Something rustled through the brush about three stones' throws off. Dale raised his musket.

"Stop, don't cut down at it," Amos murmured, "Could be one of ours."

The form slipped down the embankment about twenty feet and flitted out of their sight. Bigger than a rabbit. Could have been a deer. Amos and Dale crept toward where they last saw movement. They reached a small rock outcropping and sensed more turbulent movement directly beneath them, the shuffling of many bodies in the snow.

It could have been a herd of deer, Amos thought, but there would need to be at least twenty of them rooting around to make that much noise. He was about to peer over the edge of the snowy embankment when a low grunt rose from below. Not quite animal, not quite human.

A spasm of silent terror seized him. He didn't need a peek to see what took shelter under the outcropping. The image of their father's hand, shredded to a mess of bone and tendon, flashed through Amos' mind. He knew that grunt. Pigmen.

They inched backwards on their hands and knees, still unseen. No breeze to put them upwind of the beasts, but they were close enough that their nervous sweat would betray them soon. Some feet back from the edge of the embankment, they rose to a low crouch and picked their wary way back into the woods, back up the hill quick and quiet as field mice.

They made it about fifty feet before a hungry growl whirled the two brothers in their own tracks, and they knew they were in it. Dark shapes came forth from between the misty trees, giving chase to the hunters. Dale brought his rifle to bear and fired a wild shot that sent shrieks through the writhing brush.

"Don't shoot! Gotta leg it," Amos cried.

They ran, their deerskin-clad legs flinging snow into the air behind them. Behind, the shadowing figures multiplied and drew closer. Amos found his panic whistle and gave a harmsway call to warn the other hunters. The two brothers could try to climb some trees, but this many pigmen could get at them faster than they could climb.

Amos tripped over a fallen branch buried in the snow and knew he was finished. Frantic movement teased the corner of his eye as he turned to face the guttural pants. His hand went to his knife. A set of fangs flashed but never struck home.

Instead Amos glimpsed the blur of a skittering withdraw and heard a squeal of pain. Without giving a further thought to his wondrous salvation, he scrambled to his feet and gave chase to his brother. A short escarpment rose ahead. He pitched Dale on up with a shoulder to the rump and then vaulted after him. A hard, sinewy grip caught his foot before he had gained the edge, pulling him back down.

He dug his gloved hands into the dirt and rock for purchase and strained against the willful strength of the creature below. He heard the growling pants of other pigmen converging, all coming to eat him alive. He heard Dale cry out his name from above, helpless.

"Run, Dale!" Amos cried. "Get outta—"

A bow twanged from the top of the escarpment, and the savage grip on his leg unclenched with an animal howl of agony and rage. Bind-free, Amos clambered to the edge of the ridge, where he found a hand reaching down to help him up.

The other hunters, he thought. Thank God. But once on his feet, he beheld not his fellow clansmen, but a dark-haired young stranger with sunken eyes and a prickly face, still holding a strung bow in one hand.

"Hurry," the stranger panted, "'Afore they get to the top."

The party of three sprinted through the woods, Amos still blowing shrill warnings on his whistle. He cupped his hand around the whistle and echoed a call off a sheer cliff face on the other side of the vale. A few steps later they heard a return call from the top of the hill, perhaps three hundred paces off. The rest of the hunting party weren't far away, if the three could only reach them.

"This way!" Amos cried, already churning through the snow. "Follow me!"

They pelted up the slope, through the lonely wooden pillars of the mountain forest, the sounds of the chase behind them and the sounds of rescue ahead of them. Amos and Dale both called to the other hunters who ran down to meet them. Amos's older brother, Harvey, was among the rescuers.

"What it be, Amos?" Harvey called.

"Ready the rifles! Pigmen! Some twenty of 'em at least!"

"Muskets to bear!" one of the older hunters shouted. "Pigmen down yonder! Cut down at 'em!"

With eight able arms on the scene, the hunters leveled their weapons at the hunched beasts just entering their line of fire.

"Wai'fer a clean shot, they're a-movin'!" someone shouted.

Amos risked a glance at the stranger; never seen his face before. He'd dropped in on them like a stone from the black. The stranger took his stand with the Tuckers, having already nocked an arrow and drawn his bow with a hand quaking from fear or waning strength. The other hunters pulled back the flint locks on their muskets. Amos saw a clear shot about fifty paces off and fired. The smoke masked the trueness of his shot, but he didn't bother to check as he backed up, reloading. Others opened fire, powdering the snow with black soot, backing away while reloading to keep up the stretch between them and the pigmen and to get clear of the clouded gunsmoke. The war cries of the oncoming beasts gave way to the din of wounded yelps and howls. Amos struggled to slip the ramrod into the quivering barrel of his rifle and stuff it down through the smoky fouling caked into the grooves inside. A pigman could keep charging with a fatal wound, and battle often made them angrier.

The pigmen, with their ape-like, not-quite bipedal gait, crossed the close-fighting line before any of the Tuckers could finish their reloads, and a chorus of knives, swords, and matchets slid from their sheathes as other clansmen lowered their short spears. The pigmen were almost upon the hunters when a thunderous volley of gunfire took the charging unbreds in the flank, scattering them like pitching pins. Another group of Tucker hunters had arrived to answer the harmsway call. The creatures fled, leaving behind their dead and dying.

The assembled hunters blew on their whistles to warn any other hunters out there of the hunt's end. One of the young clansmen ran to the fallen pigmen with a drawn knife.

"What are you doing?" the eldest of the Brody boys demanded of the young clansman.

"The teeth. We can't just leave them—"

"Can't spend 'em if you're dead. We gotta get the heck out of here before more come."

The hunters took a head count before the sirens of eerie howls moaning through the woods sent them to their heels again. A throaty pigman call answered another call across the vale, and then another farther off. This wasn't a lone pack.

They made the mile or so hike back in less than ten minutes, forward runners mounting horses to warn the outlying farms. All through the woods, platoons of pigmen wriggled out of the brush like worms driven above ground by a heavy rain. The town had readied before the last hunters made it to the gates, and within twenty minutes every man waited by his home, armed for taking teeth. Here and there the pop and crack of firearms at the wall told of skirmishes that stopped the pigman onrush and kept the unbred line well within the forest bight west of town.

Amos Taylor was one of the last hunters through the gate. The mysterious young stranger had needed a shoulder to lean on, and once safe within the clan walls, nearly collapsed from exhaustion.

Chapter 2

The Drifter

Amos rammed a wet cotton swab down the bore of his rifle while he waited for the elders to gather. Outside, fear-riled clansfolk scurried to and fro, bearing arms, herding livestock, and fetching water and provender in a feverish clamor. Inside, by the dim glow of a lantern and the scant natural light that seeped in through the plexiglass windows off to the side, the stranger sat in a plastic chair, ringed in by Amos and other interested clansmen.

Such clansmen included watchman Elvin McDaniel, schoolmaster Sam Chambers, Reverend Oliver Brody, and a few on-hand elders, gathered around the young stranger on the split-plank pews of the clan's meeting-hall. The old high school was the only place in town big enough to seat the entire clan on a Sunday morning, as well as being the center of all official clan business, their marketplace, their last-ditch citadel and storehouse, and as good a place as any to question the stranger who'd dropped into their midst. Officially, he was no longer Amos' responsibility, but Amos didn't feel comfortable leaving the man who'd saved his life to the discretion of the elders.

Even after getting his first good look at the straight-faced young man, Amos still had a hard time guessing his age. The stranger could have been nearly thirty, and yet it was almost as likely that he was only a year older than Amos himself. He had dark hair, heavy eyebrows, hollow cheeks, and sunken eyes.

The eyes drew his attention—gloomy and deep, like two caverns concealing something mysterious and dangerous. In the half-light of the cafeteria-church, he seemed to stare at the world through empty sockets. His cheekbones, high and hard, formed the two points of a triangle that met down at his narrow chin like the point of a stone-head arrow. He seemed to Amos like a young man who, if he'd set his mind to it, could have stared down a raving bullhusker.

It had not taken Amos long to tell the elders what had happened in the woods, but settling on what to do with this living ghost was another matter altogether.

"Well," Sam Chambers—the clan's teacher, scholar, and middlespeaker—began when Amos had told his tale. "This doesn't happen every day."

"Oh, you don't say," Elvin quipped, the sinews in his neck spasming. The early wrinkles on the watchman's face pinched as he scowled. "Sam, I can understand if you want to sit around here on your butt wondering what to do with this feller, but I don't got time for jawing. Them's nigh-on a thousand pigmen ready to storm this town come nightfall, and you're pulling me away from the folkward."

"Um," the stranger murmured to Amos while the older men squabbled. "Did you say you folks was fetchin' me some food?"

Amos pulled the blackened swab from the muzzle of his rifle. "Yeah. Ella—that's my master's daughter—she's gone to scare up some vittles. She'll be here in a jot." The first thing Amos had done on his return was stop by the Hollands' home to air the news. Mrs. Holland had insisted on feeding the poor man found alone in the winter wilds.

"What's your name?" Elvin asked, the suspicious frown still etched into his face.

The stranger's lips moved so weakly Amos had to lean in to catch the words. "Omar. Omar ...Walking."

"How old are you, Mr. Walking?" Arnold Brody, the butcher, leaned in as well, propping an elbow on his knee.

"Nineteen. Where—where am I?"

Sam spoke up. "You're in the Tucker clan's church room, at the moment."

Reverend Brody spoke for the first time, skirting the outside of the circle of elders. Though at the edge of the lantern-light, his pale face stood out from the browned and bronzed faces of the other Tucker clansmen. "Where are you from?"

The stranger, Omar, faltered.

Alfred Bunton, the weaver, threw up his hands. "Aw, he's a drifter! We let a drifter right into the middle of our town!"

"Easy, Fred," the butcher warned, his hand reaching down to his hip as he circled behind the stranger. "We don't know he's a bad 'un."

"You don't know he isn't, neither! He isn't drifting for the scenery, I'll tell you that."

A matchet sailed past the stranger's ear from behind. The stranger flinched and ducked as the long knife clattered on the floor.

"Well, I reckon he ain't an ubermensch. An ubermensch would have caught that," the butcher said.

"Well, jump in a muddy crick to look for fish, why don't you," Shane Bunton—the weaver's brother—said. "I don't suppose that proves a thing. What if he *is* one?"

"Take it easy, Shane," Sam Chambers said. "You know full well we've never put together any clan policy towards ubermenschen outside of 'shoot if shot at.'"

"Well, this might be the time to bring it up before the rest of the elders. What if he gets the notion to 'purge the lessers?'" Shane drew his finger across his throat.

"That's a real fine notion, Shane," Elvin said, straightening up and crossing his arms. "Why don't we tell the unbreds out there to hold up a minute while we get all the elders together for a meeting?" Elvin snorted. "I don't got time for this. Kill him or put a spear in his hands and point him at the pigmen, I don't much care. I gotta see if the farmers all made it in, and Arnie, you get on up to the Griersons' settlement soon as you're able." Elvin walked out.

The weaver wove himself back into the fray, apparently unfazed. "I won't abide having some stranger with *unnatural breeding* living amongst honest clansmen of clean stock. In my mind, they aren't any better than pigmen."

Amos frowned at this but said nothing.

"I think we're hitchin' our mule backwards to the cart, here," the butcher cut in. "Don't most ubermenschen have blonde hair? And he *did* save Amos and Dale, didn't he?"

"Only because the pigmen were after him first, I'd bet," the other Bunton brother enjoined, "I'll eat my belt if it isn't so. He was betting we'd save his hide."

"Is that a bad thing, Shane?" the schoolmaster asked.

"It is if it leads a cartload of pigmen right to our doorstep. Anyhow, if he's a drifter, we can't let him stay, and I don't think he'd want to. Let him be someone else's trouble!" Shane jabbed a finger at the drifter, who stared at the floor, not answering the slander.

"Fred's right, gentlemen," the Reverend said, still lurking outside the circle. "Let us not forget what happened about five or six years ago, the last time a scruffy character asked for our stay-welcome."

The weaver nodded. "I say we stuff him with some scraps, pack his quiver, and boot him back into the woods before he marks what livestock he wants to rustle."

"We can't afford the extra food or the arrows. We've got pigmen coming. I ain't notching any extra arrows for him, for sure," the carpenter said.

Amos Taylor spoke up, turning the gathered clansmen toward him as one. "You kick him out, the pigmen will get him for sure. The forest is near overrun already. Might as well show a little mercy and cut his throat right now." The bite of sarcasm in his voice raised some eyebrows, but no one chided him for it. For one thing, he was Amos Taylor, and for another, they knew he was right.

"Aw, shucks," the butcher said. "We wouldn't throw anyone out of the clan at a time like this, overstandingly not some poor stranger what saved a brace of hunters."

"Someone will have to house him for a while, until it's safe for Mr. Walking here to be on his way." The schoolmaster scratched behind his ear as he looked the stranger up and down.

"Not my house. I've got daughters, and I won't be having this drifter anywhere near—"

"Oh, put a biscuit in it, will you, Fred?" the butcher cut in. "I swear, Christian welcomeness surely ain't your strong point."

The door creaked open behind Amos, and he turned to see Ella enter with some bread and a cut of meat. At the sight of the stranger, she balked as if at the sight of a hungry wolf. Ella took a step back.

"Come on, Ella, give him his food. He won't bite; that's just what you look like after the woods have worked you over," the butcher said.

"Who—Where—" Ella stuttered, the plate of food hanging perilously limp in her hands.

"This is the drifter what done saved Amos and Dale from the pigmen. He's a friend." the butcher said, waving Ella to hurry up. One of the Buntons scoffed at the mention of "friend".

Ella still didn't move. "But—"

"Go on, Ella. The poor feller's hungry. We don't got time for gawping at strangers, anyhow."

Ella obliged, but she backstepped away from him as soon as she'd laid it in front of the stranger. The drifter didn't scarf the food down as Amos had expected, but he'd never seen anyone savor a bite of tough, flavorless bread like the drifter did.

"Thank you kindly," Omar mumbled between mouthfuls.

"He could come over to our place," Amos said, referring to the Hollands'. He'd spent so much time at his master's home in the past month he'd come to think of it as home.

The schoolmaster shook his head. "Don't think there's enough room for him, unless you want him to bunk up with Ella or the two kids. That was a joke, Ella. Don't need to jump like that."

"How about Bill Puckett?" Amos offered. "He's got extra room since his girl got hitched."

The other men agreed, since Bill Puckett wasn't there to defend himself. Amos slid the ramrod for his rifle back into its sheath and helped the drifter to his feet.

"Don't worry, friend," Amos said as he guided the stranger outside again. "We'll get you fixed up just fine. Us Tuckers might get a little wary now and then, but there isn't a clan around that can offer a better stay-welcome than us. And there isn't a family in town better than the Hollands. Isn't that right, Ella?"

Ella Holland had fallen back a fair stretch behind them.

"Ella?" Amos asked again. "Come on, Ella, keep up! Poor fellow's had a rough day, can't you see? Now look, Omar. We'll likely have a few hours for you to rest a while, but if nobody's come to get you before nightfall, make your way back to the high school, okay? Most of the men need to—"

"Amos!" One of the Brodys rode up and plucked Amos away from his ward. "The Hadleys hit a snag a fair stretch out of rifle range. The watchman wants a posse to drag their sorry hind ends into town, and I'm grabbing you for my squad. Let's go." The scraggly farmer kicked his horse back into a trot, the rest of the posse following close behind.

Amos called to Ella as he took off with the others. "Ella, watch over the drifter, would you? He's a good man. Don't you worry about him!"

Amos turned and sprinted after the posse, carrying with him the youthful admixture of fear and excitement.

A few miles out east of town, beyond the farthest reaches of the bravest farmer's fields, a small fortress of wood and steel bristled against the wintry forest like a teeth-bared challenge. A barren path snaked from its one opening down through the sundry piles of mine tailings, on down the hill toward the main Tucker town. The smell of the incoming rider alerted the watches.

Then came the sound of galloping hooves and jangling knives, and finally the sight of the rider himself—Arnold Brody, the butcher, lashing the horse's flanks and bellowing a haunting alarm-cry in the misty dell, "Unbreds a-comin', take heed! To your heels with the lot of ye, let's go! Pigmen on the warpath! Take hee—"

"What are you carryin' on about, butcher?" A harsh voice chopped the message short as the gates swung open for the runner.

Arnold Brody didn't bother to dismount. He craned his head for a glance back at the lonely path he'd come down, and to which he'd soon return, God willing. He turned back in his saddle to face the grizzled, one-eyed Johnny Grierson standing before him with arms crossed.

"Unbred army come up from the south like the devil's own legions," the butcher breathed. "They've likely et up all the sacrifice animals the Newells and the Hadleys done left behind. I reckon you got fifteen minutes before the first pigman scouts get up this a-way."

Johnny Grierson's lip curled, the flesh puckering around the patch over his hollow eye socket. "So I reckon you come to fetch us sorry half-breeds, bring our wardfolk back to help on the town palisade."

"Watchman's orders."

"Orders for you, clansman, not for me. We got guns and spears to blunt the unbred strike, and supplies enough to last us the winter. We'll be seeing to our own palings, thank'ee very much."

"Suit yourself," Arnold said with a shrug before putting his spurs to the horse's withers and galloping off full tilt back the way he'd come, his knives rattling like chainmail.

Ella led Omar from her house to Bill's place next door, carrying a plate of food that drew Omar along like a carrot draws a mule. The men of both houses had answered the watchman's call to ready the clan's defenses. Being the clan's gunsmith and powdermaker respectively, Phil Holland and Bill Puckett would pass out powder and shot to every family that had need, without regard for wealth or standing. After the siege, if the two survived, they would reap a portion of whatever teeth the clan bagged.

"You can stay here for now," Ella said. She led him inside and wrestled a cot into place in a disused corner room, shoving sagging boxes and stacked cooking ware to the side. Omar set down his sheathed sword, a knife, and his bow and near-empty quiver.

"That's all you got?" Ella asked.

"Had to leave my gun behind. My travel pack I done ate a couple days ago."

She sat the rest of his food on the floor as she would for a dog and stepped away, trembling despite herself.

"I thank you," Omar said, his earnest dark eyes shining as he snatched up the morsels laid out for him. "I ain't had nothing but the meatier parts of a pigman and the ends of some roots since Sunday."

Ella merely stared from across the room, her hand frozen on the door handle. She found it hard to pity him. His hollow face chilled her bones every bit as much as a winter wind. "Why'd you save Amos and Dale?"

The stranger looked her in the eyes more directly than most folks did, and certainly more than she cared for. "I wasn't about to let the first humans I'd seen in—I don't know how long—get et by unbreds."

"Out of the goodness of your heart, then?"

"Didn't say that. Just wanted some food and shelter. That's all."

"Well, I reckon you've earned yourself both. Until tomorrow, if you last 'til then." Ella backed out the door.

Chapter 3

Frantic Preparations

Folks had a saying: 'Animals will cooperate as long as you aren't pressed for time'. The Tucker relief party found the straggling Hadleys at the end of a line of cattle still a quarter mile from the clan wall, and the cloven-hooved beasts didn't seem too eager to close that gap. The menfolk of the Hadley family sat atop their best horses, hawing and cracking whips at their livestock with the kind of angry energy driven only by fear.

The countryside Brody from north of town had no kind words for the last of the farmers to get inside the clan wall. "What's takin' you so dad-blasted long? I got all my luggin's packed away with enough time to come pull you out of the mud, and the pigmen ain't even coming from *my* direction!"

"It's that skittish heifer of our'n, Job," the Hadley elder shouted as the procession rumbled on. "She spooked and run off west."

The Tucker posse fanned out, not to guide the mules, cows, hogs, and packhorses laden with goods, but to turn wary eyes to the woods around. Mr. Brody cast his arms to the sky as if Hadley taxed the very limits of human understanding. "Then let her go. She'll slow down the pigmen."

"She pert near took half the herd with her, Job, and I've given up a calf and two cows already!"

Mr. Brody shook his head. "You just thank your lucky stars you ain't upwind of all that nonsense, or..." He trailed off as a puff of breeze brought the dreaded, familiar scent of pigman frenzy-sweat to his sensitive nose. "Doggone it, looks like we ain't gettin' to the town without a fight. Posse! Form a line behind the rear, muskets to bear! Shake loose a matchet, they'll be coming in fast!"

Mr. Brody leaped from his horse along with the others, the reins looped on one arm so as to keep the horse handy for when they needed a fast break out of there. He dropped to one knee, checked the powder in the pan, and leveled his rifle at the encroaching woods just as a far-off grunt echoed through the wintry cathedral of pillared trees.

The watchman's son, Ralph McDaniel, walked along the gangway overlooking the stretch of cleared land between the town and the woods. The shattered ruins of the old town lay choked in the grip of tree roots and snaking vines, and though he could not see them, Ralph could smell a host of unbred foes gathering in the cricks and crooks, waiting for the inevitable strike. When they came, they would all come at once. He wondered if they could smell him, if they knew how tightly he gripped the charred wooden spear in his hand.

His friend Nigel held up a hand to shade his eyes and scanned the brush. "How many you reckon, Ralph?"

"No way of tellin'. It's a big one." Ralph's voice cracked. "Folks been hearin' the calls clear up at the Finch's farm."

Nigel looked over at the watchman's son. "Think it could be as big as the one we had when we was little?"

Ralph drummed his fingers in a nervous rhythm on the palisade. "I hope not. Pa says we cut near two thousand pigman jaws after that one."

"I don't get how pigmen are clever enough to make an army like that."

"They've got enough human stock in 'em to know how to unscrew lids and work door handles. I suppose they've got enough to make an army, too." Ralph tried to keep his voice even, like that matter-of-fact way his father had when describing the most god-awful war wounds. "Pa says they stand on each other's shoulders and make ladders out of their bodies to get up the walls."

"Why ain't they attacking yet?"

"Still making a circle around the town, trying to go after easy pickings, I reckon. And it's still too light out. They'll wait until tonight and attack under cover of darkness." Ralph paced without realizing it.

"You hear about the drifter?" Nigel was a good enough friend to change the subject before Ralph worked himself into a panic. Every once in a while, Nigel bailed Ralph out of patrol duty, and Ralph had always rescued Nigel from the schoolteacher's critical eye. One predatory authority figure or another had warned them that neglect in a certain area of development would lead to debilitating deficiencies, and these warnings bore out. Ralph wasn't the most observant of young men out in the wild, and Nigel didn't know whether pigman jaws qualified as commodity or fiat money. Both boys were quite satisfied with this arrangement.

Ralph knew he was being pitied, and he didn't mind the distraction a bit. "Yeah, I heard about him."

"Folks are saying it bodes ill for us, him coming in at the head of a pigman army like that. Could be a Jonah."

Yes, Nigel was just the sort of calming presence Ralph needed at a time like this. He sighed and paced back the other way.

Nigel's hand shot out and grabbed Ralph by the arm. "Ralph, look."

A handful of pigmen darted out from the tree line across open ground, making for the palisade. Ralph brought his rifle to his shoulder.

"Wait, don't," Nigel said. "They're trying to tease a shot out of you. They'll turn back to the woods directly."

But they didn't.

Ella knew she needed to get a move on, but she didn't put much thought either to her family's haste or to all the stuff she carried out to the cellar. The folkward had plucked Bill Puckett and her stepmother out for clan duty, which left two fewer bodies to shutter up the houses. Seemed like everyone was worrying about this or that, except for the one thing they really ought to be worried about, and she'd left that fellow snoring on Bill Puckett's cot just as soon as she'd stuffed him with some leftovers. Was he really sleeping, or simply biding his time for some orneriness? Moving all the rations and breakables to the root cellar wouldn't matter much if that Omar character got it in his head to—

"Ella, put that coal-oil down and fetch your brother and sister," her father said, bursting from the back door of their house behind Ella and making her skip. The effort of tending to clan business and kin business at the same time had already set him puffing, and it looked like he was fixing to run back out into a fight. One hand bore a loaded rifle, the other a nine-foot spear. Bow, quiver, and the strap of a second rifle crossed his chest. On one hip he had a horn of powder and a bag of musketballs; on the other he holstered an old sawed-off shotgun to use in a pinch and a carbon-steel knife that kept its keen edge. She'd forgotten the imposing figure he cut when dressed for an all-out brawl. A fleeting swell of pride washed over her before she figured to get it all out in the open.

Ella set down the lanterns as she was told. "Papa, there's something you need to know—"

"Not now," her father interrupted, "I gotta get back to the gate. You and little Clive and Margaret head on down to the meetin'house and wait for me and your ma. The sun's gettin' low."

"But Papa, it's about the drifter. He ain't safe." Ella followed her father into the house.

A gunshot rang out yonder. Not unusual on a day like today. What cut short her pa's reply were the three shots that followed straight after.

Phil spun as the color drained from his face. "They can't be coming yet," he murmured almost to himself. "Don't make a lick of sense. It won't be dark for another coupla hours."

A distant harmsway whistle swept the spate of denial away. A surprise attack.

"Quick, Ella, get in the cellar with Clive and Margaret. I'm gonna go fetch some help, and we're all gonna run for the meetin'house, y'hear?" Her father darted out into the street without another word.

Ella ran to the foot of the stairs, calling for her siblings. "Clive! Margaret! Get on down here!"

Hearing the edge in her voice, her two young half-siblings tumbled down with one stuffed toy apiece clutched close. Ella choked down her tense tone and attempted her father's authoritative, disinterested presence. "Let's go, kidlins. Gotta wait for a bit in the cellar, hurry up, now." She hurried them through the kitchen, out the back door, to the yawning mouth of the cellar.

"Do we have to go in?" Clive whined. "It's dark down there."

"Clive, you mind me, now. Get in the cellar. I'm 'onna—" she stopped at the top of the steps with one hand on the door. The drifter. He was still sleeping inside Bill Puckett's place. No time. Couldn't go back for Omar. It wasn't like he was a Tucker anyhow; he was just a—a —She shouldn't go back.

She had to go back.

"Lock yourself in the root cellar right now! Don't open 'til I come get you!" Ella closed the door and slid a solid sheet of steel over the opening.

Ella ran next door, the red sun sinking behind her, her heart already hammering in her chest. If the stranger's half a wink got her killed, she'd really be irked. If the pigmen cut far enough into the town...

Ella burst through Bill Puckett's garage laboratory-shop, ran into the house, called for Bill, got no answer, and ran for the drifter's room.

Ella found the drifter more or less how she'd left him, only less conscious, if it were possible. She shook him like a dog thrashing a squirrel.

"Hey! Mister, wake up! The pigmen's a-comin'!"

The drifter stirred and mumbled something unknowable.

"C'mon, now, we gotta go! Hurry up!"

Understanding flared across the stranger's face. He blinked, whatever dream he'd been in finally evaporating. "Get my gear," he said, stumbling even as he said so.

He followed her back to the Hollands' house next door, rubbing the sleep from his bleary eyes all the way.

They stepped together into the kitchen. The back door hung open.

"Papa? Papa, are you he—" Her sentence cut short at the snarling pounce of an unbred.

The beast tackled Ella from the side, knocking her to the floor. Ella scarcely knew her own scream as she forced herself to stare into the wild eyes of a monster, keeping her hand braced against its sinewy neck to keep its dripping fangs away from her throat. The clawed foot-hands had just started to do their nasty work on her when they spasmed in agony. It rolled off her in a twitching heap.

Omar stood over her with a bloody knife.

"Tha—thank—," Ella stuttered, clutching her side before the drifter broke her off.

"More on the roof," he said, his gaze snapping up to the ceiling. He thrust her into the kitchen pantry and slammed the door closed. No sooner had the door latched than she heard the caw of a pigman readying a pounce. A sword rang from its sheath, and the bark of an attack sounded together with that of ripping flesh and crunching bone. In the darkness of the pantry, she heard the skittering of clawed feet overhead. She twisted at the wooden handle of something she held in a white-knuckled grasp. She looked down to see the drifter's knife. He'd slipped it into her hands, in case—

Another unbred cry tore the unsteady silence in the kitchen, right beside the pantry door. The howl cut short with only a swish of steel and a gargle to usher its departure.

There was a thump, a human grunt, and the clatter of a sword on the floor. Furniture rattled; something fell against a wall and then slid to the floor. A creature panted heavily, hungrily, struggling for fresh meat. A thud of flesh against flesh, then another, and another. Something stumbled up against the pantry door and fell away, wrestled to the ground. A human grunted, striving against unseen foes. Frenzied, scampering movement, a deadlock, a snarl, more movement, a thump and a thud, a bump and a groan, and Ella realized she was holding her breath.

She heard a shout she recognized as her father's, the loud crack of striking wood, and a pigman squeal. More struggling.

"Matchet, quick."

"Kill that sucker," she heard her father say.

A pigman squealed again.

"Kill it."

"I got it."

The pigman's weakening squeals gave way to thick, wet sounds and a man's heaving gasps. Silence settled again.

The pantry door opened. The drifter stood with a bloody sword beside her pa, both of them bent over double and heaving, but from the look of it, alive and whole. Four dead pigmen lay strewn about the kitchen amid the mess of overturned chairs and scattered cookery.

"We got help out front. Scared off the pigman scouts, but we better—Ella, what happened? You're bleedin'." Her pa sounded equal parts concerned and exasperated, like he didn't have time to spend worrying about his daughter's wellbeing, but he would if he really had to.

"I'm fine. Gotta get Clive and Margaret out of the cellar."

"Fetch 'em quick."

Ella obeyed while the two men warded the house's killways. She locked the cellar door after pulling her saucer-eyed siblings from its depths. Scarcely ten seconds later, the Holland family gathered in front of their home with the drifting stranger at their side, where the Hadleys, their blasted skittish livestock, and the bedraggled rescue posse marched past in tight formation.

And Bill Puckett was among them.

"Howdy, neighbor," Ella's father said as she and her family fell in line next to Bill. "Thought you was dead there for a bit."

"Had your eye on my shop, didn't ye? What about you? Got your whole bunch?" Bill tipped his time-worn hat to Ella before scanning the rest of the Hollands. "Where's your wife?" he asked Phil.

"Got called to the meetin' hall to char spearpoints. Clive, quit your crying. Tuckers don't flip out 'cause of a little pigman trouble. We're made of sterner stuff than that, y'hear?" Phil grabbed Clive's hand and pulled him close. Clive nearly had to run to keep up with his father's quick strides.

"I heard me some tell 'bout a drifter. This him?" Bill jabbed a thumb in Omar's direction.

"Yeah, about that. We put him in your house. For now."

“Figures,” Bill sighed. “Okay, then, Mister. What’s your name?”

“Omar Walking,” the drifter said.

“Like 'I've been walking a skinny trail', walking?” one of the nearby McDaniels—an ardent patron of all nomad music—asked.

“Yup.”

Ella’s grip on her younger stepsister tightened as Sophie’s husband, Victor Fillmore, streaked by on his mount. “Fightin’ men, rally on Market Street! Rally on the watchman!” Bleeding claw-gashes traced their way across his horse’s flank.

Chapter 4

Assault and Defense

The clan watchman Elvin McDaniel rolled a bullet between his fingers as the Fillmore boy rode in at the head of a column of town clansmen fleeing to the safety of the clan main. His rally call had brought to his beckon thirty armed men and a couple hardy widows, but he would need more to cover the final crossroads in front of the meetinghouse.

The Market and Main Street crossroads had plenty of openings, but if the pigmen wanted to keep up their surprise rush, they'd have to take the four arrow-straight lanes clogged with mud and snow. With enough men and muskets, shooting pigmen in this light would be like plugging a rabbit in its hole. If the pigmen couldn't wait until dark like sensible unbreds, Elvin would make them pay. The fighting men would cover the fallback to the meetinghouse with some fancy shooting that would have been out of the question on an overcast night.

The clan had set down a common plan for large pigmen raids on the town proper nearly thirty years ago. They had once practiced a shelter-in-place doctrine; a quick batten-down would protect their stores and keep clanfolk from being caught out in the open, or so the idea went. As it turned out, the plan preserved rations, but not clansmen.

After once losing eleven clansmen in a single night, the elders had changed their plan. Now the entire population of the clan had to gather at the high school in the event of a wall-breaching attack. This enabled a more robust defense and drew the brunt of the attack to a single strong point instead of encouraging the crafty pigmen to root around for weak spots and open windows. This tactic proved much more successful in preserving the lives of clanfolk, and both Elvin and his father before him had relied on it, while still noting the plan's two weaknesses: the vulnerability to a lightning attack, and the clan's total annihilation in the event of a ruinous failure. The clan had deemed the risks preferable to culling five parts out of a hundred clanfolk every time unbreds scaled the wall.

Elvin waved down the returning scout, and Victor Fillmore stopped his horse and leaped from the saddle.

"What's the word?" the watchman asked.

"I covered the west part, High Street to Baker, all the way to the hill. The Hadley bunch made it back all right, but I hear tell it was a near-run thing. The pigmen are keepin' themselves busy with the houses right now, so we have a little time." Victor didn't meet Elvin's gaze.

"The roundswalks?" Elvin asked.

"The ones I talked to were lightin' a shuck, your boy amongst them. Folks on the wall said it was a hefty raid, but the main body of pigmen hain't cleared the wall yet. Last I checked, anyhow."

"Everyone okay?"

The young man chewed his lip. "Some cuts and bruises, mostly. Dr. Bernhard's going to have to look at my pa's arm."

Elvin's brows inched together. "What's wrong? If you're keepin' something under your hat, tell me."

Victor cleared his throat, looking down. "They, uh, they got Billy Craine."

Elvin swore. "How?"

Victor shook his head. "Wardin' the wall, didn't mark the pigmen what scaled the palings further off. Clyde saw 'em drag him off the wall."

"If Clyde was close enough to see Billy, why the hell didn't he pull Bill's sorry hind end outta there?"

Victor shrugged and stepped back, stuttering. "I-I don't know. I 'spect Craine got his blood up and ignored the fallback. Clyde was one of the last out."

Elvin slapped his thigh, shaking his head. "Shoulda known better. He shoulda known better."

"Billy slowed them down along the whole west end."

"That's what I'll tell his widow and two young 'uns." Elvin sighed. "Mind your horse. Be ready for a fight."

Elvin looked at the men hemming him in. The men and boys still streaming in with him: some of them were kin; others neighbors; some grandfathers pushing fifty; a few boys barely past ten. All of them his clansmen. All of them his responsibility.

He looked over the sundry bulwarks thrown up at the crossroads, and the men who covered the lanes with their muskets. A fair defense, for one put up on such short warning.

"Hey!" Elvin hollered at a pair of the Evans' boys. "Only fast-twitchers ward the line here!"

"I can take care of myself," Deek Evans called back.

"Kill yourself some other time, Deek. If you can't give a horse a fair run for its hooves, head on up to the meetinghouse and cut stobs for Arnold Brody." He shooed them away. No point in a first-line hold if you can't fall back to the second quick enough.

Elvin spat and kicked a clod of mud and snow. A sneak attack at the dawn of a siege! He should have told everyone to get inside the meeting-hall long before dark. What was he thinking? His father, God rest that old bastard's soul, wouldn't have lost a single clansman. Another stain on the good name of the Paul McDaniel family.

"Everybody settle down, now. Settle down for the counting; you won't find your kin 'til we're organized." Sam Chambers tried to calm the frantic crowd inside the meeting-hall—a gymnasium, long ago. Families hollered for their kids, their cousins, their nieces and nephews, their grandchildren, their husbands, their wives, and their neighbors every which way. With over five hundred souls in the Tucker clan, it amounted to a bothersome caterwaul, and Chambers' voice carried about as much weight in the cacophony as a fly on a horse's rump. But by persistent coaxing, he whipped the nearby elders into action and enabled the heads of the big families in town to gather and steady their respective broods. The calm trickled on down the pecking order to the kiddos barely old enough to walk.

Sam did a quick walkthrough of the bustling halls to check in on those who occupied the boarded-up rooms. The Newells went to the courtyard to manage the livestock. The Fillmores made rounds checking the steel shutters on the windows. The Finches sat in a back room, calmly at their knitting. Every family not manning the line had a job. A building full of idle clansmen was one panic attack away from mass pandemonium; a building full of busy clansmen was a fortress. The watchman had scoffed at Sam's insistence, years ago, that all clansmen busy themselves when waiting out an unbred attack. But Sam never doubted the hundred trivial tasks he gave out to folks, and after a few rough pigmen sieges, most clansmen gave up their own doubts. Survival was as much a matter of the mind as the spear.

Whatever calm there was, feigned or real, shattered at the muffled drumbeat of distant musket fire. Sam dashed back to the double line of pikemen, bringing his old birdwatching glasses up to his eyes. The scarred and pitted lenses gave him a last glimpse of the smoke and flash of the Tucker rifles down on Market Street the reports shortly following.

Scanning the streets to either side, his heart quailed at the sight.

Pigmen streamed towards the Tucker clansmen like ants on an anthill. The bulk of the pigman army had scaled the town walls, and it didn't seem as if the potshots from a handful of woodsmen did anything but anger the creatures. He supposed Elvin had a point, that pulling the army toward their defenses would likely spare the town a measure of the rapine in store for it, but the move sounded like another stroke of that old McDaniel pride needing to show its feathers.

Dwindling gunfire rumbled as the men finished their reload, and the pigmen surged over their dead and wounded in a wave. The folkward broke rank and sprinted for the safety of the meetinghouse, not daring to meet so many pigmen in a hand-to-claw struggle. Sam reached over and laid a hand on his own pike.

“Can I see those, Sam?” It was Arnold the butcher, next-in-charge for now.

“Sure.” He handed the glasses over. "Only the right side works."

“Y'all string your bows now!” Arnold shouted to those at his lead. Bows groaned as drawstrings went taut.

“Oh, we got trouble,” Arnold muttered, still looking through the field glasses.

“Someone fell?”

“Looks like Shane Bunton. I don't know if anyone can get him up fast enough. Oh man, looks like the pigmen are gonna—Oh! Man!” Arnold blew a sigh of relief, then grinned. “Who needs to shoot a gun when you can club 'em like that, huh? Elvin's got him. Looks like he's got a little hitch in his git-along. All right, y'ins! Ready up, but don't cut loose until the clansmen are out of your sight line!”

The retreating clansmen rushed into the two wide-open double doors of the meeting-hall like water funneled into a spout. At the first twinkling of a clear shot, Arnold gave the order. Dozens of arrows lanced into the swarming pigmen.

All clansmen soundly inside, a man at each door pulled a rope to raise a small field of sharpened stakes. The stakes would slow the pigmen enough to give the archers more time to line up their shots. The spears at meetinghouse guardpoints rose up to form an unwelcoming wall of spikes.

The beasts made it past the stakes, crawling over the bodies of their fallen, but their onslaught met a bloody stall at the pikes. The air stank of sweat despite the evening chill. On one side of the wall of spikes, a swarm of starving unbreds slavered for the storehouse of meat beyond the last shell, darting in and out, nipping and grabbing at the keen points. On the other side, clansmen muttered and cursed, grunting with effort as they stood shoulder to shoulder with their fellows and calling out their battle-talk. Keep your pike up. Pigman's stuck on my spear. Quick pricks, clean stabs, boys. Watch it, it's jumping for ya. Don't let 'em grab the spearpoint. Let the archers do their work.

And work the archers did. Volley after volley decimated the packed ranks of the swarm's middle, the bloody chaos working its steady way to the front.

"*Faaar in the hole!*"

Dual thunder blasts shook attackers and defenders alike as Elvin revealed his last nasty surprise: two crude iron tubes packed with powder and a mess of scrap metal. The massive gouts of flame and smoke illuminated the shredded bits of unbred flesh scattering back from the entrances like chaff in the wind.

The attack faltered. The pikes were too sharp, the arrows too thick, and the battlefield ever more choked with the dead.

Elvin barked a harsh order. The pikes surged forward, shoving the swarm back. A rope slipped, the stakes dropped back down to make way for the counterattack, and the few pigmen left behind were trampled underfoot by the human stampede, alive or not.

The clansmen cheered as one, and even Elvin smiled at the pools and rivers of blood that ran from their slain foes. The pigmen might wage another raid under the cover of darkness, but he'd broken their chief attack.

Chapter 5

In Which the Stranger Fails to Fit In

After fighting a night-long battle against man-beasts, the Tucker clan came forth from their hiding place to find another dusting of snow had frosted the pigman carcasses strewn across the clan main. Scouts tested the houses closest to the meetinghouse and, finding them empty, the watchman ordered a careful house-by-house search of the town.

While both keen eyes and keen noses marked enough pigmen in the forests to keep the whole clan cooped up in the town, not a single live pigman turned up within the walls. Back on the clan palisade overlooking the forest and old town, the watchman turned to the clan's schoolteacher next to him and said with fogging breath, "We ain't out of the woods yet, but I reckon we're out of the fire."

The schoolteacher was happy enough not to be fighting for his life that he elected not to correct the watchman's mixed metaphors.

If the Tuckers were cooped up in the town, that meant the young drifter was cooped up in there with them. The elders, too busy with rations and figures and hunting parties to give the drifter much thought, settled to keep the stranger with Bill Puckett for the time being. The drifter agreed to help with the munitions and patrol the neighborhood when needed. Not that he had the liberty to choose, nor even to fuss over his lack of a choice.

The town's interest in the drifter proved to be only passing; more pressing matters bared their teeth. The clan had weathered the worst pigman attack in eight years. A strong young clansman had died, and six others were bedridden from their wounds. Doctor Bernhard nearly went frantic trying to patch up all the cuts and bites and make sure that no one got the nasty infections folks told stories about. Mrs. Bernhard still swore that the stress would kill the good doctor before anything else ever got the chance.

The ledgers showed ten fewer cattle among the clansmen, along with twenty goats, thirty-two hogs, five horses, fifty-nine chickens, and a couple good hunting dogs. The pigmen had worked a crack open in the storerooms of the Fillmores and one of the McDaniels, rendering those families destitute for the winter. There was damage to clansmen's holdings throughout, and the farmers didn't dare go back to their land. No one had the faintest notion of how the Grierson settlement had fared, and no one made the journey to find out. Their stores of powder and shot had taken a hit, and with the larger part of winter still ahead of them, the clan foresaw some tightened belts ahead.

The town watchman sent out hunting parties to thin the besieging pigmen, and they honored the passing of Billy Craine. Of the pigmen teeth, two parts out of ten went to the family of the slain, and another two to the clan watchman. The payment made up nearly a year's wages. The rest of the booty, harvested from the four hundred or so dead pigmen, went to all the wardsmen in equal parts, though it could not fairly offset the damage done. They'd cash in the jaws the moment a nomad clan came through, though that wasn't likely to happen for some weeks, and most of what they'd lost they would have to replace with good old-fashioned elbow grease.

Sam Chambers made sure that everyone was treated fairly in the spreading of such great wealth, and Reverend Brody made sure that everyone surrendered a part to the Lord's service.

Ella considered it a blessing to have the drifter mostly out of the way. The Hollands had enough of their own mess to clean up to worry about their neighbor and his ragged guest. She was even more relieved not to find Omar up and about when she brought lunch over to Bill's place.

Bill tore a hunk out of the bread she'd brought him. "He's slept all morning. It's that drifterly laziness, I'd wager," he sighed as if present circumstances had nothing to do with the drifter's slumber.

"Think we oughta wake him for some vittles?" Ella asked, looking down at the hot soup she carried.

Bill shrugged. "He's in the room yonder, if you want to splash him."

She elected not to wake the stranger, though she did set his bowl on the floor next to his cot. She halted as she turned to leave. He scowled as he slept. Did ordinary folks do that? Was it the face of a killer? A monster?

To say the drifter made her uncomfortable was to say nails made for poor bedding material. Amos Taylor was one thing, but this Omar Walking—if that was even his real name—he'd already been in her nightmares.

She left food for him and slipped away quietly. Shame they had no locks to keep him inside. When the morning came, she gritted her teeth at the mere thought of seeing him. Which meant she would always be too afraid to challenge him openly, to tell him she didn't want him here and that he'd have to go to someone else or sleep in the streets. He went about the duties given to him while she wished him gone, even as she hated herself for it.

The second evening with Omar under Bill Puckett's roof, her pa again tasked her to fetch the drifter for supper. She took him his food instead and left him to eat alone.

When Sunday came with the morning, Ella smiled at the pale winter sun. Then she remembered the pigmen who had sealed the clan into their town and the stranger who slept just next door. She frowned. The recent happenings could cast a pall even over a Sunday. She wished the pigmen would go away and take the drifter with them.

But of course he stayed, and of course he got up early to milk and feed the Hollands' and Pucketts' shared cow while Clive and Margaret cared for the goat, and of course the drifter never said a word to either of the children, though Ella watched him the whole time. Of course he cleaned his hunting clothes up for church, and of course he dogged their heels to the old high school cafeteria where the congregation met.

Her cold manner may have given the stranger pause as they entered the meeting-hall, but his unfamiliarity with Tucker pew arrangements proved more daunting. Violating one of the most rigid unwritten social structures in the clan set him backing away from first one seat, then another. A trip and a bump later, Ella found Omar sitting in the only place left available to him: directly at her side.

Ella's hands twisted at the pew in front of her as if trying to strangle the wood. The drifter shifted uncomfortably next to her from time to time, a movement she tried to ignore as she fixed herself on the sermon.

"We gather here in hard times," Reverend Brody began, "encroached upon by enemies from all sides"—he gave the drifter a meaningful glance—"and once again it seems as though we are alone in the world. I am reminded of the wickedness wrought upon us by the ubermenschen and their unbred slaves in the Evil Days, those who waged war under the banner of the twisted ladder. They sought to stamp out the Lord's Elect, those who refused the mark, untainted by the scientists' tools. But the ubermenschen failed. And the Lord poured out His wrath on the wickedness of the past age and preserved for Himself a Remnant. So again will God preserve the offspring of the righteous in their darkest hours. And be certain of this: the Elect have endured darker times than these."

The congregation mumbled an "Amen" at the doctrine faithfully dispersed. Ella herself would have murmured her assent along with the rest if it hadn't been for the drifter's palpable unease at her side. Like a cornered rat. He might have done a good deed out of necessity, but he was not a Tucker, not one of the Elect. He knew it, she knew it, the whole clan knew it. A wretch easy enough to despise, if only his wretchedness would allow her the privilege. But he was so wretched...

Pity. Dear God, not that. Not pity. Years of painstaking effort to stamp out the weakness, and here it was, bubbling up again in spite of herself.

For the first time in many years, Ella Holland had a moment of shocking clarity sitting in that church pew: she had built a house made partly on sand and partly on stone. A cornerstone had to be replaced, but which one? To allow pity for the wretch beside her would be to destroy a carefully wrought, dearly cared for home, a home that extended warmth to its keepers, but which admitted no newcomers. But a hearth too feeble to warm a chilly stranger was no hearth at all. Was tenderness so feeble? And if so, what use was it? Something had to give way. Why was pity only for other Tuckers? Had not God commanded compassion for all in His good book?

But what would it even *mean* to have compassion for a man like this? She didn't know the first thing about how to start. It wasn't possible. She wouldn't try. She couldn't try.

Dadgummit, she had to try.

Sometimes the greatest change in a life happens not in a thunderclap, but in the deepest quiet, in the slightest turn onto a different path.

"Mr. Walking," the reverend said, catching the drifter tailing the Hollands on their way out. "May I have a word?"

The drifter broke off from the stream of clansmen trudging back to their homes. "What it be, preacher?"

"If you intend to stay with us during these trying times, I would like to impress upon you the way we do things here. It is important for our clansmen to live together harmoniously. And that includes keeping the faith."

"I don't got cause to slander your church, preacher."

"I'm not worried about that. But you are liable to hear things around here that sound a bit different from what you're used to hearing out there. It is very important that you respect our customs and traditions, especially where they might seem a little ... nonsensical to you."

"If this is something important to my health—and it's sounding like it is—you're gonna have to be more specific than that."

The reverend gave him a stare, not as of a shepherd to his flock, but as to a wolf in the pen. "Walk with me."

When Ella came to fetch Omar for dinner that night, he didn't want to come.

"I'll eat dinner in here, if that's all right."

Ella fidgeted with her hands in front of her before realizing it and folding them behind her. "Don't worry 'bout being trouble for us. If we didn't want you over, we wouldn't have asked you in the first place."

"I think I should just stay here."

There might have been a touch of unfriendliness in his voice, Ella thought. Perhaps he still had not forgiven the clan for its own unfriendliness earlier. "Aw, you ain't our prisoner or nothin'. Come on over and eat like a guest."

"I-I don't want to burden y'all." Omar looked at the floor.

Ella sighed. "Listen. I, uh, think you've been a-gettin' kind of a raw deal."

Omar said nothing.

Ella's hands came back out in front and started their fidgeting again. "I think you've been a-gettin' a raw deal because I'm the one that's been a-givin' it to you."

Omar said nothing, but his eyebrows betrayed confusion. Folks didn't fess up to other folks like that, especially not to strangers, Ella figured.

She explained herself. "I'm scared of a lot of things. I've always been that a-way. I get scared of things changing." Ella stopped and cleared her throat awkwardly as her wide eyes stared at the floor. Come on, out with it. "I haven't treated you well because you've upset my neat little world, just by way of being. To tell th' truth, I never trusted you, even when you did save two of the Taylor brothers." She sighed. "But that ain't right. By rights, you ought to be one of us now. I'm sorry, Omar. A Tucker should never treat another Tucker like I done treated you. Care to come supper with us?"

Omar halted, then sighed in a slow agreement, rising to follow her. "Okay."

They left Bill Puckett's in silence. Then he asked, "How's your washboard?" He pointed to the side of his chest as they stepped out the door.

"Huh?"

"Looked like that pigman got a little piece of you the other day."

"Oh, that," Ella said with a bashful shrug, the gash along her ribs aching faintly now that he'd brought her attention to it, "It ain't bad. Nothing a couple weeks of mending won't fix."

Omar regarded her with a gaze Ella couldn't quite categorize. Perhaps respect, or maybe just careful study. "You handled that pigman pretty well. You wrestled 'em before?"

"Naw. Adam Taylor, that's Amos' pa, the blacksmith, he told me what to do when a pigman jumps you like that. He learned the hard way. A pigman gnawed off his hand a few years ago in the woods."

"Never saw a girl keep a pigman off her like that." Omar broke off his gaze and stepped ahead to open the door for her.

"You ever even seen a girl have to?" Ella grieved herself for asking it the moment the question left her mouth.

"Yeah." The stranger didn't offer any explanation. She needed none.

"Well," she started, stopped, and went on, reminding herself why she didn't talk to folks, "thanks for your help. With the pigman and all."

"No big deal."

After a silent supper, where Phil Holland's forced stabs at conversation stalled at the drifter's stiff bearing, Amos came by to greet the Holland family and bid the stranger come with him on the first watch of the night. The drifter took the offer, to the great relief of the Hollands. With a clansman, you could always ask how their children fared, or if their garden did well this year, or what they thought about Job Brody's new watering ditch. But for all their questions about the young man, he was still a drifter, and what can you say to a drifter?

"Ralph?" Elvin McDaniel caught his son sneaking in through the back door, several hours yet before the morning sun was due to peek above the horizon. "Where you been?"

"Went to check up with Nigel Bunton. We volunteered for the same watch."

"You've already got a watch laid out for you, and it don't take that long to get back from the Buntons' anyhow."

"I mighta swung by the schoolhouse to return a book. I'm—I'm not late, am I?"

Elvin didn't answer. He clomped his ancient steel-toed boots on the floor in front of his chair and pulled them on.

Ralph cleared his throat. "Uh. I was thinkin' I, uh, could take a double shift today, then—maybe have tomorrow off?" Ralph nudged the floor with his foot.

"You can take a day off when the unbreds do," came the answer, which of course meant when hell froze over. Elvin straightened long enough to catch his eldest son with a stern gaze and scoop a spoonful of boiled wheat into his mouth. "You get on out and feed the horses. I'll be along once I finish my breakfast."

Elvin McDaniel finished lacing up the old factory-made boots, bequeathed to him years ago by his own father. Together with the rusty machete sheathed at his side and the rifled musket leaning up against the door, they comprised the solemn and sacred inheritance that was the mantle of a clan watchman. A mantle his thirteen-year-old son Ralph McDaniel seemed hesitant to take up.

No matter. Elvin McDaniel would teach him, just as his own father had taught him, with scars to prove it.

He finished his breakfast, called to his son to hurry up, and loaded his rifle.

"Can I go over to the school after we make the rounds today, sir?" Ralph asked, as usual.

"No. I've got things for you to do," Elvin answered, as usual.

Ralph cast his freckled, boyish face downwards. He still had that childlike plumpness hanging high on his cheekbones, and no amount of hard work Elvin put on him could chisel it off. No doubt the schoolmaster's never-ending mollycoddling kept the boy soft. Ralph had learned there all that was useful, and a good Tucker needed more practical skills than Sam Chambers could teach.

In any case, the woods were still crawling with hungry pigmen, and there would be no rest in his household until a clansman could walk clear to the Grierson settlement without a single unbred on his tail. The McDaniel line had always been a restless lot, sleeping only half the night and still getting up with enough vigor to wrestle a bullhusker. But in times like these, even eighteen hours in a day wasn't enough to keep up with the avalanche of to-dos.

With his son in tow, Elvin placed a worn leather hat on his scarred, balding head and stepped out into the snow.

The next day, in the afternoon, shortly after Amos and the Hollands wrapped up a scant lunch, Ella molded some musketballs to replace the vast stores of ammunition used during the raid. The dishes she left unwashed in the sink. Amos came up beside her, unnoticed until he gave his offer to help. Ella acknowledged him with a gentle nod and handed him some lumps of lead to melt.

Amos placed the lead in a tray above the forge and stoked the coals a bit. "Omar seems like he'll be good help," Amos said, "overstandingly once we finish ruminating that next batch of sh—of manure. He's been grinding all day."

"Yeah, I reckon," Ella said, her cheeks warming. "Could we talk about something else?"

"Why? Drifter got your tongue?"

"No, it's just—just don't know what to think about him yet."

"I think he's rather a fine fellow, once you get to know him."

"Yeah, I suppose he is." Ella shrugged and stirred the tray of slowly melting lead without elaborating further.

Amos coughed. "Well, would you rather talk about Christmas?"

Something about Amos' tone made Ella blush. "That's still a couple weeks off."

"I know, but if I wait too long, I'm afraid some other guy's gonna beat me to it."

"Beat you to what?"

"See, all the Taylors are gonna be getting together with the Fillmores on Christmas Eve, and I was figuring if you didn't mind, I could take you along with me."

He did it. He done asked her out. And before Ella knew what she was thinking, she done took him up on it. And even though she was standing right at the forge, he picked up the softened lead and smiled a winsome smile as he handed it to her. His dreamy eyes locked on her own for a spell before he left.

The lead cooled and hardened again untouched while Ella stood wondering if this was what it felt like to be swept off her feet.

Chapter 6

Patrols and Powdermaking

If the Tucker clan hoped by their hospitality to learn more about the stranger and his story, they hoped in vain. Women of the town came together to gossip about the unbred army and the drifter and their strange simultaneous arrival. Nasty rumors worked their way into the idle chit-chat like so much yeast in the dough. Folks said the drifter was likely a fugitive murderer cursed by God to forever flee the pigman horde, and the horde wouldn't leave until the drifter did. Most folks put little stock in it, though they made sure to pass it on to the next pair of itching whisper-sniffers.

The drifter remained withdrawn to the point of total obscurity; some of the Tuckers had indeed come to believe that the stranger had moved on into the wilderness after all. To the Hollands, he yielded all the common kindnesses, though no more than was befitting, and to Bill

Puckett only silence, which suited Bill just fine as he had never been much for jawing even in the best of times.

The only soul in the Tucker clan to whom the drifter regularly deferred with something approaching real friendliness was Amos. They walked the same rounds together and kept to the same hunting parties, and Omar would hardly speak to another Tucker clansman without Amos near.

When not patrolling or hunting, the drifter had to do the grunt work for Bill Puckett. Because most of Bill's teachings were no longer than the dictums of a sage and scarcely less cryptic, the poor stranger had a rough go of it. Bill counted on Ella to help the drifter, but she didn't. Not at first. Instead, she watched. She watched him from the shadows as he shoveled manure, as he tried to spread the manure over straw in the right way, as he gave up and went out to collect more manure. On the fifth day of his manure-spattered stay, Ella left her tattered needlework to see how the gloomy stranger fared.

Not finding him up to his elbows in excrement, Ella peeked through a crack in the door to Bill Puckett's chemical shed to see him atop a high stool at a workbench, grinding powder in a pestle. The steady grinding made for dull work, but Ella suspected he preferred it to whatever life he'd fled from. It was hard to tell; Omar didn't seem to mind much of anything either way.

Omar put down the pestle on the table with a sudden, audible thump and looked up. Had he noticed her? From the side, Ella saw Omar's deep-set eyes squint of their own will. Omar reared back his head and sneezed—right into his pestle full of powder. Black soot shot everywhere, coating his face in a dusty mask.

Ella couldn't help but laugh. She tried to hide it, which made it come out like a girlish giggle, which made her blush and abashed her further when Omar turned to face her as the door swung open.

Ella laughed again, in spite of herself. Omar looked like a surprised raccoon. "I'm—I'm sorry," he explained, "I think I ruined the gunpowder."

"Oh, ha—whew. Don't worry about it, it was just charcoal. That's the cheapest part. Not even Bill would get on to you for that. Here, for goodness sakes take this rag and clean up your—" Ella snickered and burst out in her quiet laugh again.

Omar stared. He cracked the faintest hint of a smile that showed his teeth in the corner of his mouth.

Ella mastered herself again. "I won't tell anyone if you won't."

Omar dabbed the soot away with the old shop rag Ella gave him. "Who would I tell?"

"Good point. You wouldn't want to wreck your long-standing good name in the clan," Ella said with a smile she never thought Omar would see.

Omar blinked. "You, uh—was that a joke?"

"I won't tell anyone if you won't. Here, I think you've probably snorted some of that stuff. Blow your nose."

Omar obeyed noisily.

"Let's see, what have we got here?" Ella said, turning towards Omar's work. "Hmm."

"What's wrong?"

Ella rubbed some of the soot between her fingers. "You didn't put any sulfur or potassium nitrate in this."

Omar gestured to the pestle. "The powdermaker said to grind the charcoal."

"And you've done it very well. You just should have stopped about an hour ago. Here. The foremost part of the grinding is for the fixings to mix on the teeny-tiniest level." Ella pinched her thumb and forefinger together in front of her eye. "That gives it more pop. Charcoal's got little holes in it, and you've got to get the nitrates in them holes." Ella thought she sounded like a young mother talking to her curious five-year-old, but again, Omar didn't seem to mind.

"Why?"

"Well, it's kinda like this." Ella turned to the ground charcoal and fished some salt-like potassium nitrate out of a jar at the back of the workbench. "Think of gunpowder as a fire. Gunpowder doesn't blow up, it burns. But for a fire, you've got to have kindlin' and air. The charcoal's the kindlin'. The nitrates give the air-stuff—oxygen. Bill calls it an oxidizer. Any stuff you want to make explode, nitrates figure into it somehow. You know how when a wind blows on a fire, and the fire flares up? That's the oxygen making it burn faster. Well, if you already have that *inside* the kindlin', it burns just like," Ella snapped her fingers, "that."

Omar nodded, the flicker of understanding widening his eyes. "There she blows."

"Right."

"What about the sulfur?" Omar pointed to the jar of yellow powder.

"Bill says it lowers the lighting temperature and helps keep the gunpowder dry."

"You know a lot about gunpowder?"

"Uncle Bill's taught me a lot over the years. When his daughter Sophie used to live here, I'd come over all the time to sew, churn butter, fix the garden, you know. But I guess I always ended up making powder more'n anything else."

"You can teach me everything?"

Ella nodded. "Most everything, except for where Bill stores the powder."

"Ain't the recipe a big secret?"

Ella shook her head. "Powdermaking's common lore. Any old guncrank worth his teeth could stir up well enough to make a dog skip, leastways. Knowin's the easy part; the setup's the hard part. Bill's not much for secrets anyhow."

"Then what's that?" Omar pointed at the beaker on the other side of the room.

"Oh, that. That there *is* a secret, actually."

"You can't tell me what it is?"

"I can tell you what it is, or at least what it ought to be. I just can't tell you how to make it." Ella waved her hand in a grand flourish toward the beaker. "Uncle Bill's smokeless gunpowder, the same kind they use in the old ammunition. Someday, a hundred years from now, he'll crack the right recipe, and before you know it, folks'll be able to shoot these old guns we got layin' around. Not the shotguns and six-shooters, mind you, I mean the fancy chatterguns folks keep on their mantlepieces. Once we do that, you can bet it'll be only a matter of time before we tame the wilderness twenty miles out in every direction."

"You know how he does it?"

"Like I said, he ain't got the draft—the formula—quite right. And I don't really know how he got this far."

Omar nodded, scratching his stubbled chin. "How do you folks get the fixings? For the regular gunpowder, I mean."

"Well, the charcoal ain't too hard to make s'long as you can get some hardwoods, and the sulfur Bill gets from either Edward and Johnny Grierson up in the hills or the nomad traders. The potassium nitrate is the tricky part. Bill has to make it himself."

Omar's eyes went wide. "Is *that* what the manure's for?"

Ella nodded. "He mixes whatever manure he can find in with the straw and dead leaves in big piles out back. Twelve piles, one for each month of the year. Covers the heaps with animal skins to keep off the rain while the stuff marinates. He waters the beds with pee to help the right salts frost up. Then, after a year, we shovel the whole mess into Bill's crud-hopper, add water, and run it through a sluice to leach out the salts. Mix some potash into the salt and there you go: potassium nitrate, ready to use. From there, it's just some mixing, grinding, and corning."

"Simple."

"Here. All you gotta do now is measure how much ground charcoal you got there, like so." Ella scraped the soot into a notched beaker and tapped the side to settle it. She went on to walk him through the next steps and lecture him on the effects of different ratios. Omar learned quickly, even anticipating her at times. By the time Ella left, she was a little dizzy. She hadn't jawed that much in a couple years at least, not since what had happened with her brother. Even her pa noticed she seemed a good deal livelier than she usually was.

The Taylors and their guests celebrated the Christmas hoedown with a miser's thriftiness; the pigmen had whittled down the Tucker rations awfully low, and a long winter still stretched out in front of them. But the Tuckers knew how to have a good time even in bad times, and a fair number of folks turned out to dance. Arnold Brody and his butcher family even brought some meat. No clansman with a mind to host a shindig ever forgot to invite the butcher.

A young man pulled out his pappy's fiddle and played a tune, and the twenty or so-odd guests settled themselves into a line dance. Ella blushed when Amos asked her onto the shed's dancing floor. It seemed her cheeks favored their new color, because she couldn't help but blush when she tripped either, or when she got off time, or when she turned the wrong way, or when she haplessly pushed Amos into Becky. By the time they got through the first few songs, Ella wished very much that Amos' attention would go elsewhere for a while. And it did.

While Ella sat on the side to catch her breath, Amos matched up with Becky, whose sweetheart was busy sawing on the old fiddle. As always, Amos dazzled all onlookers. Ella watched them dance and tried to come around to the fact that she'd just danced with Amos Taylor, however badly. She wondered if he liked dancing with her. Did he think she was pretty? Did she care?

Of course she cared.

Ella didn't dance much more that night, but when it came time for folks to turn in, Amos walked her home. The moon was full in the clear sky, and the two could see their shadows scouting the churned-up snow ahead of them. Amos' shadow eased up a little closer to hers.

"Mighty fine evening, isn't it?" Amos said with pleasant earnestness.

It *was* a fine evening. "A little lonesome, maybe," she replied.

"Lonesome? I'm here," Amos said as he sidled up closer to Ella, close enough for her to feel his warmth in the winter night through her homespun rags. "There's no need for you to feel lonesome if you don't want."

"It's not a bad lonesome," Ella said, looking up at the night sky with bright eyes. "It's ... It's the kind of lonesome where you look up at the moon and you wonder what it would be like to see the whole world from up there. You wonder if the world really isn't as big as you used to thought it was."

Amos blinked. He drifted back away from Ella. "I don't really like to think that way," Amos answered after some thought. "It sounds awfully sad."

"Why?"

"I don't know. I suppose it's 'cause if we're small, then it's like we don't matter."

Ella shrugged. "I don't reckon we do matter *that* much. But I'm okay with that, I reckon. I think we matter where it counts."

"You don't want to be important?"

"I don't know. Maybe I do. Maybe not *important,* but—important to who?"

Amos shrugged. "Why, everybody, I guess."

Ella gave a gentle laugh. "The best we could hope for is the whole clan, and the clan's a far cry from being *everybody.* More than a couple days ride out of here, I bet most people haven't even heard of us."

"Hmm." Amos sounded like he didn't care for the turn the conversation was taking. "Really puts the ax to a guy's ambition, doesn't it? Whatever we do here won't matter out over the next mountain."

"Well," Ella cleared her throat, "maybe not me, but I wouldn't rule out Amos Taylor yet. No tellin' where that strapping young feller might end up." Ella grinned and turned away from Amos, seeing that they had come to her house. "Guess I better be a-turnin' in."

"Aw." Amos waved away her barefaced—if genuine—appeal to his ego. "Thanks for coming with me. It was real special. I couldn't think of a better way to start a watchman's night shift," Amos said with a gentlemanliness beyond his years.

Ella smiled as she looked down. "I had a fine evening too."

"I'd uh—"Amos cleared his throat and moved a little closer to Ella. "I think I'd find my night shift a bit easier if I had a kiss to warm me."

Ella's eyes widened further, if that were even possible, and she found her mouth gaping open in half surprise and half horror before she found her voice and gave her nimble answer. "I—um, could you—I'd rather—uh—I think Omar's already out waiting for you. Uh. I shouldn't keep you any longer." She eased away from Amos and turned to go inside. "I'm sorry, I—it was a good night, really, I just—good night."

She ran inside and closed the door directly behind her, then stumbled back into her room and tried her best not to pull her hair out by the roots.

Omar leaned over the top of the palisade overlooking the western gate. He turned at the creak of the ladder leading up to the gangway to see the clan carpenter, Shane Bunton.

"What are you doing here, drifter? Where's the first shift?" Shane's eyes flickered in the moonlight, and his voice had an edge to it.

"I let off the first shift. Figured the gate needed watchin'."

"I thought the Taylor boy was supposed to keep an eye on you."

Omar turned his head to face Shane. "Ain't showed up yet. I coulda maybe turned up a mite early."

"To throw open the gate for the unbreds?"

Omar's body came out of its lean and straightened up before his accuser. "No, sir."

"Well, I'm here to watch the gate now. So you best get." Shane jabbed a finger at Omar's chest hard enough to push him back a half-step.

"Don't I need someone to 'keep an eye on me'?"

"Are you being smart with me, kid?" Shane leaned in close enough to dust Omar with the fog from his breath.

Omar cast his eyes down. "No, sir."

"I said get."

"I'm gittin'." Omar slung his bow over his shoulder and started to climb down the ladder.

"Uppity foreigners," Shane muttered just loud enough for Omar to hear at the bottom of the palisade.

Omar and Amos walked along the palisade on the western edge of town, their breath clouding the moonlit air. In the tree line not far away, they could hear the not-quite-animal grunts and hoots of the pigmen.

"We can turn back at the corner past the gate, I guess," Amos said.

"The carpenter's watchin' the gate. We can turn back here just as well."

Amos shrugged and pivoted alongside Omar without comment.

A distant gout of flame sparked in the darkness like a guttering candle, soon followed by the pop of a rifle report. A single shot wasn't cause for alarm, but the two young men moseyed down the wall anyway to make sure. A couple of the Finches stood at the wall, one looking out through the arrow slits, the other up on a section of the catwalk, pushing a musketball down the barrel of his rifle with his ramrod, whistling a tune to himself.

The elder of the two answered Amos' question before he'd had a chance to ask it. "Cephas missed with the bow, so we had to burn some powder to show we meant business. Best get a move on; nothing more to see here," he said with a sidelong glance at Omar.

Farther down the wall, Amos cast a glance back. "Those Finches can sure be a cutthroat bunch in a pinch. Anything bad happens on our shift, you run and find them."

"They always work the night shifts?"

"Always. Nobody in the clan can see in the dark better than them. Whole family's like that; it's in their blood. You think they'd be good drifters?"

"How should I know? I don't know the Finches. There's more to driftin' than being able to see at night."

"I suppose so. You ever going to tell me about the drifting life?"

"No."

"Why not?"

"'Cause it's none of your business, that's why."

"Well, fine then. Seems like an awful nice night for folks to be sticking to their own business." Amos hitched the shoulder strap of his rifle a little higher up. They walked a few hundred feet farther down the length of the palisade before Amos spoke again. "I don't suppose a drifter's got much occasion to go courting."

"Nope."

"Ever wanted to?"

Omar surveyed the open area in front of the palisade. "When I was a kid, I guess."

They walked on as the night wore away. Amos shivered and shrugged off the deepening cold. Stopping to check the perimeter, he peeked through the rifle holes and arrow loops of the palisade to scan the killing space in front of the woods.

"Omar," Amos whispered.

"Hmm?"

"Pigman out on the edge of the woods. See him?"

A lone pigman rested on its haunches out in the open, watching the town with its head cocked to the side as if curious. An odd bearing, but then again, most unbred strains did not follow the warp and woof of wild-wrought beasts. It looked serene in the moonlight.

Omar looked through a firing slit as he nocked an arrow. "I see him. Eyeshine always gets 'em."

The bow twanged and a sharp howl that sounded like a man's cry rang in the night. The beast whimpered a little as its life passed into the snow.

"My dad always said archery was a waste of time," Amos said. "That and swordfighting."

"I can't speak for matchet work, but the bow is mighty cheap for sure shots."

"Dad said that if an enemy or an unbred gets past your rifle fire, go for the spear."

"And only an idiot lets anything get past his spear," Omar finished.

"Your dad told you that too, huh?"

"Yup."

"I kinda like the sportiness of it, though, you know? Me and my friends would get some dull swords, pack straw in our coveralls, and go to town on each other." Amos mimed a parry and riposte.

"Playin' is one thing. Killing's another."

"Yeah, I haven't got used to that, yet," Amos admitted.

"The killin'?"

"Only unbreds, so far. But even that..." Amos shook his head, searching for the right words. "It's not as easy as I figured when I was little."

Omar grunted. "They can be tougher than leather sometimes."

"That's not what I mean. If I had a hog and a pigman trussed up and lying on the ground, and I had to kill both of them, you'd think it would be easier to kill the pigman. I mean, it's a monster, right? But it isn't. Easier, I mean."

"Can't say I have that problem much."

"Some say that pigmen cry just like us."

"It's true. Don't make them like us, though."

"I don't know—they come from humans."

"They come from a lot that ain't humans, too."

"I know. A little bit of hog, a little bit of ant, a little bit of fish, a little mushroom, even. I heard they put some stuff in there spun out of nothing but clouds and cotton. But there's still a lot of human parts and pieces left in them. The idea curdles my blood."

"We don't hunt pigmen for the sport of it. They ain't dogs you can tame, you know."

"I just don't understand why the scientists ever made the unbreds in the first place."

"I reckon they made a mistake."

"But I don't get what they was even *trying* to do that they messed up so bad they made all these creatures. None of the old folks ever talk about it, and we've hardly got any books about the breedcrafting in the school. But you know there had to be *some* reason for the unbreds."

"They was—" Omar stopped.

"They was what?"

"I guess I don't know," he shrugged.

"Yeah, I reckon so," Amos said.

They walked on for a while before Amos spoke again. "Did you ever see any ubermenschen while you were out drifting?"

"I ... I don't make it a point to go a-lookin'."

"The nomad traders say some of them could fly and punch through walls and peek inside people's heads."

"That would be something to see."

"But you haven't ever seen it?"

"No."

"Sam Chambers thought there couldn't be many ubermenschen left anymore, 'cause they weren't suited for this belt-tightening kind of life. But most of the ones still around are otherworldly cunning."

"Not cunning enough to last, though."

"I suppose they're still human, like the rest of us. I've heard a story that in the old days, before the unbred outbreak and the plague and the war, an ubermensch and a regular person fell in love. They couldn't be together because of the breeding laws, so they killed themselves rather than go on with their own kind. The Reverend says it's a wicked tale, but I always thought it was really... I don't know. Really something."

They got on with their patrol. The moon's placid face hung over a black forest seething with ill-will. They reached the gate, where the murky shapes of the two Finches stood just outside the ring of light cast by a lone lantern. They didn't move as Amos and Omar drew near.

"Evening again," Amos said.

"*Shhh*," one of the Finches hissed, his gaze locked on the road beyond the wall. "Douse that glim."

Amos and Omar stopped in their tracks. Amos reached out and shuttered the lantern hanging on a peg. A low, meditative, horn-like call glided across the forest. Two rifles bolted to their shoulders and leveled themselves at the darkness.

"That isn't a pigman call," Amos muttered.

The elder Finch made no move but whispered back, "Wasn't sure what I was seein' 'til I heard it. Can you make it out?"

The four of them peered into the moon-pale darkness of the woods and the sloping hills before they heard one last call, this time within rifle range. And they saw it briefly against the velvet night sky before it flitted away. It stood upright, and if they had not known better, they might have mistaken it for a man.

Chapter 7

From Bad to Worse

"All four of us heard it and saw it. It's a shadower for sure," Amos reported to the gathering of clansmen. Omar and the two Finches nodded in agreement beside him. A shared sigh droned among the gathered elders, but not of relief. Someone cursed.

"I thought them pigmen were staying around a little too long," Elvin McDaniel mused. "I figure they already ate most of the game around here."

"There'll be nothing left of our farms by now," the elderfather of the Hadley family moaned as he swept a hand through the scant gray hairs on his scalp.

"They've already gotten most of our winter stores, and with a shadower guiding them, this whole area will be overrun until way into spring," Shane Bunton said.

Shane's brother followed on his heels. "They'll starve us out for sure if our farms are wrecked."

"If this goes on, it'll be the worst pigman siege in more than a decade."

"We've barely got any powder left—"

"I'm already running low on foodstuffs—"

"My whole family'll be down with scurvy in a couple more weeks—"

"Now let's all simmer down, now," Elvin shouted, his voice commanding. "We keep our heads, understand? So the pigmen are here to stay for a while. That's fine. We can pull through that. We've dealt with shadower armies before. I'm sure the clan can keep up all our farmers to get them back on their feet—the Craines, the Newells and Hadleys, the Brodys, even my nephew's little upstart. You folks built your farms for this sort of thing, and they can take a beating even when a shadower's playing general to the pigmen."

"I ain't worried. I'd bet teeth I'll bag this shadower, too," Deek said.

"This ain't helpin', Deek," Arnold Brody snapped. Deek had snagged a lone shadower once, six years back, and he hadn't stopped bragging about it since.

"We don't got no reason to panic yet," Elvin continued. '"Just gotta tighten them belts and grit your teeth. We're gonna have to hunt down that shadower. Rick Fillmore and his boy can track for us, and I reckon if we get our manpower behind 'em, we'll fetch that shadower 'fore your feet get cold."

The Tucker clansmen struck out in spear-point raids, clearing swaths of forest with blades and what little ammunition they had left. Rick Fillmore and his son, Victor, took leave of their wives and led the clansmen in an effort to track the shadower. Amos followed, taking heed of every mark they made, every bent twig and footprint, every nest and cranny. The trackers worked up a map of a series of oft-used trails bearing signs of a shadower passing. As best they could tell, there was only one shadower in the area.

Both of the abandoned shadower nests they found spanned only a few feet across and bore only one imprint. In one of the two nests, they found a breech-loading Greenbrier rifle—an odd find this far out from Greenbrier territory—and the gnawed remains of a couple human fingers. Elvin reckoned the fingers came from somewhere closer to home and pocketed them, if only to have something left of Billy Craine to put in the ground outside the church.

With some of the paths and trails found, the clan regrouped its hunting parties into teams that stuck together in groups of ten or more. Most of the team set up a wide hem while a couple clansmen worked to place snares and traps at strategic points along lookouts and pigman trails, marking and noting the placing of each snare. The last thing they needed was for a clansman to get caught in one of their own traps.

All of their wariness, however, did not save old John Hadley from the ravages of a stray, starving pigman. The creature had laid in waiting until most of the posse had passed by, then blindsided the easiest target at the back of the line. Pigman claws opened Mr. Hadley's thin skin like a plow opening fresh sod, and Doctor Bernhard did not give the frail old man long odds for living. He didn't. Two days after the clan's first hunt for the shadower, they buried one of the clan's few grandfathers in the cold earth. Morale sank. When the clan next ventured out, the only traps that hadn't been disarmed had only pigmen caught in them.

They reset the traps in other places, again without result. They tried hunting the shadower down the old-fashioned way, sneaking out in teams of two and three, but there were still far too many hungry pigmen out, and no shadower with an army at its beck and call would risk a tooth-and-claw grapple with a clansman. A few too many close shaves did nothing but use up the last of the Tuckers' powder and shot, and Elvin scrapped the whole scheme. If the snares wouldn't get the shadower, nothing would.

And nothing did.

To the chagrin of many clansmen and young folk, Sam Chambers refused to let out school. But bad news and scant calories had a way of making even the younger folks more restive and testy.

"Mr. Chambers?" One of his students slouched in the back with a raised hand the morning after the clan's latest death.

"Yes, Jimmy," Sam said.

"My pa said all this science stuff is what killed the world and made the unbreds in the first place." The student's eyes challenged Sam from across the classroom.

Sam frowned and pursed his lips in thought, as if finally caught out. "The idea being that your education is just laying the foundation for the next disaster."

The student shrugged.

Sam went to the chalkboard and swept the diagram of a cell away with a dusty cloth. "I'm glad you brought this up, Jimmy. I hear this kind of thinking a lot, but I haven't had the chance to face it so directly. The problem," Sam said, turning to face the class, "wasn't that the ubermenschen knew too much. It's that they didn't know nearly enough. What have I always talked about? Cause and effect. Ideas and consequences. What was the major cause of the Great Catastrophe?"

"Human genetic engineering," a student blurted without raising her hand.

"And why did scientists rush headlong into human genetic engineering without an adequate understanding of what it means to be human? Or where a person's value comes from? Or even something as simple as how to grant equal access to a technology that would change humanity forever? Total, blind ignorance. And in scarcely two generations, they paid the price. They went from an age of abundance to the last vestiges of government offering ration bounties for pigman jaws. Let's go through the stages of the Great Catastrophe. What was the first stage?"

"Social instability," a student answered, again without raising her hand.

"Good, but how did genetic engineering *cause* the social instability? Well, the most obvious reason is that it turned a class divide into a race divide," Sam answered his own question, counting the steps on his fingers. "You had the normal, unmodified folks like you and me, and then the superior race of ubermenschen, who were demonstrably better at everything. Who would want to give jobs or important positions to lesser humans? But no one stopped to think what would happen if they continued to exclude the 'lessers'.

"Which leads us to stage two. They didn't understand that when medical science turned into an ubermensch-only profession, knowledge of diseases unique to unmodified humans would grow dangerously weak. So when a nasty flu strain emerged among the natural-bred humans, doctors didn't know how to stop it properly. They underestimated the impact of the virus, and they misjudged how badly the loss of a billion so-called 'lessers' would damage their societies and economies."

"The Reverend says the ubermenschen created the plague to wipe us out," a student interrupted.

Sam rolled his eyes. "Not even the ubermenschen would be that diabolical. But when things went from bad to worse, the ubermenschen weren't above graverobbing. There were millions of empty homes and lands ripe for picking. When they gobbled up the land and resources our dying people left behind, they didn't know that those of us left alive could hit back harder than they could have imagined. Imagine what a country of unmodified humans with nothing to lose and a few nukes could do.

"And finally, in stage three, they didn't know why the unbreds went feral to finish off a world wounded by plague and war. We still don't know. Just like we don't know why so many of the ubermenschen disappeared. With a well-rounded education, all of these dangers should have been obvious."

Sam Chambers stopped his pacing and faced the class. "The Reverend says the ubermenschen were evil, but they were also stupid. And you don't cure stupidity with more stupidity. Science isn't just a how-to manual. It's a way of thinking, one that demands we be careful when there are so many things we don't know. Which makes us better scientists than the ubermenschen, don't you think, Jimmy?"

Old Man Brody shivered in the cold of his house underneath a pile of furs. He could never warm himself in the winter months. He'd come to terms with the fact a long time ago, but he still hated winter just the same. The cold, the death, the scant edibles—it was like holding your breath for three months out of the year. Sometimes he hobbled over to his neighbor's house to sleep with them on especially cold nights, just so he could ensure that he would indeed wake up in the morning. He tried not to trespass upon their hospitality too often, especially during a pigman siege. If his long life had taught him anything, it was that the clan's forbearance ran lowest when tested by an army of monsters at their door and meager foodstuffs in their pantry. Everyone knew what happened to a freeloader.

So he spent most of his time sitting and trying to keep as warm as possible when not on duty at the palisade. He sat alone with his thoughts for hours on end, the only idle occupation he could ever seem to keep up. The second and third generations had their share of troubles and cares, no doubt about it, but none of them had to live with the memories of his generation.

Sometimes it seemed like the memories didn't really belong to him, but rather to a monster or a madman. Sometimes he wondered if it had all been a nightmare, time having blurred the distinction between memory and dream. Other times, it seemed like it was just yesterday that he'd strangled his academy roommate over the keys to his car. He didn't wake up screaming anymore, but that was mostly because he was too weak to scream now.

People were different now. Quicker to react, but less likely to panic. He'd never forget the collective deer-in-the-headlights stare that swept the country when the unbreds went wild. Surely it won't get as bad here, they'd thought. The police always handled the uprisings and riots before. The CDC had controlled the spread of the Pandemic. It couldn't happen to us. Not us.

But Brody had known. He'd known even before the military had hastily recalled him from his tour abroad. He was supposed to support a special project, but the hens had come home to roost, and there was no telling how far civilization would fall before it finally hit the bottom. A second outbreak of the Pandemic crawled up from the lower classes to feast on the middle class, and the wavering economy finally collapsed. The power never came back on, the grocery stores went empty, the riots turned into massacres, all communications failed, and soon even he hadn't known what was going on anymore.

When they'd given his unit a couple cans of ammunition and tasked them with house-to-house eradication, he'd had enough. He took whatever supplies he could carry and went AWOL. If he was going to die, he would do it at home, back in the mountains. When he last saw his unit-turned-ragtag-extermination-squad, he was certain they all marched to early graves.

It had all fallen apart so perfectly it felt like it was meant to happen, like an act of God. Maybe the world had known, deep down, that they deserved it.

If the disease favored the poor—not the right medical histories—the unbreds showed no distinction. And the crushing despair might have been the worst killer of all. One of the women in the group—she'd been a middle school principal, he thought—cried every night, all night, until folks couldn't take it anymore and told her to go weep somewhere else. She went outside one night and never came back.

He remembered when they'd left the city and struck out on foot toward the east, toward the supposed safety of the Appalachian Mountains. When they camped in an old church one night, one of their lookouts came crashing down from the bell tower with a bullet through the back of his head. They figured it was some sort of robber party, and they waited for hours, bracing for an attack that never came. When morning arrived, they realized they'd walked into a killing field. Unbred and human corpses lay everywhere, all killed by precise, carefully placed shots.

They never solved the mystery. Of course they eventually tracked down and killed the sniper, but they could never figure out the smile they saw on the face of the long-haired, thirty-something shooter they cornered on his throne of canned goods and bottled water. They couldn't explain the sack of severed human ears tucked beneath his bed. They never understood why anyone could enjoy the end of the world.

The madmen came out of the woodwork as the world burned. Old Man Brody never knew there were so many, or why they seemed to survive so well. One of the men in his own party had turned out to be one of them. Brody should have seen it coming, should have known it when the man shrieked in glee as he fired an Armalite into a knot of marauders and their bastard children. He'd just seemed so useful at the time.

Old Man Brody shivered in the cold. When someone came knocking, he considered not answering. An open door wouldn't do his frigid hands any good.

But folks didn't come knocking without good reason, especially during times like these. His eldest surviving son stood on the stoop when he opened the door.

"Morning, Oliver."

"Morning, Father," Reverend Brody said. "How fare you?"

Old Man Brody shrugged. "Still okay."

"The shadower hasn't..." The Reverend didn't finish his thought out loud. He didn't need to.

"No. I think it's too wrapped up with its army to worry about persecutin' an old has-been like me. I'm having more nightmares, but I expect most folks are."

The Reverend nodded. "I'll check in again tomorrow, if I can. Come to me right away if anything changes."

Chapter 8

In Which Desperation Comes Knocking

Young Ralph McDaniel, the watchman's boy, stole from the penning walls of his home after supper in early January with a package tucked under one arm, hoping his father wouldn't heed his leave-taking. He met with his cousin just past his uncle's house and with one of the Varner boys just beyond. The three of them made their way to the schoolhouse without a lantern between them, happy to find their way by moonlight. A faint light burned inside the school, and the side door opened for them. Three more Tucker boys huddled inside, hiding from the cold and the prying eyes of their elders. A few tallow candles were all they had to light the small room.

"You bring it?" one of them asked, his whisper fogging the frosty air.

"Yeah." Ralph unwrapped the package and began to pass out little plastic odds and ends from it.

"How much are we going to start out with this time?"

"I say two hundred dollars. Mack hasn't ever played before."

"Seven cards?"

"Yup." Ralph started dealing the cards to the other boys.

"Are we gonna let 'em trade?"

"Not this time."

"Okay, Mack, here's how it goes," Ralph explained. "It's the old days, and you've just graduated from school. You have to make your way in the world. Depending on what you spend your time and money on, you could choose to become a soldier, a doctor, a businessman, an actor, or whatever. Depending on which one you choose, you unlock different sets of story cards as we get on through the game. Think you can pick the rest up as we go?"

Ralph had bought this game from some nomads a little more than a year ago, and the purchase had been a hit with town boys of a certain bent. Some of the young men could not resist the imaginative allure of a bygone world, where money flowed like water and a thousand different possibilities presented themselves to someone every day. Their fathers and mothers, however, did not share their enthusiasm. If they had to waste time, why not waste it on something more active, like horseshoes or rugby or swimming? Imagination was a guilty pleasure, pursued only when the chores were all done and parents weren't watching. Which meant, in Ralph McDaniel's view, that pigman sieges weren't *all* bad.

Winter was hard for the Tucker clan that year. They celebrated New Year's Day with root vegetable rations. Two weeks later, they took rations down by a third, with Elvin going house-to-house to make sure no one was skimming the cream. All unneeded work ceased as clansmen scrimped dear energy and calories. The clan could not count on renewing its food stores until a nomad clan came through, and no nomads would try to run a blockade of starving pigmen. With the shadower and its mysterious ways of guiding and controlling the pigmen, the horde could besiege the Tucker clan until every last unbred starved, which could take years. The pigmen would cannibalize each other to keep up their strength. The clan had never stooped so low as to eat the flesh of their fellow man, though that is not to say some of the older folks had never been tempted.

Halfway through January, Omar stood in line at the miller's for Bill's weekly ration of flour. The miller measured out the allotted amount of flour to each family representative, then made a chalk-mark on the giant slate placard in the shop behind him to keep track of the disbursements. Siege or no siege, rations or no rations, the miller would collect his due when folks came into money again. The fact that he was now cutting the flour with sawdust made no difference. Supply and demand were uncompromising masters.

When Omar's turn came up, the miller dropped his measuring cup back into the barrel. "You, drifter. My boy says you came here twice for rations last week."

"I picked up for the Hollands last week," Omar explained.

"Well, that's a shame. I ain't got any flour for you this week."

"Check your slate. If the Hollands came here aside from me, you'll know I'm lyin'."

The miller's nostrils flared. "Did you hear me, boy? I said I ain't got any flour for you this week!"

"This is Bill Puckett's rations."

"Serves him right for taking in a scheming drifter to suck the lifeblood from the clan. From now on, Bill needs to come and get his rations personally. I don't want to see you skulking around here again, you hear?"

Omar gave the miller a hard look before removing himself from the line. All the Tuckers still waiting for their share followed him with their eyes, their whispers nipping at his heels.

"He's a Jonah for sure."

"The pigmen won't leave until he does."

"And my kids are going hungry to keep him plump."

A cold shock blasted the side of Omar's face with the force of a brick. He blinked and staggered as the remnants of an icy snowball fell to the ground. Someone had packed rocks into it. Another one sailed past his ear, and he ducked to the ground, darting a glance behind him.

A passel of young teenage boys stood on the other end of the street, scooping up snow and bits of ice.

"Look at the big, bad drifter. Not so tough when he can't take the butter off your bread," one of them said, chucking his snowball.

Omar ducked and ran.

When Dale Taylor came over to the gunsmith's shop to fetch his older half-brother for dinner, he found young Clive and Margaret Holland lounging outside on the faded plastic lawn chairs left out for company.

"Hey. Amos ready to go yet?"

Clive and Margaret both shrugged. Clive didn't even look from the whimmy-diddle he was half-heartedly sawing on.

"Amos!" Dale hollered inside. "Dinner!"

"Gimme a minute! I'm helping Bill!" came the answer from Bill's shop next door. Ordinarily, it was common for an apprentice to eat with the family of his master, but during a famine or pigman siege like this one, each family looked after their own.

Dale sat down next to the two young ones to wait.

"Whatcha eatin' for dinner?" Clive asked.

"Turnips. Same as you, I guess."

"Yeah. On Sunday, we're gonna have some toasted bread with hog grease." Clive kicked out languidly at a mound of snow, sliding a bit further down into his seat as he did.

"That's somethin' to look forward to," Dale said in the half-fatherly tone eleven-year-olds will sometimes put on when talking to younger children. "Amos! Mom's gonna have a fit if you don't come soon!"

"I said hold on! Sheesh..."

Dale sighed, already too exhausted to press the matter further. "Mom gets after Amos a lot," he explained. "I think it's 'cause he's her stepson, and she never got used to the idea. Is your mom like that?"

"She gets after us when we're bad," Margaret said.

"No, is she that way with Ella, I mean."

"She don't ever get after Ella," Margaret said, incredulous. "Ella's a grown-up!"

"Okay. Never mind. How's Amos been working with your dad?"

"Papa says he's a good help," Margaret said while trying to stop a bored but exhausted Clive from slouching.

"My brother Harvey says Amos should've gone in with Mr. McDaniel to apprentice as watchman. Dad wouldn't have it." Dale slouched a bit himself.

"Papa says I can't apprentice with the watchman, either," Clive said, now nearly sliding out of his seat.

"Me neither."

"We ain't never had a girl watchman, Margie!"

"Ma said I can be whatever I want!"

"Mr. McDaniel wouldn't ever let a girl be watchman!"

"Ah," Dale said, then thought better of it. "You know what? Never mind."

"What took you so long?" Amos asked as Omar slipped inside. "My arms are killing me."

"Got stuck jawing with the miller." Omar returned to his hand crank and got back to work. At the end of a foot-long shaft, the crank turned a ball mill with a small batch of powder encased inside. Powdermaking was one of the few professions still in full swing, and the arms of two apprentices suffered for it today.

Amos had wondered aloud earlier why they couldn't fill the ball mills up to the brim and get it all over with in one batch. Bill's response was that keeping the batches small made it somewhat less likely to kill the mixer if the powder sparked off, a reassuring answer if there ever was one.

Bill Puckett entered with Ella trailing behind.

"Y'uns done grinding yet?" Bill asked.

Amos and Omar opened up their ball mills for Bill to check

"Hmmm," he mused, rubbing the mixture between his fingers. "Pretty good. Ella, start corning this."

Amos flexed his aching hands while Bill lifted a bunch of charcoal onto the bench and crushed it with practiced quickness. "Omar, measure out thirty grams of sulfur into there, then one-hundred-fifty grams of that nitrate over yonder. Then come out and help me with the niter beds."

"I gotta go. Got dinner waiting and I've got the shakes something awful," Amos said.

"Have yourself a sit down if you're dizzy. You'll hit your second wind in a bit. Fill the mill the rest of the way with sulfur and grind it in before you take off." Bill had crossed over into his house before he heard Amos' sigh.

Omar had just measured out the foul-smelling sulfur into a cloudy beaker when a cry emanated from the house.

"Omar, you lazy good-for-nothin'! Where's the gol-darn flour I sent you after?"

Amos and Ella looked at Omar.

"Pardon me," Omar said, leaving the workbench to face the music in Bill's house.

Bill beat him to the door, storming into the shop to get an answer for the missing flour. "Have you been out playin' hooky when I sent you on an errand?"

Omar stared deadpan at his master. "The miller thinks I'm a cheat. Said I've been stealing rations. He won't dole out rations to me no more."

Bill looked as if he'd been slapped. "He didn't."

"Said you'd need to come get your rations personally from now on."

"*He didn't.*" Bill looked ready to take a swing at Omar.

Ella jumped in. "It's my fault. He went in for my family last week. I didn't think—"

"I don't care what happened! If that old screw Joe Garmen is bad-mouthin' *my* apprentice in front of half the clan—" Bill shook his head, fuming. "Let him try sticking a musketball up his butt and farting at the unbreds, 'cause I don't know where he's gonna get his gunpowder from now on! Not from me, no sir! Uptown millers, casting aspersions on my apprentice, wasting workin'-time like I don't got nothing else better to do."

Bill looked at the Ella, Amos, and Omar. "Well, don't just stand there. Get on home or help me turn the niter beds. I'm about through having my time wasted."

"I'm not finished with the ball mill yet," Amos said.

"No, go on home. You done enough," Bill sighed. "Ella, you too."

"Want to come on over for dinner again tonight?" Ella asked.

"Yeah, we might. Ask your ma."

When Bill and Omar were alone, Bill sighed again. "Fetch a lantern. We'll leach out the January pile before bed, I reckon. Take it easy tomorrow." He grabbed a wooden pitchfork, stained brown with use, and headed for the back door and the deepening dark of an early winter evening.

A knock at the door interrupted them before Bill could exit out the back. It was Ella, already cringing at the news she bore. "Uh, Johnny Grierson is outside."

"Aw, hell." Bill cast weary eyes to the ceiling and leaned on his pitchfork. He straightened up and strode to the door like a man getting ready for his hanging, but a man barged in past Ella before Bill could make it outside to meet him.

The man had one eye and what looked to be burns on that side of his face. The other side, lacking the advantage of an eye patch, looked less pleasant.

"Johnny Grierson!" Bill said with forced neighborliness. "Decided to crawl out of that settlement of your'n and join the rest of us?"

"Just for tonight. We've come down to get some supplies and deliver some powder. Had to gather every able body in the settlement to break through the unbred patrols. Stuff's a-getting' real scarce up yonder."

"Stuff's getting real scarce here." Bill leaned the pitchfork against the wall and folded his arms.

"Easy, Bill. I'm just here for your manure."

"You got some charcoal and potash?"

"A few pounds of each." Johnny jerked a thumb back at the hand truck behind him.

Bill sighed, whatever shred of pleasantness he could muster fading. "Let me see it, then."

Johnny came up with a couple pokes, which Bill went over with a keen eye.

"I'm not giving you shit for this," Bill said, pushing the offered payment away.

"Bill, this is all you're gonna get from me. You wanna risk your neck to the pigmen to find a good hardwood tree yourself? Who's gonna help you haul it back? Him?" Johnny said, waving to the drifter. "You got your own weight to pull, same as me. We've brought in five pounds of gunpowder from our workshop to help fight the pigmen. How much have you ground?"

"Not as much as I could have made if I didn't have y'all trying to stiff me."

"Don't blame this on us. Your ill fame ain't caused 'o cheatin'. You manage that all by your lonesome. You should have left the powder-making to us Griersons."

"Then I will. Get your own manure. Pull that stick out of your behind; I bet you could supply the whole clan."

Johnny threw his hands into the air. "I don't know what's the matter with you! If anything is your calling, surely shoveling crap is! Isn't that what you were doing when Martha blew herself up in your shop? If that ain't a sign—"

Bill grabbed the wooden pitchfork and gestured toward Mr. Grierson. "Johnny, is there *any* reason you came here besides getting your ugly face busted in?"

"Well, since you mention it," Johnny said, stepping back. "I wanted to see the drifter. Folks up at the settlement don't cotton the way y'uns took him in without even asking us. Edward and I are still elders, you know."

"Elders who can't be troubled to come on down in the middle of a pigman attack. If you didn't want him here, you should have said so. It's not like *I* asked to keep him. I didn't get a say in it any which way. No offense, Omar."

Johnny turned to face the drifter. "Is that what they call you? Omar?"

Omar nodded.

"Is he behaving himself around here?" Johnny asked Bill.

"He is."

"Well, we'll see what he does after we kill that shadower, and he finds himself a chance to leave." Johnny gave the drifter a good looking over—from a sound distance. "I heard some of the folks around here don't fancy the extra mouth to feed."

"Yeah, well, whatever folks those are, they got the wrong idea. I haven't been taking any extra rations," Bill said.

"That's horse malarkey. Everyone knows you're living off the Hollands and that pretty little daughter of your'n. You might want to tell your drifter what we do to folks who don't pull their weight around here." His parting shot taken, Johnny hastened away while Bill wrung the handle of his pitchfork with white-knuckled fists.

Omar paused for a moment, then wordlessly walked out to spread straw on the niter beds. Bill stayed in the shop with the ball mill, and when alone in the shop once more, performed some action that brought forth a loud thud and a clatter. When he emerged from his shop, his shoulders sagged, and all he could manage was, "When it rains, it pours."

"What about the charcoal?" Omar asked.

"We've got enough to make a few more batches of powder. Then, I suppose I'll see what I can do with the firewood we have already. It won't be very good, but I can make it work."

"And after that?"

Bill sat down with a sigh. "If the pigman siege hasn't ended by then, I reckon we'll go ahead and starve."

The Hollands—Phil, his wife, Leah; his eldest daughter, Ella; his younger daughter, Margaret; and his remaining son, Clive—together with Bill Puckett and his drifter apprentice Omar Walking sat down at their table one dark Tuesday night in late January to a meal of salted mashed turnips. Mr. Holland threw some ashes into his for better flavor. They said grace and dug in.

"Ella," Mrs. Holland said between mouthfuls, "this is great!"

Clive and Margaret agreed with smacking lips and choruses of "Mmm!"

Ella paused. "It's good?"

Her stepmother nodded. "I think you finally did it, sweetie."

Phil Holland shook his head. "Ain't possible. Turnips can't taste good, it's—" He caught a glance from his wife. "All blazes, it's a miracle! Congratulations!"

And so the family finished their meal in happy silence, and not a soul betrayed the fact that they were all starving.

Chapter 9

In Which Omar Outstays His Welcome

Two weeks into February, life slowed to an unending crawl. Even Elvin McDaniel felt the pinch. Many Tuckers didn't leave their homes during the day. Those that did usually only went out to scavenge and beg for food. The Hadleys paid Reverend Brody three pigmen jaws for a ten-pound sack of cornmeal just before the second Sunday. The Newells butchered their two milk cows to keep the clan in meat. The longer the siege went on, the more the Tuckers would eat into their livelihoods to survive.

Then the inevitable ugly news came: someone was hoarding food beyond what their work required. Old Widow Finch, laid up more often than not, was seen feasting on a whole chicken that hadn't shown up on her ledger. Word of the outrage spread like wildfire. A whole chicken for a worthless old woman! That very morning, Elvin McDaniel went to call on her to check out the rumors.

"Mrs. Finch!" Elvin knocked on the door a second time. "It's the watchman. Open up." He waited a beat, then knocked again, harder.

"Let's take it easy, Elvin," Sam Chambers said. The schoolteacher had joined Elvin on his visit to the old lady. As to why, Elvin had not the slightest idea.

He hammered on the door again, and again he received no answer. "That old bitch knows we're coming for her."

"Elvin!" Sam's reproach came sharp and sudden. "Innocent until proven guilty."

"Her lollygagging ain't doing her any favors." Elvin pounded on the door. "Mrs. Finch, if you don't come and open this door right now, I'm gonna bust it in."

No answer.

Elvin shrugged, braced himself, and placed a pile-driving heel right below the doorknob of her old door. The hasp broke away with a snap, a rusty wood screw skittering across the floor like a cockroach exposed to light.

The watchman shouldered his way inside, the schoolteacher following. The house was as cold as an icebox.

"Mrs. Finch?" Elvin called, his breath fogging the air as he walked toward the kitchen. "Mrs. Finch, I'm gonna need to talk to you about—"

Mrs. Finch sat in a rocking chair, a pair of knitting needles in her throat and a frozen pool of blood clinging to her dress in her lap. Her unseeing eyes bored holes into the two men who had violated her tomb.

"Oh my God." Sam recoiled from the sight.

"Well, that's that." Elvin grabbed a poke, walked over to her pantry, and loaded up what grub she still had left.

"She up and killed herself," Sam murmured, stating the obvious in that irritating way of his.

"Didn't think she'd have it in her." Elvin paused to look back and nod in respect. "Just as well. Better for her. Better for the clan."

"How can you say that?"

"What did you think was going to happen to her, Sam? She went ahead and got it over with and saved us a big headache dealing with it in the middle of a pigman siege. Instead of being remembered as a miser and a cheat, she'll be remembered as an eldermother who laid her life down for the clan. If the unbreds or the Greenbriers don't get me, this is how I want to go." He motioned to the corpse. "I'm only sorry she did it after eating a whole dad-blamed chicken."

"I thought we were moving past this sort of thing." Sam shook his head. "It's been ten, no, probably twelve years since we last banished a clansman. I thought we'd be able to work this one out. I didn't want it to come to this."

"This is the natural order of things, Sam. If this siege goes on much longer, we'll be trimming the fat some more. I got me a list of folks I wouldn't mind kicking to the unbreds, and that list includes some elders." Elvin gave Sam a hard look.

"I suppose that would make sense, if you believed a person's value only comes from their worth in a fight."

Elvin inspected the seal on some canned tomatoes. "I didn't say that. I take a high-minded view. Fighters need support, too." He looked at Sam and gave the jar of tomatoes a little shake.

"So the fighters and those who 'support' them? Those are the ones worthy of life?"

"That's how we've survived."

"We've survived by keeping *this*"—Sam pointed at Mrs. Finch—"to a minimum. There are invisible ties that bind us together. Or invisible to you, at least. The more this happens, the more those ties strain. If they break, we break."

"Yeah, but see, I ain't interested in pie-in-the-sky hullabaloo. I'm interested in the real world," Elvin said as he walked over and slapped the back of Mrs. Finch's rocker, "and I'm sorry to say it, but in the real world, we're all gonna end up like this sooner or later. Best we can do is decide when, where, and how."

"And my 'pie-in-the-sky hullabaloo' makes 'it' happen later, in your own bed, peacefully. It's called trust, Elvin. A lone fighter won't survive long. Which means he needs a community. And how long will a community last if they think they'll be kicked out the moment they can't heft a spear anymore?"

"We done it that way for fifty years, no problem."

"And we'll keep on doing it for the next fifty?"

"If we have to." Elvin slung the full burlap poke over his shoulder and walked past Sam toward the door.

Sam, apparently, wasn't finished with the watchman. "My aim is to make sure we won't."

Elvin stopped and turned. "And how you gonna do that?"

"I build that future a little more every day I spend teaching the youngsters in this clan, including yours."

"You're makin' 'em soft, if you ask me." Elvin snorted and hocked a wad of phlegm out the open kitchen window.

"I'm making them *smart.*"

"I don't got a problem with smart. But I worry that when the time comes, my boy won't be able to do what's needed."

"You think I haven't done battle, watchman? I know what's needed. And I know what isn't. With you, it isn't about what's needed. You *need* this life to be hard, to *stay* hard, even if it ends up costing you your own kin. Because this nature red in tooth-and-claw business gives you the only purpose you can have. Because apart from the Paul McDaniel in you, there isn't much else to you."

Sam appeared to regret saying that last bit, which was exactly Sam's problem, Elvin thought.

Elvin grinned without mirth. "I'll take that as a compliment." He left that spineless little man with the old widow.

"What about the burial?" Sam called after Elvin.

Elvin shifted the weight of the sack he carried. "I don't want clansmen to waste calories digging a grave right now. It's cold. She'll keep just fine for a few weeks."

The eldermother's death promised to calm things down a bit, even if it did little to raise anyone's spirits. The contents of her larders did not go far to supplement the diets of her neighbors. Sunday came and went, and Reverend Brody continued to preach on the story of Jonah, marking for the second Sunday in a row how the storm only ceased when the one cursed by God was thrown overboard. When morning peeked on Monday, a few Tuckers milled about in the freshly churned mud of an icy thaw. They were dazed, closing in on despair, but at least it was peaceful.

It seemed safe enough for Omar to make a powder delivery for Bill.

"Hey, drifter," someone called as he passed by. A scrawny, scuzzy-looking fellow leaned up against a hitching post, his arms folded in a stewing languor.

Omar kept going without giving the man a further glance.

"Hey, drifter! I'm talkin' to you!"

Omar stopped and turned to see the man had straightened and was now following him with haphazard strides. "Have we met before?" Omar asked.

"Bert Daly. You stole food from me. I want it back."

Omar turned to walk away. "I ain't stole nothin'."

"You've et, ain't ye? That's *my* vittles you've been a-chowin' on!"

"You're crazy, Tucker. I been gettin' the same rations as ever'body."

Bert kept following, gaining on Omar. "The rations you get come from somewhere. They come from me. The elders don't cotton to half-breeds, so they figger they can screw me sideways anytime things get tight. Weren't for you, I wouldn't be plumb outta bread. I'm *hungry*, goddammit."

"Not my problem."

"It will be if I tell folks you been stealin' stuff."

Omar stopped and turned to face Bert again. Omar's eyes narrowed. "Good luck arguin' that." Omar went on his way.

He'd barely made it to the next street up the hill when Bert hollered "Thief! Thief!" behind him. Omar slowed before waving it off disgustedly.

Bert Daly didn't slow down until he got the attention of another clansman, that clansman being Shane Bunton.

The burly carpenter burst from his home, already red-faced. "What's all this caterwaul about?"

"The drifter's a thief!" Bert shrieked as he jabbed a trembling finger at Omar.

Omar threw up his hands. "That half-and-half's a liar—"

Shane didn't even look Bert's way. "You drifting leech!" Shane stomped toward Omar. "You little cockroach, bringing them doggone pigmen with you!"

Omar remained frozen as the carpenter stormed up to him.

Shane walked up to Omar and thumped a heavy hand on his shoulder. "About time we teach you a thing or two ab—"

It was a mistake. Omar spun under Shane's outstretched hand, seizing his arm and kicking his legs out from under him. Omar had him face down in the mud in a second, with Shane's arm cocked behind his back, ready to pop right out of his shoulder.

"Gaa! Son-of-a—" Shane bellowed into the frosty mud as Omar planted a knee on the Tucker's back to keep him there.

Other clansmen gathered like vultures. "What are you doing?" Reverend Brody's voice rang out from the coalescing throng, indignant. "Get your hands off of that clansman!"

Omar looked up at his surroundings, released Shane, and backed off. "He attacked me," Omar said, but Shane hadn't yet said his piece, and his was the only piece that mattered.

"Son-of-a-bullhusker jumped me," Shane muttered, wiping mud from his face with the back of his hand, half-starved murder in his eyes.

Omar looked around him. Bert Daly was already gone. "Listen, I—"

"Get him, Fred!"

Two arms grabbed Omar from behind, holding him fast. He struggled while Shane drove a clenched fist into his gut. The Tuckers who'd gathered to witness the beating winced but did nothing. Shane was just getting ready to sock Omar another good one when Elvin broke in.

"What's going on here?" the town watchman hollered, his trusty rifle cradled in his arms. "I don't got the energy for this kind of crap. We got some trouble going on?"

Shane stopped mid-swing and stood at attention, and his brother, Alfred Bunton, lessened his grip on Omar.

Elvin's narrowed eyes jumped from person to person before settling on Omar and narrowing further. There were no words necessary. Omar broke free of the hands that held him and took to his heels, heedless of the calls to *halt*, to get his *worthless behind back here.* No one had the energy to work up a quick run after him as he disappeared between the houses and shops at the edge of the street.

He ran back to Bill Puckett's place and slid inside. He snatched up his meager belongings, suiting up as fast as his hands could fly. He looked out the window. The clan watchman, along with Alfred and Shane Bunton, came marching down the street.

Omar paced the room. No options. Pigmen infested the woods, and he wouldn't make it more than a mile on his own in the dead of winter. He grabbed Bill Puckett's rifle. Put it down. Picked it up again.

Ella walked in. "Omar?" She stopped short at the sight of him armed and panting. She took a step back. "Somethin' wrong?"

He said nothing. His grip tightened on the barrel of his rifle.

A thunderous knock on the door made both of them jump, and Elvin's voice burst into the room from just outside. "Bill? You in there?"

Ella and Omar looked at each other. "Take it easy, Omar," Ella warned in a low voice, her hands moving as if to keep down the desperation. "Put the gun down."

"It wasn't my fault."

"It's okay, Omar. Just put the gun down."

"What am I going to do then, huh?" Omar said, his voice rising.

Someone muttered orders outside. "Clyde, you cover the back exit. Someone watch the windows. Make sure your pan's primed; he's a fearsome one." Then the Tucker watchman called out again. "Hello? Someone in there? Come on out right now, with your hands where I can see them."

Ella stepped to the door to open it. Omar tried to stop her, but she pushed him gently away. "I'll talk to them," she explained. "You stay here. And could you please put that gun down? No one's gonna get hurt."

She opened the door and stepped outside, closing the door behind her. "How are things today?" she asked in the plain, soft-spoken way she would have used in happier days.

"It's the drifter. Seems there's been some orneriness," Elvin said.

"Omar? What's he done?"

"Well, from what Shane here tells me, the drifter attacked him and pushed him into the ground."

Ella's eyes darted from Elvin to Shane, then back to Elvin. "For no reason?"

"Bert Daly's sayin' Omar stole food," Elvin grunted.

"I knowed he was a bad apple, Elvin. The Griersons were right!" Shane said from behind Elvin.

Ella scanned the handful of gathered clansmen in the background. "I don't see Bert Daly anywhere. Why didn't he come along? Are we sure Omar stole food?"

Shane thumped his chest. "That's what I was a-tryin' to find out when he took a swing at me!"

Ella looked genuinely concerned for the carpenter. "Are you hurt bad, Shane?"

No one answered. Everyone knew the only thing really hurt was his pride.

Elvin's voice was firm. "Now, Miss Holland, we've got that drifter upsetting the peace. We just can't have that during a pigman siege like this. Can't say that I abide by him being here in the first place. He's not safe, and I'm not about to let a drifter get the best of a clansman."

"What'll you do to him?" Ella stared down at her feet.

"He might have to get himself a move on."

Ella looked up again. "In the middle of a siege?"

Elvin shrugged. "He can always take old Widow Finch's way out."

"All because *Bert Daly* said Omar stole food? Bert Daly? The first clansman to get fired from an apprenticeship in who knows how long?"

Elvin didn't answer.

"Has Omar even told his side of the story? If we're talkin' of banishment and whatnot, I'd like Mr. Chambers to sit in on things."

"We don't need any of that," Shane interrupted. "Half the clan saw him jump me!"

"Shut up, Shane," Elvin hissed.

"Well, his word doesn't matter anyway; he's a drifter!"

"I said *shut up*, Shane!"

"His word should matter," Ella reasoned, "just as much as any one of ours. He *is* a fellow human, ain't he?"

"The clan hasn't settled on that, and you know it!"

"Shane, if you don't shut your gol-darned yap, I'll bust in every tooth you've got in that empty head of your'n." Elvin rapped his temple hard enough to look like it hurt.

Ella shrugged as if she didn't much care how the discussion went. "Well, if you are going to banish Omar, make sure you have a replacement apprentice on hand. Bill's been getting quite a bit of use out of him, and it would be a shame to lose a workhorse when we need so much gunpowder. I don't figure he'll be too keen on trying out Bert Daly again."

Shane spoke up again in utter disregard for the soundness of his teeth. "This is all a bunch of hooey. I say we kick that guy out of here, pigmen or no pigmen. I can't stand him sticking around any longer. It's an extra mouth to feed, and I'll bet a hundred jaws that he's just waiting for the right chance for him to spring something on all of us. I'm surprised you're taking his side in this, Miss Holland. You've got more cause to be skittish than anyone else in the clan."

"Now, Shane," Ella said, "I think the problem is that we're all hungry and we aren't thinking straight. We ought to save our energy instead of arguing about this. If it ain't worth it for Bert to come and call Omar out to his face, it don't seem to me like there's been any real harm done."

"Well—" Shane started, but couldn't seem to come up with anything more to say.

"You don't know that Omar's like other drifters. You don't know nothing about him, really. He's been a good help for us, and he hasn't really hurt anyone. Y'all should just bide your time a little while longer and bear with him. When we kill the shadower, the pigmen'll leave, and you won't have to worry about the drifter no more."

Shane didn't look like he wanted to budge, but the surrounding clansmen had turned away, casting sullen looks over their shoulders as they went. Alfred Bunton pulled his brother away, saying, "Come on, Shane, there isn't anything we can do now."

Ella watched them go, and not until Elvin McDaniel had herded the last of them down the street did she dare turn around to come back inside. The door sighed softly as she opened it to see the drifter still clutching his rifle. "They're gone, Omar."

"They'll be back," Omar said.

"Try not to think badly of them, Omar. They're not bad folks, not really."

"Tell me that after they've hung me from the gates."

Ella looked at the floor and gave no answer.

"Why'd you do it?" he asked after a stretch of silence.

Ella gave Omar a long look before she answered. "How can someone claim to love God, who he ain't seen," Ella said, "and hate his brother, who he has seen?"

"But I ain't your brother, strictly speaking."

Ella looked away. "No, I reckon not."

Someone pounded on the door, and they both jumped again.

"Hey, it's me, Amos. What's going on? What were all those folks doing outside?"

Ella opened the door to let Amos in. "Folks are gettin' tired of having Omar around."

"What are they tired of? Him stealing their precious manure?"

"They think I'm a thief and a rabble-rouser," Omar explained.

"Who does? I'll beat up anyone who needs it."

"Take a breath, Amos. It's all over. And don't you worry, Omar. Our clan's bark is worse than our bite," Ella said.

"I ain't so sure," Omar said.

"I'm not either," Amos said. "I'm not so sure nobody would even—you know—do him in." Amos nodded to Omar.

Ella shook her head. "They wouldn't. Not like you're thinking. Not like that. Not Omar."

Amos scratched behind his ear. "Last time we had a drifter come through here and raid us, Elvin got a posse that trailed him for fifteen or sixteen miles. They took his body back and staked it out on the road for the buzzards and unbreds to pick clean."

"But they wouldn't get a bunch of people to try to hurt Omar. At least not in any sorted-out way like that."

"Maybe. But we can't put them off for long; he's got to be taken in, not just put up with, and the clan won't take him in until he earns their respect."

"And I suppose it wasn't enough to save you and your brother," Omar mused.

"Hold on," Amos said with a hint of a smile and the kind of crazed twinkle in his eye which his family had learned to fear. It was the same look he'd had when he'd set on the idea to raft the Bird Run creek on the mountain stretch with his feet strapped to a log.

"Hold on," Amos said again.

Ella and Omar held on for some seconds, but Amos felt the need to repeat himself one more time. "Hold. On. Just a minute," he said with growing enthusiasm before he left the two standing in Bill Puckett's shop.

Ella looked at Omar. Omar looked at Ella. Amos didn't come back.

"Sooo—" Omar began.

Amos burst back into the shop. "Omar! I've got it!" He grabbed Omar by the shirtsleeve and pulled him toward the door as he spoke. "Come with me, and I'll tell you everything. Sorry, Ella, no girls allowed." He slammed the door behind him right in Ella's face. She blinked.

"You want to *what*?" Omar cried in as loud a voice he'd dared since he'd first faced the pigmen alongside Amos.

"Not so loud, Omar." Amos peeked out of the root cellar where they held their secret meeting. "I swear, did you think we snuck down here to start caterwauling?" he said as he closed the door.

"You're out of your head, Amos," Omar hissed.

"Of course not. I'm clever. I've thought this out. Killing the shadower will help both of us. None of us will starve, the clan will be able to get back on its feet come spring, and not even Reverend Brody or the Buntons could get at you after you bring back the shadower's head, even if they wanted to."

"I'd rather wager my chances with the clan."

"You don't have any chances with the clan." Amos sighed. "I—"

The root cellar door burst open, and Amos clapped his mouth shut. Ella looked down at the two young men looking like they'd been caught plotting murder.

"What are you doing here?" Amos demanded.

"What am *I* doing here? What are *you* doing here? This is *my* root cellar."

"You've come here to eavesdrop, haven't you?"

"No, I came for the turnips and canned beets." Ella leaned up against the doorframe and held out a hand.

"Fine. Here." Amos handed her the vegetables. She slowly closed the door, her bewildered stare never breaking.

Amos turned back to Omar. "Aaaanyway, I didn't want to tell you this, but folks are stirring. More than you know. There's been talk among the Tuckers that you're one of the really nasty drifters—one of them crazy murderer types, maybe even an ubermensch, after all. And since you don't talk very much and haven't been one for fellowshipping, well, I suppose it's been pretty easy for the hearsay to get on. If we don't kill that shadower—if you don't come waltzing down the center street with the shadower's head in your arms, well—"

"You really think we got a better chance going out into pigman-overrun woods hunting for a shadower without any other hands or help with us?"

"Don't worry," Amos said with a sideways grin, "I already told you I've got a plan."

That night, Amos and Omar went to their post to make their rounds, armed to the teeth and dressed for an ice age. Their stand-ins came to unburden them just after midnight and, not finding them, cursed the two for leaving their roundswalk early. It wasn't until Elvin McDaniel came to Phil Holland's place to chide the young men that folks grasped the truth. By the time they had found their tracks leading briefly into the woods and disappearing right before the untrained eye, by the time they had gathered a party search for the two, everyone knew they would be searching not for Amos and Omar, but for their chawed bones.

Chapter 10

The Best Laid Plans

In the early morning twilight, when the chill of a long winter night still clutched the air in a stony fist, a chorus of pigmen shouts and barks greeted the thin dawn. In a glen next to a frozen stream, a young man hung upside down in a trap of his clan's own making, wounded in the leg from the part of the snare meant to kill its victim. The remains of a fire smoldered a few paces away, a line of sharpened stakes laid nearby, ready to char. A ring of pigmen hemmed in the young man, hungry and eager but unable to reach the upside-down human. His rifle, his bow and quiver, and his knife lay scattered on the ground underneath him.

"Omar," Amos moaned. "Omar."

His pleas brought forth no answer from the woods, save the hungry snarls of the pigmen beneath him. Omar was nowhere in sight. They'd taken precautions, but on a deathly still night with a slight breeze and an army of starving pigmen scattered about, all the sneaking in the world only went so far.

Amos couldn't call it bad luck that he'd been caught in one of the clan's own traps, since it granted him a temporary reprieve from the pigmen jaws, but now he'd drawn a small crowd with his blood. No way to tell where the drifter could be. That didn't stop Amos from calling his name, though.

"Omar, help. Help me. Please." He curled up as he did every few minutes or so to try to keep the blood from pooling in his head too much, but he was getting tired.

The pigmen had tried to get at him for about an hour now. Jumping had proved fruitless, as had climbing the tree that housed the leader line and the snare's engine—in this case, a heavy log hung out over a short bluff. Pigmen and their ilk were known to be clever enough to disarm snares before, but the clansmen took every measure to make sure that their catches stayed caught. Hence, the pigmen's little snag.

When they had spent their options, they huddled together, watching their prey. A couple pigmen came, and a few more went. Amos had nearly lost interest in their movements when, without any noticeable communication among them, they burst into action, fanning out and rooting through the ground in a lively frenzy, searching for other snares. They scoured the entire area before they changed direction and abandoned the grounds, leaving only two sentinels. When they came back, they came guarding something else among them.

The shadower. The pigmen had been readying the way for the shadower, acting under its orders. Finding a lone human caught in a snare in the middle of the woods might be an unforeseen treat for the starving hordes or for the shadower itself, but it was also unusual, and either instinct or cleverness told the creatures never to trust the unusual. Even now the pigmen kept wary eyes for the shadower, skittering here and there without any clear command to guide them. Some folks said that shadowers controlled the other unbreds by sheer force of evil will, but Sam Chambers and a few of the older, more learned clansmen said that it had something to do with scents or small tremblings or whatever.

The shadower's thick hide, cracking here and there like parched earth, steadily smoothed itself up on the neck and head until it became limpid and milky, like glass. Veins and strange fissures snaked their paths across the skull just beneath the skin. Its enormous black eyes swiveled around in the misshapen head before settling on Amos, not as prey, but almost as something ... curious. A toy to be played with, perhaps, or a trinket for studying.

The shadower that walked across the frozen stream with a nearly human gait wore a covering made from the dried skin and shredded clothes of what was once a living person. Amos guessed that this skin was all that remained of Jim Craine, the Tucker who was dragged off in the first onslaught. The shadower peered at Amos again with growing interest. Then it waved at him, like a neighbor on a Sunday stroll.

The cold had not been enough to make Amos shiver until now.

"Omar—Omar—" Amos cried with greater urgency. The pigmen might not have been able to get to him, but the shadower would unravel the snare's riddle.

The pigmen watched as the shadower stopped beneath Amos and turned its gaze to its surroundings. Still wary.

"Om—" Amos began before trailing off as he locked eyes with the shadower. His breath caught in his throat in a way he hadn't expected. He could have sworn he'd heard someone talking. It seemed like several someones, somewhere far enough away that he couldn't make out anything for sure. His mind worried at trying to fathom the words in vain, like trying to work loose a stubborn shred of meat stuck between his teeth.

The shadower's eyes closed, and Amos' hand went to his head as if suddenly struck by a headache. Amos' mouth gaped open and closed like a fish's, unintelligible sounds tumbling from his throat as he tried to find his voice again.

The spell passed, and Amos turned his head away, as if in fear. Then, careful not to change his tone, he sobbed gentle instructions to the empty air. “Not yet, Omar, not yet...”

The shadower turned its own gaze again to the surroundings and walked around, tracing knife-like claws through the frostbitten leaves on the forest floor, trying to understand the mystery. One pigman lunged forward, gesturing and tittering and fogging the air with chilled breath, apparently trying to show something to the shadower. The pigman quickly went silent at the shadower’s glance and backed away.

“Not yet, Omar—almost ready—”

The shadower sifted the smoldering fire about twenty paces away, up the slope a little bit. Satisfied, it turned and walked back down to Amos, and all eyes turned to his up-hung form.

Still whimpering so as not to alert the shadower, Amos said, “Okay, Omar. Take him.”

The smoldering fire came to life in a whirlwind of spent ashes as Omar pushed the animal skin covering off of him and rose from the shallow trench dug out beneath the fire. They had wanted the pigmen to find Amos, to smell the blood of the hog they had drained before they left. They had *not* wanted the pigmen to take heed of Omar until it was too late, and a good hiding place and a scent-masking campfire was all they needed to that end.

Omar rose with his bow already strung and an arrow nocked. He had it drawn to his ear by the time the pigmen marked the sudden racket behind them. The shadower turned just in time for Omar’s arrow to skewer it through the lower chest.

The shadower’s howl of agony drowned out Amos’ cheers. Its jaw unhinged and its mouth opened in an unending shriek. The shadower turned to flee, only to find that a string tethered the arrow stuck between its ribs to the quiver at Omar’s side, keeping the shadower from escaping. The unbred creature snapped the thread with its claws and scarpered away. Omar leaped into the tree next to Amos and scrambled up beyond the reach of the pigmen rather than worry about sticking the shadower with another arrow.

"What are you doing?" Amos cried, fumbling for the sword he had hidden under his clothes.

"Gettin' away from the pigmen!"

"We've gotta go after that shadower!"

"Why? That thing's a goner! It'll be dead by tonight at the latest!" A pigman squealed as Omar fought off the creatures trying to climb his tree.

"Who cares? If you don't bring that thing's head in yourself, none of the clan will believe it was you that killed it!"

Amos cut his legs free, dangled for a moment one-handed to get his bearings again, and landed more or less on his feet. One more arrow from Omar and one less-than-deft swipe from Amos' sword was all it took for the already surprised pigmen to flee in every direction.

"Quick. Gimme my rifle," Amos said, stumbling as the blood drained from his head. He grappled with the gun, checking the powder in the pan and sprinkling a little more from his powder horn. Omar scanned the forest, bow drawn. Beyond the yelps and leaps of the back-stepping pigmen, there was neither sight nor sound of any living creature. The pigmen would soon be back in force, and if they didn't nab the shadower soon—

"It went up over yonder. I reckon we can see it from up on the cliff," Omar panted.

The two young men scrambled up the short hill overlooking a bend in the stream and peered into the woods. "There it is! Just past that brush yonder."

"I see it." Amos snapped the rifle to his shoulder, lowered it, then raised it again more slowly.

"Got a bead on it?"

"I got it. Relax." Amos brushed dusty brown hair out of his narrowing eyes as he set his jaw firm. Barrel had a good rifle and a fine charge.

Allow just a hair for bullet fall. Steady the hand. Breathe easy. Mind the trees. Lead the target just a mite. Squeeze the trigger—

The rifle bucked. Amos' musketball threaded the dense woods and drove the fleeing shadower face-first into the ground a good hundred long strides away. The forest echoed with the yowls of confused pigmen bereft of their leader.

Omar whistled softly, took a sword, and ran for the downed shadower.

The morning light haloed the two young men as they strolled in the front gate with the shadower's head. It was still winter, but the warmth they brought with them banished the chill for the day.

Unbeknownst to the rest of the clan, Amos took an extra souvenir from the shadower's corpse: a ceramic locket from a bygone age, with an inscription he could not understand and an image of a twisted ladder. Perhaps just a trinket picked up by a shadower, or perhaps indicative of something more.

Chapter 11

In Which Omar Makes a New Friend

The older, wiser Tuckers knew that life's pleasures occurred not in spite of life's hardships, but often because of them. There's a kind of joy only relief can bring. Most folks would have preferred the unbroken peace to the eleventh-hour rescue, but you wouldn't have guessed it from the way they carried on when Amos and Omar came back with the shadower head in hand. The two heroes hardly had room to breathe that evening. The Tuckers doubled all rations and threw as big a hoedown as they could with only turnips and beans in their store. The meeting-hall was packed with well-wishers.

"I still say I would've had that sucker in a few more days," Deek Evans said, a disappointed frown darkening his face. He hadn't meant it as a joke, but everyone around him mercifully took it as one.

"You two are nuts, that's what me and Victor say," Sophie Fillmore said, a hand on her pregnant belly.

"But she means 'thank you', both of yun's," her husband qualified.

Amos and Omar sat together at a table in the Tucker's lantern-lit cafeteria-church. Amos basked in the glory and enjoyed the attention more than he thought he would; Omar sat hunched over his meal, back to his old brooding manner, though perhaps without his hackles perpetually raised.

"Whose idea was it, anyway?" Becky Brody asked. Amos and Omar pointed at each other. Everyone laughed.

"Excuse me, everyone," Reverend Brody cut in as the laughter cut short, "may I steal Amos away for a moment? The clan elders would like to thank him formally. Good to see you all here in the Lord. Ms. Brody, Mr. Craine, Ms. Hadley, Mr. and Mrs. Fillmore." The Reverend greeted everyone with a vulture's stooped forward head and furrowed brow, though his tone of gentle disapproval only emerged for the latter two of the names. Sophie and her husband shifted under his gaze. Marriage was supposed to rubber-stamp the baby-making, but Reverend Brody always seemed to prefer breathing space between the "I-do's" and the infant's first wail. But there she was, with child and ready to burst, scarcely married a year ago. It didn't say anywhere in the Bible that such passion in marriage was sinful, but he checked just to make sure. It was a pity folks couldn't marry on their twentieth anniversary.

With all conversation and mirth murdered and the more charming of the two heroes now gone, the small knot of Tuckers scattered, leaving Omar alone. For about fifteen seconds.

"So, the triumphant drifter," came a voice from behind Omar. He turned to see an unkempt man with a wild look in his eyes.

"Hey, I remember you," Omar said, his voice as flat as his expression. "Bert Daly."

"Look, friend, I figger we oughta sort things out. Get off on the right foot, you know. Folks say lots of nonsense about me, and you probably got the wrong idea." Bert moved to sit next to Omar, though Omar had made no move to invite him.

"Huh," Omar said, his voice daring Bert to step one inch too far. "Tell me what wrong idea I gotta get sorted out."

"Now see here, I don't blame ye for a second," Bert said with a grin, wagging a finger at Omar and leaning in like a conspiratorial old friend. "I don't blame ye for thinkin' ill of me, seein' how things went yesterday. You was takin' food from me, sure, but lookin' back, I mighta been a little hasty with you. You gotta understand I got a family to take care of. Got a nag of a wife and a little anklebiter with a stomach like a borehole. My wife, she gets after me all the time about food, always pesterin' me, and I gotta get what's owed my family somehow or another. It's a hangin' shame, I say. Folks with breeding like ours oughta be *runnin'* this clan, but just because we're outnumbered, they can keep us on the edge of beggary. Steal from us with one hand so they can pretend to be generous with the other."

Omar turned his head like an owl to stare Bert right in the face. "What do you mean, breeding like ours?"

"You're not like the others here. You're like me. Better than them. It's in your blood. That's why they can't stand you. A bunch of scared, jealous weaklings is what these Tuckers are."

Omar paused, then repeated the essence of his question with more pointedness. "What do you *mean*, I'm like you?"

Bert gave a knowing, squinty-eyed smile. "I know what you are, drifter. I know the Reverend's stitched your lips. I wasn't sure what an ubermensch would look like up close."

Omar poked at a whole boiled turnip with his knife. "You tryin' to threaten me again?"

"No, no, no," Bert said, eyeing the knife even as he kept inching closer. "I'm reaching out as a long-lost relatiff, you might say. I'm a half-breed, see."

"Didn't seem to matter to you yesterday."

"Yesterday was dog-eat-dog. Today, you're a big shot who could use someone on his side when the wind blows the other way."

Omar gave a chuffing laugh without humor. "You are the slipperiest little feller I ever did see. Sic the elders on me, then the very next day I'm your closest friend."

"If I get you what you want—what you *need*—do you care who you got it from?" Bert asked.

"Okay, I'll bite. What you sellin'?"

"See, a bunch of things we got taught around here don't add up."

"Well of course they don't. Half the things your parson says are so bent-headed I wonder if he makes it all up as he goes along."

"It's all how they keep control over the clan. You want to keep someone under your thumb, you got to control the way they think. Me, they can't hardly control, but the likes of me don't got nowhere else to go. What the elders say about the ubermenschen is the way it is, and that's that. But I got me an inkling what bones they got buried. You're the first honest-to-goodness ubermenschen I've ever seen up close, and likely the first most Tuckers have ever seen. My parents is gone. Every half-breed in this clan is an orphan. Don't that hit you kinda funny?"

Omar didn't answer.

"The elders buried my folks out in the old town, but never told me where, nor why neither. Not even sure what to look for. But a full-blooded ubermensch from outside the clan might know what this is all about. And whatever it is about the ubermenschen them elders don't want us to know, it's dangerous enough to knock 'em off their high horse."

"You want me to tell you what I know," Omar said.

"It'll help us both."

"You're a persistent little piss-ant, ain't you?" Omar said. "I thought you was gonna try to buy me off, keep me from knifing you in the middle of the night. Instead, you just want me to stick my neck out even further for a cause I don't give two shits about."

"You should. This is *your* cause."

"Only cause worth my time is what keeps me alive another day."

"I don't believe that. You ain't some leaf blowin' in the wind, or else you wouldn't have gone after that shadower. No sir, you're your own man. Not about to be told what to do and how to be. But look around you. Ain't nothin' but a prim and proper slavery we got goin' on here. You want to keep on lickin' the boots of these uppity cranks in charge?"

Omar shrugged. "It's a clan. Uppity cranks come with the territory."

"So you don't care?"

"You pick up on things pretty fast, don't you?"

"Then why'd you become a drifter in the first place? Why not stay under a clan's thumb?"

"I didn't *choose* to become a drifter."

Bert nodded as if Omar had made the point he was trying to make all along. "The clan rules *forced* you into the wild. It was the only place you could be free."

"You're so set on seeing things your way that you've got everything exactly back'erds. These uppity cranks you got stuck in your craw are the only reason I ain't cut your throat yet. You might not like who's in charge right now because it ain't you, but you take them away, and nature's all you got left. Nature's as hard a rider you'll ever bear, and she don't brush you down any when the day's done."

Bert's gaze darkened. "You're making a mistake. You need me, like it or not."

"I need you about like I need a new asshole."

"They'll come for you," Bert said. "Then you'll know. Then you'll know." He turned and left, his last words still ringing in the air.

While Omar was busy making and entertaining new friends, Amos was busy shaking hands with the elders of the clan: Elvin McDaniel, Sam Chambers, Reverend Brody, Dr. Bernhard and his wife Helen, Old Man Brody, and others. Amos grinned and took the praise in his good-natured stride, for he and Omar truly had saved the clan.

"I've got my eye on you now, Mr. Taylor," Elvin said with more geniality than he addressed even close friends. "You don't know how close we were to a royal mess. Another month or two, and we would've been strangling each other for rats."

"It's true," one of the other McDaniels said with the same sagacity as he had once remarked on the relative harmlessness of shadower armies. "These big sieges can wipe a clan clear off the map. Anyone remember what happened to the Lancaster clan up north just a few years back?"

Amos' father entered the circle and faced off against his son.

Amos saw the serious expression on his father's face, and his gaze lowered. "Hey, Dad."

His father answered with a cuff from his remaining hand. "Doggone fool of a son, what in the world were you thinking? I could skin you alive!"

"I'm sorry, D—"

His father crushed him with a bear hug. "Doggone it, Amos, you've done us real proud. Real proud."

Elvin interrupted. "Alright, enough of this touchy-feely stuff. I need to ask the kid some questions. What things looked like out there, how the pigmen were acting, that sort of thing."

The debriefing lasted only as long as the celebration, and that only as long as the clansmen had energy to celebrate. In a time of low supplies and cold temperatures, most folks were dog tired at about eight-thirty. The party broke up to the relief of both Omar and Amos, though perhaps more so for the former.

As Omar left to return to his precious cot at Bill Puckett's place, a figure emerged from the shadows.

"Hey, drifter."

Omar whirled to see Shane Bunton following him, bundled against the winter cold.

"What's your name again?" Shane asked.

"Omar. Omar Walking."

"Listen, Omar, I, uh—no hard feelings, huh?" Shane extended his hand after a cough and a pause.

Omar stood silently, staring, gauging. Then, slowly, he extended his own hand to shake that of the Tucker. Shane shook with a firm grip, even if he didn't lift his eyes from the ground.

Mr. Bunton cleared his throat. "You did good out there. If you need some arrows when you go—if you go—I'll be sure to hook you up."

Omar nodded, unsmiling, as Shane walked away.

Ella watched the party leave the cafeteria and head home. She had stayed inside the whole day, fiddling with some shoes she was supposed to be mending. The shoes still sat on the ancient dresser in her home, still unmended.

When the search parties had gone out for Amos and Omar that morning, she'd immediately gone to her room, not to worry, not to pray, but to think. To prepare herself for the inevitable news: that the two young men had foolishly thrown their lives away; that desperation had claimed two lives, with more surely to follow. And maybe she did pray a bit. She prayed for Amos, because he was a valuable young member of the clan, and because he was nearly Pa's last hope for securely passing on the trade before he died. She had prayed for Amos because she liked him, and he seemed like a good young man in spite of his recklessness and his stubbornness and his nonconformist streak; maybe he was even a good man because of it. She had even prayed for Omar.

When the news had come that Amos and the drifter had not only returned but had returned unharmed and with the shadower's head, she could not help but breathe a sigh of both relief and anger. Boys. Careful, sensible people died horrible deaths all the time, and yet somehow a young man could fool himself into thinking he was invincible in spite of it all. But she couldn't stay mad. They were alive, and they had succeeded, and all question of the clan doing anything to Omar had been banished. He was well-nigh a Tucker now. He wouldn't need her to protect him again.

Before, she had hidden away to prepare herself for bad news. She hid now because she was shy, because she didn't want to claim their attentions. She didn't want to intrude.

But the party was over now, and there was Amos, escorted by his—by her—friends, by Sophie and her husband, by Becky and her beau, and by Amos' little brother, Dale. Ella sighed and prepared herself. There was a familiar fluttering and lurching of the stomach—the same she'd felt when she was ten and first jumped off Jeb's Rock into the Gooseneck Run thirty feet below. She wouldn't be shy, not this time. She would congratulate him and tell him what she really thought of him. That she was proud of him. That she thought of him often. That—

"Amos, I—"

"Later, Ella," Amos brushed her off with a good-natured smile. "Oh, tell your pa I might not be in for a bit, okay?"

He left without another word, swept away in cheerful conversation with his fellow clansmen.

Ella stood alone in the winter night for a bit.

She went home alone, the moon and the stars her only companions.

Now we're here with Stephen Moore, head analyst for the Bioethics Research Institute and author of No Turning Back: Our Transhuman Destiny, *to talk about the unrest that's been springing up this last week.*

Good to be back, Alice.

Federal officials are calling this an escalation, with five reported fatalities and dozens of serious injuries to modified citizens so far. Your institute predicted worse violence to come. Why is that?

Talking with law enforcement officials on the state and federal levels, as well as collaborating with experts overseas, we're starting to see serious coordination on the international level now, with evidence that some of these extremist groups are even receiving funding from foreign anti-engineering governments like Nigeria and Saudi Arabia. These are scary groups, very zealous, capable of pulling off bold attacks, as we saw with the assassination of Senator Redlin last year. Now they've got infrastructure and funding from what are essentially nuclear-capable rogue states.

What groups are we looking at here?

Obviously, there's a growing number of religious fundamentalists, especially after the Pope failed to speak out against the violent anti-engineering protests. But we're also seeing fringe elements splitting off from the NAACP and various environmentalist groups like the Sierra Club. What's particularly disturbing here is that various high-profile lightning-rods for this issue from the past have come out in support of, essentially, the murder of modified humans. We have the ex-director for the Institute of Health, the ex-President of Notre Dame, ex-Senator Cora Martinez, even Brittney Kellerman came out of retirement to say that, basically, we had this coming. So we're seeing a growing number of previously pacified, unmodified people radicalizing, and we're seeing that the police are having to—

Amos Taylor woke in a strange place, cold sweat standing out on his forehead in spite of the nighttime chill. In a moment, he recognized the roof over his head as that of the Hollands, and thus reassured, he rolled over to go back to sleep.

Then the chirp that had first woken him from a strange dream pierced the silent darkness a second time.

Amos gasped in surprise, reached for the oaken nightstand beside his cot, and withdrew the hard, ceramic talisman that had made a high-pitched squeak almost like that of a bird's, but different somehow. He should show this to somebody. The small little thing didn't look dangerous, but what did that chirp mean? A third and final beep sounded in the dark, and Amos dropped the thing as if it were hot.

It was some time before Amos could again find sleep, and that time was spent staring at the thing and wondering what the beep foretold.

Chapter 12

Expectation Is the Root of Heartache

It took the better part of the butter churning the next day for Ella to decide that she had been too hasty in dismissing Amos. A slight is not grounds for abandoning a clansman, or a friend, or whatever Amos was. She thought about going to see him in the morning, but with the pigman horde already dispersing and the solid assurance that the clan would indeed make it to spring, the gunsmith had fired up his shop again and put Amos back to work. They were well into their morning work when Ella had finished her chores. Fortunately, it was a Tuesday, and she looked forward to seeing her two good friends again without young men getting in the way.

Ella sighed, stretched her aching arms, and left the butter churn. Folks were saying a nomad clan would come through any day now, and Tuckers were eager to open up the last dregs of their larders. She took a pan of cornbread and beans from the oven—the last real foodstuffs they had left—took a hefty portion for herself, her stepmother, and siblings, and brought the rest out to Amos and her father.

The heat that blasted her face told her that the furnace was working, but no more efficiently than usual. Ella's father must have had great faith in Amos to start him so soon managing the cantankerous heat of their smithy.

"Now, the important thing to remember is that rifles got tighter tolerances than a regular musket. So if you don't get the barrel right the first time, you'll probably just have to start over," Phil instructed his astute new apprentice.

"I have a question," Amos began as Ella watched the two huddled around the workbench. "Do we have to make only muzzle-loading rifles? What about breech-loaders?"

"Waste of ammo. We got plenty of old shotguns and six-shooters around if you want to make that work, but they don't shoot like a rifle. If they're far enough away to use a rifle on, you don't need a breech-loader. Them's bust too easy, anyhow. Too many moving parts. Break action's just about as simple as I can manage, and I don't like the idea of gunpowder having anywhere to go but forward when you pull the trigger."

"What's break-action?"

"That's the same way you load an old double-barreled shotgun. It's hinged, so you can snap the gun open to load it. The only people I've heard of who use breech-loaders very much are the Greenbriers, and they don't do break-action; they do some sort of lever-action to drop the breech lock." Phil pantomimed the action.

"Can you copy their design?"

"No. For one thing, Reverend Brody doesn't exactly approve of the whole breech-action scheme to begin with. Them Greenbriers are Satanists, you know. Their technology was given to them by the Devil. So the Reverend ain't too keen on us copying the Devil's designs. And anyways, they don't sell their guns to the nomads, mostly because they don't want us to get our hands on one, and if we ever kill one of their men, they're more likely to fetch his gun than they are to fetch his body."

"Nice folks."

"They're a robber clan. Marauders who only settled down when there weren't no more food to steal or scavenge anymore. They ain't the kind to give much thought to the dead, even their own."

"Hey, Pa? Amos?" Ella dared to interrupt. "Fixed y'uns up something special. I'm afraid it'll have to be back to turnips again after this until the nomads come, but—"

"Nomads comin' up to the east gate!" one of the neighbor's kids shouted into the shop as he streaked by. "Grab your teeth; they're bringing enough food to feed an army!"

Sam Chambers welcomed the elder of the Schnider clan at the eastern gate with arms spread wide. A host of other Tuckers in the streets behind Sam waited to greet the nomads with great fanfare. Even the Schnider scouts who'd first made contact that morning were heralded as heroes. Never were money-grubbing merchants so lauded.

"We've been camped out up on the highway for nearly a month, just waiting for the pigmen to clear out long enough for us to get through," the Schnider elder explained. "From the look of you, it doesn't look like we came too early."

"Not by a minute."

"We've come with every scrap of food we could get ahold of, along with medicines from up north and that order of lumber you put in last time." The elder was a salesman, but anyone could see he was itching to sell just as much as the Tuckers were to buy. The aftermath of a pigman siege made the biggest windfall of the year for a nomad clan scrappy enough to swoop in quickly.

"Food first, accessories later." Sam waved the Schnider elder on toward the clan main.

Someone approached Sam from behind. "Excuse me, Mr. Chambers?"

Sam turned to see the young apprentice gunsmith approaching. "Something on your mind, Mr. Taylor?"

"I was wondering if you could give me a thought on this." Amos fished the small ceramic talisman out of his pocket.

"What is this?" Mr. Chambers inspected the item with a keen eye.

"Found it on the shadower we killed. I thought it was just one of those whatsits shadowers are liable to pick up, and I thought I'd hold on to it as a keepsake of my own. But the other night, it made a little noise, like a cricket or a bird. So I thought there might be more to it, and I brought it here to you."

"Fascinating," Sam Chambers said, his nimble fingernails seeking a crevice he might force open. Not succeeding, Sam brought the piece up to his ear and shook it. "Would you mind if I kept this for a while, Mr. Taylor?"

"Do you know what it is, Mr. Chambers?"

"I'm ... not sure. Certainly some old-world item, battery-run. Very interesting, whatever it is. I'll have to have a talk with some of the elderfathers and eldermothers, see if any of them can give me some clues. I'll let you know if I find out anything, okay?"

Nomad clans and the market days they brought with them often made occasion for a fair shindig even in the best of times—amused customers tended to buy more things they didn't need. On the far side of winter after a pigman siege, however, the clan was ready for an outright hoedown.

Most folks sat and watched the nomad performers, but Amos Taylor somehow had energy to get up and dance with all the exotic nomad girls. The kid was unstoppable.

Elsewhere, wizened nomad eldermothers told tales of their travels through far-off lands, like the blasted and flooded ruins of New York City. They told of fierce battles the nomads had with marauders to open up the stack interchanges on the big interstates.

The only killjoy in town was Doctor Bernhard, who insisted that everyone keep to broths and simple soups for at least a week until folks had their strength back.

Melissa Daly was quick to close the door behind her as she brought in a sack of flour and some salted pork. It wasn't until she put little Earnest down and locked the door that she finally turned around to see her husband waiting for her with arms crossed.

She jumped a little. "Bert! Hey."

"Where you been, darlin'?" Bert asked, his eyebrows raised.

Little Earnest toddled back to his mother and grabbed her leg. Melissa patted the runt on the head and forced a smile. "I been buying food from the nomads. I'll fix us up somethin' to eat real quick."

Bert didn't move. "The nomads are on the clan main, and you just come from the other way."

"Uh, I stopped by to see—"

"Who you gettin' food from?" Bert asked, his jaw clenching.

Melissa shook her head. "Bertie, honey, it's not what you think—"

"*The hell it ain't!*" Bert roared, and little Earnest's eyes went wide. "You're at your old tricks again, ain't you?"

"Hon, it's for Earnest—"

He cut her short with a neat box to the ear. "Who you ruttin' around with?"

"I ain't goin' with nobody, I swear!"

He knocked her back straight again with a jab to the other side. "You lyin' bitch."

"It's from Earnest's father!" Melissa wailed, flinching.

Bert grabbed her by the hair and forced her to look up at him. "*Who. Is. It?*"

Reverend Brody bade his wife goodnight, picked up the lantern, and started down the lonely road to his father's house. Except that tonight, he wasn't alone. A bundled figure, which had leaned up against the fence for the past two hours, followed him at a distance. The protrusion of some piece of wood or metal extended downward from the figure's hand.

The Reverend continued on his way until he came to a crossroads. He stopped and turned.

The figure following him ducked into the shadow of a nearby tree.

The Reverend followed through the turn as if he hadn't been watching his backside and went up the side street, up towards the schoolhouse side of the clan meeting hall. The figure waited nearly a full minute before following again.

The Reverend opened the door to the schoolhouse as the figure poked a hooded head around the bend. Brody doused his lantern, threw a brief look around him, and stepped inside. The schoolhouse lay still as the figure watched.

Scarcely a couple minutes later, another clansman came up to the schoolhouse from the opposite direction. He, too, cast a brief look about before dousing his lantern and stepping inside.

The figure slipped from the shadows, crossed the open space to the schoolhouse window, and leaned close enough to hear the voices inside.

"I think it's homing in on something," Sam Chambers' voice rumbled, muffled by the intervening wall. "The chirps reach a steady frequency on one side of the town but fall off completely on the other side of town. I think whatever it's homing in on must be a bit outside the walls, maybe out in the old town. I just wondered if I could poke around—"

"No," came the Reverend's abrupt answer. "Give me the talisman. I'll consult with my father, but this chip will probably have to be destroyed. Its function most certainly is forbidden knowledge."

Sam muttered something that sounded like grudging acceptance of the verdict. Only a few seconds later, the schoolhouse doors swung open, and two men went their separate ways without a word.

The figure at the window watched the Reverend go the whole way, marking the small white chip he put in his pocket as he trudged off. When finally alone, the figure dropped its club and removed the hood. Bert Daly's eyes gleamed in the moonlight with a wild hunger.

The very existence of men and women together in the human species was a mystery to Ella, not that she had really been interested in solving it until recently. Nevertheless, she was grateful, as she had always been, for the company of the female half of the species. Men might never cease to frustrate, but Sophie and Becky made sense. When Ella came inside, the two of them were already talking about something.

"I'm in the mood to make a mashed turnip sculpture today," Ella announced as she came in.

"Not now, Ella. We have more important things to talk about."

"What is it?"

Sophie looked over at Ella with a girlish grin. "This Amos Taylor you got apprenticing with your pa—"

"You know him pretty well now, don't you?" Becky asked, her voice heavy with implication.

"Care to tell us a little about him?" Sophie asked.

"Everyone already knows everything about him; he's the clan hero," Ella evaded, blushing. "What's this all about?"

Sophie and Becky glanced at each other and grinned. "I'm not sure," Becky began in almost a whisper, "but I think Amos might be wanting to court me."

"What?" Ella exclaimed with more astonishment than she really cared to express. The color drained from her face as quickly as it came. "Becky! You already have a man! Think of Oliver!"

"Oh, Oliver—you didn't hear?"

"Hear what?"

Sophie explained. "Mary Hicks told me the other day that Oliver was giving her younger sister the googly eyes."

"Cynthia," Becky said, as if the very name inspired incredulity.

"But why don't you try to—" Ella's dismay was beginning to alert Sophie, but Becky kept going. "We haven't been getting along that well recently, and if he were really serious about me, we'd be married by now anyhow. I'm thinking I'm about ready to move on. And who better to move on to than Amos?"

"But—"

"And Oliver never bagged a shadower like Amos!"

"But—"

"But what?" Becky asked. Sophie cleared her throat to catch Becky's attention. A meaningful glance was all it took. Becky looked from Sophie to Ella. Back to Sophie. Becky's eyes widened. "But what do I know! Amos? Court me? Ha! The butcher's daughter? Covered in hog grease more often than not? I need to stop running my mouth about these kinds of things; I'm wrong about them so often, I hardly know if I could tell the weather in the middle of a thunderstorm! Is it hot in here? I'm just gonna step outside for a little bit and soak my head in a bucket of water."

Becky left the two girls in silence. Ella stood staring at her hands.

"I'm sorry, Ella," Sophie said.

The Tuesday afternoon was ruined even by Becky and Sophie's standards, but Ella decided not to let it go any further. She refused to jump to conclusions. Amos was a good guy who'd let the attention go to his head a little. It could happen to the best of them. There wasn't any need to make a scene or cause trouble. No reason to be emotional or angry. She would just wait and see. He'd come around after a while, and then things could go back to the way they should be.

So, ever forbearing, Ella waited for Amos to come back, which, of course, he never did.

Chapter 13

Labor

Bill Puckett woke up with what seemed like half the clan clamoring at his door for gunpowder. Spring would be here within a month or so, and when the game came back everyone would want to get some fresh meat. After the siege, the clan never seemed to have more than a couple hundred charges at any one time.

Bill ran a weary hand through his hair and stroked his close-cropped beard as he looked into the barrel of potassium nitrate next to his workbench. It all had to be ground meticulously into the charcoal and sulfur, which would take hours for every scrap. He'd have to get Omar and Ella to help, and wouldn't you know it, Ella seemed to be in one of those womanly moods for the last few days, scarcely coming over to visit at all, and rarely focusing on her work when she did. Omar would have to pick up the slack. A week full of late nights might get the short-term stockpile up and going again, but the long-term stockpile would take a year or more to save up. And if folks couldn't get it from him, they'd get it from Johnny Grierson. He could see that one-eyed upstart mocking him now. Another knock sounded at the door. He felt powerful tired.

He sat down at his work bench, pulled a tattered volume from a hidden, hollowed-out compartment in the wall, and opened it up. The logbook of his experiments. Before he tried any new formula, he'd make sure to write down the entire procedure in exact detail, down to the exact cc's needed of each acid. He'd highlighted any formulas that had shown promise at some point and, flipping through the book, he could see one or two underlined formulas on each page, most of them furiously scratched out when further exploration revealed their inherent flaws.

Bill read through each experiment, his fingers gliding over the familiar rumples and stains on the brittle paper. The faint smell of charcoal dust reminded him of Martha. She'd worked with him on this project of his. She'd been the only one to back him up when the rest of the clan thought it a lost cause. Perhaps it still was a lost cause. So many failures. He was so close, he could feel it—but he had so many orders to fill, and it would all come to nothing if he didn't keep up with the daily grind. He turned and looked at the two beakers of weak sulfuric and nitric acid he'd synthesized earlier.

It's pretty cold outside, and I've got a new thermometer, he thought to himself. *I have more than enough sulfuric acid, and it won't take me long to distill the nitric acid. If I tweak the ratios just a bit...*

Ah, what the heck. The gunpowder could wait. He stood up and went out to barter for some baking soda. But first he had to shoo away the clansmen at his door.

Bill slowly poured the sulfuric acid into the flask. The acid absorbed quickly into the mass of white powder already inside: potassium nitrate of the highest quality, leached from his own niter beds and purified in his own shop. He stoked the flaming coals outside under the lean-to and placed the flask over them to start boiling the liquid. Then he hooked the flask up to his distillation setup. It wasn't really that different from the stills folks used to make whiskey, except his had a water-filled pipe wrapped around the distilling column, fed by a rainwater-filled bucket on the roof. Also, he wasn't distilling alcohol.

He broke up some chunks of ice he'd cut from a nearby pond during the last hard freeze and placed them in a wide bowl, followed by the receiving beaker. He watched the glass thermometer perched at the top of his homemade fractionating column. Finally, he dropped the curtain down over the entrance to the lean-to—nitric acid was sensitive to light. He had to let the reaction happen outside because of toxic fumes inevitably leaking out, but also had to enclose the whole process to keep light from getting in. Whenever he did make nitric acid, he always had to use it within the next day or so, or otherwise it would decompose into a yellowish mess. The stuff was a royal pain.

Soon, clear droplets of liquid dripped from the condenser into an empty glass flask. He left for a minute to get some grub and came back with a damp neckerchief. He watched the distillation process from a distance while he ate, occasionally coming to stoke or spread out the burning coals to control the temperature of the reaction. When the flow rate slowed to nearly a stop, he put on safety goggles, tied the neckerchief over his face, and removed the flask. The liquid inside fumed a little at the slightest breeze. Valuable stuff.

He carried the concentrated acid back inside and was reaching for some tongs when he bumped into his workbench, jostling the flask of leftover sulfuric acid he'd left there earlier. It wasn't enough to knock the flask off the desk, but it was enough to make him flinch, which sent a drop of fuming nitric acid splashing out onto his hand. Even this wasn't too bad; he'd had multiple spills of nitric acid, and while the stuff would eat through copper like candy, it only caused slight discomfort and discoloration on exposed skin.

But it was enough of a surprise to make him recoil a second time, and this was enough to upend the sulfuric acid and spill some on his shirtsleeve. His skin bubbled almost instantly underneath, hot needles raking his nerves every which way. He ripped off his shirt in a fury. A bucket of cold water lay nearby. He doused his hand in it as he swore and swore and swore. He tossed a handful of baking soda onto the burn and swore again. Omar came running into the chemical shed just back from collecting manure.

"You okay?" he asked.

Bill turned his red face towards Omar and answered by swearing. He stomped around the room, clutching his hand, kicking at benches, and pushing Omar out of the way. Omar took the hint and stepped back. Bill ripped the ancient safety goggles from his head and threw them to the ground.

"Papa, what's the matter?"

Bill whirled around, and there was Sophie standing in the door with a bunch of decaying vegetables.

"I done burned my dad-blasted hand," Bill growled, showing her the small spot of bright pink skin on his forearm.

"Oh, Papa, I'm sorry." The basket was already on the floor, and Sophie was at her father's side.

"Damn thing hurts."

"I know, Papa, I know," Sophie said, her voice like milk and honey. "Come here, let's clean you up." Bill sat down while Sophie got a bucket of water and began gently pouring it over the burn. Bill winced but didn't swear. Instead his lip pouted out a little bit in a way that seemed much more appropriate for a child.

"Omar, could you go and fetch some water from the pump? We'll need to flush Pa a little more."

Omar nodded and left.

"Stupid beaker slipped off the stupid metal stand when I was taking it off the stupid fire," Bill explained.

"I'm sorry, Papa."

"Can't do a blasted thing around here without screwing something up."

"That's not true, Papa; you're the smartest man in the clan."

"Should've just stuck to making regular powder like the Griersons."

"You'll get it one day, Papa. Remember when you thought you'd never get the nitroglycerin to work?"

"I'm just a washed up ole' has-been. I used to be able to work all day back when you were little and your mother was alive; didn't bother me none. Didn't burn myself then. I didn't blow up no chemical sheds. I didn't ruin any gunpowder."

"Ssh, Papa. It's okay."

Water ran down Bill's arm, over the sundry scars from old burns, past blotchy discolorations; it trickled down his hand and dribbled from his fingers, where it pooled on the dirt floor. Sophie cooed and consoled while Bill murmured and grumbled. She patched up his arm and wrapped it in clean strips of linen and nodded and listened and stayed with him much longer than was necessary. When Victor came over to see what was keeping her so long, she shooed him away and told him she'd fix him supper later that evening. It was dark when she left Bill, now smiling, at the door of his deteriorating house.

Sophie walked home, no longer smiling. A groan escaped her as she eased her way into her house to Victor in the process of preparing a hide for tanning.

"Y'okay?" her husband asked.

"I—Oh! Not sure. Think you ought to go get Mrs.—Oooh! Mrs. Bernhard."

Bill heard Victor knock on the door of his shop to tell him that Sophie was having the baby. He smiled to himself. His daughter, having a baby of her own. That would make him a grandpa. Even by Tucker standards, most folks likely thought him too young for that gray-haired position.

He thanked Victor for letting him know, and then sat down. He looked at his bandaged hand. He went to bed to wait for morning and the news it would bring; there wasn't anything he could do to help his daughter give birth.

As he lay down, he looked at his bandaged hand again. He sighed. Sleep eluded him. He clenched his wounded fist and returned to his work in the shop more intently than before, eyes narrowed in the dim light of the two doubly shielded lanterns.

"How's she looking?" Ella asked as she walked into Sophie and Victor's ramshackle home. Becky Brody was already there, kneeling at Sophie's side.

"Fine, fine. She's looking fine," Mrs. Bernhard said, more to Victor than Ella, patting the former on the arm.

"I don't feel fine!" Sophie cried, her hands on her belly.

"That's how I know you're fine. Just ride it out, ma'am. One thing at a time," Mrs. Bernhard said with the calm authority of a woman who had delivered most of her patients. "I think we've got too many cooks in the kitchen, though." She looked around at the crowded room.

Ella turned to go. "I can wait outside—"

"I want them here," Sophie said, coming out of her latest wrestling match with her own womb. "Let them stay."

Mrs. Bernhard nodded her assent.

"Looks like our baby got tired of all the pickles and gravy you've been eating," Victor joked weakly, fidgeting with his hands.

Mrs. Bernhard turned to Victor. "We'll need some hot water. Can you heat some up, Victor?"

"Yeah, sure," Victor said, jumping up out of his chair and tripping on his way toward the door.

Bill paced the floor of his shop as the sulfuric acid bubbled and boiled in a beaker on the reaction throne outside. He kept his eyes on an old wristwatch as the second hand ticked its way around and around the white face.

"Jake. The contractions are coming closer together."

Doctor Bernhard came inside to help his wife. "Have her drink this, if she can."

In spite of the evening chill, Bill dabbed beading sweat from his brow before he rested the large canning jar into the icy water of a waiting bucket. The nitration reaction was powerfully exothermic, and it had gotten away from him before. Bill poured the nitric acid in with the sulfuric acid at precise ratios he'd made note of at the outset. Both acids were valuable, and he couldn't stand wasting any. The nitric acid was, of course, responsible for the nitrates, but the sulfuric acid helped by sucking up whatever water the reaction produced. Without the sulfuric acid, the nitration would stop, and the nitric acid would start oxidizing—violently.

Then came the really touchy part. He measured out a specific weight of cotton on an old balance scale—just enough to absorb all the nitrates without any leftover—and placed it into the waiting acid solution. He poked it down below the surface of the oily liquid with a glass stirring rod and let it soak. *Come on—come on you bugger—*

"How's she doing?" Victor knocked on the door of his own bedroom and placed an ear to the wood paneling.

"We need more hot water!" Ella said through a crack in the door.

Bill used tongs to pull the dripping cotton from the deadly mixture. He dipped the cotton in water, then placed it in a supersaturated solution of water and baking soda. When the remaining acids had neutralized and the foaming mixture had died down, Bill pulled the cotton out and laid it on a metal grate to dry. In the intervening hours of night, he went out to prepare the next step in his process.

Becky stepped out of the birthing room to find Victor gnawing on the end of a corncob pipe, staring out at naught. The springtime birds had mostly quieted down, and there wasn't much else to mask the intermittent caterwauling of his pregnant wife.

Becky cleared her throat. "Been thinking of names?"

Victor jerked as if wakened from a nap. "Huh?"

"What'll you name it?"

Victor shrugged. "Well, if it's a girl, me and Sophie thought we'd name her Jessica."

"Jessica?" Becky asked as if she'd just smelled a punctured intestine.

"You don't fancy it?" Victor sounded surprised.

"Oh, no, it's fine. If you're planning on naming your grandmother, that is."

"I liked the name." Victor waggled his head from side to side. "Thought it sounded ... I don't know ... quaint."

"Why don't you try for a sensible name, like Ruth or Mabel?"

"I like Jessica." Victor held his ground.

"Well, then let's hope it's a boy." Becky rolled her eyes.

"If it's a boy, then we'll name him Justin."

"Oh, no. *No.* You're earnest, ain't you?"

"And what if I is?"

"You'll be kicked right out of the clan, mark me." Becky slapped Victor on the shoulder, and the two of them smiled before Sophie's groans from inside pulled them back to the situation at hand. Becky took her leave.

Bill watched his precious nitrated guncotton dry. He checked his watch. About two o'clock in the morning, assuming Sam Chambers had kept up with maintenance on the town clock. He'd need to wait a little while longer. Once it was dry, he'd know if he had material good enough to move forward with. Probably not, but even if he did, he wasn't done yet. Pure guncotton wasn't reliable as a propellant. He'd need a powder of much greater density.

He lifted a bottle from the shelf inside, set it firmly on the bench, and removed the rubber stopper with careful precision. It took a pretty strong physical shock to set off nitroglycerin, but he'd learned the hard way never to underestimate his capacity for messing up.

"What's all this hot water for, anyway?" Victor asked, trying to force himself into the room.

"It's not fit for you to know," Becky said as she closed the door in his face. She promptly handed the pan of hot water to Dr. Bernhard, who in turn promptly tossed it out the open window.

"Okay, Sophie, dear. I'm going to need you to stand up. Hold onto these handles here." Mrs. Bernhard moved a contraption into position around Sophie.

Sophie sobbed and moaned as she heaved herself to her feet with the help of her two friends Ella and Becky. She grabbed onto the proffered handles for support.

"Just—Just kill me," Sophie sighed, almost serious.

"Okay, Sophie, this might sound hard for you, but you're going to have to start pushing. We're almost done."

"Can I come in?" Victor called through the closed door.

"Not yet!"

"Is there anything else I can do?"

Becky ran to the door. "We need more hot water!"

Bill took a small piece of cotton and dropped it on the wooden workbench. He rubbed it with a stirring rod, then tapped it with his fingers to check the compound's stability. Good enough. He opened one of his lanterns with both hands, heated up a small piece of oak bark in the flame, and touched the glowing end to a tiny piece of guncotton. It disappeared in a flash of light and heat. His eyebrows rose. Good nitration. Surprisingly good nitration. He looked back at his notes to make sure he'd taken down the ratios.

He took the rest of the guncotton and dropped it into the nitroglycerin, followed by a pinch of baking soda to stabilize things. He watched it gelatinize before his eyes.

"Come on, Sophie! The baby's coming! Push!" Mrs. Bernhard encouraged.

"Push, Sophie, push!" Victor cried at the closed door of the bedroom, begging now.

Now a thick gelatin, the explosive mixture could be formed into grains. Bill dumped it into a funnel feeding into a tube, the end of which was capped with a perforated metal plate. Pressing down on a plunger with one hand, Bill cut the extrusions erupting from the tube with the other. The result was roughly oblong granules spread out over a sheet.

He left the material to dry.

"Ugh—I can't do it, Victor!"

Bill scraped the translucent, orange-yellow granules into a hollowed-out bull horn and capped it off. As he stepped outside, a thin band of morning smoldered on the horizon. He put out a small charge, tamped it down, and reached for a burning match.

"It's a boy!"

"Wait, Helen, she's still contracting!"

An explosion. A pop two feet away that bruised Bill's fingers. Bills eyes opened in shock. He looked back at the note he'd written just before his test: only a gram of powder.

"Twins! A boy and a girl! And both healthy!"

Bill touched a match to a second charge. Again, the same explosion, this time splintering the stump. The energy density of the substance was high enough to use as an explosive. As a gunpowder, he would actually have to *slow down* the burn rate. Unbelievable. He had finally done it.

Bill ran through the copse of trees fifty or so paces behind his home and laughed. He topped the hillock that peeked over the distant palisade to reveal the hills and mountains beyond. "I did it!" he cried to the first smile of the morning sun. "Martha! I told you I'd do it! I told you I'd do it, sweetie!"

Victor ran from his house into the street where the men and women of the clan were just beginning to stir. "I'm a daddy!" he cried to the golden sun and the sky and anyone who would listen.

"And mommy's fine, too!"

Chapter 14

Tests and a Mystery

Phil and Omar stared across the table at each other. The chickens clucked outside, waiting for feed they had yet to be fed. A pot of porridge bubbled on the stove with no one to tend it. Clive and Margaret clomped in, took their places on either side of the table, and waited for their breakfast with legs swinging under their chairs.

Phil cleared his throat. "Folks been sleepin' kinda late, ain't they?" he said.

Omar shrugged.

"Mama's a-checkin' on Uncle Bill," Margaret said.

"Can I fetch the porridge?" Clive asked.

Phil waved his son off as Ella stumbled to the table, bleary-eyed and frazzled.

"What happened to you?" her father asked.

"You didn't hear Victor come a-knockin'? Sophie had her babies last night."

"Babies?"

Ella gave a languid nod that ended with her staring up at the ceiling. "Bwuah. Twins. I was up 'pert near all night."

"Is that where Bill is? Over to see Sophie?"

Ella yawned. "Never came over."

Phil examined the bowl of porridge Clive set up onto the table. "Well, it's good to see the Fillmores growing the herd, I reckon. Them's got some good, hardy stock in their blood." He spooned himself out some goop before reaching for the molasses.

Bill followed Leah Holland inside, rubbing his own eyes with the tired but satisfied smile of a new grandpa.

"I guess you heard about Sophie's twins?" Phil asked.

"Oh, twins, huh?" Bill said, taking his seat at the table. "Good to hear, good to hear."

"What's got you in such a good mood, Bill?" Leah Holland asked.

Bill leaned back in his chair and swept a sprinkling of crumbs from the table. "The guncotton is stable."

Phil almost choked on his breakfast. "You serious? You did it?"

Bill nodded. "I'd like to test my charges on one of your guns."

"Sure, Bill." Phil faltered. "You ... you need any other help? Want me to send Ella over?"

"Not yet. I still need to sort out a bunch of some such. I got a lot of things need more lookin' into. I've got an inkling that the powder burns a little too quick for most guns, so I'll need to add something to slow the burn rate. I want to be able to recycle the by-product of the nitric and sulfuric acid reaction. I could cut down on waste all through the goings-on, and I need to get this ready for mass production. Need to make a bigger distillation outfit. I need—how many charges do you reckon we'd need to really get this going?"

Phil opened his mouth to answer, then simply shrugged.

Ella chimed in. "Will you be selling to the nomads?" she asked.

"If I can. This could be the Tuckers' new big export, if I can get some solid production underway."

Phil whistled as he ran a hand through his hair. "Bill, this is ... you got me flat-footed here, Bill. I'd half expect you could leave black powder behind. The Griersons can take over, if they can keep up. You've might have yourself a new full-time job. Why, if you pitch it to the clan, you might get a right fancy shop big enough for you and, say—five shop-hands."

"Where am I gonna get five apprentices?"

"You'll get them from all over once families realize their sons'll get rich here. Think about profits, Bill. At, say, a quarter tooth per shot—"

"It costs more than that just for materials. I'd likely have to a take a full tooth per charge, but I won't know for sure until I start testin'."

Phil's eyes widened again. "Can anyone afford that?"

"If I can smooth the rough edges off the formula, I can bring the cost down maybe to half a tooth. Even so, folks would be stupid not to buy this stuff."

Phil whistled again. "How'd you figure all this out? What'd you do to get 'er beat?" Phil asked.

"Well, the problem up until now has been findin' out how to balance stability with—" Bill stopped himself to meet Omar's intent stare. "Uh, Omar, if you've finished your bran, why don't you go start grindin' whatever powder you started yesterday?"

Bill didn't continue until the drifter was safely away.

Bill swore the entire Holland family to secrecy until he'd run some tests. Although Bill kicked Omar out of his ramshackle shop while he cooked up a fresh batch of guncotton, he permitted both Omar and Ella to help him with tests later that afternoon, just as the sun was setting on the lingering chill of late February. They marched to the outskirts of town, beyond the wall, where the wintered forest had reclaimed much of what had once been a town before the unbreds changed everything.

"Okay, test one. We've got one gram of compacted nitrocellulose over by stump number one. Everyone clear?" Bill looked up from his dusty clipboard and glanced at Ella and Omar, who gave him a thumbs-up behind the cover of a makeshift bunker made of old barnroof tin. "Let 'er rip."

Ella did nothing. She was too busy staring elsewhere.

"Go ahead and strike it," Bill said.

"Ella?" Omar brought her out of her reverie with a gentle prod.

"Oh, right." Ella yanked a string that sparked a whetstone on steel, igniting the charge of guncotton. A loud pop showered the tin above Omar's and Ella's heads with dirt and bark.

Bill checked the middle-sharing circles marking distance around the test site. "Now for the control. We've got a one-gram charge of 76-17-7 gunpowder. Hit it."

The explosion produced by the second test was more a puff of smoke and flame than an actual explosion. Some flecks of dirt coaxed into the air by the spark landed about ten to fifteen feet away. Bill busied himself with measurements and meticulous margin notes on his grease-stained clipboard with a nub of charred wood.

"Doin' some thinkin'?" Omar asked Ella.

Ella blinked, awakened from a further distraction. "Oh? Yeah, I reckon."

"It'll be spring 'fore long."

"Can't come soon enough. I'm tired of breathing cold air." Ella sighed as if winter amounted to breathing problems. She changed the subject as Bill set out the next charges. "So, Omar. That's a funny name. Where did you get it?"

Omar turned from watching Bill and looked at Ella. "I'm named after a general. My full name's Omar Bradley Walking."

"Why'd your folks name you that?"

Omar turned his attention back to Bill. "My grandpa'd come from a military family. Both he and my pa always thought of themselves as military men. Only seemed right to him I'd have a military name."

"Are you a military man?"

"I don't think military men exist anymore," Omar said.

"Then what do you call fightin' men?"

"Cutthroats, I reckon."

"Fair enough." Ella had the good sense not to ask if he were a cutthroat.

Bill called out to the two of them. "Omar! Bring me a hammer! Ella, weigh me out some charges."

They completed tests for blast strength, impact sensitivity, and damp combustibility before they even began testing it on the rifles Phil had loaned them. It was full dark before they could test the guns. The sulfurous smell of black powder mixed with the acrid smell of Bill's new concoction.

"Okay, you two. This'll be the last few tests we run until we've got some daylight again. Load up this gun, Ella. We'll start off with a small charge—about that much, how 'bout?"

Ella loaded the gun while Omar set up a wooden target.

"Double that up," Bill instructed. "I reckon the bullet will penetrate a bit."

"Where you from, Omar?" Ella asked as they set up their last tests by lantern light.

"Huh?" Omar turned.

"You weren't born a drifter, were you? Did you have a clan?"

"Yeah. A few years ago."

"Where was it?"

Omar gestured out into the wilderness as if he were casting a stone. "Way down south and east."

"Beyond the mountains?"

"No. The mountains go on forever, as far as I care to know."

Ella set the rifle on its stand and clamped it there. She tied a string to the trigger. "What was it like?"

"What was what like?"

Ella tested the strength of a nearby fallen log and sat down. "Your clan."

Omar didn't answer for a bit. He fiddled with the lantern burner in front of him. His face remained passive in the glow of the flame. "It was nice."

"You had to think that long for 'nice'?"

"Well, there were some things I liked and some things I didn't," Omar said.

"What didn't you like about it?"

He sat down on the log next to Ella, keeping with the warmth of the lantern between them. "Awful lot folks shuttin' their eyes and stickin' their fingers in their ears," he said. "Or some of them thought we were the center of the world or something. Like we got something special in our veins that makes us different from everyone else."

"Sounds mighty familiar," Ella laughed, but added with a whisper, "but don't tell anyone I said that."

Omar nodded and said out of the corner of his mouth, "I won't tell anyone if you won't."

"I guess most clans are like that some way," Ella mused. "Folks will prefer their own over strangers, even if they can't stand their own half the time. I hope this smokeless gunpowder thing don't puff up our chests too much."

"Hmm. Yeah, me too."

Bill called out from behind the barn-roof tin. "Y'uns got that charge ready yet?"

Ella spun around on the log to face the other way. "We've been a-waitin' on you, Bill!"

"Then git on back here and let 'er rip. I want to hit the hay."

The two of them joined Bill behind the makeshift bunker. Ella pulled the string, and the rifle bucked off of its stand, the report loud enough to make all three of them flinch. They peeked out from behind their cover to get a look at the rifle.

"Looks like it's still okay," Ella said, inspecting the trigger mechanism and barrel.

"We'll see how it holds up with several more shots," Bill said.

"Good grief, Bill, the barrel's completely clean."

"Look at this, you two," Bill said, waving them over to the target and holding up the lantern. The bullet had punched a hole through both planks of wood. "Add another layer of wood," Bill instructed Omar, "we'll try the test again."

The third additional plank successfully stopped the next bullet at the cost of its shape and a few splinters from the back side.

"Looks like a charge with a standard .55 caliber ball will penetrate almost four inches of solid walnut. Is the gun still holding up?"

"Looks that way. But the barrel's getting mighty warm," Ella said.

"Watch—out—for—overheating," Bill said aloud to himself as he scribbled a note on his clipboard. "Where is it warm? At the end of the barrel, or right around the firing chamber?"

"A little bit all along."

"Good. That means the gas is pushing the bullet all along the barrel and not just right at the beginning. All right, kids. Let's call it a night. I'm going to get the clan together as soon as I make some more of this stuff and figure out what to call it."

Bill left Ella and Omar to clean up, muttering to himself about remembering to set up more space for something or other.

"Hey, Omar?" Ella said without looking his way. "How do you feel about ... killin'?"

Omar inspected the ragged hole punched through the splintered planks. "Not my first choice of work, I reckon."

Ella rammed a cloth rag down the muzzle of the rifle. "I think it's a sin."

"Always?"

Ella pulled the cloth free and found it nearly clean. "Always."

"Not even to save your life?"

She pressed her lips together in thought. "Thing about sin is, folks are always tryin' to make themselves feel better about it. This talk I hear about self-defense and whatnot squawks the same as anyone else tryin' to explain what they shouldn'ta did in the first place."

"How's a powderman like Bill supposed to scrape a livin' if folks ain't even 'lowed to defend themselves?"

"That's just the thing I'm wonderin' about." Ella straddled the log and gestured with an open hand toward Omar. "If I never shoot a gun in all my life, never harm a living soul, but I help make a better gunpowder, we'll go sell it to the nomads, and they'll sell it to who-knows-who, who will use it for who-knows-what, and that's just taking it for granted that our own clansmen won't use it for ornery doings. I'm wondering if we'll end up realizing one day that we're well-nigh killin' folks just to scrape a livin', as you say."

"Folks make their own choices, and you ain't responsible for that."

"Folks ought to make choices what ain't likely to cause harm."

"You can't tell whether this'll cause harm or not."

"It's a risk."

"So's making regular powder. Did that ever stop you? Cause you to think?"

"You think I shouldn't be worrying about this, Omar?"

"I think I wouldn't expect a powderman's apprentice to fret about the rightliness of shootin'."

"Before it was mostly for huntin' and shootin' unbreds. The only humans we had cause to shoot were Greenbriers, and we ain't had a run-in with them since..." Ella looked down.

"Since what?"

"The point is, this stuff ... folks won't spend a tooth per shot just to go shoot squirrels."

Omar shrugged and looked away, scratching at his earlobe. "Thing about killing power is it tends to warn off the killing before it starts. Folks ain't too apt to fight each other if they know the fighting is as likely to kill themselves as it is the other."

"I don't know." Ella shook her head. "Seems to me humans don't think that a-way. I think if folks have a new tool, they'll wonder why they ain't usin' it. That's fine if you're talking about a hammer or a drill, but what if you look that a-way at the nuke-bombs, or the breedcrafting?"

"It's a long way from shootin' powder to nuke-bombs."

"Wouldn't never have made either of 'em if we hadn't been making spears first."

Omar grimaced. "That ain't a problem with killin' tools, that's a problem with science. You reckon we oughta have stayed in our tents eatin' berries for all time? Science always came with a cost. But don't pretend it ain't given us the world on a silver platter. Or that this new powder won't make a nice living for you and yours."

Ella turned away, picking up the rifle they'd tested. "I ain't sure a nice living for our clansmen is worth the price of killing a bunch of folks, though."

"Not sure how much say you got in the matter."

"Yeah, I ain't either. Just airing my mind."

Sam Chambers dismissed his students and turned to wipe the gigantic slate hung on the wall. The classroom door swung open behind him.

"Did you forget some—" Sam stopped as he turned. "Something the matter, Reverend?"

Reverend Brody didn't answer at first. He stared at the schoolmaster long and hard.

"Wha—" Sam began.

"Did you take it?"

Sam opened his mouth to ask the obvious, then stopped. "The chip is gone?"

"I looked everywhere for it. I think someone broke into my house, but only the chip is missing. You were the only one who knew about it."

"No. I got it from Amos first. I didn't tell him you confiscated it, though."

"Do you have anything else you'd like to share?" the reverend asked.

"Reverend, do you really think I'd do something as stupid as burglarizing your home just to satisfy my curiosity?"

Reverend Brody exhaled slowly through his elephantine nose. "No. But I know everyone in this clan, and you're the only one who's got any cause and means to know about it. Unless..."

"Unless what?"

"That drifter helped take down the shadower. He may have seen the chip."

"Would he know about what it was?"

"Maybe not." The reverend scratched his face in thought. "But if he *did* know what it was, and wanted it bad enough to steal it, then he's far more dangerous than we gave him credit for."

Many summers of overgrowth and as many winters of decay had rendered the old town nearly as wild as the forest. Even small municipalities of the bygone years stretched far further than the clans of today could wall off. So at the clan's founding, the leaders had parceled off what they deemed the most valuable land of the city around the high school, stripped the rest of valuables and salvageable building materials, and left everything outside the walls to nature and the unbreds.

By now, only vine-choked foundations and the shattered wreck of a wall or roof here and there remained. The rotting remnants of a home trailer, or maybe a heap of trash not even fit to burn clogged the spaces between the undergrowth. Most of what could be called a town had long since been picked clean by two generations of Tuckers trying to shore up the palisade and patch their homes.

Because it was so close to the wall, most of the old town was usually safe enough for folks to wander around. Few did, however. The kids were afraid of ghosts, and maybe the adults were, too.

Bert Daly didn't give credence to hearsay.

It didn't take him long to find the cemetery, with the steadily increasing chirp of the ceramic talisman guiding him through a narrowing cone of territory. By the time he approached a lonesome collection of runic stones marking old graves, he was more or less walking in a straight line. The steady chirps blended together to form a single tone, and he knew he'd found his X marking the spot.

The remaining gravestones lay scattered like a giant's broken teeth, tucked into the folds of an old copse of trees. He recognized none of the names, and the inscriptions meant nothing to him. An hour's labor produced nothing he could use. These graves all came before the Pandemic.

He had to be close. He circled out from the overgrown graves, kicking at tufts and bundles of dried weeds to check for a buried headstone somewhere. A town this small, the cemetery couldn't stretch too far. If only he knew what he was looking—

Bert froze in front of what he'd assumed was the remnants of a cheap concrete wall, pieces of cement already falling off to reveal field stone aggregate. Lilting to the side in a losing death-struggle with roots and tentacle-like tendrils of ivy, the pockmarked face still bore the spray-painted image of a twisted ladder.

Chapter 15

In Which Omar Learns About the Greenbriers

"Bill, you mind telling us why you dragged us way out here? You still haven't filled any of our orders for powder," Elvin asked with crossed arms. The morning sun had risen far enough over the tops of the trees to cast everything in a golden light out in a flattened part of the old town. Spring was fast approaching, and the forest was nearly clear of unbreds, but that didn't stop Elvin from being a stickler about security. He resented his absence from the wall. Perhaps a few of the other Tuckers who had gathered in a small crowd there were inclined to agree, but curiosity won out over caution or busy schedules.

"I've got Omar out yonder setting targets at one hundred, two hundred, three hundred, and then four hundred yards." Bill motioned to clear on the other side of the bare plateau on which they stood.

"What for?" Elvin asked.

"I've cracked the formula for smokeless gunpowder. I'm thinking of calling it nitrogel. But I ain't tested it on ranged targets yet, so I wondered if y'all would mind helping me out while I demonstrate how you're supposed to use it."

"It's just fancy gunpowder, ain't it? We just use it the same," one of the Fillmores said from the back of the group.

"If you use the same amount of this stuff as regular gunpowder, you'll bust your gun and your shoulder both. And you can't use just any gun. That pea shooter Job's got from the nomads there won't cut it. I can only guarantee Phil Holland's rifles, since he made them with my powder especially in mind. Any other rifle you want to use, I'll have to test it.

"You'll use about two-thirds of a normal charge, to be safe," Bill said, loading his rifle. "Any volunteers?" He held the rifle out to anyone who wanted to give it a try.

The Tucker men looked around at each other as Omar came back from placing the targets.

"Aw, shucks. I'll give it whirl," Ricky Brody, Job Brody's youngest son, said, stepping up. He took the loaded rifle from Bill and stepped out in front of the line of targets.

"Bullet won't fall as much, at least until you hit about two or three hundred yards."

"Aim with the sights, then?" Ricky asked, rifle at his shoulder.

"Yeah, I reckon. Haven't really tested accuracy yet, but that's what I'd—"

Ricky pulled the trigger. The report blasted the ears of the men watching and echoed off of the shattered husks of buildings far away.

"Dadgum! Dang!" Ricky said, clutching his shoulder.

"Yeah, you should expect a sight stronger recoil," Bill mused.

"Feels like I done been kicked by a dad-blamed mule!" Ricky said.

"But imagine how it would feel on the other end of that gun." Bill smiled. "It'll make it all worth it. Omar, go check the target."

Omar ran out and returned grim-faced. "Pert near a bull's-eye."

"Really?" Ricky asked, shocked. "I didn't aim high at all. Just shot straight."

The Tucker men whistled, and a few women who came out to see what all the commotion was about stood entranced. More volunteered to shoot. They quickly passed the one-hundred, two-hundred, and three-hundred-yard marks, and by the time they had run out of ammunition, the Tuckers had put a spread of bullet holes only a foot or two wide on the four-hundred-yard target, almost a quarter mile away—all with the same rifle.

"Bill, I think it's taking the bullet longer to hit the target than it takes for me to reload." Job Brody whistled as he swept his tattered hat from his head.

"I never woulda believed it if I hadn't of seen't it," Bill's naysaying cousin said, stroking his beard.

"Fellers," Bill Puckett spoke grandly to the assembled clansmen, "what we've got here is powder-ized nitrogel. As you can see, it's good at taking out targets at *real* long ranges without losing its kick. Since it leaves behind so little soot, you can use more shots with a single rifle. *And* I'll be a-workin' on the formula so it keeps longer. Aside from huntin', this new powder will let you pick off unbreds from safer stretches. You can punch holes in the hide of a bullhusker with this ammunition. *Human* targets won't stand a chance. Imagine sniping a Greenbrier at four hundred yards without even a puff of smoke to give yourself away. That," Bill said with a clenched fist, "is the power of my nitrogel."

The impromptu audience broke out into applause.

It was a rare calm day at the Grierson settlement. Debris had clogged up the old mine ventilation shaft again, so it wasn't safe to work the ore for the time being, and the spell of good weather and easygoing wildlife made it a good day to be aboveground. For a little while, anyway.

"Eddie," Johnny Grierson growled as his cousin came out from the brush with a dead bird in hand, "how come you're so deadly with a flip out in the timber, but you can't hit a target to save your life?"

"Can't eat a target," Edward answered, grinning.

A ruckus at the gate pulled Johnny's attention back behind him. A lone figure sauntered up the path from town to the settlement gate where the watchman on duty tipped back the brim of his hat to better see.

"What brings you way out here, Daly?" Johnny heard the watchman call down from the palisade to visitor.

Bert Daly. "Need to talk with Johnny," Johnny heard him say. "Clan business."

"Since when do you come talking about clan business?" The watchman sounded almost ready to believe this was all a joke.

"Since I learned the clan's dirty little sec'ert." Bert cackled.

Johnny Grierson may not have given the town good-for-nothing the time of day normally, but the mention of a dirty little secret brought him to the gate before the watchman could even announce it.

"Bert Daly, you low-down varmit!" Johnny hollered as the settlement gates swung open to receive the visitor. "What in blazes you talkin' 'bout?"

"I saw it, Johnny." Bert leaned up against the inside of the palisade with the kind of ease borne of newfound swagger. He giggled as if half mad. "I saw the grave. Dug 'em up and saw our forefathers with my own eyes."

Johnny scowled. "Then what are you doin' here?"

"I know why the elders didn't want us to know the truth. The powers of the ubermenschen can be *ours.* Even watered down, the ubermensch stock is strong enough to make us like them. I knowed it all along. I could feel it. Now I *know* it. I can already feel it. Just do as an ubermensch does and let the breeding blossom. The body knows what to do." He sucked in a lungful of air as if the wind itself gave him strength.

"Bert, if you know what's good for you, you'll turn right around and march back on home and forget whatever you think you saw in the old town."

"Don't you see, you one-eyed coot? The clan elders won't stand a chance once the half-and-halfs tap into their ubermensch blood!"

"The hell they won't. I'mma kick your ass clear over your head. *I'm* an elder. Any secrets they keep, I'm keepin' too. If you wanted to kill yourself, why not do it the fun way and jump off a cliff or something?"

"Did you know all along?"

Johnny hitched his shoulder toward Bert as if he was getting ready to charge. "Why do you reckon I'm way out here in this settlement? Why ain't I a town Tucker?"

Bert didn't answer.

"I left of my own free will in the end, but not without a bit of unfriendly encouragement on account of what I knowed—from my mama's deathbed. I struck a deal to keep my mouth shut, and they'd give me first shot at the labor and apprentices from the clan, the watchman's protection, and a seat among the elders if I turned up enough jaws. I wasn't supposed to bring it off, but I did. But if you start running your big fat mouth about the truth, they're going to look for someone to blame. Someone they never were too fond of to begin with." Johnny stabbed a thumb at his own chest.

Bert's lip curled in disgust. "You don't deserve your ubermensch blood. The only way you can become an ubermensch is to *act* like one."

"Yeah? And how in holy hell is an ubermensch supposed to act?"

"It ain't layin' down and takin' it right in the ass, I'll tell you that."

Johnny grabbed Bert by the shirt and pulled him close. "Does this look like I'm taking anything lying down? Took me *fifteen* years to get where I am!"

"You got some grand plan, then?" Bert's lip curled.

"Yeah." Johnny eased Bert back down and let him go. "Not gettin' banished and et by unbreds, that's my plan. Turn this mining operation into a respectable little clan in its own right. *That's* my plan. You want to help the cause? You can—" Johnny stopped, the red in his face fading. "You apprenticed for Bill Puckett once, didn't you?"

"'Bout four years back. Why?"

"I'll pay you to tell me anything useful about Bill Puckett's powder-making operation. The more useful to me, the more I can pay. You interested?"

"Hey, Omar, you busy?" Amos knocked on the door of Omar's room.

"No," came the answer from within.

"Come on outside. I got something to show you."

The house was open to the night air, Amos standing in the doorway, already extending one of two rough-cut swords to Omar.

"Defend yourself," Amos said as he tossed the sword to Omar, stepped out into the open, and assumed a defensive stance.

"What?"

"I picked them up from my dad's smithy. I want to see who's the better swordsman."

Omar stepped outside, kicking the door shut behind him. "Swordsman? You've been reading fantasy books, haven't you?"

"No harm in it. Sam Chambers collects whatever books he can find from the nomads. Enough talk, Omar. Let's see how you do in a straight fight!"

Omar gave Amos a gormless stare. "I'm tired, Amos. I haven't done this sort of thing since I was a kid. I'm out of shape—" Omar lunged mid-sentence, trying to catch Amos off guard.

Amos parried just in time and deftly hopped back one step. "Ah, ha ha! Nice try!" Amos returned the stroke, shifting his feet forward in a near leap. Omar staggered back again, keeping his distance, watching and gauging.

"I've been thinking," Amos said, still keeping the point of his sword up but not making a move yet.

"Ain't a good sign, knowin' you."

Their blades made contact, but neither moved. They would use their swords to feel for the slightest changes in pressure that signaled an attack before the eye could catch it.

"About what makes a good swordsman." Amos struck, but Omar darted back before counter-attacking a split second later. "I know people think matchetwork's the stuff of pirate stories, but Paul McDaniel—that was the watchman's old man—he was supposed to be this crazy berserk warrior with blades. This one time he was out following some tracks when he and his second were ambushed by a big pack of pigmen. Anyway, Paul McDaniel had his second-in-command get out of there while he worked himself into a little cove with his back to the wall, sword drawn. When the second-in-command came back with reinforcements, they found Paul McDaniel picking his teeth with a pigman claw. There were twenty pigmen corpses piled up around him."

Omar scoffed audibly, backstepping a lazy engage on Amos' part. "That's a fisherman's tale if I ever heard one. Twenty?"

"The exact number was twenty-one. I know 'cause they used the jaws to pay for Elvin's first rifle. All with just a machete."

"How could he take on twenty pigmen in one go?"

Amos dodged a thrust and shifted on nimble feet out of Omar's range. "I think I figured it out."

"How, then?"

"The only way to get a really decisive victory like that," Amos said, feinting to the left, "is to be *unexpectedly* bold."

Amos spun out of his feint and stepped in to the right, close enough to bump heads. Omar flinched, blocking Amos' sideswipe but leaving his flank open. Amos used his momentum and a well-placed foot to trip up Omar, and by the time Omar had recovered from his stumble, Amos had tapped him on the ribs with his sword.

Omar accepted his defeat and dusted himself off. "Remind me not to tangle with you hand-to-hand."

"Well, playing around with a dull matchet is one thing. Risking your life is another." Amos rested the machete across his shoulder. "Even Paul McDaniel's grit didn't keep him from catching a Greenbrier musketball."

"Folks keep talking about Greenbriers. What's a Greenbrier?"

"They're another clan about twenty, oh, twenty-five miles south or southwest. Nasty bunch. Skin you alive. Folks don't ever go more than a day's hike down that way unless they've got some sort of death wish. We Tuckers have been feuding with them for God knows how long."

"Why?"

"Why what? Why are we feuding with them, you mean? Well, I suppose it started back probably thirty years ago, maybe more."

Omar stood as if expecting Amos to elaborate.

Amos used the machete to scratch a hard-to-reach place between his shoulder blades as he settled in to tell the tale. "The story goes that Old Man Brody and some of his kin went out to trade with them. A couple of the clansmen were sick—real bad. We needed some special medicine, but it was the dead of winter, and we didn't have any nomad clans around. Well, apparently we'd stumbled across an entire hidden basement filled with goodies just a few weeks earlier. When our clan came down sick, it looked like there wasn't anything we could do. Well, that's when Old Man Brody remembered the outpost the Greenbriers had at the time. They were camped out on one of the old interstates, so they'd run a trading outfit from an old gas station outpost. But they were mean, I'm telling you. Real thugs. They had a road tax they used to have out on that highway. The men had to give teeth, and the women had to go for a toss in the sack if they wanted to pass soundly. People didn't take children through there, 'cause there was no telling what the Greenbriers would decide to take from them, and you'd just have to leave them behind if the kids didn't have anything to give. No exceptions. If you didn't pay the tax, or if they didn't like you, Elvin McDaniel's told me that they used to eat a couple of their victims and let the last one go to tell the stories of how mean the Greenbriers were.

"Anyway, we came up to their outpost with a band of clansmen aiming to trade for the medicine and some food. Well, the Greenbriers get a look at the goods and figure they could take advantage of us. They told the Tuckers that the medicine would cost the whole lot of loot. The whole bunch! It was probably all worth a couple hundred jaws. Anyway, our boys wouldn't have any of it, so they tried to haggle. But the Greenbriers knew we'd have to be in a desperate situation to come all that way for medicine in the middle of winter, so they didn't budge. Well, we started arguing. Maybe we even begged. The Greenbriers just invoked the road tax like we were passing through or something.

"So the Tuckers made like they would just walk away with the loot and take their chances with someone else. But the Greenbriers wanted that loot about as bad as we wanted the medicine. But instead of bargaining with us, I supposed they figured they could just steal it. Anyway, they turned loose while our backs were turned and shot most of our clansmen. Old Man Brody got away, and a couple of others, but that was it. We were finished with that whole business then. They could get away with doing that sort of thing to lone travelers, but we wouldn't let it pass.

We came back in late spring and burned their little trading outpost to the ground. We've been fighting them ever since."

"Been fighting recently?"

"Off and on, here and there. No real battles to speak of for about six years. No, we've scared them off for now, for the most part. Might go after them again sometime soon. There's plenty of folks here who can't sleep too well knowing the Greenbriers are just a two-day march away, and with this new nitrogel, we've finally got an edge on them."

"Hmm," Omar mused, poking the ground with the point of his sword and staring at some point far below them.

"What?"

"Just thinkin'. Maybe Ella was right."

"About what?"

"She was frettin' over nitrogel. Figured it would make the clan more warlike."

Amos folded his arms and cocked his head to the side. "Huh. Seems to me Ella's got more cause than most to want the Greenbriers taken down a peg or two."

Omar looked up. "Why's that?"

"They killed her brother a couple years back. Almost killed her, too."

"Some sort of a raid?"

"Something like that. She'd gone out to visit with him on a roundswalk. He went out into the timber and never came back. They were pretty close, too, as far as I understand."

"Hmm. That why you were courtin' her?"

"Wait, what?"

Omar dropped his gaze again. "Never mind. Not my business."

"I'm not courting anybody."

"My mistake."

"Why'd you think I was?"

Omar shrugged. "Just seemed like you ... I don't know ... felt sorry for her."

Amos sighed. "You know what? Now that you mention it, I guess you're right."

Chapter 16

Springtime

Sam Chambers greeted his wife, along with his six young sons and daughters, as he sat down at the table for breakfast. He got up and stoked the fire when his youngest complained of the cold. She was always cold, always wrapping herself in patchwork blankets and animal skins until she looked twice her actual size.

"Honey, you smell that?" his wife asked.

He stopped and sniffed. He ran to the door of their house, instinctively bracing himself for a blast of cold air. He opened it and stepped outside into what felt like a mellow warmth. "Hey, kids! Come on outside. It must be sixty degrees out here."

His children piled outside, sucking in the unmistakable smell of spring like parched deer panting for water.

Elvin McDaniel whipped his son, Ralph, for not being up early enough before dragging him out on the roundswalk. They'd nearly made half of their one-hour roundswalk of the town's palisade when the sun inched through the stark net of the forest canopy. Elvin looked over briefly at his son to notice tears—tears, for crying out loud—standing out on his face. Thirteen years old and crying like a baby.

"Ralph, you're gonna need to toughen up, plain and simple," Elvin lectured. "You act like this, you're gonna embarrass the whole family. You be glad I'm raising you and not your grandpa. You never had it so good. Your grandpa beat the soft outta me by the time I was half your age. Now get on up there and wipe those silly baby tears off your face!"

Elvin panted, disgusted. His pa never would have stood for this. His pa had been a great leader of the Tucker clan; shoot, he'd *saved* the Tucker clan more than once. Elvin respected that. A hard man? Sure, no one would deny that Paul McDaniel had been a hard man. No one knew it better than Elvin. His back still had more scars from his pa than from the unbreds. But it was a hard world, and it took hard men to survive, not the Sam Chambers kind of man. What would Paul McDaniel have done with a son like Ralph?

He stopped. A breeze from the south brought fresh smells to his nostrils and the sound of a singing warbler. He looked through an arrow loop and saw the flit of an animal deep in the woods, probably a deer. There hadn't been any sight of pigmen in at least a week and a half. Other animals were returning. His son had stopped too, looking into the forest that stirred after its deathly sleep.

Neither father nor son could keep from smiling a little.

Old Man Brody hobbled outside his sagging clapboard house where he lived alone. The winter had taken its toll on the place, as every winter had done, adding a host of chores that the old man would never quite get done. Patch the roof, tear out that rot, borrow the Craines' mule and pull up that sapling growing into the wall, try to fix that disaster of a lean-to he'd used to smoke meats—there was no end to it, and each year his home looked a bit more like a boxer barely holding on between punches. Another winter, another reeling blow, another stagger close to the brink of collapse. But it hadn't fallen yet.

Another spring. He greeted it gratefully, if without a smile. The girls of the clan would start rubbing buttermilk into their cheeks, and the boys would soon get into competitions to catch some fair gal's fancy. Folks would get out to the springs in the backhills to forage peppery watercress and hunting for small game and fowl coming back into the area. Time for him to get back to work. Ignoring the pain of his arthritis, he set to work prepping his garden. His neighbors, the Timothy Craines, always offered to help him with his tasks, but he usually did it himself, the exception being last year when he broke his leg tracking a screevler. Not that he didn't appreciate the gesture, but folks tended to forget too easily what kind of world this was. It was a world that didn't forgive weakness, and no amount of human kindness would change that. The moment he couldn't pull his own weight would be the moment the clan would have every right to boot him out into the wild.

It wasn't like that in the old days when he was a young man in college. The old were kept in nice homes made especially for them, where they could sit in wheelchairs until the long ravages of time finally wore their lives away. He'd wondered often what had happened to all of them when things had taken their final turn for the worst. They'd probably all been abandoned in the mad rush for survival. He'd heard from the band of survivors he'd joined in the early days that a couple doctors had gone crazy and euthanized every patient in their hospital before they lit out for the hills. Maybe that's what happened in the nursing homes. Would have been better that way.

A lot of folks died then. The Pandemic was bad enough, and that was even before the unbreds went wild. There had been a wide variety of special little critters back in that time, critters which couldn't really survive outside of a laboratory but which were still so useful at the time: organ donors, meat factories, drug test subjects, who knew what else. They called it a biological revolution when he was in school, the next step in human evolution. And so the ubermenschen arose—designer babies grown into designer people.

The best of intentions, the dream of a heaven on earth, had driven the revolution of his father's and grandfather's youth. But there were ... complications.

There were as many theories about what went wrong as there were survivors. What had driven the unbreds wild? How did the Pandemic spread so efficiently? To Old Man Brody, even from the early days, the answer was clear as it was simple: God had measured mankind and found it wanting.

He was a survivor by nature, thankfully. He'd learned to forget the old ways, the comforts and luxuries of a bygone age. He'd learned to forget air conditioning and central heating. He'd learned to forget virtual reality. Digital music. Electric lighting. Cars. Indoor plumbing. Not that he never missed them; he did. He missed antibiotics when his second wife was down with an infection that Dr. Bernhard's garlic and herbs couldn't stop.

One way or another, you learned to adapt. You didn't hear the hundred-year-old oaks complain of the wintertime.

"Becky! Quit lollygaggin' and get on out here! Archie Fillmore brought by a whole fresh deer this morning, and it ain't gonna clean itself! Plus, Amos Taylor is here to talk to you!" Charlotte Brody called to Becky, the butcher's daughter. Becky went out to meet Amos, who beamed at her approach.

"Morning, Becky! It's a mighty fine day we've got here."

"Yes, I reckon it's pretty nice having the temperatures up a little. It'll get cold again soon, though."

"But it's springtime. It'll be getting warmer more than it'll be getting colder."

"Yeah, that's the way it usually goes, isn't it?"

"Say, I was wondering if you cared to take a little turn up the road with me. To enjoy the sunshine and such."

Becky raised her eyebrows. "Oh? Any reason you'd want my company in particular?"

"Well," Amos explained, "I couldn't help but notice a while ago that you're a mighty fine dancer, that you're pretty, and people say you cut up a chicken pretty well. But with the pigman siege and all, it didn't really seem like the right time to get acquainted much. But now that it's over, well—"

"Well! That's a funny thing," Becky said in a tone that should have been a warning to Amos, though he didn't realize it until too late, "'cause I could have sworn you was becoming pretty well acquainted with my good friend Ella."

"Well, about that—"

"Yes? I'm all ears. Please explain."

"We've gotten to be pretty good friends, you see, but I don't think there was ever any real—"

"'Cause I'm *sure*," Becky inbroke, "that if, let's say, you actually *were* courtin' Ella and playin' around with her heart, you wouldn't be stupid enough to come waltzin' over here to try and court someone behind her back, someone who happens to have been her best friend longer than you've been alive."

Amos stood on Arnold Brody's front porch, mouth agape, the abruptly-closed front door staring him in the face.

"Well," he said to himself, turning slowly, "that could have gone better."

The pliant loam peeled away under the edge of Job Brody's plow. The winter freeze and early spring thaw had left the grassy sod greedy for water, and the plentiful rain sucked in like liquid on a wool blanket. His feet sank in a bit before springing back out as he trailed behind his two workhorses. He lived for this time of year. It was like nature was having itself a good long stretch with the rising sun.

"Hey, Job!" A voice from behind him lowered his spirits somewhat. It was Sam Chambers, which could only mean one thing—

"Clan meeting back in town! Come on back with me, and I'll have you back before sundown."

Job sighed. "Aw, Sam, I'm right in the middle of something. I got corn to plant."

"Sorry, Job, it's a big one. The Griersons are coming down from the settlement for it."

This elder business wasn't all it was cracked up to be. At forty-two, Job was getting too old for this sort of thing. But he supposed this was why they were called elders. "Fine. This really slaps my crackers, you know that, right? Help me put away Biscuits and Gravy and brush them down and unhook the plow."

"Can't you have your boys do that?"

"They're tending the hogs. And if I keep making you help me every time you come up to fetch me, then maybe you'll stop fetching me for these gosh-darned meetings."

"Okay, everybody, quiet on down, now," Sam said, trying to settle the clan elders. Most of them hated coming, but once they got there, trying to get them to stop talking about crops or lumber or hunting was like trying to herd pigmen. And Edward Grierson was here now, and good Lord, that man could talk the ears off an elephant.

"We've got some old business to take care of, the Newells' new fortifications, the barn for the Fillmores, and help for the Craine family. But first we need to take care of the new business that's come up recently."

He didn't even need to mention it. The gunpowder. Even the womenfolk were talking about it. Bill Puckett had changed the game overnight, and some folks were restive. A lot of people in town had been pushing for a new water-powered mill down on the Gooseneck Run, and the clan had been saving up for it. The Pucketts now had a say in a different project, and there was no telling who would go over to the other side.

Sam wasn't totally sure he wouldn't go over himself. The implications of this invention were huge. Not only was this a giant leap forward for firearms, it was the first serious industrial chemistry done in this part of the world in fifty years. Sam knew something of the different chemicals that needed to go into the making, and any one of them could sell for a hefty price. That Marion clan way out west got filthy rich from baking soda. Baking soda! What would folks do to get their hands on sulfuric acid? But how would the elders react?

"It's a new-fangled luxury item, is what it is," Johnny Grierson cut in as soon as the necessary formalities were out of the way. "I reckon it'll be too costly to make. Even if it isn't, our black powder's the finest there is around here. There ain't no need for smokeless powder."

The Reverend Brody nodded in agreement. "We've made such progress toward the new mill, and if we pull honest, hardworking Tuckers into this fly-by-night operation, we'll put a much more dependable project behind for several more years!"

So there were two elders against expanding Bill Puckett's business, but that wasn't much of a surprise. And since Dr. Bernhard was basically at the Griersons' beck and call, that meant another vote against.

"I second that," Dr. Bernhard chimed in. Just like clockwork. He'd probably follow Edward Grierson right off the edge of a cliff.

Shane Bunton dissented in his usual mild manner. "You're all crazy. This nitrogel will be the best thing that's ever happened to our clan since Alfred got his loom set up. We can keep on grinding our grain over up at the old mill like we always do. I don't know about you, but I'm signing my boy up to do the grunt work for Bill."

There was a surprise. The Buntons usually went with the Griersons these days. How much of the clan did the Griersons really have under their thumb?

"How'd you work up the nerve to think that a-way, you ole' turncoat!" Johnny exclaimed.

"Don't make waves. Bill Puckett's got me feeling a little entrepreneurial, you might say."

"I'm in agreement with you, Shane. I was never all fired-up about the mill anyhow," Job Brody said.

"Who asked you what you think?"

"This is an elder's meeting, Johnny. If y'uns didn't want to hear me, you could have told me before you pulled me off of my dadgum cornfield."

"Just what is Bill asking for anyway?"

"He wants several new buildings for his business: a separate shed for each bit of cookery that goes into this, a," Sam Chambers checked to make sure he read it correctly, "distillation tower for the production of sulfuric acid, as well as three apprentices, not including the drifter he already has working for him."

"Besides the three young clansmen getting pulled off of other important projects, how much will this all cost the clan?"

Chambers hesitated. "Four hundred jaws for materials and supplies."

Mr. Newell jumped. "Great baby-eating bullhusker! How in blazes is this going to cost us more than a watermill?"

"Lots of little specialty items we'll need to pick up from the nomads. Bill thinks he can turn a four-hundred-jaw profit by this time next year, though."

"I don't cotton to pouring a bunch of money into something we don't have a market for yet," Johnny Grierson groused again. "The watermill is already set to turn the clan a profit, and inside the clan walls to boot. Once we get it up, it wouldn't be too hard to run some wires and get the town a steady supply of 'lectricity."

That got some heads turned. There'd been some private discussion about using the Gooseneck Run for hydroelectric power, but it had never before been discussed in an elder's meeting, mostly because those who'd worked with any old AC generators knew the logistics behind getting a large-scale electrical operation going were prohibitively complicated and expensive. But why let practicality get in the way of politics? Grierson did have a point when it came to the plain old profitability of a watermill, Sam admitted to himself, and the mechanical possibilities intrigued him. But those possibilities paled in comparison to the prospect Bill Puckett offered.

"As long as we're proposing ambitious goals for the future, I think Bill's chemical experiments bring up some interesting ideas of their own. I've had a few conversations with Bill about all the different ingredients he includes in his process, and I can tell you all that I've never seen this kind of chemical wizardry anywhere. If Bill can figure out how to make these powerful acids in his workshop, imagine what other chemical discoveries we can make? We could have a chemical research lab if we get enough people and resources together to try new ideas. Heck, it wouldn't be long before we've got neighboring clans sending their best and brightest to do research here."

"That ain't never gonna happen, not on my watch," Elvin said. "The nitrogel and everything about how it's made is a clan secret, and I'm not about to have any foreigner poking around in the name of some empty-headed notions about science or progress or whatever."

"Speaking of foreigners," Johnny Grierson said. "How long do we mean for this drifter to stick around anyway?"

"That's not on our agenda, Johnny—"

"Well, I make a motion to discuss it."

"I second that."

"That's a separate item," Sam said, sighing, "and we haven't voted on—"

"It's related. If the guncotton's such an important secret, how come we got some foreign-born drifter apprenticing under Bill?"

Chambers sighed again. This was going be a long meeting.

"Well, crap, Johnny," Edward Grierson said to his one-eyed cousin as they mounted their horses and got on the road up to the settlement six miles away. "That meeting could have gone better."

"It couldn't hardly have gone any worse if I'd said 'Ma'am' to the watchman."

"We'll get that mill built somehow."

"Not with Bill swinging all the town Tuckers against us like a barn door in a tornado."

"Relax, Johnny. Bill ain't ever been too big a problem before."

"He's never been a big problem before 'cause the fool ain't got a lick of business sense. But now he's got this fancy powder, and it's only a matter of time before our powder won't be worth busted teeth no more. Then what'll happen to our little settlement up there? The Coles ain't far enough along with their coopery to keep us going; we'll all wind up pitchin' hay for the Brodys and the Newells."

"I still think we could have tried mining some of that hematite, bring the Taylors up, and start smelting some iron."

"Even if we could get enough ore, we'd need some raw mechanical power. Which we don't have without that mill. What we *can* get from the mines is feedstock for Bill's chemistry set. Coke. Lime. But especially the sulfur."

"Well, there you go. If Bill can't keep things going without the sulfur—"

"That ain't how it works no more, Eddy. We're beholden to him now, not the other way around. If I raise the price any more, he'll up and get it from the nomads. He'll probably start getting it from the nomads just to spite me. The best we can do with our mineral goods is to keep the settlement afloat, and that's only if Bill wants to keep buying from us! Either way, we can kiss goodbye all our big plans for the settlement."

"We can give the whole sulfuric acid thing another try."

Johnny sighed. "We can try it, but I ain't got the faintest idea what we been doing wrong. Can't purify things the way Bill can. Don't got the knack for it."

"Or we could work for Puckett. I reckon he'll need the help if the nitrogel picks up like folks think it will."

Johnny pulled up his horse to make sure his cousin was serious. Seeing that he was, Johnny shook his head. "You flippin' idiot."

"Well, what do you have in mind?"

Johnny gave the reins a frustrated shake. "That Daly kid's been watching. He ain't told me much, but there's still an angle I don't got worked out yet. Maybe we can use something there."

"What's that?"

"The drifter."

Omar jumped when Ella burst into Bill Puckett's shop.

"I'm a genius!" she announced, holding a stained sheet of paper in the air. The springtime weather had put the whole clan in a good mood, but none more than Ella Holland.

"Is Bill here?" Ella asked, unhinging a lantern from its blackened hook and carrying it over to a bench on the other side of the room, away from the elements that did not react well to flame.

"No. Why?"

She smiled ear to ear. "I did it."

Omar sat back and waited for her to elaborate.

"I figured out where he hides his formulas and notes." Ella removed the double shields from the lantern, exposing the flame.

Omar turned to face her. "You don't say."

"He hides it in plain view! It's so simple! He uses invisible ink!"

"What?"

"He uses some sort of chemical you can't really see with the naked eye. But if you heat it up a little bit, there it is, plain as day."

Omar pointed to the paper in Ella's hand. "You've seen it?"

"See for yourself."

Omar took the proffered parchment and held it up to the lantern on the bench. "I don't see nothin'."

"Look closer. It has to heat up."

Omar leaned in, eyes squinting. The thin parchment glowed against the lantern light. Omar's eyebrows furrowed in concentration. Then, in a literal flash, the paper was gone. There was a spark of heat, a knife of light, and then nothing. His hands jerked back and grasped at thin air. Omar cried out in surprise and nearly fell backwards from his seat. He stared at his inexplicably empty hands. "Wha—"

"Bahahahaha! Perfect!" Ella slapped her knee as she doubled over in laughter.

Omar turned his bewildered gaze to Ella. "What's goin' on? What happened to the paper?"

Ella didn't answer. She leaned back against the wall, wheezing in silent laughter.

"What's so funny?" Omar asked.

Ella wiped the tears streaming from her eyes. "Oh, oh, ho ho, I just, whew—that was great. It's flash paper. It's like the guncotton, except you nitrate some paper instead of cotton. Anything with starchy-type stuff in it, you can nitrate it. All it needs is a little spark, and poof! And you were right up there with your nose in it!" Ella snorted in spite of herself, which only made her laugh harder.

"Then you don't know where he keeps his formula?"

Ella shook her head. "No, I just thought this would be funny."

"Does Bill know about this?"

"Oh, it was his idea, partly," Ella said with an ear-to-ear grin. "You should actually be thanking me. Bill wanted to nitrate your britches—" Ella tried to stifle the bout of laughter that forced its way out at the image of Omar's britches flashing into nothing. She failed. Omar did, too, for that matter.

Omar had a nice laugh, Ella thought. She wondered if she was the only person in the world who had heard it.

It was Ella's turn to jump when a heavy fist pounded on Bill's workshop door. Not the kind of knock an eager customer would make.

Ella opened the door to see the watchman standing there, stone-faced, with the Reverend behind his shoulder.

"Is something the matter?" Ella asked, a firm hand on the door.

"Dunno, miss," Elvin answered. "Need to talk to the drifter."

"Is he in trouble?"

"I said I dunno, miss. Reverend had some property stolen. Gotta check him off my list. Let's go, drifter." Elvin waved Omar out into the open.

"What's been stolen?" Ella asked as Elvin propped Omar up against the wall and patted him down.

"Dunno, miss," Elvin sighed. "Reverend, you can go on in and check out his stuff while I watch the drifter."

"Wait, you don't even know what's been stolen and you're—"

"Miss Holland, if the drifter ain't done nothin', you got nothing to worry about. Now I've had me a long day already. Spent the last two hours splittin' hairs, and I've about had it. Now you best get on after whatever you gotta do and let me do my job."

The Reverend stepped inside the shop and began poking around. "Where's the drifter's room?" he asked her.

"Does Bill know about this?" Ella asked, spinning back and forth between Elvin and Mr. Brody. "This don't seem right by clan rules."

"Take it up with the Reverend," Elvin said. "He's got claim to his property, and cause to suspect, besides."

Ella moved to follow the Reverend inside, then stopped to shoot a glance at Omar.

"I'll be fine," Omar said.

Ella went in after the Reverend, crossing the shop and into Bill's house to find the preacher tossing Omar's travel pack on the floor of his little room.

"What is going on?" Ella put a hand to her head. "Can't you folks leave the poor feller alone for one moment?"

The Reverend rifled through Omar's straw-packed cot. "It's not your concern, Miss Holland."

"It *is* my concern. Mr. Walking's my friend."

The Reverend grunted in frustration. "He wouldn't have hidden it here," he muttered to himself before turning to Ella. "*Mr. Walking* is certainly not your friend, and he may be more dangerous to you than you can imagine."

Ella crossed her arms. Not many beside her pa had known it, but Ella'd always had an all-fired stubborn way about her when she fixed on it. "Try me," she said.

"Miss Holland, I cannot tell you everything, but I have very good reason to believe that drifter is an ubermensch."

Ella didn't budge. "Pffft. I knew that from the first moment he stepped into this room. He told me he ate pigman, and apparently he didn't know that was something only ubermenschen could do."

The Reverend looked astonished for a moment, but soon recovered. "I don't know what ideas he's put into your head, but—"

"He ain't put nothin' into my head. I happen to think he deserves a little decency. And as his friend, I think *I* deserve to know what you're after here."

"I can't tell you. Only that it involves the safety of the entire clan. Friend or not, Miss Holland, you have your own kin and many fellow clansmen to think about."

"How's clan life been treating you?" Elvin asked without any of the pleasant intonations folks usually had when exchanging small talk.

"Fine," Omar answered, now leaning with his back to the wall while the Reverend pored over his effects inside.

Elvin kept Omar in his careful gaze, even if the drifter refused to meet it. "Thinking of making the stay permanent?"

"It's crossed my mind."

Elvin sucked his teeth as he stared at Omar. "We've got us a bit of a situation here," he explained, "aside from whatever the Reverend's upset about. Spring's come. The pigmen are gone. On top of all that, the clansman you're apprenticing under cooked up a handy milit'ry tool. There's folks around a-startin' to wonder why you're still here."

Omar frowned.

"Now," Elvin continued, "You've done us Tuckers a couple of good turns, and it seems like you ain't caused too much trouble neither. But you're still a stranger, and as a watchman, I don't like strangers much, overstandingly not around something so all-fired useful to us. So you've got two options. Option one: you agree to get initiated as a Tucker. There will be a tax you'll have to pay. Come up with a few pigman jaws, and we'll ink you as an honorary clansman. We ain't done that since the Scavenging Years, but we've got the means and willingness to do it, for a price."

"I make an apprentice's wages. Where am I going to come up with a couple jaws worth of money?"

"A clansman can sponsor you, provided you're useful enough."

"What's the second option?"

"Option two? You clear on out and get back to your drifting life. And we'll be checking your saddlebags before you go."

"How long to I have to think on it?"

"I'll give you a week."

The Reverend came out, shaking his head, and both he and the watchman strode off without a word. From across the street, between a couple houses, Bert Daly watched the party break up.

Chapter 17

In Which a Smoldering Ember Flares Up

Two days later, the Brody boys spotted a large party out on the highway while watching over their hogs and raced each other like fire to relay the news. It was the Penskes, Elvin came to discover, and the nomads were delighted to find themselves the first buyers of a hot new invention.

Bill was a powdermaker by trade, not a salesman. Conscience demanded that Bill include as many warnings about safety and proper use as he could, but the demonstration banished all skepticism. The nitrogel needed no pitch or slant. When the armsman put a bullseye through a sheet metal target at two hundred paces, he demanded all of Bill's nitrogel. When he found out Bill only had about forty shots worth of ammunition—the powdermaking chemist had only completed the formula a few weeks ago—he cursed his poor timing and placed an order for the next time the Penskes would come through. Bill ended up selling the lot of it for five jaws—the better part of a month's income.

Other merchants flocked to Bill's home as he read the calculated list of items he'd need to continue making his powder, baking soda and alcohol among them. If it hadn't been decided earlier, it was now. The Griersons no longer had a leg to stand on; nitrogel would be a great boon to the clan and anyone smart enough to jump on the wagon.

Omar sat watching a Penske merchant juggle while waiting for customers. He'd been working long hours for Bill Puckett recently, and this was the first day of rest he'd had in over a week. The sight of the one-eyed Grierson approaching banished the calm scarcely five minutes after he'd sat down.

"Howdy there, drifter. Omar, isn't it? Mind if I sit down?"

Omar didn't protest, so Johnny took it as an invitation and rested next to Omar on the grass. He leaned back against the wall behind him. "We haven't been properly introduced. I'm Johnny Grierson. My family started a neat little settlement up in the hills yonder. Up to about fifty people now. Real nice operation."

Omar didn't shake the extended hand. "I know."

"Word gets around, I guess. If the word's coming from Bill, I can't reckon it's very good."

Omar shrugged.

"You seem like a practical sort of feller. Which means you'll hold off on judging me until after I explain myself. Did I read you right?"

"Go ahead."

Johnny smiled. "Right to the point. So I'll get to my point as directly as I know how. You're a drifter, Omar, so I wouldn't expect you to know a lot about how our clan works, but around here, we have a democracy. But the thing about democracy is that it's never really a democracy. That's not what Sam Chambers would want to say, but it's true. Power's like money: even if everyone has a lot, there are always some with a little bit more than the rest. When my cousins and brothers and sisters started up that settlement years ago, our say didn't count for nothin' around here. The whole thing was crazy talk. The thing is, us Griersons saw farther than the rest of the Tuckers. The first Tuckers didn't settle here because this was a great spot to grow and become a powerful clan; they settled here because they needed shelter and all the buildings they needed were already built. But I took the long view and started from scratch up near the old coal mine. We've got a river what runs near there, and a fair stretch of flat land besides. All crazy talk, but guess which won out in the end?"

"I think I missed where you were heading to so directly."

"My point's that now I run enough of this clan, you'll want to be on my good side," Mr. Grierson said.

"I done aught to get on your bad side?"

"A little birdie told me you mighta stole something from the Reverend."

"The little birdie told you a lie. I ain't stole nothin'."

Johnny leaned in, his voice nearly whispering. "Then how did that little birdie know the truth about the ubermenschen? You know we don't talk about that nonsense around here. He got it from you. I know he did."

Omar didn't answer at first. The Penske merchant across the way had long since given up on the idea of customers and moved on to greener pastures. Omar watched the juggler disappear up the street, leaving him alone with the one-eyed half-breed. "You Tuckers don't care much for the truth, I guess."

"Ain't a soul out there who cares for the truth if it don't serve his purposes. It gets out you spilled the beans, the elders won't care if you bagged a shadower."

"Bill would vouch for me. He's got pull with the elders."

"You willin' to bet your life on it? Bill's a flash in the pan. I've seen his kind before. He ain't likely to get much pull, and he ain't likely to use it to save you if he did. You're throwing your hat into the wrong ring."

Omar examined Johnny the way one examines a maggot found in the porridge. "You'd rather I throw my hat into yours?"

"I'd rather you'd help me deal with Bill."

"Thought you said Bill was a flash in the pan."

"A match don't have to spark long to burn down a forest."

"So what do you want?" Omar said.

"I could use some information."

"What about?"

"How does he make the nitric acid?"

"Why do you want to know?"

Johnny tapped his chest. "You can let me worry about that. All I need from you is what you know."

Omar heaved himself to his feet. "Sorry. Can't help you. I work with the small stuff. Bill never explains any of the tricky stuff to me."

"And you can't find out?"

Omar shrugged. "I got everything I need right now. Ain't keen on biting the hand what feeds me."

"Whatever you're getting from him, I'll do you better."

"No. Whatever you're wanting from me, I don't want no part of. You got yourself a clan spat a-brewin', and I got no reason to be part of it any which way."

"You're in it, drifter, whether you like it or not."

"Yeah, but I ain't sure which way the wind'll blow, and all things bein' even, I'd rather stick with someone who ain't tried to get me twisted around his finger."

Johnny Grierson nodded. "I'll be around to see how that shakes out." He flashed an ugly parting smile before he left.

"Nice to meet you, too," Omar muttered to himself when he was alone.

Ella went to fetch Omar for the dinner prepared to celebrate the end of winter. She knocked on his door, and receiving no answer, called his name. "Omar? Suppertime. Omar?"

No answer. Something clattered in Bill's attached gunpowder shop. "Omar, is that you?" Ella said, turning toward the door leading outside. "Omar, Bill and the rest of us are waitin' to eat. Come on..."

The smell of something burning teased her nose as she laid her hand upon the latch. She stepped back from the door, and then the whole house shook. Thunder crashed on the other side of the door, and though the cinder block walls and the heavy oak door held, a rush of black soot and fine debris raced under and around the door, swirling around Ella's curled-up form on the floor.

She was still on the floor, stunned, when Bill rushed in, followed by her father and stepmother. Bill rushed forward to throw open the door to the shop, but Mr. Holland called out for him to stop. "Check it from outside, Bill! You don't know if it's done or not."

Ella heaved herself to her feet and followed the other adults outside.

"Are you okay, Ella? What happened?" her stepmother asked, taking her by the elbow.

"I-I dunno. I was fetching Omar. Don't know where he went. Thought he was in the shop. I—" She stepped outside the front of the house to see the contents of Bill's shop thrown out into the street in a jumble of blackened wreckage.

The explosion had snuffed out most of its own flame as soon as it had erupted, but it had also gutted Bill's shop. The powdermaker was on his knees amid the rubble, senseless to the bucket brigade that had already formed from the gathering neighbors and onlookers.

He turned toward Ella as she came up next to him. "I'm ruined," he said.

Elvin oversaw the cleanup when the fire was for sure out and most surfaces were cool to the touch. Tucker volunteers picked through what was salvageable, minding Bill's warning that there "might be some nasty stuff spilled somewhere that'll cook your fingers cold".

Bill himself stood off from the wreck, more or less in the same place he'd ended up when he first arrived on the scene. His daughter was there by then, trying to pick up his spirits somewhat, promising that the clan would help him rebuild, that he'd be back at it in no time. Bill, for his part, wasn't having any of it.

"I wasn't even in the shop this time. Wasn't even around. Wasn't distilling nothin'. I never leave a flame unwatched. Must have left a lantern out..." Bill was mostly talking to himself, and he barely came around when Elvin walked up to question him.

"Seems Miss Holland heard a clatter inside when she was fetching the drifter. Ain't no one seen that feller, so ... No, we ain't found his body, so he weren't in the shop when it went up. Best we can figure, there was some fire loose, and that set off your powder store."

Bill nodded. "Must have been the black powder. The nitrogel I store somewhere else."

"Well, that's some good news. How much do you—Ralph, don't go wand'rin' off now, I need you here. How much do you think that nitrogel reserve is worth?"

"Enough to buy me a fresh batch of ingredients. But most of my tools, my glassware, my distillery, and a chunk of my potassium nitrate's ruined."

"How much can we replace from the nomads?"

"Not the nitrates, for sure. I reckon I could salvage some of it, if it's just got ash in it, but what's the point if I'm gonna blow up the shop again."

"Pa?" Ralph McDaniel called out, looking at something on the ground.

"Not now, Ralph. Mr. Puckett, I don't think you understand what will happen if you get this place runnin'—"

"Sir?" Ralph called out again.

"*What*?" Elvin turned his attention to his son, but not without audible irritation in his voice.

"I ... I'm not sure the fire was an accident."

Now Ralph had everyone's attention. He was staring down at the charred remains of a couple sticks. They were mostly blackened, though clearly more burnt at one end than the other. But the odd thing about these two sticks, the thing that had grabbed Ralph's notice in the first place, was that—

"They're from a tree branch."

Elvin looked to Bill's shop. There were no trees in front of or behind the building, and no odd piles of brush nearby. "Bill, did you have some sticks in your shop today?"

"Not that I know. Why would I? What are you thinkin', Ralph?"

Ralph pointed to other similar twigs nearby. "I think these were put into a bundle. And if Bill didn't put it in there, someone else had to. I reckon someone started a fire with this."

The life returned to Bill with a fury. "Son of a bitch."

Elvin turned now to look around him. "Where's that goddamned drifter?"

No one breathed a word.

"I want that drifter found *now!*" the watchman cried as he stormed into Bill's house and kicked open the door to the spare room to find it empty. The drifter had flown the coop.

The posse poured from the western gate on horseback, fanning out in a wide search pattern until one of the Fillmores picked up his trail fifteen minutes later. They dragged him back into town a mere fifteen minutes after that. He hadn't even left the beaten path out of town yet.

Chapter 18

Internal Affairs

Ella made her way down the dim hall of the clan's meetinghouse. The building served just about every purpose the clan could think of, the town jail being the most recently added function. Though daylight outside, they needed lanterns to see in this part of the meetinghouse. A young Tucker sat in a chair next to a locked door, whittling something by the light of a lantern. Upon seeing her approach, the guard nodded to her, lit another lantern, and unlocked the door.

"Visitor," he said to the darkness within, and handed Ella the extra lantern.

She stepped inside while the guard kept watch. "It's okay, Nigel," she said to him. "You can close the door. I'd like to talk to him alone."

"I got my orders, miss. What if he—"

"I hear your worry, and I take it in hand. I'll be okay."

When the door had clicked shut behind her, she spoke to the man bound in the corner. "How you holding up, Omar?"

"I've been better."

"They haven't done anything to you, have they?"

"Aside from hauling me in by the scruff of my neck? Not much. But I'll hang for this, sure as shootin'. I'm surprised they didn't gun me down on the road."

"Mr. Bunton said it would dishonor the clan if you weren't given a fair shake. The elders haven't settled on what that'll look like and likely won't for a couple days. In the meantime, there are some folks lookin' into it. Now," Ella said, rubbing her forehead with two fingers, "is there anything you want to tell me? Just between the two of us?"

"I didn't do it."

"But you taking off without telling anyone—"

"I'm a drifter. Figured most folks would have been glad to see me gone anyhow."

"Well, I wasn't one of them."

"My mistake. Most folks who *matter* would have been glad. I didn't even know why they was galumphin' after me on the road until it were too late. If it *were* me, I woulda been sneakier than I was."

Ella crossed her arms and looked at the floor. "I believe you. But that won't do you any good if all you can tell us is 'I didn't do it'. Why'd you leave, exactly?"

"Stayin' much longer was liable to get dangerous."

"Why?"

"Can't say."

Ella grunted in frustration. "*Why?*"

"Talkin' would be as dangerous as stayin' quiet." Omar sighed before continuing. "But I think I've been framed."

Ella's head snapped to attention. "Good grief, Omar, why didn't you say this earlier?"

"Nobody else would've cared to hear it."

"Do you know who did it? Who would want to frame you?"

Omar's eyes flicked to the door. "Maybe the one-eyed feller who lives out of town."

"Johnny Grierson?"

"He's worried about Bill Puckett's new formula, and he's got it in for me."

"Why's that?"

"'Cause ... 'cause I don't much get along with half-bred humans."

The guard knocked on the door from outside. "You okay in there, Miss Holland?"

"Just wrapping up, Nigel." Ella turned to leave, but not before putting a hand on Omar's shoulder—a more forward notion than she was used to—and trying to offer some sort of hopeful cheer. "Don't you fret none. You got friends here who won't let you down."

His eyes met hers, and the two shared a look that lasted longer than Ella intended and said more than words could utter.

Ralph McDaniel could barely keep his gait down to a lively stride. "Following a downwind scent" was what his pa had said when Ralph had aired the idea of a deeper look, but Ralph had plead his cause well enough that the watchman had warily granted his son the leeway to sniff out whatever he could for the entire afternoon.

So far, Ralph didn't have much to go on, but his first hunch had turned up more clues. Volunteers had gathered all the twigs and scraps they could glean, most all of them blown outside by the explosion. But the thing that tied it all together, so to speak, was the length of charred, broken string woven from hemp. All of it lay in front of him on a table while Ralph scratched his head.

The shop had been empty, and no one recalled marking any strange folks hanging around. But then again, it had been a Sunday afternoon, and most folks were taking their Sunday rest.

Omar taking off without telling anyone made him look guilty, no doubt about that. But the thought of Omar burning the powderman's shop seemed so ... dumb. After living with the Tuckers for four months and grinding their black powder, why would a drifter, even supposing he wanted to cause mischief, use a torch, of all things? Why would he risk blowing Ella or Bill or someone to smithereens?

The torch pointed to a low whim, and neither Ella nor Amos, whom Ralph had interviewed, thought the drifter whimsical. Unless Omar wanted to make it *look* like some hothead did it, knowing his standing among the clan as ... No, if that were so, it would be the stupidest gamble anyone ever took. If any wrongdoings were done in town, the first person tapped for it would be the drifter, and the drifter would have known that.

It was lazily done. Whoever did it figured Omar would take the blame without a further look into it. Which meant that maybe whoever did it wasn't really after Omar at all, as Ella seemed to think. Maybe he should start looking at Mr. Puckett's enemies.

It was time to head up to the Grierson settlement.

Ralph McDaniel let his horse trail a bit behind Amos Taylor's on the way up the road.

"If you really needed the extra clout, you should have brought your dad," Amos said.

"My pa doesn't think it needs any more looking into."

"Then why'd he let you come at all?"

Ralph grimaced. "He doesn't quite know I'm out here. He just said I could poke my nose around a bit, since I noticed the torch. I elected not to press him on the finer bits."

Amos was quiet for a moment. “Okay. How do you want to do this, then?”

“I don’t know. I figured we’d just go up and ask some questions, see what turns up.”

“But if you think the Griersons were behind it, how will you get them to own up to it?”

“I don’t know,” Ralph snapped. “This sort of thing isn’t exactly in my wheelhouse.”

“Your pluck isn’t exactly catching.”

“Just stay limber.” Ralph rolled his shoulders as if trying to follow his own advice. “We’ll take it as it comes.”

A cry in the brush not far to their right broke out. “Ho, there! Who’s that?”

“Amos Taylor and Ralph McDaniel up on clan business,” Amos answered before Ralph had a chance to speak.

Edward Grierson came out of hiding. “It’s always that-a-way, ain’t it? Ain’t no one comes up here for kick-ball or skeetin’. Come on, I’ll walk you in.”

“Patrolling kind of far out from the settlement, aren’t you?”

Edward shrugged. “You know what they say. Gotta keep the unbreds and drifters guessin’.”

“Speaking of drifters, I guess you heard about what happened yesterday,” Amos said.

Edward nodded. “That’s a rough deal. That’s what you get for trusting a drifter, though.”

“You don’t think Bill should have taken Omar in as an apprentice?”

“I surely don’t. But it was the whole clan suckered into it, though. Us Griersons knowed better.”

“It worked out for you folks in the end, though, didn’t it? Your biggest competitor got his business blown up.”

Edward cleared his throat. “It’s a doggone shame what happened. Wouldn’t wish it on my worst enemy.” He shook his head.

Ralph shook his head as if concurring. "I just can't imagine why the drifter would go ahead and do such an ornery thing. We were hoping Johnny might be able to give us an idea, since we know he was talking with the drifter when the Penskes came through the other day."

"I think the drifter's just a low-down feller. Johnny tried to be friendly to him, and he just clammed up, mostly."

Amos took up the thread again. "So Johnny *did* talk to Omar. What were they talkin' about?" he asked.

"Oh, uh, you know, the weather and powdermaking and stuff. Uh, likely a bunch of chitter-chatter. For sure nothin' about what happened yesterday," Edward answered, scratching the back of his neck and looking aside as his cheeks flushed.

Amos nodded and sucked his teeth. "Yeeeah, Omar didn't want to say what they talked about either."

"Wha..." Edward's jaw was agape.

Amos waited in vain for him to say something before turning to Ralph. "Actually, I think we've about got what we came for, wouldn't you say, Ralph?"

Ralph had the presence of mind to agree. "I think you're right, Amos. See you later, Mr. Grierson. Tell Johnny to keep about."

When they'd left Edward safely behind, Amos was the first to break the quiet. "You were right, Ralph. There's some sideways stuff going on here. Johnny had a meeting with Omar he doesn't want folks to know about."

"Still doesn't make Omar look a whole lot more innocent, but things look a mite trickier than before. We'll see what Johnny has to say when I get Pa to question him."

They didn't even have to wait until the next day. Johnny came down that very afternoon. This turned out to be a fair bit earlier than Ralph either expected or wanted. He'd planned to talk about his new lead over dinner and break the news to Elvin easy, so as to make sure his side of the story was the one his pa heard first, and in a neutral setting.

Ralph knew he'd made a poor call when he answered his father's beckon to see a red-faced Johnny Grierson standing on their porch.

"What's this I hear about you going out and wolf-cryin' arson of our clan elders?" Elvin asked, his stare hard, one knee resting on their porch railing.

Ralph didn't answer. He was too busy turning a lighter shade of white.

"You got any reason—*any* reason—to go traipsing off to the Grierson settlement without asking my say-so?"

Ralph looked down. His freckles stood out on his cheeks like splatters of ink on parchment.

"When I said you could look into things, this wasn't what I had in mind." Elvin turned to Mr. Grierson. "Many sorries, Johnny. I'll get this straightened out."

Johnny gave Ralph one last look before he left to go harangue Amos' pa. When he'd left, the storm he'd brought with him remained. Ralph didn't look up.

"Boy, go fetch my belt. Git."

"Hey, Omar," Ella said, closing the door behind her, this time carrying a hot sweet roll. "Still keepin' your chin up?"

"Well, they agreed to tie me to this post frontways instead of hands behind my back, so I'd say I'm coming out ahead."

"That's good news. I would've had to feed you this treat by hand otherwise, and that would've made things a mite awkward."

"What's got you in a good mood? Was it Grierson?"

Ella gave Omar the sweet roll. "He likely didn't do it, if that's what you mean. Nobody saw him or any of his kin in town the day it happened. But he knows something. He said he never spoke to you, let alone what you two actually spoke about."

Omar looked at the floor. "He wanted some of Bill's chemistry secrets from me."

"Were you gonna give it to him?"

"Did it look like I was a-headed his direction when I jumped the fence?"

"So you left because, what, you figured he'd beat the snot outta you or something if you didn't cooperate?"

Omar shrugged. "Yeah."

Ella shook her head. "Omar, I don't think you got a lick of sense. You act like everyone in this clan is out to get you."

"'Cause they is."

"Oh, hogwash. You've got the watchman's own son tryin' to clear your name even now. You coulda asked for help then, same as now. You wouldn't have had to mess with Johnny Grierson at all."

"I can take care of my own problems."

"Yeah, I can see that," Ella said, looking at his bindings. "You'd rather go into exile than be beholden to me?"

"It's not—It's not that simple."

"Then tell me."

Omar looked at the ceiling now. "I was being blackmailed."

Ella took a minute to soak in the new information. "Okay. What about?"

"Grierson seemed to think I'd stolen somethin' from the Reverend."

"Is that what the ruckus the other day was about when the watchman and the Reverend came over?"

“I guess. Still don’t know what it is I’m supposed to have stole.” Omar took a bite of the sweet roll.

“Maybe,” Ella said, gauging him, “but I get the feelin’ you ain’t tellin’ me everything.”

“I’m not,” Omar admitted.

“Care to bring me up to your level?”

“I likely already told you too much, and I can’t see how it has anything to do with Bill’s shop.”

Ella sighed. “Then I guess I’m gonna have to do this the hard way.” She got up to leave.

“What’s that?”

“Blackmail the guy who was blackmailing you.”

It was one of the Coles who spotted the young woman riding up through the piles of mine tailings. A young woman, alone, a good number of miles beyond the safety of the town walls, and likely the furthest she’d ever ventured from home, with or without an escort. Her coming turned some heads in the Grierson settlement, and Johnny’s hackles were already raised.

“I don’t got time to bandy words with a young girl. Tell me why you’re here and make it quick.”

Ella squared her shoulders and attempted to look Johnny in the eye. “The drifter told me what you were meeting about.”

Johnny’s face grew red. “You better watch yourself real careful, girl—”

“And I know he didn’t start the fire—” Ella’s voice was already trembling.

“Now you mark me: I did nothing against clan law, y’hear? Nothing.”

“Please, sir. You have to know how bad this looks for you if—”

"Who the hell do you think you are?"

Ella's lip trembled now. "I-I know you know something about it—"

"I said *who the hell do you think you are?"* Johnny took a dangerous step toward Ella.

"And I just want to save Omar from the noose!" she sobbed.

Johnny stopped as she cowered. Others in the settlement were looking. Johnny turned aside and spat.

"I don't think you did it, sir," Ella said, her voice still quavering. "But you know something, I know you do, and to just stand by while a clansman suffers for it and an innocent man takes the blame ... that just makes you as bad as the one who did it, you know it does. And I know what you'd stand to lose by fessing up, but you know if I figured out this much, someone else will—"

"That's enough," Johnny growled, finding his bluster again. "I'm sick and tired of ignorant young folks coming up to point fingers at me. I ain't fessin' up to nothin', 'cause I ain't *done* nothin'. You want to get to the bottom of this, you go talk to that Bert Daly character. He's the only reason—and I mean the *only* reason—for any of this nonsense, you understand?"

"So you'll help me?"

"Get on your ass and get out of here. Now," Johnny said, pointing to her mule.

She ran off to saddle up again, wiping tears from her face.

"And if anyone asks, you never spoke to me, and I never said nothin' to that drifter, you hear?" he called out after her.

Johnny's cousin sidled up next to him as she left. "What was that all about?"

"It's all coming apart, Ed. If we don't step light, that Daly kid could sink us."

"They could end your eldership and replace you with Bill if it gets out what you was tryin' with the drifter."

“That was gonna happen anyhow. And mind you this, I’m still gonna get something out of this that favors us. The trick is,” Johnny said, gritting his teeth, “how to dodge banishment while doing it.”

Ella rounded a corner in a bad part of town to see a rundown little house on the edge of a muddy cul-de-sac. She ambled on up, casting sideways glances as she did. It stank. Out behind the house, she could see a large collection of mostly useless garbage stockpiled high.

It took Ella a bit to work up the nerve. But it needed to be done. She knocked on the door. No one answered, but she heard movement inside. Her heart quickened.

She was about to knock again when the door opened just a crack. Just enough for her to see an eye staring back out at her.

“Go away,” a woman’s voice said.

“I’m ... I’m sorry Miss ... Daly?” Ella said when she got a good look at the woman’s face behind the door.

“What do you want?” Mrs. Daly asked.

Ella blinked. “Um, could I ... I want to talk to your husband.”

“He ain’t in. Sorry.” The door slammed closed in Ella’s face.

“Could you tell me where to find him, then? It’s important!” Ella called without receiving an answer.

A small child wailed somewhere inside. Melissa Daly’s frazzled head poked out once again. “Look, you seem like a nice girl. I don’t know what put the notion into your head to come out here, but you’d best take the notion out.” Melissa closed the door in Ella’s face without a further word spoken.

A thought occurred to her. "It's about something stolen from the Reverend! They're going to send the watchman after it, and Bert might know who has it!"

She waited a few minutes before giving up.

In the dark of night, a hand fumbled at the window from outside. A sliver of metal wedged itself between window and sill, and then it whooshed up. A shadowy figure crawled into the room. The drifter's confiscated things lay in a pile on the cot.

Before the figure could get all the way across the room, a hand tore away the shroud covering a lantern, catching Bert Daly with a small white chip clutched between his thumb and forefinger.

"So *that's* what went missing," Ella said.

Bert swallowed, his eyes darting between Ella and the comely Tucker maiden holding the lantern next to her. Becky Brody.

"Ella figured if this was a frame job, and if they ain't already found what they wanted when they tossed Omar's stuff earlier, that meant you never got around to planting your last little seed there," Becky said.

Bert smiled. "Now why would I go ahead and want to do a thing like that?"

"I don't figure it matters too much, since two witnesses just caught you red-handed. But how did you guess, Ella?" Becky said.

Ella took a breath. "I know you put the finger on Omar during the siege for stealin' food, so I knew you had it in you to twist things your way. When Omar got himself into the clan's good graces, you were likely a-fear'd Omar would come after you some way or another. You needed to take care of him before he took care of you, and that meant getting him out of the clan's good graces as best you knew how. You'd been an apprentice for Bill some years ago, so you knew his shop, and when Bill got his breakthrough, you had a way to get back at Bill for firin' you, as well as takin' Omar out of the picture. That's what I'll tell the watchman, anyway, and he'll have good cause to believe me."

"I didn't set no fire. Ain't got anything to do with any of this." Bert pointed at the white talisman.

"Yeah, still not quite sure how this fits into the picture, except that there's something Omar don't feel like he can safely talk about. I reckon this has something to do with it, and you want folks to think Omar blabbed about something he shouldn't have, and this here is the proof that he did."

"It *is* the proof," Bert said. "He blabbed to *me*. He's the one that stole this and gave it to me. I didn't want to be caught with it, so I was putting it back where I got it from."

"Oh, goose-feathers-on-a-bullhusker!" Becky shouted. "You expect us to believe—"

"What did he blab to you about?" Ella broke in.

"Wouldn't you like to know?" Bert grinned as if he had the upper hand. "Everything you know about the ubermenschen, about the old world, is a lie. A lie to keep folks like you on top and half-breeds like me on bottom."

"What's the lie about?" Ella asked.

"The great things that the ubermenschen were supposed to be able to do, most of them couldn't do it," Bert said. "It was locked up inside them, and most of 'em didn't even realize it. They didn't realize an ubermensch is as an ubermensch does. It weren't enough for the ubermenschen to be born better than you folks; they had to *transform*, like a butterfly breaking out of its coffin."

"Why would the Reverend care to lie about that?" Becky asked.

"'Cause he's afraid of us half-breeds. He's afraid of what we could become. What do you think ended the world? A butterfly has to break its house to spread its wings."

Ella's brow furrowed. "So you burned down Bill's shop to 'spread your wings?'"

"I didn't burn down the shop. But if I did, it would only be the beginning. You folks are termites. Gotta make sure everyone's a drone so you can build your little houses and keep everything nice and orderly. But half-breeds like us ain't made to crawl like you want us to. We're made to fly. And it's about time you termites quit holdin' us back." Bert squared his shoulders.

If Bert meant to intimidate the two girls, Becky wasn't impressed. "I'm done listening to this. Let's go fetch the watchman and tell him what we saw."

Bert scoffed. "What are you going to tell him? You saw me with a little white rock? I ain't done nothin' wrong, and there's no way to prove I did!"

Ella and Becky left him there.

"It was the drifter's fault, you hear?" he called after them. "He forced me into it. I ain't done nothing I weren't forced to do to survive. Y'all act like your shit smells so sweet, but y'all are the ones who put me here! You cockroaches! You termites! You dig your tunnels and then blame me for seein' daylight!"

Only silence answered him.

In the church part of the clan meetinghouse, Reverend Brody opened the door to Bert Daly.

"Welcome," the Reverend said, smiling. "You asked for counsel?"

Bert looked like he hadn't slept all night. "Not exactly. But I'm in need of a favor."

The Reverend's smile faded. "Favor?"

"A couple girls are making a charge against me. I need a few elders to see things from my point of view." Bert looked at the floor.

"As long as it's the point of view of the truth, you have nothing to worry about."

"The truth is what you make it. And I'd like you to make it mine."

Reverend Brody curled his lip at Bert's insinuation. "This smells of skullduggery."

"You can't afford not to help me, Reverend."

"Why?"

"Now that little Earnest is going to turn three soon, I've noticed he has your eyes." Bert returned the Reverend's stare with his own.

The Reverend went white. "Come in," he said after a lengthy silence.

Chapter 19

Loose Ends

The meeting had lasted hours, and the elders weren't getting anywhere. Sam had argued for acquitting the drifter, but Elvin and the Reverend had opposed him at almost every turn. Most of the elders settled into their slots based on their own fragmented ideas of the case they'd brought in with them, and few of them changed their mind.

"Every time we gave the drifter a chance, it's done us good," Shane Bunton said. "Now, I know that isn't an easy thing to say, much less easy to do, and Lord knows I wasn't too keen on the idea myself. But I tell you what, we'd still be fighting those pigmen if it weren't for that drifter. We can't afford to lose a fighter like that who's clearly willing to fight for us."

"I don't care how good a fighter that drifter is," Elvin said, drumming the school desk he sat at with a fist. "He's causing a heap of consternation, and since it's my job to keep the peace, I say he's got to go. For the good of the clan."

"Well, my, my, my," Sam roared. "Did I just hear the watchman imply there's more to a clan than its fighting capabilities? I thought you didn't care for that mystic mumbo-jumbo like 'the good of the clan'."

It did nothing to calm the debate, but dear heavens, it felt good to say that to the watchman.

By the time the elders were ready to give their decision, most of the clansfolk who'd showed any kind of interest in the hearing had left. Ella, who had dozed for a minute or two, shot up when the door opened and the clansmen emerged. None of the elders looked happy. Ella wasn't sure if that was a good sign or a bad one.

"Hooookay," Sam said, exhausted. "After much deliberation, we've made our decision. On the first question: Was the drifter Omar Walking responsible for intentionally destroying Bill Puckett's powder shop?" Sam paused for what Ella thought was supposed to be a dramatic effect. "The elders believe there is not enough evidence to convict him of a capital offense, and Mr. Walking's testimony is credible enough to save him from the noose."

Ella saw Omar exhale a bit. Perhaps she sighed a bit herself.

"As to the identity of the alleged arsonist, the elders have decided, upon further review of the available evidence, that there is not cause enough to assume intentional sabotage."

"What?!" Amos cried, standing up.

Sam shot Amos a severe look. "Based on the evidence on hand, we consider the matter closed, and any further *independent* dredging about will be seen as sowing unnecessary discord among our clansmen and will be met with the appropriate consequences." Sam caught his breath before he continued. "We consider the fire an unfortunate accident, and the clan stays committed to rebuilding Mr. Puckett's shop and making his business profitable again."

Bill nodded his head. Ella stirred, about to get up, but saw that all the other elders remained where they were. None of them looked happy.

"Now," Sam Chambers said with a sigh, "the question remains as to what kind of accident the fire was. Some accidents are unforeseeable. Others, preventable. The elders have decided that this accident was of the second sort, and that someone must be held responsible for their carelessness. The elders have returned to the soul in question, Omar Walking, to determine his guilt or innocence with regard to gross carelessness."

Ella's breath caught again, just as she'd started to breathe normally.

"Because the decision was not unanimous, the elders will show their votes on the matter. Those who did not find Mr. Walking guilty of gross carelessness?"

Job Brody, Arnold Brody, Shane Bunton, and a few others raised their hands. No one else moved among the elders.

"Those who found him guilty?"

A number of hands shot up, Johnny Grierson and the Reverend Brody's among them. Enough that Ella started counting votes.

"As it stands, with a couple abstentions, the elders found a tie. I was the deciding vote." Sam Chambers raised his hand. "Guilty."

Amos Taylor shot up again. "This meeting is a damned joke! A *damned* joke, I say!"

Elvin jumped up to meet the dissident, red-faced. "Get him out of here!"

One of the elders came up to escort Amos out of the room, but Amos was already gone, shaking off the dust off his clothes at them as he went.

The peace restored, all eyes returned to Sam Chambers. "Having been found guilty of gross carelessness, Mr. Walking has been sentenced to banishment. The terms of the banishment are as follows." Mr. Chambers cleared his throat. "Mr. Walking is to take nothing more than what he first arrived with, excepting one day's provisions, thirty rounds of ammunition, and one travel pack. He is not ever permitted to return to Tucker clan territory, on pain of death, excepting the full compensation for Bill Puckett's losses in the fire, amounting to"—Mr. Chambers swallowed—"one hundred pigman jaws."

One. Hundred. Jaws. Ella sat in stunned silence, as did the other few clansmen sitting in to hear the ruling.

Amos paced the floor as Omar rubbed his wrists.

"It's not fair," Amos said. "They're protecting Bert Daly."

"Drop it," Omar answered. "If they know he did it and he gets away with it, it's because there's more scandal wrapped up there than the elders are willing to grapple with. I'm lucky I got off so easy."

"Banishment isn't an easy thing. Most folks would call it a death sentence with an unknown date."

"*Life* is a death sentence with an unknown date. I'm a drifter. I'll manage."

Amos reached the end of the hallway ahead of Omar and opened the door for him. "I can't stand the idea of someone getting away with something like this. It isn't right."

"Way of the world. But," Omar said, stepping out into the daylight for the first time in two days, "I do welcome your regard. You're a good man, Amos. This clan don't deserve you."

At Bill Puckett's house, Omar's effects were laid out on the kitchen table for the watchman to go through. Anything out of order, and Omar would start his banishment crippled in one leg. When Elvin had accounted for everything, he watched as Omar packed.

"No rifle?" Elvin asked, leaning against the kitchen doorpost.

Omar lashed a water-filled plastic jug to his travel pack. “Lost mine fleeing the unbreds. Always preferred the bow anyhow. Easier to keep up.”

“I’ll allow for a full quiver of arrows instead of the powder charges, then.”

“I could trade the powder more readily out there.”

“One or the other. I won’t ’low for both.”

“The powder, then.”

“No nitrogel, you hear? Just the regular stuff.”

“I hear.”

Elvin turned to leave. “I’ll see you outside in fifteen minutes.”

Ella walked in as the watchman left. “Hey,” she said, looking at the floor.

“Hey.”

“Came to say goodbye.” Ella kept her head down.

“Goodbye, then.” Omar kept his head down in turn.

“Yeah.”

Neither of them moved.

“What is it?” Omar asked.

Ella fiddled with her apron. “Nothin’.”

“You seem hurt.”

“Didn’t figure it would end like this.”

“Ended a lot better than I expected, with this lot and all.”

“Try not to think too badly of us Tuckers. All any of us want is peace for our families. I know that’s not an excuse but ... they’re still God’s children, same as everyone. There’s goodness here, if you know where to look.”

“I don’t think there’s much goodness anywhere. But you’re giving the notion a run for its money.”

Ella sniffed.

“Hey. Who knows? One hundred jaws ain’t impossible. Give it four years or so, I might wind up around here again. It’ll give me a chance to make things up to you, seein' how you bailed me out of this scrape here."

"No," Ella said. "Don't waste your make-ups on me. But I'd think it a real favor if you'd make it up to someone else."

"Who?"

"Anyone. Overstandingly if it's someone who don't deserve it."

Omar smiled his sideways grin. "Huh. They broke the mold with you, sure thing. I'll do my best. You stay out of trouble, now."

"You too, Omar."

Omar paused with the strap of his new travel pack slung over one shoulder. Thinking, Ella reckoned.

"What is it?" Ella asked.

"Well, since I'm leavin' anyhow, figured you ought to know. You've got some pretty eyes. Don't know if folks around here ever told you that."

Omar shouldered his way outside.

Amos Taylor stood next to the watchman at the western gate. "So long, Omar," Amos said, shaking his hand.

"So long."

"Listen, some of us weren't feeling too fine about how things turned out. Bill was sayin' you was pretty good help over the winter, and it's plain you pulled your own weight during the siege, and what with the shadower, and you saving me and Dale and all—well, some of us folks figured you'd probably get tired of going everywhere on foot, so we got together and chipped in and, well, here's your new horse."

Shane Bunton stepped forward, leading a sturdy mountain-bred horse over to Omar.

"Us Tuckers may be rough on the edges sometimes, but we don't forget a good turn," Amos said.

Omar looked from the horse to Elvin. "Is this going to get me shot as a horse thief?"

Elvin looked from the horse to Omar. "Horse? What horse? There ain't no horse here," the watchman said, deadpan.

Omar nodded and saddled up. "Thanks."

"So long, you young good-for-nothing apprentice," Bill said with a sigh. "Sorry about things."

"So long, you old slave driver," Omar shot back. "Sorry about your shop."

Ralph watched the drifter disappear into the woods through one of the palisade arrow-slits. Against the background of green buds stippling the forest canopy, purple streaks of redbud and wisteria blooms burst forth in a springtime blaze of glory, while white sparks of wild cherry flashed from low-hanging branches.

"Why'd you do it, Mr. Chambers?" Ralph asked when the drifter was gone. "You were the deciding vote. You could have cleared him."

"He was causing division in the clan," Sam Chambers said with a sigh. "He was festering here."

"But he didn't do nothin'—"

"I know he didn't. It wasn't his fault. But he was causing division, all the same. Two camps, drawn up in scarcely a day, and before long you wouldn't have been able to tell what the elders were arguing about in the first place. Little cracks and fissures that had always existed, that drifter trickled down into them and forced them wide open. We were deadlocked, and the only thing more stubborn than a mule is a clan elder whose hasty opinion is on the line.

"A good leader can heal the wounds in a community, Ralph. I could have dug in my heels, demanded justice and truth carry the day, and we would have been left with a drifter still amongst a bunch of hostile neighbors, only this time with Tuckers taking swings at other Tuckers on top of it all. Compromise sounds like a beautiful thing in the history books, but in practice it looks a lot like Mr. Brody's butcher shop.

"I struck a deal. We wouldn't execute the drifter, we'd let bygones be bygones among the clansmen, and now some of the hawkish elders see me as a man who can see their point of view. Which means in the future, we can maybe get past some of the egos keeping us from solving any of the clan's problems. That drifter might have done our clan the biggest service yet just by way of being banished.

"And part of the deal I made specifically with your father. You'll be coming to special tutoring sessions with me, two afternoons a week, from here on out."

Ralph couldn't exactly say he was happy with the price paid, but he couldn't argue with the reward bought. Two afternoons every week, free of the belt.

Melissa Daly answered the knock on the door the next day. Elvin McDaniel stood there, unsmiling, his son a few paces behind, also unsmiling.

"Whatchu want?" she asked from behind the half-closed door, sweeping little Earnest aside behind her.

"Where's Bert?"

"He's out."

"Huh. Everywhere I've asked, folks been sayin' he's in."

"I don't know where he is."

"I'm not busy. I'll wait for him. Mind if we come in?" Elvin asked as he shouldered the door open and tromped through the front hallway into the kitchen, heavy feet threatening to break through the thin layer of worn carpet and rotten floorboards. Ralph followed in, murmuring an apology as he passed Melissa and her toddling son.

Melissa brought up the rear without a word. She found Elvin already sitting in Bert's chair, leaning it back against the wall, his feet up on the kitchen table. Elvin was a wiry fellow, but he seemed to take up the entire kitchen like a seething bull.

"Can I get you somethin'?" she asked, still blinking.

"We're fine."

"What's this about?" Melissa's hands fidgeted behind her back, then in front of her before tucking themselves under her apron.

Elvin let her simmer under his gaze. "Nothin' important. Just needed to clear something up."

They waited, Elvin staring directly at Melissa, and Melissa deliberately keeping her own gaze everywhere else. Little Earnest started fussing. Melissa picked him up but didn't dare move. Earnest's cries grew in pitch and volume.

"You know what?" Melissa said, trying to keep Earnest from wriggling out of her arms. "I think he might be takin' a rest. Let me see if I can go fetch him."

"Good."

Melissa retreated into the back room behind Elvin. The watchman and his son heard some muffled shuffling, a hissing whisper, and a stumbling thud. Elvin was already out of his chair, following Mrs. Daly into her bedroom. Earnest was still crying, but he was sitting on his parents' raggedy mattress on the floor, his mother and father locked in some sort of struggle in front of an open closet.

"Mister?" Elvin asked, the tone of his voice communicating none of the politeness his words implied. "How about we step outside for a minute?"

Bert snapped a look at his wife, his nostrils flared and his hair wild. He jumped at her a little, just enough to make her flinch and Elvin say, "Now."

Elvin marched Bert out the front door, past a bewildered Ralph still stutter-stepping around the kitchen table.

Once outside, Bert turned with a sigh. "Okay, watchman. What's this—"

Elvin's fist caught his jaw right in the middle of his turn. Bert stumbled to the side at the blow, his arms shooting up to cover his head. Elvin kicked him in the back of the knees to drop the half-bred bastard into a crouch, then grabbed Bert's shirt and pulled it up over his head to expose his back. The watchman whipped out a switch he'd tucked into his pants, the fresh green kind with the supple tip, yet thick enough to keep its shape with vigorous use. Without a word, Elvin laid into Bert's hide with practiced, furious strokes.

Ralph, who'd finally mustered the gumption to come outside when he heard the commotion, winced at the sight of pink stripes blooming under Elvin's switch. Bert writhed as Elvin beat the living daylights out of him, with special attention given to Bert's hands whenever they went out to protect his sorry behind. Elvin knew how to get a grown man wailing in a jiffy.

The pink stripes turned bright red. Elvin showed no sign of slowing down, but neither Ralph nor Melissa Daly dared stop him.

Elvin stopped when the thin bark on his switch had frayed from the flailing. He tossed the bloody switch to the side and muttered, "All right, now get up," between pants.

Bert struggled to his feet, still bent over double, his shirt still mostly up over his head. When his arms came down enough for Elvin to get in another shot, Elvin clocked him one more time in the face, sending him back to the ground. Elvin gave Bert a stiff kick in the ribs for good measure.

"Now we don't got enough proof to kill you, but I don't give a damn. You try to make fools out of us again, so help me God, I will blast your nutsack off with a shotgun."

Elvin left Bert whimpering in the dirt. He spat over his shoulder as he went. "By the way, your turn for patrol is up. Be ready bright and early tomorrow."

Old Man Brody answered the door and beheld young Miss Holland, the great-granddaughter of a tough-minded colonist and friend of his back from the Scavenging Years.

"Hello, Mr. Brody. I brought over some bread and cheese, if that's agreeable to you," she said, holding out the proffered edibles.

"What do you want?"

"I had to know what Bert Daly said."

"What did he say?"

"That you lied to us about the olden times. The Reverend won't say anything about that white chip. But I know that's why they kicked Omar out. He's an ubermensch, and they're afraid of what he could do. Is it true? That they can ... change?"

"Miss," the old man said with a sigh, "we kicked that drifter out for a reason. You'll just have to believe me that it was a good one."

Ella put her hand on the door to stop it from closing. "A good reason for harming the innocent is a bad reason."

"There's no one innocent, miss. Not even one."

"So it is true, then? That you lied about the half-breeds?"

Old Man Brody took a long time to answer. "Have you been lied to? Yes. But the Reverend didn't lie when he said the ubermenschen waged an unholy war against the natural-bred humans. The ubermenschen got what they deserved," the old man growled. "The founders lied because we cared about you, about our children and grandchildren and descendants we knew we'd never meet. Because not all truth is good for surviving and thriving. You don't have to like it. But before you decide to herald the truth as you know it, I want you to count your blessings. You live in a house. You have friends and family, and plenty will live a good many years yet. You've likely never had to kill anyone. You've never watched a loved one die of starvation, or eaten that loved one to keep yourself from the same fate. And I'll bet you've never been raped, not even once. All of this, you owe to a lie."

When the Holland girl was finally gone, Old Man Brody turned away from the door, his shoulders sagging. The palsy had already started at his fingertips, and by the time he'd settled into his chair, his arms and legs had joined in the fun. The seizure would not be far off.

Doggone those ungrateful kids, stirring up all that black mold in the brain. His head jerked, and his eyes rolled back into his head.

Ella made her way through the tangled brush in the old town. In one hand, she held a note scribbled on valuable parchment:

Found this in my pack. Figured one of the elders thought I was an easy way to get rid of it. Do what you want with it when I'm gone. Don't know what it is, but you're the only one I'd trust to find out.

In her other hand, she held the talisman. It was chirping with a steady frequency now, which meant Sam Chambers had been right. It was homing in on something, just like a bloodhound sniffing out the trail of some prey. She'd asked him what had been stolen, and, not knowing she had it, and being the helpful teacher he always was, he had told her.

She nearly stubbed her toe on a gravestone before she noticed the great heap of freshly excavated earth. She walked to the edge of a hole to behold a mass grave filled with bones. Mixed in with the various human bones and skulls, she saw the distinct shape of unhuman, unbred creatures. The generals of the unbreds. Underneath the sign of the twisted ladder, she beheld the unmistakable remains of a host of shadowers, enough to call and control every unbred creature for many miles around. If these were the butterflies, she thought, better to be a termite.

Chapter 20

The Bullhusker

The clan came to life in the wake of Omar's banishment as trees blossomed and the spreading warmth called forth the wildlife again. Song sparrows tweeted from the brush. Hunters took down most of the pigman snares and replaced them with smaller game snares for squirrels and rabbits. The Tucker greenhouse a block away from the clan main went down, the plexiglass windowpanes stored away until fall came again. Young lovers snuck off to whatever isolated glens they could find, and vigilant clansmen went out after them with willow switches.

The Brodys, the Craines, and the Newells had to put their corn in the ground, and when the weather was fair, many of the town Tuckers went out to the fields, either to help with the planting or watch over the workers as they sowed. One field safely done, a hundred-odd folks moved on to the next, toiling from sunrise to after sunset until the fieldwork was done. When June came and the wheat was ready, the Tuckers would turn out again. It was a chore, to be sure, and it kept the tradesmen from their shops at a time when they could ill afford it, but on the other hand, it kept the tradesmen from their shops at a time when they dearly wished it. Either way, it had to be done. The farmers couldn't manage the planting and harvest times on their own with the threat of unbreds or raiders overlooking every outlying field.

On Planter's Eve, a host of clansmen traipsed out to the Newells with fancy foodstuffs bought from the nomads. A week previously, Sam Chambers had set his brood to working shifts on the bicycle-powered compressor on an ancient refrigeration unit he'd fixed up long ago. It was a bothersome chore, but when Planter's Eve came, Sam had enough ice cream made for the whole clan to have a helping. Sophie, Becky, and Ella brought their own handiwork, much to the chagrin of the other Tuckers who were loath to forget what had happened last year. The three young Tucker women couldn't account for the weight of the scandal, because—and they took particular care to point this out—no one had died.

But, this Planter's Eve feast having gone off with much less puking, and the corn having been planted without overstanding trouble, Phil Holland and Bill Puckett found themselves back in their own shops, swamped with work and armed with spring fever. With money raised by the clan, Bill paid the nomads for whatever building materials he could get and promptly had Victor and his brother and Phil Holland's nephew come and help him make a proper new chemical shed, complete with shaded recesses for lanterns and a number of removable ceiling panels to help with ventilation. He made it big enough to fit any stretching his business might see down the road.

Phil Holland dusted off his treadle-powered metal lathe to cut some new rifle barrels. The lathe was a dear piece of workcraft. The electric motor had been stripped off long ago, backfitted with a bicycle flywheel and belts made of leather. Amos watched and learned, starting with the gauges and micrometers. Two things every craftsman needed, Phil said: a steady hand, and a high regard for fine-cut benchmarks. With some help and no more than a couple failed tries, Amos had cut his own perfectly centered barrel by the end of the month.

And Ella went back to the life she knew before, wordlessly attending to both her father's and her stepmother's beck and call and helping Bill Puckett when she could, inwardly wincing whenever Amos addressed her as "Miss Holland". She stayed out of sight of whatever young man was applying to become Bill's apprentice, of whom four came by in as many days. Bill hadn't come to any firm understandings yet, but the only ones who weren't "head-addled slackards" were Ricky Brody, Job Brody's boy, and Nigel Bunton, the carpenter's oldest.

It was a rainy day in April when one of the young Hadley men came rocketing into the clan main, kicking up a storm of mud behind his exhausted horse. His alarm whistle brought Elvin running, rainwater pouring off his hooded cloak and muddy clods flying off his boots.

"Bullhusker! Bullhusker out on our south forty! It got my cousin! It got Alice!" he cried, a hand over his pale face. The alarm bell crashed. Arnold Brody emerged from his slaughterhouse, his apron still stained in blood, and ran to get the Hadley clansman a fresh mount. The two Bunton brothers and their sons were suited up in a flash, as were the Taylors and one of the Garmens. Deek Evans came up, as sure a glory hound as ever there was.

"It's probably tuckin' into some of the cattle by now," Arnold said as he checked the flint on his rifle.

The watchman saddled up. "If he came straight away from the south forty, the homestead wasn't warned."

"Mighta heard the town bell," the butcher said.

"Not in this weather."

Two more Tuckers rode up, armed and ready to answer the bullhusker call. The horses stamped in the rain, whickering and champing at their bits, fogging the air with their bated breath. Elvin counted heads. Eight. Not a bad posse.

"Who else is up for folkward duty?" Arnold Brody asked.

"Phil Holland and Amos Taylor is," Elvin said, squinting into the rain. "Where they at?"

"Might've forgot. Let's drop by Bill's and pick us up some of that nitrogel while we're at it. I want to see what this stuff can do."

Elvin nodded and turned to his right. "Shane, we need a tracker. Head on over to the Fillmores and meet us at the western gate after we pick up Bill. We leave in three minutes, by meetin'-house time."

The three minutes came and went, and with Amos, Phil Holland, and Victor and Richard Fillmore now joining them, the Tucker hunting party shot out from the gate and headed west, bearing watertight nitrogel cartridge bandoleers. The young Hadley man led the posse to the field about a mile and a half distant, horses galloping the whole way.

Even in a gallop, the clan's tracker couldn't miss the bullhusker's rut scarring the earth as they neared the field. The party slowed their horses to a walk and scanned the perimeter. The misty pitter-patter of a gray rain shrouded the distant trees and the tops of the hills.

"Bullhusker went through here. Could come back out this a-way," the elder Fillmore remarked as he examined the massive footprints of the quadrupedal monster.

"You smell that?" Elvin said, raising a hand to halt the party.

"Too much rain. It's your imagination," Phil Holland said.

"Everyone dismount. We're heading to the tree line over yonder," Elvin ordered.

Everyone but the Hadley guide got off their horses. "We were lighting out of there full tilt," he murmured, his eyes staring, gripping the reins in white-knuckled fists. "That thing caught up with Alice and took her down, horse and all. Didn't know they could run that fast."

Elvin left him there on his horse rather than try to coax him out of it. They had enough rifles without throwing a shell-shocked clansman back into the fray. The Tuckers filtered into the tree line, ducking to keep their low profiles, eyes and ears sharp for any movement or sound. About a hundred yards into the open field, a huge smear of blood marred a trampled patch of pasture. Neither human nor horse victim were visible. Not any identifiable pieces, at least.

"There it is," Shane Bunton whispered softly, pointing out to the east. The movement of a large mass disappeared behind the gentle slope of the terrain.

"Move in. Set up a stand-off line and keep your range. Plant your spears if it charges."

The Tuckers backed out of the tree line and crept swiftly along through the neighboring field, picking through the sparse and scattered trees, looking for a clean shot. Their boots stuck and squelched in the soggy earth. Perhaps it was the stormy weather or the scent of a fresh kill, but the air sparked with an electricity the hunters could smell. Amos tried to calm his nerves and felt them draw to a steely point. The tips of his fingers, nose, and ears tingled. As he approached closer with the rest of the fanning roundswalk, he could see the bullhusker steadily eating and tearing to shreds the carcass of what must have been Alice's horse. The pinpricks of rain haloed the gory swatch of mud and guts. So it was true what they said about bullhuskers: they could dissect a cow and empty out the innards in about eight minutes. They had to move quickly to catch the creature—Elvin said it was smart enough to know there'd be more humans coming soon, and since it had been a good fifteen minutes since the attack, it was already starting to make movements to leave.

Amos found a position and planned his shot. Phil Holland had had the foresight to bring a tarp, which they stretched over their guns like a blanket. Rainwater ran off the tarp in thin rivulets, pooled in their eyebrows, and soaked their knees where they knelt bringing out the powder charges, careful not to get them wet.

Both Tuckers loaded their guns as the bullhusker finished its meal and began to head out, trotting toward the southeast, making for the dense woods in the hollow. Amos powdered his pan while Phil held the tarp in place. The hulking creature stopped midstride about two hundred yards off and froze. Its gargantuan, knotty, bald head rose in alarm. A scattering of Tucker hammers clicked back to full-cocked. Amos could hear Elvin swear not too far away.

"Get it, get it, get it!" Elvin said as he fired.

A thunderous chorus crashed over the pasture. The bullhusker's bellows rose up over the echo of gunfire as it jerked about, limping and heaving. It charged off for the cover of the trees and did not stop when it had broken through.

The Tuckers packed in their gear and ran for their horses.

"We wounded it pretty good, I think," Phil guessed as he thrust his rifle into its sheath on the saddle.

"Everyone reload," Elvin ordered.

"But the rain—"

"We ain't going into those woods after that bullhusker without some powder and shot in our guns. Period."

No one answered. Elvin was right. They loaded their weapons under their cloaks and tarps and wrapped the firing mechanisms in plastic or leather. Even so, these precautions would not stop some of the guns from misfiring if the need for shooting quickly arose. The Tuckers spurred their horses over to the point where the bullhusker broke into the forest.

"It's bleeding," Amos observed.

They followed the wounded bullhusker down into the lowest part of the vale, then up a stream where the bullhusker tried to lose the riders it knew were following it. The rain worsened to a downright gully-washer, soaking the Tuckers to the bone.

"I don't like this, Elvin," Arnold said, casting nervous glances this way and that. "If that bullhusker jumps us, I don't think half of our guns would fire."

"Let's reload our guns, then."

"This isn't getting us anywhere," Alfred Bunton muttered. "It's headed south, and it looks like it's favoring the low places. I think if we run up ahead and set up a good firing position on the bluffs over the crick by Clint's new farm, it would walk right into us."

Elvin slowed up his horse, thinking. "You might have a point. But supposing it doesn't show up?"

"We're not gonna get it this way," Bunton argued. "We're not gonna pop it from horseback in this kind of weather. This rain's got my gun all gummed up. Walking around with a bunch of damp firecrackers is just asking to get another one of us killed."

The Tucker party honed in on their course of action. The two trackers with them, warded by Arnold Brody and Joe Garmen, would carry on trailing the bullhusker without grappling with it while the rest of the party would head to the bluffs, stopping by the Newells to warn them of the situation and hopefully pick up a couple more riflemen.

The plan took little longer to carry out than it did to lay it down. The Tuckers set up their places high on the bluffs overlooking a broad swath of the short mountain across the valley, enough shelter raised there to keep off the unceasing rain. There they waited for five solid hours. Near the end of the fifth hour, the trackers came up to tell them that the bullhusker had gone far off the expected path and looped clear around the other side of the mountain. The Tuckers had lost it for the day.

They were not going to give up yet, however. The party would rest up for the night and begin tracking the unbred afresh in the morning. The wounded bullhusker could not keep up a fast pace for very long, and they would catch it tomorrow.

Chapter 21

Greenbrier Territory

The other Taylor boys—Harvey and little Dale—joined the Tucker hunting party the next day in what was fast becoming a hefty attack force. They picked up the trail on the south side of the mountain and followed it like shrewd housewives tracking a mouse, finding the remains of the ill-fated horse strewn along a game trail and the wounded bullhusker's abandoned resting place not far beyond that. Poor Alice Hadley had been spared the depredations wrought upon her mount—not enough meat on her to go to the trouble of dragging her carcass over hill and dale. It was one of only two consolations her widowed husband and five kids would get, the other being the assurance that she had not suffered—perhaps she had not even known what had hit her.

The blood trail ended sooner than any of the hunters would have liked, but not so quickly that blood-sniffing wolves and pigmen were not a danger. Over a campfire, the Tucker hunters sharpened stakes and speculated about how much they could get for the bullhusker's tusks and giant razor claws. They broke camp early and beat a hard trail the next day. Early on into the morning's ride, Victor Fillmore noticed a freshening in the bullhusker's tracks. They were all but upon the south-fleeing bullhusker by nightfall that day, but Elvin forbade them to go any farther in the dark.

"We'll catch it tomorrow," Elvin surmised as the hunting party set up camp again.

"We'd better," Arnold Brody said. "We'll be stretching our rations mighty thin by the time we get back."

"Isn't anybody worried that we're right smack dab on top of Greenbrier soil?" Harvey Taylor asked.

"I don't reckon there's a single Greenbrier within ten miles of here," Elvin said. "We go in, bag the bullhusker, and get out, and double watches until we're clear. No sightseein'. We do it right, they'll never even know we were here."

"Too bad," Deek Evans said after a pause. "I never killed me a Greenbrier."

"We ain't kitted for that sort of thing," Elvin said. "You go lookin' for a fight with them, they'll skin you alive. I mean it."

"It isn't a lie," Shane Bunton growled. "Gutted my dad and left him to the unbreds."

That shut Deek up for a while. But not forever. "Who here's killed a Greenbrier?" Deek asked.

The Tuckers in the party all looked at Elvin. "I done three or four," he said. "Arnold's done a couple. Rick here got one, a few years back. Apart from that, the rest of this posse's nigh well unblooded."

"What, shadowers don't count?" Deek said.

"No, they don't. You got lucky and killed a monster. You ain't killed a person."

"Greenbriers ain't people."

"You can say that, if it makes you feel better," Elvin said, leaning forward. "But when it comes time for killin', you'd best do away with the notion. 'Cause if you keep thinkin' that a-way, you get arrogant. Then you get careless. Then you get skinned alive."

"I don't like this," Harvey shook his head. "A pair of bullhusker tusks aren't worth this sort of risk."

"It ain't about the claws. I don't want some scarred bullhusker wandering back onto one of our farms looking for revenge. I never seen a critter hold on to a grudge like bullhusker can. We're putting that thing down tomorrow."

The next morning brought with it a thick, low-lying fog that clung to the hills even when they had finally caught up with the wending bullhusker, deep into Greenbrier territory.

The bullhusker got wind of its pursuers and, panicked, made to charge, but a volley of three or four musketballs blinded it in one eye and turned the beast back the other direction. Now seriously wounded, the bullhusker could do little but limp away from the pursuers, who surrounded it and herded it into the cleft of a sharply sloping dell. A few rounds of flanking fire from either side made short work of the ugly man-beast. When they were sure it was dead, Arnold Brody oversaw the butchery.

"Let's hurry," Fred Bunton said, hands twisting on the forestock of his rifle, eyes darting to the surrounding stones and discarded leaves as if nature this far out was liable to grow teeth when he wasn't looking.

"We can get the tusks and razor claws back to camp in about an hour, I'd reckon," Elvin answered as he buried an ax in the bullhusker's jaw. "Whoever's not helpin' cut this thing up, fan out and set up a watch around here."

Dale and Amos took to the south, just over the hill. Harvey posted up on a tree nearby and surveyed the unfamiliar scenery. The sun had yet to break free of the clouds in the eastern sky, and fog still clung to the low places. "You guys keep close now, you hear?" Harvey ordered his two younger brothers. "This is Greenbrier territory."

Amos and Dale gave their agreement in a nod that was forgotten as soon as it was given. They picked their way down the hill towards a ravine that snaked its way around the mountain before forking at a wedge-like cliffside staring down at them.

"Think I could climb that?" Amos asked his brother, motioning up to the crumbling face of the cliff that loomed across the canyon from them.

"Why? You going to?" Dale sounded skeptical.

"I might. It'll take them a good fifteen minutes at least to get the tusks loose from that husker. I could be back by then."

"I'll tell Harvey!"

"Good gosh, Dale, give it a rest. I'm just fooling. I'd bet you'd have heart attack if you ever thought to break a rule."

"You're just jealous 'cause Ma says..." Dale's sentence drifted to a halt along with his stride.

Amos stopped and turned and face Dale. "Dale, what is it you're—"

Dale tackled him from behind before Amos could finish his own sentence. There was the sound of a cracking whip as a bullet whistled past and ricocheted a split second after. The thump of a rifle report echoed down from the sheer cascade of weathered rocks that blanketed the opposite cliffside.

"Quick! Under cover!" Amos cried, scrambling on his hands and knees to the shelter of a thick tree. Dale followed right behind him. Together they clutched the ancient bark on the lee side while another gunshot sparked off.

Up the hill behind them, Amos heard the distant warning call of his older brother. "Greeeeenbriaaaaars!" A soft, far-flung cry, but one that made Amos' heart seize as much as the gunshot did. They were in it now.

"Where did that shot come from, Dale? Are we covered?"

"I-I think so. They haven't shot at us any mo—" The shocking thunder of a Tucker gun somewhere up the hill from them—friendly side—punctured the brief, tight-as-a-drum stillness.

"Yeah, chew on that, you Greenbrier sons-of-bullhuskers!"

"I'm gonna tell Mom you said—"

"Give it a rest, Dale!" Amos stood up, checked the powder in the pan of his gun, peeked around the edge of the tree, and jerked back. A bullet tore the bark off the tree right above his head. Without faltering, he dropped to a knee, put the rifle to his shoulder, and leaned back around the big silver maple. Another musketball whipped the air above Amos' head where he'd allowed himself to be seen earlier. Amos saw the puff of smoke up between a cleft in the rocks and fired. The recoil of the rifle knocked him back behind the tree on his butt. A bullet kicked at the ground.

"Thanks for tackling me, Dale." Amos began reloading.

"N-no problem," Dale stuttered, "I thought I saw some moving a-ways away. Saw a rifle when I looked again." Dale tried to sound calm, but his hands were shaking, a cold sweat beading on his face. No more shots for a moment—the shooters were either reloading or searching for other targets. The brief cessation of gunfire lent no semblance of safety; Dale flinched at the caw and sudden flight of a crow overhead.

"Amos! Dale! Get outta there! You got the Greenbriers zeroed in on ya!"

"We're pinned!" Amos called back to Harvey. "Give us some cover fire!"

"How many of them are there?"

"How should I know? Two or three!"

"Run on our shots!"

The rapid drumbeat of rifle reports just over the crest of the hill on the Tucker side jolted the Taylor boys from their cover. The other clansmen had come to give support. Amos and Dale burst into the open and ran not backwards, not straight up the hill, but parallel to the Greenbrier line. They pelted across the face of the hill, dodging around trees and through the underbrush. The Greenbriers managed a shot or two, but it was hard to track a side-winding target on rough ground at a span of seventy yards.

Amos continued his zig-zag through the trees, Dale following behind. They dropped down about forty feet on the hill, heading west-north-west to where nature had hammered a smoother flee path. The sharp cut of the ravine wall ironed out around them, stretching and yawning into a tree-covered slope as they pelted their way to safety.

If you're in a gunfight, Amos remembered his dad telling him, *you've got to figure out where all the shooters are.* Then, if you need to run, run crossways to them. You've got good odds, even in the open, if you're running crossways. Not good if you find yourself running straight away or straight to a shooter. Amos figured they could get around the rump of the hill, move out of the Greenbriers' range, then loop back around to the rest of the—

"Holy crap! Down! Down!"

A posse of eight to ten horsemen came riding up from the misty washout below, curving back to head straight towards them, cutting them off. Amos and Dale snapped a right angle turn to the left and sprinted deeper into the ravine. The cavalcade redirected and drove the two Taylor boys back south, deeper into enemy territory. Couldn't outrun the horsemen. Amos turned on his heel, took a knee, drew a bead as calmly as his shaking hands and heaving lungs would allow, and shot one of the horses out from under a charging Greenbrier. With the few brief seconds afforded to him by the fanning cavalry, Amos and his brother spilled down into the sharpest downhill slope, where it was too steep for the horses to follow. Slinging the rifle over his shoulder, Amos bounded down between footholds where tree trunks met the ground. The two brothers found some cover behind an outcropping of scalped bedrock as the misty shapes of Greenbriers loomed in the fog like wraiths.

"Dang. We're cut off. Where the heck did these guys come from?" Amos scrambled in vain to look for a workable escape route, and a fresh volley of musketballs sent the two brothers diving into cover.

The Greenbriers took up positions above them at a murderously close battle range. A spurt of three rapid-fire shots split the air. An automatic gun. Both Amos and his brother flattened themselves behind a boulder and grabbed the soil for purchase as if for fear it would drop away from them and leave them uncovered. The rifle fire chipped bits of stone from the ancient hillside and dropped lichen-covered flint pieces onto the bed of pine needles around the Taylor brothers.

"What are we gonna do, Amos? What are we gonna do? I wanna go home! I wanna go home now!"

Amos knew they couldn't stay put for long. Unless the Tuckers could make it forward to flank the enemy from the other side soon, the Greenbriers would move in and surround them. Two Tucker muzzle-loading rifles couldn't keep up with eight Greenbrier breech-loaders. What to do, what to do—

"Dale, reload my gun! Gimme yours, quick!"

Dale obliged, eyes wide with a wild, animal terror.

With both of them behind one rock, they gave only one firing position for the Greenbriers to worry about. He needed to get to a different spot, get another line of fire. "Nock an arrow and watch out for a wiseacre Greenie tryna get at you from the right!" Amos pointed, remembering the combat advice he'd heard from Elvin McDaniel some years ago: *Greenbriers like to wait until they think you've touched off your charge, then they rush you. If you can keep them zoned, you can hold the cowards pert' near all day.*

Amos waited for two shots to snap past him into the shallow brook below, then sprinted for the cover of another tree. The automatic gun chattered, and he heard the bullets buzz through the new spring leaves around him like small, angry bees. He dropped into a roll that put him firmly behind cover and gave him a bruised shoulder. I'm being too risky, he thought to himself. Quelling the panic he could feel rising in his throat, he posted up on the Greenbrier he reckoned had the automatic and waited for a clean shot.

Come on, come on ... There! The Greenbrier rolled out from behind his cover squarely into Amos's sights, and the young Tucker threaded a bullet clean through the brush and right into the middle of the machine-gunner's chest. It was the only shot he could afford to take before rifle fire rained down on his position.

Elvin had just inched up to Harvey's tree to get a better sense of their footing when he heard more gunfire far down the hill on his right flank, echoing in the distance. He swore. More Greenbriers. The Tuckers who had come up to lay down cover fire hardened up again, waiting for orders.

"What are they a-shootin' at?" Arnold the butcher asked behind Elvin.

Deek Evans ventured from his cover to move right but ducked back again with an oath when a Greenbrier bullet from across the canyon nicked him in the leg. "Ah! They done stove in my shin!"

A rifle boomed way on down the hill to the right. "That was one of our guns just now! That's Amos and Dale down there!" Harvey hollered.

Elvin cursed. "Okay! Listen up, boys! They're trying to surround us. Those shooters on the cliff want us to get in a long firefight with 'em. Hold us here while the others close the loop. We gotta get out of here fast and smooth. Garmen, Shane, Fred. Move on back to our camp eastwise and watch our left flank. Somebody get Deek up and get him to quit his yapping. Pull out. The rest of y'uns, on me. We gotta go pull Dale and Amos out of a hornet's nest. Rally back at camp, y'hear? No tomfoolery. Go," Elvin ordered.

Elvin, with his support, ran through the woods to rescue Amos and Dale. The sounds of gunfire went on and on like the uneasy popping of corn, and Elvin's gut lurched a bit when he heard the chatter of an old assault rifle. He could feel his deceased father slap him on the back of the head for that, for feeling dread in the face of better weapons. That wasn't the way a watchman behaved, and certainly not a McDaniel.

Amos tried to reload, but the *thwack* of bullets hitting the tree behind him nearly sent his mind over the brink. Where were the other Tuckers? He heard the automatic gun again. Someone else had picked it up.

The next burst of gunfire all but drowned out Dale's cry as he fell backward out of the corner of Amos' eye.

"Dale!" Keeping his cover between him and his attackers, Amos backed away from the tree, down the hill. When he was more or less below the line of fire, he ran back to the rock where Dale sat slumped over, a rifle on the ground beside him. Blood stained Dale's clothes scarlet. The kid's eyes stood open in silent, frightened pain, swiveling to and fro, framed by frantic questions in his eyebrows. Amos swore in spite of himself and tried to stop the world from spinning.

"Hold on, Dale. You'll be okay. We gotta—"

Amos looked up from where his brother lay and saw a Greenbrier run up to the very tree he'd run from, not twenty paces from where Amos now kneeled. He was so close Amos could make out the features of his face. Did he not see Amos? Slowly, the Greenbrier turned his head to look Amos right in the eye. The Greenbrier had a round, pug-like face, and a smug, brutish expression. The man smiled and made a show of reloading his gun. He ratcheted out a lever under the trigger guard, pulled out a cloth-bound cartridge, and slipped it into the breech.

"Better hurry, boy," he said. "If you hurry up now, I'll even give you to the count of ten."

Amos choked back his impotent rage and scooped his little brother up into his arms and over his shoulder. He heaved himself to his feet. With no gun, no bow, only his sheathed machete at his side, Amos marched off down the hill. If he was going to get shot in the back by a filthy Greenbrier, he would do it on his own terms.

"I'll get you out of here, Dale. Don't you worry," he breathed into his brother's ear, "I'll get you out."

Staying low and trusting himself to pure, stupid luck, he jumped down the hill as fast as his feet could carry him. No following shots, no bullets hitting him in the back. A shallow stream lay at the bottom of the ravine about fifty feet away. Thirty. Twenty. Ten. Then he was in it, and then he was across it, and then the bullets kicked up the earth around him. One, two, three shots, one right after another.

Then he was back in the trees, ducking through cover, lungs chugging and heart hammering, praying that pure, stupid luck would smile on the two of them for just a little while longer.

Elvin and his accompanying clansmen rounded the remains of a ruined country house and crossed the battered remnants of an old driveway to see, near the bottom of the ravine, a knot of Greenbriers concentrating their fire on a target fleeing across a shallow creek. The Greenbriers were pretty distant, but all their backs were turned against Elvin.

"Spread out and take up positions there, there, and there," he ordered, pointing. His men obeyed. Then, as he brought his nitrogel-charged rifle to his shoulder and rested his cheek against the stock, he whispered a prayer to his father, patron saint of war if there ever was one. "All right, old man. Let's see your good-for-nothin' son pull a headshot from a quarter mile and see what you have to say then."

Elvin lined up his shot, breathed out a little, and squeezed the trigger. Even from his distant vantage point, he could see the spray of red that told him his aim was true.

A second Greenbrier fell to a well-placed Tucker shot, and the five remaining figures bolted for their horses and rode off, taking only the rifles of their fallen. Elvin and his fellow clansmen ran down to the scene of the skirmish. One of the corpses was missing half his face.

"Clear?" Elvin asked.

"Clear!"

"Dale? Amos? Y'all okay?"

No answer.

"They were here behind this rock, looks like," Nigel Bunton observed, kneeling over a discarded rifle.

"I saw at least one of 'em light out into the woods yonder. Amos! Dale!" Elvin called.

Still no answer.

"Should we follow them?"

"Shit fire!" Elvin kicked the ground. "No, we can't afford to chase them around. They got themselves a topo map and they know where we're camped. We gotta make a beeline outta here. This place'll be crawling with Greenbriers in about ten minutes tops, and we're just about plumb out of ammunition. Don't even got time to raid the bodies. Sound the whistle."

"It's okay, Dale. I got you. We'll fix you up real good when we get back to camp. We shook those Greenbriers. You hear me, Dale? Gotta take you back to Mom and Dad, okay?" He felt Dale's grip tighten on his neck and continued his arduous trek through the forest, stopping to rest every couple minutes.

"I'm s-s-sorry, Am—,"

"Don't worry, Dale. You're doing fine. Don't need to talk now. Just hold on a little while."

Harvey Taylor shook his head. "I don't like this. I gotta take care of them, and if they run across some screevlers or pigmen, I—"

"Too bad, Harvey. If they ain't gonna make it, they ain't gonna make it. There ain't nothing you can do for them. If you stay here, the only thing you'll do is give your scalp to the Greenbriers. Now we gotta move, and I mean now."

"Hey, Dale, remember when we were little, and you and I kept on wanting to play 'ride the bullhusker' with Dad? That was your favorite

game. You nearly rode Dad to death. You were too little to remember much, but I remember Dad telling us that we'd bring in a real bullhusker hide someday. Won't that be great when we give Dad that tusk? Yeah, that'll be pretty great."

Amos' throat burned with thirst, and his face glistened with sweat. He could feel something warm soaking his clothes where he held Dale against him, and for some reason could only think of when he was seven years old and had wet his britches in the middle of school while Sam Chambers told all the kids about bacteria and washing hands.

He stopped halfway up an unending uphill slope and sank to one knee. His lungs chugged the air and tugged at his ribs. How much further? He couldn't make it. He just couldn't.

But he had to.

Amos struggled to his feet again and readjusted the limp weight in his arms.

"Come on, Dale. We'll be okay. Almost there. Just—a little—further."

He topped the hill, expecting to see their morning campsite, their rallying point in case anyone got separated, but it was empty. The Tuckers had moved on.

"No. No." He sank to one knee again. He was alone. He couldn't accept it. He wouldn't accept it. He took a few deep breaths, got on his feet again, and headed north.

Amos stumbled onward, fighting back the sobs of despair with the same inner strength with which he had fought back earlier panic. He remembered exactly the course they'd taken into Greenbrier territory, seemingly ages ago. The odds were good he'd run into them eventually if he retraced his steps. But distances always seem less *before* a return journey with a wounded brother. Now the distance stretched out like a hundred long miles. By the time he reached the crest of the next hill, Amos was so hot and thirsty that he didn't notice Dale's skin had gone stone cold long ago.

"You're doing great, Dale. We're gonna make it. When we get back, we'll have Mom make you some special strawberry rhubarb pie with whipped cream. Extra sugar. It's too bad you didn't get that for your birthday. We're gonna make it up to you, I promise."

"We don't know they didn't make it," Harvey muttered, pacing. "They could be trying to catch up with us. They'd know where to go if they got back to the base camp and we weren't there."

"Problem is, they ain't the only ones following us. Won't do either Amos or Dale much good if we get ourselves surrounded."

"We can bull-work this hilltop, ward off on the slopes," Arnold Brody said. "I reckon we can spot friend or foe from a-ways off if we post up right."

"Fine," Elvin said. "We'll hold up for a spell. We can leave tomorrow morning. But we'll have to foot it out of there then, or we'll be pigman bait for sure."

"I got you, Dale. Don't worry. I won't let you down."

After trudging through the underbrush and hills for two hours, Amos finally heard low voices ahead of him. "We—we made it, Dale. I told you. Help!" he called out. "Dale's hurt!"

"It's Amos!"

"You okay?"

"Good God!"

"Look at him!"

"Amos, you thirsty?"

"Here, put him down here and let's have a look."

"Sit down!"

"Amos."

"Amos."

"Amos!"

Amos blinked and found himself staring at Harvey. It was a Harvey he had never known, grim-faced and care worn.

"Amos," Harvey began.

"Did you look at Dale?" Amos broke in. "Get him something to drink, quick. I think the bleeding's stopped, but I haven't looked at the wound."

"Amos."

"I'm sorry I took so long getting here. I went as fast as I could, I really did."

"Amos, listen to me. Dale's dead."

"Wait, what?"

"He's been dead for at least a couple of hours."

"No, he's fine, he's going to be okay, look at him—"

"Look for yourself," Harvey said, his voice thick with blame and pity. Amos looked over and saw Dale's pale body, arms and legs frozen in rigor mortis, eyes staring without seeing. Amos' own eyes stared as they mounted up, as they made camp that night, as they rode through the next day, and as they clumped into town after their week-long hunting trip. He didn't breathe the question, but his stare asked it just the same. How did this happen? *How did this happen?* He asked of his clansmen.

How did this happen? He asked of the birds that still sung. *How did this happen?* He asked of the trees and bushes and hills and abandoned cars and homes they saw scattered along their way. None answered.

Chapter 22

The Aftermath

Sam Chambers was just putting the finishing touches on the next chapter of his memoirs when his wife called up the stairs.

"Sam! The hunting party's back."

He detected something different in her voice. "What's wrong?"

"There was a run-in with the Greenbriers. Dale Taylor's dead."

Sam Chambers set down his quill and rested his head in one hand. Good God. Poor Mrs. Taylor. The boy had been her only natural son; the others had been the children of the blacksmith's first wife. What would he tell the other schoolchildren? He couldn't remember the last time a clansman so young was killed in a battle against other humans. Killing kids was the sort of thing he'd expect an unbred to do. Not people, not even the Greenbriers.

Sam sighed deeply. "The hunting party just getting here?"

"They're just coming in the south gate. Most of the town's come out to pay their respects."

"Then let's go along, too."

Sam silently watched alongside a number of other Tuckers lining the street as the hunting party wove its somber path through the town, a bundled corpse draped across a trailing horse. The silence was grim and absolute until a warbling wail rose from the throat of a mother held aghast. Mrs. Taylor ran forth from her husband's smithy, one hand hiding her face twisted in despair. Most of the rest of the clan looked down.

"Not Dale!" she cried as she reached the body just beginning to smell of decay. "Not Dale! My baby!"

Amos tried to lay a hand on her shoulder. "I'm sorry, Ma, I—"

But his stepmother pushed Amos away with a trembling hand, recoiling in disgust. "Don't—Don't you dare touch—" she stammered before burying her face in the bundle with heaving sobs.

Amos kept his distance, his head bowed.

"Tell me, Elvin. Where do we stand?" Arnold asked, pacing the floor and periodically looking out the window at the town Tuckers milling about the street, gossiping and speculating about the same thing he and the watchman were worrying about inside.

"We traded one of our own clansmen for at least three of theirs, plus a pair of bullhusker tusks, coming out of an ambush, outnumbered, in *their* territory," Elvin murmured to Arnold Brody in his butcher shop. Elvin looked uncharacteristically tired. "I know what I'm supposed to say. I ought to say we've got our first real test of the nitrogel, that we can now go toe-to-toe with any clan around and take them down if we wanted. But I don't cotton to sacrificing our young'ns to those damn Greenbriers, even if we do end up carving three more notches in our own stocks. And I just don't know if I'm man enough to finish what this run-in's got started."

"Just what do you reckon this run-in's started, Elvin?"

"War, Arnie. We've started us a war."

Sam knocked on the door of the clan watchman the day after Dale's funeral. He hated doing this.

Elvin opened the door, dressed as usual in his worn but functional buckskin and vest, and as many weapons on his person as possible. Elvin greeted the clan schoolmaster by his surname without mentioning his title.

"Ah, Chambers. Just caught me leavin'. I'm headed over to meet with some of the clan's elders. Care to join us?"

"I was actually wanting to speak to you about that," Sam said, walking alongside Elvin and finding himself having to quicken his pace to keep up with the watchman's mechanical stride. "Might I advise some caution as we think about how we will, that is, how you and the fighting men will carry themselves when and if—"

"I'm nothing if not a wary man, Chambers," Elvin said without shortening his stride.

"Never meant to imply that you weren't. The problem is that there are a few clansmen who are a little riled since our contact with the Greenbriers and—"

"You talking about the Taylors?"

"Mainly, yes."

"Why should I care about that?"

"Well, they're upset, pretty understandably, I'd suppose. Mrs. Taylor has been overstandingly distraught and—aside from her remaining two sons—she has placed some of the blame with the leaders of the hunting trip. She says he was too young to be in a war party."

"It wasn't a war party when we started. And anyway, we were cutting our teeth at twelve years, same as Dale. Even you. Same age, same risks. His number came up, is all."

"Maybe we should rethink that custom, then."

"And wind up with a generation of sprightly young warriors who can't tell a muzzle from their own ass? I'm going to a meeting to wrangle over war plans, and you're talking about hamstringing the folkward."

"I'm not arguing for that, I just think we ought to let things simmer down a little before organizing a war party. The Taylors have got quite a few good fighting men, and I don't suppose they'll be too eager to get back into danger after one of their own's just died. At least the women won't stand for it."

"That's funny. It ain't what I heard. Seems they're itching for some justice to get served."

"They don't know what they want, they're just—"

"Sam, look." Elvin finally stopped and turned to face Sam, his forbearance losing strength. "I know what you're doing. You're going around and sticking your nose in places it don't belong."

Sam pinched the top of his nose and closed his eyes to focus. "Elvin, I'm just saying that we've got bigger and more important things to worry about."

"No, what you're saying is that we should all sit on our hands while them Greenbriers get away with murder."

"I want some peace. That's it. I've got a lot of bright young boys and girls in my school, and they can make something of this clan if they don't all get killed. Dale was one of the best students in his class. He'd wanted to build watermills when he got older. Think of what the clan could have done with a clansman like that if we hadn't gotten him killed. Think of your son, Elvin. Ralph's got a gift. We can't afford to waste it."

"I'll decide what's best for *my* boy, thank you very much," Elvin spat back. "You do your job and I'll do mine. Some of us got more important things to do than sit around and wish for a world that don't exist no more."

"Elvin, your problem is that you can't see two inches past your own nose."

"What? And you can? Mr. Too-Afraid-to-Teach-Our-Kids-to-Defend-Themselves?"

"Remember what our folks told us about the old days, with the Pandemic, and the unbreds going wild, and the die-off during the Scavenging Years?" Sam asked. "None of that happened in a day. In fact, it never really stopped. Most folks figure things are more stable now, and if we just keep trucking on, our kids will replace us and the human population will get its numbers back up again. Well guess what, Elvin. They're all wrong. I've looked at my father's journals. When the Tucker clan was first started, there were five hundred and eighty people. Now there's only a hair more than five hundred. The number of babies we're having isn't enough to balance out those of us who are dying."

"Which is why we've got to be tougher than the Greenbriers and whatever other clans are out there."

"That's not good enough. The only way for us to steady our numbers is for us to rediscover medicine, machinery, agriculture, chemistry, commerce, and that will only happen if our bright young minds survive long enough to make some progress."

"Sam, I've got a meeting to go to. You're real cute when your eyes light up like that, but I've got the real world to deal with. I can't worry about my grandchildren starvin' to death fifteen years from now when some peckerwoods are a-wantin' to kill my children tomorrow."

Elvin turned around and entered the school cafeteria, closing the ugly metal door behind him and the thirty or forty grown men who stood waiting inside. Sam Chambers hated talking to that man.

"Sorry I'm late, everyone, but let's get to it," Elvin said, unslinging his rifle from his shoulder and leaning it against the wall behind him. "How's your leg, Deek?"

"Doc says I'll manage."

"Sorry, Elvin, but could you hurry? My fields need tendin' to, and I don't reckon my kids can go about it too long without burning down my farm," Job Brody said.

"This won't take any longer than it needs to, if ya'll settle down and we can get started." The murmuring among the men there stilled at Elvin's commanding voice. "Now y'uns have heard by now about the run-in with the Greenbriers we had earlier last week. We lost a fine young clansmen in the skirmish, as you all know. Looks like the father and one of the brothers of the deceased have joined us today."

The men all nodded to Adam Taylor and his silent son, Amos.

"What you don't likely know," continued Elvin, "are the particulars of the Greenbrier attack. From all I've been able to figure, and the Buntons and Arnold Brody will agree with me, is that the Greenbrier attack was coordinated. Somehow, they probably picked up our trail some way or spotted us from a distance some time before we killed the bullhusker, and set up an attack as fast as they could. That would explain the flanking horses and the chattergun they had with them. Yes, an automatic. But here's the point of all this, folks. They got the drop on us and used a machine gun against us, and we still killed at least three of them. They killed one of ours and injured one other."

The clansmen waited in silence for Elvin to get to the point.

"Two of our kills were made at a range of about three hundred and fifty yards, a good deal beyond what the Greenbriers could ever hope to hit. What we have here," Elvin picked up a small bag holding a charge of nitrogel, "is the first real tactical advantage we have *ever* had over the Greenbriers, or anyone, for that matter. It works. We've tested it in the field, and it works even better than we expected it would.

"The problem is we've used up most of what Bill had stockpiled before the accident, and Bill tells me he can't start up production again until the next nomad clan comes through. So you all are gonna chip in again"—he paused as groans swept the room—"without caterwaulin' about it. Five teeth each, and we're gonna get Bill working again.

"Now, until that time, we'll send out patrols along the whole five miles south of the clan. I wager the Greenbriers will send up a war party of their own before too long. The Newells will need some extra sentries. The southeast overlook will be manned at all times until I say otherwise."

"What if they try to loop around and hit us from the north like they did a few years back?" one of the Craines asked.

"With this nitrogel, we can spread out our scouts and roundswalkers. If we place our men right, they'll be able to take a couple shots at any approaching enemies and be half a mile away before they ever figure out where the shots came from. Sure, put a couple of our boys out there on the ridge by your place."

"Hold on," Clyde McDaniel, Elvin's cousin, said with a frown. "I ain't committing any of my boys to a fight unless I'm sure about this. You think for sure the feud's flaring up again?"

"Clyde, I'd bet fifteen jaws that we'll be trading shots again with the Greenbriers in less than two weeks."

Ella risked a laugh, perched on the moss-covered stone. Jim took a swig from a discolored plastic jug with the swagger of a young man certain of his invincibility. They shared the same color of hair, his own cropped close and covered with a tattered baseball cap. He had the same long face as hers, too, though his stubbled whiskers made him look less like a horse, by her reckoning.

Jim had assured her the roundswalk hadn't taken them far from the clan walls, and she trusted him when he wagered on a peaceful lunch of cornbread and beans. Despite her teasing to the contrary, she trusted his judgment. The wrecked skeleton of an ancient convenience store offered a tidy fallback point further into the woods. The trickling brook next to them masked their hushed voices, and the hills going on up to either side were enough to hide them from anything further than a stone's throw away.

Neither the hills nor the stream were enough to mask the unearthly shriek that shattered the calm. The two dropped their things and darted into the cover of the trees without a word spoken between them. They stirred the reeds no more than a passing breeze as they flitted through the greenery for a few short seconds, went still, and disappeared. The agonized screech, some three hundred paces out and up, carried on, warbling in and out before going quiet. Neither of the two stirred. The brook trickled on and the birds sang as if nothing were amiss. The young man shifted toward his sister.

"*This* is why you always bring a weapon with you, dingus," he muttered.

"What was that?" His sister hugged the ground beneath the spreading brush.

"It was a screevler, I reckon. I think it got caught in a trap."

"We don't trap around here, do we?" Ella asked, her voice rising again, even if her body remained in a low crouch.

"Naw. Must be Greenbriers."

"You think they'd be this close to the clan?" The fear returned to the girl's voice with a hissing breath.

"Two miles out—I don't know. Could be planning a raid."

They waited a while longer. Ella watched as her brother fiddled with his rifle's improvised cigarette lighter flint lock.

"I'm gonna go check it out."

Ella tried to stop him without moving. "The watchman said to never go after a screevler alone, and I ain't even got a knife on me."

"Pretty sure it's dead."

"But what if it ain't?" She reached out far enough to lay a hand on his arm, to pull him back. "Might've just yanked off one of its arms instead."

"I need to know if it's a Greenbrier trap or not. If it is, then it was a trap meant for us." Jim shook his head. "Those psychotic sons-of-bull-huskers."

"We should go back and fetch help. Don't go, Jim."

But Jim was already moving, shaking her off and climbing to his feet. "Stay here and keep hidden 'til I get back. You mind me, now." He stole into the forest, the butt of his rifle tucked into his shoulder.

Ella's low breath rustled the dead leaves underneath her as she waited. The birds sang their frivolous songs, and the brook bubbled steadily away. She waited and peered through the leaves for any sign of movement, but she did not move. Time oozed.

A human scream of pain pierced the woods.

Ella laid the last of the springtime flowers on Jim's grave. The ground had settled over it, as if the earth thought it were time for folks to move on and forget the corpse rotting underfoot. But three years or thirty years likely wouldn't make much difference. She looked over to Dale's fresh grave.

No, on occasions like this, time didn't seem to make much of a difference at all.

Chapter 23

In Which Miss Holland's Naivete Causes Trouble

When another nomad clan came through at the end of that week, the bullhusker tusks fetched a handsome price, and the clansmen, true to their word—or at least to the word of Elvin McDaniel—fronted the bill for all sorts of chemical feedstock. Bill's nitrogel shop was back up and running, bigger than ever scarcely more than three weeks after the fire. Ricky Brody and Nigel Bunton moved into the room Omar had once used, working slavish hours to meet the demands war brought to the clan's powder supply. Ella returned nearly as often to help Bill keep up with the sundry tasks around the new shop. Bill, though he never said as much, was glad for the help, and Ella was glad to give it, if at least to get out of the house and away from Amos, whose ringing silence reminded Ella too painfully of her own.

Amos went back to his apprenticeship with barely a word, and most folks left him alone to his grief after a week or two of unending condolences. He didn't dance with the girls when the nomads came through; it all seemed a little silly to him now. But every morning he woke up to find a hot sweet roll waiting for him in the shop. An unspoken "I'm sorry" every morning with an unspoken promise to go on until the hurt went away. Amos accepted the anonymous treats, though everything tasted the same to him now.

Of course Ella was culprit behind the sweet rolls. Whatever Amos had or hadn't done, Ella wouldn't have wished this on anyone, and so the baked treats kept coming without either speaking of it.

Johnny Grierson was directing his daughter to stir the flaming coals in a roasting kiln when his cousin came up to tell him that that Holland girl had come out to see him again. Johnny Grierson blinked his one good eye and wiped the sweat and grime from his face. "What? You serious? What's she want this time?"

"Ask her," was the reply.

Johnny went to the gates of their small settlement to find Ella wandering meekly about inside, hugging herself as she coughed and sputtered in the smoke of the wood fires and the dust from the mine tailings.

"What do you want?"

"Bill sent me."

"Alone? For what? To gloat?"

"No. Bill wanted me to give y'uns something."

"Well, let's see it," Johnny said with arms crossed.

Ella removed a satchel from the horse she'd taken up to the camp. "Twenty charges of nitrogel, our first batch," Ella said, "and a pound cake. The cake is from me."

Johnny sneered. "What for?"

"Bill was wanting to bury the hatchet. Maybe one day he could use a business partner."

Johnny spat. "That's bull, little missy. Bill didn't say any of that. Or if he did, he didn't mean it. What's he trying to get at?"

Ella blinked, unsure of what to say. "I-I thought ... You don't want it?"

"No, I don't want it. Bill can take his fancy powder and blow it out his butt."

"But business hasn't been good for you, and—"

"What do you know about my business?"

"I-I didn't mean it like that. I figured it would help to say no hard feelings."

"No hard feelings? Did Bill put you up to this, or was this your idea?"

Ella looked at the ground. "My idea."

Johnny Grierson laughed. "You silly girl. You don't got the slightest notion how a business works. Ain't none of it personal, so there's no hard feelings to worry about. There's just getting back on top."

Ella looked up a little. "It seems pretty personal to you."

"I don't think you get what I'm drivin' at. I stick to my business, you stick to your'n. Everyone's happy."

Ella frowned. "I'm sorry, Mr. Grierson, but a life like that wouldn't make me happy at all, and I don't reckon you'd really like it that much yourself."

"Then you don't know me too well. If you did, you'd know that I don't cotton to an uptown Tucker girl thinking she knows diddly about what it's like to be a half-breed *anywhere*, let alone one scratchin' out a living a day's ride from everywhere. You'd know that after *years* of blood, sweat, and tears, and with nary mor'n a teacup's worth o' piss from the clan, I still ain't worthy of a handshake. You'd know that after my fancy uptown competitor muddles through without setting something on fire, and then the clan bends over backwards to save him because he's set something on fire I ... Where was I?"

"Your fancy uptown competitor," Ella prompted.

"You'd know I don't need a treat and a hug from a pampered, bleeding heart. I need respect. I need a fair shake. If I'm not gonna get that, it's not because I made it personal. Your kind made it personal. So if I'm going to make any kind of peace with anyone, I'm going to do it on my own gosh-darn terms when I'm the one calling the shots. I'm not going to wait until some brainwashed son-of-a-bullhusker has me over a barrel to accept mercy. I won't have me and the rest of us Griersons humiliated that a-way."

"I-I'm not trying to humiliate you. I just—"

"You just what?"

"I just wanted folks to be friendly with each other again."

"Well, I'm sorry, girl, but that just ain't the way things work. In the real world, it takes a lot more than some hand-holding to make folks friendly again. I told you what I want, what I need. You want a real peace offering? You got fifty years of clan history to undo." Johnny folded his arms. He'd said his piece, and he wasn't sorry he'd said it.

The Holland girl didn't break down crying this time, though she still seemed like a hefty wind would blow her down. "This pampered uptown girl ain't *so* uptown," she said, "that she can give you what you want. But I can give you a cake. So I thought I'd bring you what I can and hope you wouldn't hold it against me for what I can't."

Johnny stopped for a moment. The sincerity was refreshing, even if only momentarily so. "Well, if you can't give me what I really want, the best your kind can do is stay off my turf. So run on back to your clan, little missy, and take your nitrogel with you."

Johnny shooed her away as he would a whipped dog, and Ella left with her head hung, embarrassed and chastened. When he turned back to his work, he saw that she'd left the pound cake on the rough-cut oak table, right next to his pickaxe.

"What are you gonna do with it, Johnny?" one of the Coles asked.

Johnny sighed. "Welp, can't let it go to waste." They cut up the cake and savored the break it brought with it. For something that tasted so good, though, it sure left a sour taste in Johnny's mouth.

"Well, that didn't go how I was hoping," Ella muttered to herself on the long ride back down to town, her cheeks still hot with shame. "Yeah, yeah, I know. Looking out for your enemies is how you get et by unbreds," she said in her best mockery of Omar's voice.

She crossed over the narrow springtime creek that marked the halfway point between the Griersons and the town before she spoke again to the empty air. "I know it's not that simple, but what do I do? I can't undo the past. I wish I could. I can't fix the clan, I can't fix wrongheaded ideas, Lord knows I can't fix Johnny Grierson. All I can do is what I done. I don't know how else I coulda done it."

She allowed a silence to pass for how she figured Omar would answer. He'd probably say something about minding your own business.

"But to me, that's just settling for the lesser of two evils. I'm sick of having only bad and worse choices. We're stuck living this way because we don't have a lick of imagination, nor the mettle to dare it."

Who are you to lecture me about not having the mettle to dare, Ella?

Her frown faded into a wince. "That's a low blow. That's not fair. Ugh, but you're right, I guess. I reckon I got me a yellow streak. But if that's true, then my talk of livin' by faith is all a show. 'Cause faith is just courage by another name." Ella sighed. "But if I'd never been a coward, I wouldn't be alive today. I'd be layin' alongside Jim in a grave. That's what makes it so hard. I'm trying to be better, but every small brave thing I manage, I turn around and cower at the next thing. I never hashed things out with Amos. I never told Bert Daly to stop beating his wife. Never dared before just now to even think about the lot that's been given to the half-and-halfs. Not because I didn't know; because I didn't *want* to know."

She shook her head, angry with herself. "And I never told you the truth about me and you. Never had the time. Never had the courage. And now it's too late."

Her horse snorted, long since weary of her spoken thoughts. She ignored it. "Did you mean it, what you said about my eyes?"

Elvin was busy teaching his son the finer points of a lethal unbred snare, a lesson Ralph actually took some amount of interest in. Elvin was beginning to worry his son had no interests outside the clan walls. They'd finished making their rounds to the eastern outposts, going almost as far as the Grierson settlement. Elvin had been displeased to find several of the posts out here manned by women. He didn't mind women fighting in a pinch, and the Tuckers had often used women as fighters in the past, but this was just lazy. He'd have to talk with the Newells and the Craines about that practice when he was done with Ralph for the day. Daughters, no matter how well-trained, were no substitute for a seasoned clansman on the roundswalk. Elvin looked at his own son. Good heavens, that boy needed some seasoning.

"Now the thing to remember," Elvin instructed as he tied a knot in the thin leather cords that crossed a game trail, "is that the unbreds are smart enough to recognize trap bait when they see it. You put some meat on a stick, you might get a wolf or a bear, but a pigman is going to wonder why this is so easy. They'll start looking around for the trap. Now what's the easiest part of a trap to spot?"

"The engine."

"Right. So they'll go and find the log or rock you've got hanging off a cliff, and they'll start gnawing on the rope to disable the trap. So what you do is put the tripwire on the way to the engine. You got to play mind games with 'em. Best thing is, it works on humans, too."

"But how do we keep other clansmen from getting caught in them?"

"That's what we got the notches on the bait stick for: they tell us where the tripwire is."

"Pa?"

"Huh?"

"Can I ask you a question?"

"Go ahead."

Ralph paused in spite of his father's permission. "I been thinkin'," Ralph said, "'bout my future and all. Bill Puckett's still needing more help with the nitrogel and whatnot, and seein' how the nitrogel will help with the clan defense and all, I was wondering if I might start on with Bill as an apprentice."

Elvin didn't answer immediately. "Well, I don't know..."

"I think I could be really good at it. We use sulfuric acid as one of the ingredients, and my science book was saying that sulfuric acid could be used for a lot of things—"

"Hold on," Elvin said. "Did Sam Chambers put this idea in your head?"

"N-no," Ralph said.

Elvin wasn't convinced. The mere mention of science-y school nonsense settled the debate right then and there. "I'm not going to let you skip out on your roundswalks so you can do chemistry experiments. You are a McDaniel, and the safety of the clan comes first."

"But the nitrogel is important to—"

"Let other folks worry about how to make the nitrogel. Our family has a job to do. I didn't ask for this job any more than you did. It's high time you get used to the way things are."

"But—"

"Any more arguing is gonna have to be done with my belt. Do you under—"

Elvin and Ralph both froze as they caught a new scent on the westerly wind. All of the McDaniels in the clan had some of the most sensitive noses. This scent almost certainly belonged to a horse, but that meant there would be a human along with it.

"Into the brush quick-like, now," Elvin ordered his son in low tones.

Father and son both crouched in the concealing undergrowth as the wind picked up and the smell came in stronger.

"Shouldn't we ought to get further on up the hill, sir?" All traces of Ralph's boldness had vanished, replaced with the respect due to necessity and Elvin's position in the family.

Elvin shook his head and whispered back. "Could give away our position if he's close enough. He's already given himself away. No need for us to do the same, not until we have a better idea how close he is."

They waited. Presently, they picked up the scent of the rider, unfamiliar. They agreed that the rider was too far off yet to notice them if they got a better lookout place, and straight away started on up the slope.

"Ralph, scamper up that tree yonder. Leave your rifle down here, I just need you to see."

Ralph obeyed, finding a perch just high enough to give him a fair view of the westward downhill slope.

"I don't see nothin'," he said.

"Keep lookin'. Watch for movement."

Ralph's eyes strained to see through the foliage, to spot any odd rustle or sway in the leaves and branches. Like as not, the whoever it was would keep to the low places. The rider might be tough to spot, but the horse ... There!

"I see him."

"Just one?"

"Looks like it. Wait, no. There's another'n next to him, I think."

"Any others?"

"I ... I can't say," Ralph said, squinting. "There's movement down there, for sure. I just can't make out all the shapes."

"That looks like a war party, all right."

"What are we gonna do, sir?"

"They're still a good mile or so out from the Hadley farm, and they're slow going. We need to warn the Hadleys and muster the folkward. Get on down. Look sprightly, now."

Chapter 24

War Is the Province of Uncertainty

The watchman sent out runners to the town, the Newells, and the Craines the moment he reached the Hadley farm. Being the furthest away, the Craines would get the news last and be the slowest to send help. Clansmen at each of the stops would send out their own folks to gather the scouts and pull them back and muster whatever fighters they could to send to the Hadleys.

Meanwhile, Elvin would use whatever men and women he had at hand to harden the bulwarks set up on the inner side of their biggest field. If he'd had more time, he might've tried to prepare an ambush inside the far tree line, but without knowing their true numbers, he'd have to settle with making a good show of force and hoping the oncoming posse would either get wise and leave or get dumb and charge across open ground.

There'd been no sign of their quarry when fresh fighters and their help came in from the town. With the Tucker war force now tripled, armed clansfolk manned the full length of the Hadley's irrigation ditch. Most of the Tuckers from the west side of town had turned out, as well as every arms-bearing Taylor. Dr. Bernhard and his wife were already here, with boiled white bandages and horsehair sutures, splints, and a wicked sharp saw that made folks shudder. Sam Chambers answered the call, probably to slow down the planning and generally get in the way, Elvin figured. Many of the young womenfolk had come out as well to carry supplies and relay messages. Arnold Brody rode in with his own daughter in tow, jumped from his horse, and made for the watchman with quick strides.

"Found us a war party, I hear," Arnold said, handing Elvin the pair of field glasses he'd brought along.

Elvin took the proffered binoculars and scanned the distant tree line for movement. "I want to know where the Newells are. If they got beat by the town Tuckers *and* our camp followers, they must be dragging their feet something awful."

"Send another runner?"

"Yeah."

"Becky!" Arnold Brody hollered at his daughter, who'd broken off to join Ella on the homestead fence. "Take my horse and head on over to the Newells'. Ask them what the holdup is."

"Can I go with her?" Ella asked, hopping off the fence with Becky.

"What? Heck no. This is a battle we're about to have, not a picnic. You get over with Dr. Bernhard and make yourself useful. On the double, now."

The butcher turned away as his daughter scrambled onto his horse and Miss Holland went off to get Bernhard's oft-repeated refresher on how to apply a tourniquet. "See anything?" he asked Elvin.

"Still nothing."

Sam Chambers stepped up behind the two. "Let me take a look," he said, reaching for the binoculars.

"Sam," Elvin said, jerking the binoculars out of Sam's reach, "I think we got us too many cooks in the kitchen. Why don't you go teach some Shakespeare or something?"

Sam murmured an apology and backed off.

Arnold Brody cleared his throat after a moment filled by the trilling of the cicadas. "Maybe we scared 'em off."

"Yeah, maybe. Wait ... I see one of 'em." Elvin pointed, and the nearby Tuckers all shielded their eyes to follow his finger.

Way out yonder, right at the edge of their rifle range, stood the outline of a man atop his horse, unmoving, as if daring them to take a shot.

"Orders?" one of the Hadleys asked, putting his cheek to the stock of his rifle.

"That's their watchman," Elvin said to Arnold. "It's him for sure."

The horse and its rider trotted out into the field towards them.

"What's he up—"

The horseman raised a piece of cloth tied to a stick and waved it as he rode out.

"Ralph," Elvin said without lowering the binoculars, "get me my horse."

The horseman stopped in the middle of the field, his banner still raised.

"Does he want to talk?" Arnold Brody said.

"Looks like it. Keep me covered. Blast him if there's any funny business."

"Like what?"

"How should I know?" Elvin said, handing Arnold the binoculars, and with them the responsibility to take command if something went awry. "Just keep an eye out."

But as he swung into the saddle, he saw Sam Chambers already trotting into the field on his own horse.

"Sam, what the hell do you think you're doing?"

"My job. If he wants to talk, it should be with someone whose idea of a dialogue isn't grunting and flinging dirt in the air."

"Uh uh. I'm a-comin' with you," Elvin said.

"This one's mine. Why don't you go strangle some puppies or something?"

Elvin swore softly as he got off his horse and chucked the reins in frustration. "That little cuss."

Arnold chuckled, returning the binoculars. "You know you prefer this to his hand-wringin' and sooth-sayin'."

"Yeah, but the hand-wringin' ain't what's gonna get 'im kill't."

The Tucker schoolmaster rode out to meet the messenger. When he was still a good ten paces away, the man said, "That's far enough, mister."

Sam pulled up and got a good look at the man. He had a hatchet face and dead eyes long grown used to killing without pity. It was a different breed than what was found among the Tuckers. Even Elvin at least had some sass to him.

Different contexts required different tactics. For this one, he let the dirt he had spent years scrubbing from his voice back in. "What brings y'uns this far out this time of year?" Sam asked, as if talking with a nomad chieftain on an unexpected visit.

"I've got a message," the man said without breaking his unblinking stare, "from the headsmen and all the matrons of the clan. We've put up with you Tuckers long enough, and your last attack on our clan was the final straw."

"Attack? What attack? Us Tuckers don't go out of our way to throw rocks at beehives."

"For your crime," the Greenbrier said, ignoring Sam, "we demand the following: give us the heads of three clansmen of your choosing. Tear down your walls. Abandon your settlement. Move north at least fifteen more miles, and never set foot south of Picken's Ford again. Also, your clan leaders will give us five of your young ones for us to hold in thrall, to make sure you abide by our terms."

"And if we don't agree to your terms?"

"Then all your lives belong to me. Down to the last suckling babe."

Sam made to look like he was mulling over his options. "This is clearly an unfortunate misunderstanding. Surely two reasonable fellers can talk this out."

"The price for your survival is now four heads. Dick around with me some more, Tucker. I dare you."

Sam raised his hands in surrender. "Whoah, there, sir. I meant no provocation. I—" Sam sighed and threw a look back to the defenses where he knew Elvin was eyeing him through those field glasses. "I got most of the elders right here," Sam said. "Let me talk with them, pass on your terms, and meet here again to give you our answer."

Without a further word, Sam wheeled his horse around and ambled on back, without looking to see if the Greenbrier had done the same.

"What'd he say? Does he want to negotiate?" Arnold asked as Sam approached.

"No, he wants to fight while still making it look like we're the warmongers. His terms are marauder's parley."

Elvin's eyes narrowed. "What did that hatchet-faced sumbitch say?"

"Something he figured would rile us up, make us do something stupid. I told him we needed to discuss, so I suppose I bought us an hour."

Elvin nodded. "An hour's plenty of time. I need another messenger to ride over to the Newells' lickety-split."

"I'll go," Ella Holland raised her hand, having escaped Dr. Bernhard's graphic instructions on how to hold down an unwilling amputee.

"Tell the Newells and the Craines we've got men a-plenty here, and that they oughta take whatever gunhand they can find and push directly south, and then swing west and north to the Hadley's south forty. I'll try to hold these Greenbriers here as long as I can. With any luck, we can surround these assholes."

When she was gone, Elvin returned to the bulwarks.

"So we wait 'em out?" Arnold asked.

"For now, yeah. Every minute they sit on their hands, they're digging their own graves."

"Then how come you sound uneasy about it?"

"I don't know," Elvin said. "It just don't feel quite right. If I were leading a raid and saw they'd mustered half the folkward to greet me, I wouldn't sit around in the tree line across the way. I'd get out of there. Just doesn't quite make sense."

"Maybe he was hoping to provoke you, like Sam said. Make you cross the open ground instead."

"Maybe," Elvin said, still scanning the tree line with his binoculars, still unsure what mischief they were about.

The distant sound of gunfire reached Ella when she was over halfway to the Newells'. What made her stop short was the fact that the sporadic pops had come from up ahead, not from the Hadleys' behind her. Her breath, which had just returned to a calmer rate, picked up the pace again.

Gunfire up ahead. At the Newells'. But the battle was supposed to be west of here. Was it unbreds? Could the Greenbriers attack in two places? And if they turned up at one place unforeseen, where else might they lurk?

Ella turned to the quiet forest around her. Her horse nickered as if to remind her that standing still, whatever the reason, would never do. Willing her limp hands to move, she gave the reins a tug and turned the horse around. Best get back to the Hadleys', tell what she'd heard to the watchman, and let the fighters lay down what to do next. She put her heels to the horse and galloped back the way she'd come, only to stop up short a few paces later. The horse gave ample air to its annoyance, but Ella turned him around again with a grunt of frustration. She needed to make sure. Becky had gone before her, and she had to make sure.

"Not again," she prayed aloud as she kicked the horse into another gallop. "Please, God. Not again."

The sound of galloping horses turned Elvin back away from the defenses. Two of the Newell farmhands had no sooner leaped from their exhausted mounts than they stumbled over each other to bear news of disaster and death, cutting short Elvin's sharp rebuke for their tardiness and sloppiness.

"Greenbriers! They ambushed us outta nowhere!"

Elvin whirled back to the distant tree line, his heart falling into his gut as he imagined the hatchet face of his foe staring back at him through the foliage. The whole farce came clear, too late. The joke had been played, and he was the punchline.

Chapter 25

The Shootout at the Newell Homestead

Becky pulled the rifle from the dead hands of one of the Newell brothers. She hadn't known him too well, but well enough to wonder for a moment whether this was all a dream. A bad dream. She'd been given the run-around when she'd first arrived, with the menfolk running this way and that, getting ready for the big battle and telling her she'd need to find the boss and give him the message face-to-face, and Leonard Newell was still coming in, trailing the last of the recalled patrols.

Then came the shots from the south, no sooner than the scouts had all returned. She'd seen the survivors skittering helter-skelter off over the heath as she'd come around the barn for the third time to talk to Mr. Newell, but she hadn't grasped what was going on until she saw the Newell boy go down with a couple arrows in him not far off. A moment of doubt kept her from bolting back to the house, back to her horse, and back to the Hadley's farm. Instead, she'd hid in the gol-darned barn.

Having worked up the gumption to sneak out and arm herself again, Becky checked the gun in her hands while she hugged the ground. No powder in the pan. Not loaded. Figures.

She scrambled to her feet and ducked back into the nearby farm-hand's hut out on the edge of the Newell homestead. The old hinges creaked as she swung the door to, but she didn't hear anything outside. She tried to rein in her chuffing gasps and peeked out through the cracks in the oak boards.

Nothing outside. A ghastly quiet simmered in the late spring heat, a quiet teetering on the edge of chaos.

Becky strained her ears for any hint of sound, even if only from an errant bird or squirrel. She stepped to the other side of the shed, spears of sunlight stabbing at her through knotholes and decaying planks in the wall. No one out yonder. Did they already leave? Didn't burn none of the buildings or take anything yet. They'd have to be in the trees yonder. They'd be coming this way soon, she knew it.

A voice not far off and an answer even closer nearly jolted her into the mad dash for home that had eluded her earlier. Greenbriers. She had to get out of there. The mud-and-straw patch over the back of the hovel yielded to her foot, and she slipped out as quietly as she could.

Not quietly enough.

An order barked for someone to check the shed, and Becky didn't waste any time to see who was coming. She sprinted up through the narrow field, jumped across the ditch, and wormed her way through the overgrown weeds to the Newell fence. In another thirty seconds, she was over the fence and in the open yard. Becky bolted across the stretch of patchy cropped grass and bare earth in a half crouch, whipping around the north side of the house and scattering the goats in the yard before slipping inside through the back door, quiet as a mouse. There was not a living soul to be seen or heard. She was safe, for the moment.

The bad news was her horse no longer waited for her outside. Likely someone had taken whatever mount was handy in their headlong flight from danger.

There was a rifle on the floor among the other scattered items the Newells had left behind. A shotgun lay across the kitchen table. She picked up the extra rifle and loaded it with the ammo strewn across the table, along with her own gun. The shotgun she packed with black powder and buckshot. Now she was properly armed. Even if the Greenbriers hadn't noticed her sneaking into the main house, they'd be here to plunder the homestead. Becky probably had enough time to run out the back and make her way across the wide-open field beyond—Wait, what was that on the floor?

A thin trail of blood snaked across the kitchen floor, over into the tiny living room and up the stairs. Becky followed it up to find a middle-aged woman propped up in a corner, a hand pressed to a bullet wound in her leg, still breathing.

"Mrs. Newell!" Becky exclaimed.

Mrs. Newell looked up at Becky with a face used to famine and misfortune. She'd already resigned herself to whatever was about to happen. "A ball took me straight off. Ain't no one knows I'm here. They all think I'm dead."

"Can you walk?"

"No mor'n ten paces, I'd wager."

"Well, I'll just have to take care of you, won't I?"

"You'd better leave, girl. You might have a bit of time left. Just tell me, did you see everyone make it out okay? Lennie? The kids? Did they make it?"

"I-I don't know. Right now, let's worry about you."

"I'm not worth it right now. Ooooh. Once they get finished looting down at Jesse's, they'll come back here for me."

"Quit frettin' about that. Help'll come soon, and we'll live until then," Becky said as she wrapped Mrs. Newell's leg. She hoped she was right.

Someone let out a harsh cry not far off outside. Becky jumped up, snatched both loaded rifles, and made for the second-story window. She'd grabbed a powder horn with some weight to it along with a handful of musketballs from the downstairs table. Across the yard, the flit and rustle of enemy outlines stirred the brush and grass beyond. Most of them would probably come from the patch of woods about three hundred feet out from the house, but there was cover until about one hundred feet from the porch. She stuck a gun out the window, waited until one of them was out in the open, and shouted at the top of her lungs, "Stop right there!"

The men fell back into the cover of the woods and brush, down into the ditch in front of the fence. Becky herself pulled further back into the house, lest someone try to take a potshot at her. For a moment, there was only silence, then whispering she couldn't make out. God, they were close. Close enough she could nigh well smell them. She wondered if they could smell her, smell her fear. There was a low, hoarse laugh that pricked her ears and the hairs on the back of her neck. Then came the catcalls.

"Just put down that gun, little girl, and we'll treat you real good."

"You think that pea-shooter's dangerous? We'll show you a real gun."

"Come on out, girl, show us a turn! Show us that pretty little behind of your'n!"

"I like it when they play coy!"

Becky saw movement in the bushes but didn't fire. Not enough ammo. Wait for the good shot. Wait for it.

"Aw, come on, honey, talk dirty to me!" They were distracting her. Trying to get around, catch a flank. She had them bottlenecked, though. The Newells had designed the yard to withstand a pigman raid, to funnel them through a single killzone. There were fences on either side of the yard, and if they tried to climb over, she could catch them with an easy shot. Becky switched to another room and posted up on another window to get a better angle. She had them stalled, for now, and they knew it. Or were they toying with her? Becky tried to push the thought from her mind and gripped the stock of her rifle a bit tighter.

"Don't get anxious, honey, we got all day to play. Hey, there's someone you might like to say howdy to. We figured you'd know him."

As if on cue, a scream burst forth from the woods to the south. There was movement in the brush, and then someone tumbled out into the clear area behind the Greenbriers in the ditch. He tried to get up, but there was something wrong with his legs. Becky's eyes narrowed.

It was Jesse Newell. The Greenbriers had hobbled him with a couple vicious gashes to the back of his legs.

A bow twanged, and Jesse jerked as an arrow pierced his thigh. An anguished plea for mercy rent the air before someone shot him again near the rump. They cackled like boys pulling a crude prank. Becky's vision swam. *They're torturing him for sport.*

"What's happening? What's going on out there?" Mrs. Newell cried out. Becky turned to face her. Gone was the resignation. The look that replaced it was something like fear, only more ghastly. "Who have they got?"

Becky didn't answer. Couldn't. Jesse was Mrs. Newell's oldest surviving son.

They shot him again. His screaming shudder made the arrows in him quiver like porcupine quills.

"*Who have they got?!*"

Something inside Becky snapped, but rather than drive her to panic, whatever broke in her stilled the tremor in her hands and cooled her mind. She fired her rifle, and all screams ceased.

This was the fool move the Greenbriers were looking out for, and Becky knew it. When the first Greenbrier rose up from the ditch to rush the house, she had already brought up the second rifle and pulled the hammer back to full-cocked.

Becky took her time and lined up her shot, just like her father had taught her. She squeezed the trigger and stopped the intruder with a lead ball to the gut. The Greenbrier jerked and stumbled, falling forward on his face with his gun just beyond his reach.

Becky grabbed the shotgun and brought it to her shoulder. The Greenbriers scrambled back into the ditch. She waited for someone else to risk it. No one did. She waited for a beat, then reached to reload the first rifle. She fumbled with a prepared cartridge and rammed it on down, ball, paper, powder, and all.

The man she'd shot wasn't dead yet. He began moaning, bleeding and writhing on the ground.

"Aw, what's the matter?" Becky called out. "I'm fresh out, I promise. Come and get me."

They didn't answer. The downed Greenbrier went silent for a moment, then began moaning again.

Becky sensed movement downstairs. How did they get in? Becky reached for the shotgun, then relaxed as she heard a whisper she recognized.

"Becky?" Ella hissed below.

"Up here. Keep it down. Greenbriers out in front."

"I heard. I got a horse out back," Ella said as she crept up the stairs.

"Good. Help Mrs. Newell. She's hurt. I'll cover until you get downstairs."

Ella stepped forward to help Mrs. Newell up, offering her shoulder for support. Mrs. Newell barely seemed to notice her.

"Come on, Mrs. Newell. Time to go," Ella said, kneeling down and rubbing the woman's back.

"Kill me. Please," Mrs. Newell said without tears in her eyes or a crack in her voice.

"Ella, I don't know—" Becky said.

"Shh, we're okay," Ella answered before turning to the wounded woman. "Mrs. Newell, I know you done been laid out somethin' awful, but I just want you to stand up for me right now. Can you do that for me? Good, good. I know it hurts, Mrs. Newell. Lean on me. There now."

Though Mrs. Newell turned a lighter shade of white, getting her to her feet seemed to put some life back into her. "My babies, I want to see my babies—"

"I know, I know. Don't think about them right now. Just take a step for me. Just a step, now. One thing at a time; you can do it."

Once Ella coaxed Mrs. Newell into moving, the two of them got downstairs at a limp.

Becky turned her attention back to the Greenbriers just in time to receive a barrage of gunfire. She threw herself away from the window and hugged the floor as bullets punched up through the window into the ceiling. Age-old plaster rained down on her head. Becky snatched up the rifle at her side and switched to another bedroom, keeping her head down. She knew what was coming. She peeked out the window to see five Greenbriers running for the house. Ready or not, here they come. She pulled up her rifle and fired, dropping one of them with a bullet to the hip.

Becky slung the rifle over her shoulder, grabbed the remaining rifle and double-barreled shotgun, and bolted down the stairs. "Ella! We've got to get out of here right now!"

Becky hit the first floor running and heard the footsteps on the front porch. She spun and leveled the second rifle at the front door as she backed out through the kitchen. A Greenbrier head poked around the corner. Becky gave them a parting shot that missed but made them think twice before sticking their heads out again.

"Come on, Becky, let's go!"

Becky turned and kicked open the back door. Mrs. Newell sat astride the horse, with Ella supporting her from below.

"You ride up front with Mrs. Newell," Ella ordered.

"But—"

"I'm not a good enough rider to keep Mrs. Newell in the saddle and get away fast enough. You know that."

Becky jumped into the saddle without further protest, but she tossed the shotgun to Ella. "Take that, just in case."

Holding Mrs. Newell with one hand, Becky helped Ella up behind her with the other. Becky put her heels to the horse's flanks as the front door exploded open on the other side of the house, and the three women were off as fast as the horse could manage.

With thundering hearts and hooves, the three women rode out across the wide-open field for the safety of the vale a half mile away. Ella struggled to keep seated on the horse's rump, her sweating hands wrapped around Becky's middle for dear life. A low stone fence separating the garden from the field jumped towards her, then under her as her horse sailed over it, and Ella was a bit closer to safety, and still in her seat.

Ella heard the bang of gunshots and the whizz of bullets dangerously close around her. She ducked and prayed she wasn't as big of a target as she thought she was. A more carefully aimed shot missed them, but only barely. The horse wasn't as lucky. A bullet nicked it in the rump, and when the world stopped bucking and spinning, Ella found herself facedown in the grass.

When Ella came out of the stunned shock of the fall, her surroundings assaulted her senses. The blue sky stretched above, and the roots and dirt and coiled grass spread out beneath her splayed fingers. She could feel the ridges on the blades of grass with her fingertips. She could even feel the pounding of the horse's rapidly retreating hooves and those of approaching Greenbrier horses. And the smells—damp, cloyed earth and her own nervous sweat mixed with a pungent vibrancy. Did imminent death always make a body feel so alive?

Ella couldn't move. She'd had the shotgun in her hand when the horse threw her, so it must lay somewhere nearby. But could she find it? The sound of horses drew closer. She chose not to move. It was an easy choice to make, seeing as how her limbs wouldn't work even if she wanted them to.

"We've got one down, here."

"Is it her?"

"Can't tell. Want to keep chasing the others?"

"No. We're pushing our luck. Let's light up the house and get out of here. Wait," one of the Greenbriers said. Ella held her breath, feeling two pairs of eyes on her, studying her.

"We've got a live one." A saddle creaked, a pair of feet hit the ground, and a machete slid from its sheath.

Ella's brain somehow found the strings marionetting her arms and legs again, and she bolted.

"Hey!"

She ran away from the two Greenbriers and their horses and glimpsed, out of the corner of her eye, the wooden stock of the shotgun poking up through the grass ahead of her. She dove for the weapon and fished through the hay, her lungs choking for air.

"Well, look what we have here," the dismounted Greenbrier mused behind her, scything the tall grass out of the way with the blade of his matchet.

Ella rolled upright, leveling the shotgun at a Greenbrier not much older than her. She ticked off the safety. The Greenbrier froze, sword in hand, his partner fumbling with a breech-loading musket not far behind.

Ella struggled to hold the shotgun steady. The older Greenbrier behind had aimed his own gun at her, but he didn't shoot. At this range, the young Tucker woman was liable to hit them both with one shot.

"D-drop your gun," Ella stammered.

"Bullshit," the older Greenbrier spat. "You drop your gun."

"We all know what happens if I drop my gun."

"Well, we know happens if we drop ours, don't we?"

"I've got the both of you outgunned."

The young Greenbrier in the front motioned for his partner to stop. He squinted at Ella with keen eyes and said, carefully, "Take it easy, girl. You don't want to hurt anyone, do you?"

"But I will if I have to."

"But you don't want to."

Ella didn't answer for a couple decade-long seconds. "Yes," she said finally, "I do. I *really* do." The barrel of the shotgun shook a little more. "You all killed my big brother. You likely killed half of the Newells. You almost got Mrs. Newell, who was the nicest lady what ever lived. Why would you do something like that?"

She got no answer. Maybe there was none. She was a bug to them—a bug with a shotgun, but a bug no less. She had every right to blaze away at them.

And yet...

The barrel of the shotgun stopped shaking and lowered to the ground as Ella clicked the safety on. Her shoulders sagged as she surrendered herself to the mercy of the enemy.

The foremost Greenbrier cocked his head in bemused curiosity, but only for a moment. He strode forward with grim purpose. His sword came up for the killing stroke, but Ella didn't look away. If she would die, she wanted this Greenbrier to see her eyes as he killed her.

The killing stroke never came. Ella heard what she thought was the wind picking up, and then the young Greenbrier hitched backward with an arrow bristling from his shoulder.

Ella dove back to the ground, covering her head as both Greenbriers remounted their horses, one of them shrieking and clutching at the arrow buried inside him. At the crest of the hill, a single hooded figure strung another arrow and sent the bolt whizzing just past the two Greenbriers. The horses and their riders galloped off, but Ella did not watch them leave when she raised her head. Rather, she looked up to the dark silhouette of her rescuer.

She gasped. “O-Omar?”

The figure turned and walked back the way he’d come, disappearing over the hill to the north.

Ella stood up, wavered, and then collapsed again, shaking and heaving, finally alone.

Chapter 26

On the Warpath

Elvin thundered onto the Newell homestead at the head of some thirty clansmen, himself a fearsome avenging angel, his son a whipped dog. Already the advance scouts were dousing the fire at the entrance of the house.

Elvin leaped from his horse. "Goddamn sons of bitches! How'd it happen? How'd it happen?"

"Greenbriers come up from the south!" Leonard Newell cried, on the verge of hysteria. He'd returned with the advance scouts as soon as Becky Brody's miraculous escape with his wounded wife had become known. "We were so busy readying ourselves for an attack to the west, we never gave a thought to our defenses. They were all supposed to be at the Hadleys'! And they stole my children from me, my dear-born children..." He turned away, a shaking hand rising to cover his mouth.

"What are you gonna do about it, watchman?" one of the gathering clansmen shouted.

"As surely as I'm the son of Paul McDaniel, I'll spill two drops of Greenie blood for every one of ours."

Someone among the outraged Tuckers muttered, "Paul McDaniel would have spilled ten."

Elvin whirled to face the grumbler. "Who said that?" No answer. "What scum-sucking coward wants to say that to my face? Who thinks I won't take out a war party this very night?"

Elvin ripped a machete from its sheath and leveled it at the crowd around him. "You think I ain't Paul McDaniel enough? Face me like a man and you'll see how much of my father I got in me!" His eyes went wild in that way those who had known his father had seen. No one took up the challenge.

Elvin stormed off, his son following at a safe distance. Ralph would sleep outside tonight. Experience had taught all the McDaniel children to avoid their father at times like these.

Becky found Ella sitting on the stoop of the Newell house, staring out at nothing.

"Ella, you're alive!" Becky came running to Ella's side. "I'm so sorry. The horse went wild at the shot. I thought you were a goner."

"They thought I was a goner too. I guess that's why I'm alive."

Becky paused. "Are you okay?"

"Sure. I just need a minute." Ella kept staring off into the distance.

Becky sat down next to Ella and put a hand on her shoulder. That was all it took. In an instant, Ella was shaking and holding onto her friend for dear life. Becky held tight, too. She'd seen what Greenbriers did to their prey.

The night was a grim one. The Newell family had lost two daughters and a son, cutting their family in half. Five other Tucker farmhands had been killed. The Greenbriers had damaged the house and the barn, slaughtered more animals than the Newells could afford to lose, and ran off with a great store of supplies. After such a hard winter, the raid pauperized a once great family of the clan.

The safe return of Mrs. Newell—whom everyone had thought dead—marked the one bright spot. It made for small comfort in the face of such loss, a loss made greater when Mrs. Newell's wound went sour. Dr. Bernhard's saw took her leg amid her poppy-addled wails. Still, one-legged was far better than dead, and Mrs. Newell pronounced Becky Brody as the cause for her escape. The clan took care to honor the young woman that very evening. Becky, in turn, owed her escape to her friend Ella Holland, who in her own turn bowed her head and withdrew into her home and her room to think about what she had done, as her father ordered.

"Dadgum that girl. What a headache and a half. She'll be eating nothing but dry biscuits for a week for pulling a stunt like that," Phil Holland muttered as he helped Amos saddle up.

"She did save a couple Tuckers, though. And Becky Brody turns out to be quite a fighter," Amos mused. "Well worth the saving, I'd say."

"That's all well and good, Amos, but it's going to get her killed or cause her family trouble, or both. We can't brook that way of thinking all the time. There ain't no call for it."

"I suppose I don't quite understand it either, sir."

"She won't ever learn. It's good to fight for the clan, Amos. Don't you forget that. It's a mighty high standin,' as standin's go. But she's my daughter, and that oughta stand a mite higher. It's good to do a good thing, but you can carry it too far. You got to pick your battles and know when to drop something."

"Like when I carried Dale back when he got shot?"

"I'm sorry, Amos, I didn't mean that. That's a different thing. Gimme the tongs, will you? I got to heat it up a little before we give her a layer of polish." Phil pursed his lips in concentration. "You and Ella are different. How can I say this?" Phil sat down and wiped his hands on a rag dirtier than he was.

"Ella's always been like this," Phil said, sighing. "A little mousy thing with a glass heart. She would always come home from school crying because Cephas Finch pulled her hair, or because he pulled some other girl's hair, even. Any little thing. She wouldn't make too much of a fuss about it, more often than not, but she let things get to her. I remember when she was ten years old and I caught a rabbit out in our garden with a trap. It was still alive when she found it, and she actually tried to free the dumb thing. She wanted to nurse it back to health. Can you believe it? She cried for days after that."

Phil shook his head. "She didn't have the right temper for this life. Too frail. If you were to ask me which of my first two children would have died, I would have said her. Jim was a strong boy, stronger than me. He would have grown up to be a clan elder for sure. I was startin' to teach him the trade, and he was learnin' fast. He killed his first pigman when he was nine years old. He had himself a good sense of humor, too. He was a real goofball. Always roping around. But he knew how to get steel-eyed when he needed to. How does a kid like Jim die before his time while a kid like Ella survives?

"I tried to toughen Ella up. When she found that rabbit in the trap, I kept her from saving it. She had to know that there weren't no call for that kind of behavior. I put an ax in her hand and made her kill the critter. I reckon it was a mean thing to do, but life is a mean thing. She toughened up a bit when Jim died, at least."

"I guess that's what it takes for some of us," Amos said.

The town bell clanged, and both master and apprentice dropped their things and froze. The bell clapper's easy backswing set their shoulders at ease: it was a call for a town meeting, not an alarm.

The clan packed the meeting-hall tighter than a Sunday morning service. Nearly all the women and a good chunk of the men had come in from the farms, and even half the Grierson settlement filled a seat.

Sam Chambers rose from his own seat and walked out in front of the seated elders to give air to their decision. "Our fine clan," he began, then broke off, his voice choked with feeling. "Our fine clan didn't set out for a fight. We had no want for it. But the Greenbriers have brought a fight to us, laid it on our doorstep, and threatened the lives of our loved ones. This we cannot bear. The Newells have suffered a foul blow, as have many of those here in town. This we cannot bear. Our farmers are not safe to till the land, not safe to bring in the harvest, not even safe to walk out their own door. This we cannot bear. And so, until our lands are safe again, the elders have chosen to give Elvin McDaniel the final say in clan matters." Sam returned to his seat.

Elvin McDaniel stood to address the clan as its leader. "Now see you here. I don't aim to drag this out any longer than we need to, so we're all gonna get this done. We're right in the middle of the growing season, so everybody—and I do mean *everybody*—is going to chip in here somehow. I want a fighting force not less than two hundred. I want men and women to turn out, bear arms if needed, tote sundries otherwise. You have until this evening to gather again with whatever you plan to bring into Greenbrier territory. I want shotguns, rifles, sixers, bows, spears, swords, and knives. I want draft animals and carts. I want yards of whatever cloth you can lay ahold of. I want bandages, shovels, and pickaxes. I want rope, dried meat and vegetables, dry cheese and stale bread. If I say you're in the attack force, you're in the attack force. If I say you're in the baggage train, that's where you are. And God have mercy on any of you poor bastards who turn tail without my say-so."

The Reverend closed the meeting by giving his blessing. "God is on our side, and if God is for us, who can stand against us?"

The clan assembled itself into the strike force Elvin called for. Tuckers aged fourteen to fifty turned out and waited for Elvin to look over each kit in person.

Elvin made his way down the line. He'd taken the family's Kalashnikov—a piece with as much stormy history behind it as his own breedstock—from the mantle. He wore it slung over his shoulder in place of his musket.

"Nigel, where's your brother?" Elvin stopped in front of the carpenter's boy.

"We drew straws for it. Ma didn't want both of us out in the shootin'."

"I don't care what your ma thinks. Tell him to get his ass out here."

On down the line. "You. Finch. Get that peg leg of your'n out of my line. Get your cousin to stand in for you. Hal, where's your family's Armalite?"

"Elvin, I only got fourteen rounds for it—"

"If you've got more than none, that's enough for me. Go fetch it."

The watchman kept on, casting off unwanted volunteers here, drafting more family members there, until he stopped in front of the butcher.

"Arnie."

"Elvin." Arnold nodded to the watchman.

Elvin sighed. "Arnie, I've got some news for you. Gonna have the clan near emptied. Somebody's gonna have to stay behind and look after things."

Arnold's face twitched a tick, as if Elvin had slapped him. "I never asked you to spare me a fight."

"If I got something wrong, if the Greenbriers get a mind to jump us again, I won't have spared you nothing."

"You got someone to nay-say you?"

"I got a plan, Arnie."

"Don't give me that, Elvin. Everybody needs a naysayer they can trust. I ain't heard your plan."

"Fine. We go down, single-file, quiet-like, hit 'em from the east."

"And if you're spotted?"

"We'll have the numbers on whatever scouts come our way."

"I don't know, Elvin. We've never had us a war party this big, not even since the Scavenging Years. If something goes wrong—"

"Things always go wrong, Arnie. I never stick with a plan longer than I need to. And I have you here if the worst should happen."

"This ain't the job I want."

"That's why I'd want you to have it," Elvin said. "Only a fool wants to be a watchman."

"Find yourself a naysayer, Elvin. I won't abide by you running off and gettin' killed because you didn't have enough sense to know when to run and when to stay." Arnold Brody slapped a hand on Elvin's shoulder, a gesture which Elvin returned before moving on without a word.

Elvin stopped to look at the remaining Taylor boys, Amos and Harvey.

"Y'all ready for a fight?" Elvin asked.

"We are," Amos answered. "We're here for Dale."

At the end of the line, Elvin's own son stood at silent attention. He'd gotten taller in the last year. A wisp of fuzz teased his upper lip and chin. The freckles remained, but his cheeks had drawn down.

"You ready for a fight, son?" Elvin asked.

His son didn't meet Elvin's gaze. "I'll do my best, sir. For the clan."

Elvin's own father wouldn't have accepted that answer, but it was enough for him. "It's all we can ask of any Tucker. I've taught you all you need to know when the time comes." He turned to mount his horse, then stopped. "And son?"

"Yeah?" Ralph looked up at his father.

Elvin placed a curved knife in Ralph's hand. "When you kill, you do it without pity, without mercy. Unbreds and ubermenschen alike look at you with people eyes when they get up close. Don't let that shake you."

Ella Holland knocked on the schoolmaster's door. When he answered, she noticed he'd already dressed out for the journey, a sheathed sword at his side, an unstrung bow attached to his travel pack.

"Miss Holland? What's the matter?"

Ella chewed her lip, having already drawn back the hand she'd knocked with and folded it behind her back. "I think this is a mistake."

Mr. Chambers shook his head. "I ... don't know what you mean."

"I mean we ought not go to war."

"I'm afraid there's not much you can do about it, Miss Holland."

"But *you* can. That's why I came to talk to you."

"What exactly do you think I can do about it?"

"Talk to Elvin. He's running things right now. We can try us some middlespeakin', 'fore it comes to killin'."

Chambers shook his head. "It's already come to killing, Ella."

"It's not too late to stop."

"I'm afraid it is."

"The Greenbriers done had their smack-back. They won't be traipsin' here again if we don't give 'em cause to."

"You willing to bet your life on that?"

Ella folded her arms. "Sure."

Sam sighed. "What do you want me to say to the watchman? We should let the Greenbriers have the last word and hope they don't get the idea to come in and finish the job?"

"You could tell him the truth. That war means signing away the lives of our own, only for the chance of hurting them worse. We hit them now, even if we win, we're marking the gravestones of some honest clansfolk on down the road."

"Ella, I don't like this any more than you do. Believe me. But times like these, trying to stop the Tuckers from avenging their kin, you might as well try to stop the rain from falling."

"Revenge is a lousy reason to kill a person."

"You'd better be careful repeating that idea." Chambers' face darkened. "If the wrong clansman heard you say that now, you might find yourself banished for befriending the enemy."

"They wouldn't do that."

"Elvin would. He'd see it as an insult to the memories of those killed."

"I've lost someone, too. And as much as I'd like to see the ones that did it hung, I'd much rather not lay down the lives of other Tuckers to do it."

"It's out of my hands. As much as I want people to get along, politics don't work that way. If another clan senses weakness in us, we're just carrion for the vultures to pick at."

"There was a time when they would have been our fellow Americans."

Sam Chambers grimaced and looked away. "I'd give anything for those days. You know I would. But it's not that simple. We don't think the same anymore. We aren't the same. I know the history better than most people in the clan. It's not just us and the Greenbriers. This fight went back before even the world ended. Our kind stood for the old ways, for science guided by right and wrong. Their kind, and everything they represent, are only interested in *can.* Not what the effects will be, not who it will hurt, not what it will cost, but only whether they *can* do it. I don't think much of the Reverend's moralizing, but he's right about this: the arrogance of the ubermenschen ended the world, and the Greenbriers carried that torch on past the end. To their kind, the end of the world was just the price they had to pay to get rid of *us.*" Sam Chambers straightened up. "I don't want a fight. But there's no fixing that rift. The Greenbriers wouldn't stand for it."

"You don't know that."

"I don't know that the sun will set this evening, but you won't see me betting the lives of my fellow Tuckers on the chance it won't."

"Sounds like something the watchman would say." Ella was already turning away, her shoulders sagging.

"Maybe so. Like I said, he's calling the shots now."

Chapter 27

Plans Are Useless

As the first day drew to a close, the sun slid down the dome of a massive hill that rose up from the bottom land like a cornbread muffin. A narrow glen plunged wedgelike into the side of the hill as if someone had cut a piece out of the cornbread. The great Tucker war party filtered out of the woods, crossed the meadow at the base of the hill, and filed into the wide mouth of the glen. The few pigmen who'd tailed the war party for the last several miles broke off now that there was no longer any hope of picking off stragglers.

One of the older Tuckers who had visited this glen long ago said it had once been a limestone quarry. A seasonal trickle worked its way down the craggy riprap at the back of the glen before wending through the more or less bare ravine floor. Time or human activity had pulled down the once sheer walls of the quarry into steep banks of sun-bleached gravel. The dell's original U-shape had weathered into more of a V, and only scrubby weeds had wormed their roots into the hardscrabble slope.

Still, the little dell nestled itself far enough into the mountain that it made itself nearly invisible unless approached from the mouth, and the forward Tucker scouts had found it still neatly abandoned. Some three hundred Tucker fighters and transport folk made for a tight fit, but it would only be for one night, and Elvin preferred the close packing. Better hidden that way.

Folks laid out bedrolls on the softer deposited silt of the valley floor and raised up some shelter here and there, but Elvin made it clear: no fires, no foraging, no hunting. Lookouts cast about not more than a hundred feet from the mouth of the canyon, more to make sure the camp stayed well-hid and quiet than to watch for enemies.

And the Tuckers *were* well-hid, except for the big wrinkle in Elvin's plan that lay in the woods across the meadow.

"You worried about the unbreds, Pa?" Ralph McDaniel asked as they set up the watchposts for the night. The pigmen were out of sight, for now, but the watches could hear their calls further out.

"I am, a mite." Elvin swore softly, shaking his head. "There ain't enough to tangle with us, but we'll be dragging a stuck plow the whole way. We get much further into Greenbrier territory, we might as well toot a horn while we march."

"What do we do?"

"Can't do nothin' now. Wait and see. Maybe they'll get wise and clear out on their own. Too risky to go chasin' after them now."

Elvin and the war-fighting elders met outside his tent in a close circle, some standing, some sitting, some leaning up against the canyon wall. A couple topographic maps lay splayed out underneath them in the waning evening light. A young man came up to the circle and rested his chin on one fist as he sat down.

"Amos, this is an elder's meeting," Johnny Grierson said, his brow furrowing over his one good eye. "Best get a move-on. Don't need too many cooks in the kitchen."

"He can stay," Elvin said.

"Why?"

"'Cause I said so, that's why."

"Are we letting youngsters make our battle plans?"

"I'm letting him watch. Drop it." Elvin's irritation passed as quickly as it had boiled up. He pointed down to the map in front of them. "So I reckon this puts us about halfway between town and the Greenbrier clan. The camp followers and most of our supplies will stay here. We'll get us a couple runners to keep in touch. I want this to be our fallback place if aught goes awry."

The elders nodded.

"The plan is to get down there as sneaky as we can with two hundred fighters. Scouts stay within eyesight. If we make it to Greenbrier territory okay, we'll push in and hit 'em from the east. I want to take advantage of our numbers and hit them in as many places as we can. Which means we'll split up into three groups, spread out over a few miles, and march until we hit something. We'll also have runners keep in touch with the strike teams, so as we can support each other if need be.

"Now, this is all saying we don't get found on the way down there. If we do, we go after whatever found us, and hard. Then we change directions and hit 'em from another angle. If they try to hit us out in the woods, we beat the living tar out of 'em. Whatever happens, we stay loose and limber now, y'hear? I don't want to hear anyone hollerin' at me that we're not following the plan. We fight where we can hurt them more than they hurt us. That's what we're here for. Questions?"

Amos raised his hand. "Is that the best plan we got?"

"You don't think this'll work, Mr. Taylor?"

"It might work, but it seems pretty shaky to me."

"That's why I'm telling you to stay loose."

"But they'll be expecting us. And really we're doing the same thing they did, just with more people. Seems like they'd have a plan for that."

"Like what?"

"I don't know, I'm not a Greenbrier."

"Well this is a fine howdy-do," Johnny said. "Glad we're bringing the young upstarts into our war meetings now. They don't like our plans, but they don't got any better ideas."

Amos squared his shoulders. "I think we should do something that puts Bill's nitrogel to good use."

"Like what?" Elvin asked, arms crossed. The other men stared at Amos.

Amos shook his head and shrugged. "I ... I don't know."

When Elvin shook the morning dew off his sleeping roll to check up with the last sentry of the night, he found several of the elders already up with the sentry, sharing a pair of field glasses in the dim early dawn.

"Anything new?" Elvin asked.

One of the elders pointed, handing Elvin the binoculars. "Look at that. Up in the timber, yonder."

They could make out the distinctive pink skin of a pigman waiting and watching in the woods, barely hidden by the surrounding brush. One of the Tuckers drew a bow, but the pigman skittered away.

"It'll be back. Just keeping tabs on us, seeing what we'll do."

"Well, what will we do?" Shane Bunton asked. "Fred could hear enough commotion during his watch, he reckoned twice the number we saw yesterday. That's enough to give us a headache, no matter what we do."

"Even a hundred pigmen couldn't take on our war party," Clyde McDaniel said.

"No, but they could pick off our scouts or harass our back line. I don't want to march fifteen miles today with these unbreds dogging us over hill and dale."

Clyde didn't yield. "We've got the numbers to take 'em if'n we can keep 'em from running away."

"And how do you reckon we do that? We only got one direction we can attack them from. You can see from here how loose they're playin' it," Johnny Grierson said, spitting to the side. "Just waitin' for us to screw up."

"What if we scatter 'em good enough we can break out and put a mile or so between us before they can regroup? I reckon we could lose 'em that a-way."

"I reckon we will. But what do we do when they come back here where all our wives and young'uns are holding the camp? You think they can hold out?" Job Brody asked.

The elders went silent.

"I don't reckon we've got a choice," Elvin said. "It's a risk, I'll grant you, but so is wasting time jawing about it. If we go down, hit the Greenbriers hard, and hightail it on out of there, we're liable to make it back in time."

None of the elders said anything.

"Fellas, I got kin here, same as you. I got kin back in town, same as you. If you thought there wouldn't be a risk, then you've been drinkin' some mighty strong whiskey. I'm sorry, I just don't see any other way to do it."

"There is another way," Amos said.

Johnny Grierson threw his hands up. "Not again."

"You all agree that if we run out and attack, the pigmen'll just run off, yes?"

"What's your point?" Elvin asked.

"And if we leave with most of the fighters, the pigmen'll break off and stake out the camp again, yes?"

"Your point, Amos."

"We could loop back around and trap them right here in this box canyon."

The elders looked at each other. "It would take care of the unbred problem," Shane said.

Elvin crossed his arms. "Okay, well what about the fact that our bait for this little trap has to sit in a *box canyon*. We picked this place for a hideout, not a fortress. If something bad happens, we'll have half the clan tryin' to climb these banks with pigmen nippin' at their heels."

"But what would that take? Three hundred? Four hundred?" Amos looked around for an elder to give him an estimate.

"I'd be surprised if there's fifty," Job Brody said, stroking his beard.

Elvin shook his head. "So you want us to hold off our main attack for a full extra day to go beatin' around in the timber huntin' pigmen. We can't afford the time."

"I don't think we can afford not to, Elvin. You wanted sneaky, but a company of pigmen raising Cain is just about as unlike sneaky as you can get. Have people back at the camp set up a bunch of stakes, and I bet they can hold them long enough for us to get around them. I say we put it to a vote."

"This ain't a democracy, Shane. I'll keep your advice in mind if I'm in the mood for it."

"Fair enough, fair enough. Then what'll it be, boss?"

Elvin sucked his teeth, scratched the back of his neck, and sighed. "We're far enough away from Greenbrier territory yet ... I reckon we can try Amos' plan and not have to worry about a patrol picking us up. But whatever we do, we do with bows and spears. That's it. No gunpowder." Elvin leaned down and drew a crude outline in the dirt, explaining the plan as if it were his own. "We charge out here, whoopin' and hollerin', not so many that the pigmen think we're all leaving, but enough to get 'em runnin'. I don't much care which way they run, as long as we can get them moving and break line of sight. Once we've pushed out far enough to make a good show and break contact, we wait until noon and head back. Sooner if we hear a gunshot. And I better not hear any shooting unless it's a goddamn emergency. Understood?"

Heads nodded.

"We come back, catch a passel of pigmen if we're lucky. If we're luckier, we'll have scared them all off and won't have to worry about 'em.

The town was empty like Ella had never seen it before. Only a smattering of able-bodied clansmen remained, and those few kept narrow watches within a mile from the walls, and not beyond the farthest edge of the farthest field. There were more hogs and chickens around now than people. Children, their mothers, and the old folks seemed about the only ones left inside the city, and if the Greenbriers had known it, they likely could have marched straight through the gates without taking so much as a stray arrow from the Tuckers. Arnold Brody's butchery had ceased entirely, with patrols and check-ins taking up both his and his wife's time now. Mr. Brody's nerves seemed to set everybody else's on edge, including Ella. No telling where an attack might come from, no telling when the war party would be back, and with how many survivors, if there even were any survivors to speak of.

With her pa gone off to battle and Bill Puckett out on patrol, Ella gave herself to the watching of the young ones alongside her friend Sophie. The kids, it seemed, had caught the same nervous energy that lay low on the town like a stifling fog. The children were cantankerous and moody, arguing and fighting one minute while whooping and carrying-on the next. The handful of volunteers could not corral the riotous imps to the clan main where they belonged, and Ella found herself chasing some stirred-up five-year-old down the street when he didn't heed her call to return.

"You're a bullhusker! You're a bullhusker!" he shouted over his shoulder at Ella in a mix of defiant orneriness and playfulness that had become mighty wearisome in the past half hour.

"If you want me to be the bullhusker, you have to go back to the main!" Ella called back, but too late. The boy had darted around the corner, down an alley. "I know you can hear me, Noah Hadley. Just because your pa's gone, doesn't mean the whole town's your playground."

She chased the rascal all over, losing his trail more than once, finally finding herself at the wall. Surely he didn't climb over? She scrambled up a ladder to the gangway and peered across the kill-way to the forest. She saw movement in the brush and was about to call out to Noah when the boy called out to her from the town side of the wall, behind her.

"You're a bullhusker, Miss Ella! A big, fat bullhusker!"

Ella looked back to the town to see Noah retreating the way he'd first come, then she turned again to the woods, where she'd seen movement. Could have been an animal—possibly an unbred—but it had seemed human. There! She saw the movement again, further in the woods, and picked out a head of thinning white hair from amidst the greenery. What in tarnation? Noah would go back to the clan main when he knew Ella wasn't chasing him anymore. Whichever of the clan elderfathers was running around in the woods, though... She thought of old Mrs. Finch, dead by her own hand when she'd outlived her usefulness. Ella slipped down from the wall, crossed the open kill-way, and broke through the tree line.

Arnold Brody chawed on the same piece of sassafras root he'd been working on since he'd gotten out of bed. He'd had more than his fair share of the stuff yesterday after the war party had left town, and he'd scarcely slept a wink last night. With luck, the Tuckers would hit the Greenbriers today, light out for the hills, and be back safe and sound in two days' time. But he knew better. Luck didn't care to grace his clan too often. Hence his long hours in the crook of a great oak tree with a primed rifle in his hand and a chaw of sassafras between his teeth.

The danger wasn't great, he reminded himself. The war party stood to take the most risk, which was why he'd forbidden his daughter to take up with them. It so happened to be the same reason Becky had gone against his wishes and lit out for a tussle in the hills anyway. There was no stopping her; she'd taken that all-fired mulish turn from her mother, and he'd never known a disagreement in his married life he'd come out on top of. He was too proud of his daughter to lock her up anyhow, but he knew what happened to folks when things went bad out there. Hence the sassafras.

But Elvin knew what he was doing, and he'd taken men enough to balance out the risk. If they got in a scrape, they'd likely claw their way out of it through sheer manpower. It was a luxury he didn't have. There were scarcely ten able bodies in the whole town for him to call up when the need arose. Hence the—

A twig snapped a-ways off, drawing Arnold's eyes to a slight rustling of leaves. He froze, wide-eyed, the sassafras hanging from a now open mouth. He slowly pulled the hammer back on his rifle, but he didn't move otherwise.

What he glimpsed through the shrouding brush was far, far worse than even his nightmares last night had churned up.

Chapter 28

Mind Games

Ralph McDaniel stepped up beside his schoolmate, Nigel Bunton, along with some thirty other camp watchers left behind to form the anvil to Elvin's hammer. It had been four hours since his father's big war party had sallied into the woods, and the settling heat of a summer midday was sapping their energy. Job Brody had ordered the tall meadow grass scythed back up to the first scattered trees about fifty paces beyond the hollow's entrance. It would make for a kill-way neat enough to handle a nasty pigman rush.

The forest finally stirred again.

"String your bows, lads," Job ordered, though he himself still held his prized thirty-aught-six bolt-action.

Young men and women both bent bows to their strings and stuck arrows in the ground at their shooting positions as a full line of pigmen came out of the woods in front of them, walking nearly upright. Ralph scrambled to nock an arrow, but the pigmen stopped out in the open.

Job put his hand up. "Wait. Hold your fire for a second."

The pigmen stared across the open meadow between them.

Becky Brody broke the silence. "What in tarnation's goin' on, Job?"

The pigmen turned and walked away as calmly as they'd come.

Ralph eased off the string, his mouth agape. "What the—"

Nigel's cousin jerked as his collarbone split open with a loud *pop*, a red mist in the air where he had stood. A gunshot cracked from near the top of the steep-walled glen. Ralph turned to look to the source of the sound behind their line, up and to the right. A smattering of dark human shapes looked down on him.

Ralph blinked. His senses gave him all the information he needed in an instant, but his brain lagged like the report of a distant rifle.

A volley of flanking gunfire rained down on the thirty forward guards from the right side of the canyon, kicking up dirt, ricocheting off stones and steel, and cutting down another unlucky Tucker to Ralph's left.

Job turned on his knee to face the new threat. "Sheeeiitfire! Back to camp!"

The Tucker defenders abandoned the forward line at the edge of the meadow and scurried back for the scant cover in the dell. Ralph saw the dozens of men and women back in the camp scamper about like so many rats, except for the few scattered heaps where a guard or camp follower seemed to founder. Ralph skidded to a halt—still twenty paces off from the canyon wall—when he realized Nigel Bunton was no longer at his side. He ducked behind a rock and turned to see Nigel wailing in despair as he tried to heave his cousin up onto one shoulder.

"Help me, Ralph! You gotta help me!" Nigel called.

Ralph waved him over. "Leave 'im, Nigel! You're gonna get kill't!"

Nigel's face twisted as if he'd been shot, but he dropped his cousin and dashed back for cover next to Ralph, his body, at least, intact.

Nigel's cousin writhed on the ground a few paces off from them, reaching out with a shaking, bloody hand, eyes wide and frightened.

From behind them, Job Brody called to the two young men. "Get your hind ends outta there! Move!"

Ralph struggled to his feet again in a low crouch and took off toward cover at the base of the steep slope, Nigel on his heels. Ralph sensed the whump of a Greenbrier rifle atop the hill and heard the bullet ricochet off the flinty canyon floor to his right. His heart stuttered as his feet forgot how to run and he scrambled across the last distance on all fours.

They're trying to kill me, he thought to himself. *Somebody up there saw me and tried to kill me.* His face felt fuzzy, prickly. His brain still hadn't caught up.

His fellow Tuckers squirmed in around him on their bellies or backs, crawling over each other to buy a couple more inches of cover.

Nigel hit the dirt next to him, his eyes welling with panicked tears. "We left him, Ralph. Just left him lying there..."

Amos Taylor wiped the sweat from his face and sighed as a Tucker hawed at a straggling pigman staring at them some fifty yards ahead. It had been like this all morning. Every time they'd thought they'd scared and scattered the pigmen enough to quit the chase, the pigmen would double back and tail the Tuckers instead of the other way around. It was like the pigmen were taunting them.

It had become tiresome enough that Elvin had ordered the war party to string their bows and stick any pigman they saw. They'd bagged a couple, but the pigmen kept up their game, never attacking but never quite running away.

The echo of far-off gunfire froze Amos where he stood and raised gooseflesh all over him as he realized what should have been obvious all along. They'd been had.

Elvin might have had the same thought because the moment he broke out of his rigid tremor, he whipped the war party into action. "Back to the camp, you lazy bastards, lickety-split!" Elvin hollered.

The war party's frantic dash through the brush drowned out the sound of the battle, but not Amos' racing thoughts. There was an emergency back at camp, but the strange unbred behavior betrayed something more than coincidence or bad luck. The pigmen had drawn the war party far away from the glen, too far away to help in an emergency. But in order for the pigmen to do that—

Elvin slowed to a gasping halt, the rest of the war party stopping a few strides ahead of him. Amos looked back at the watchman.

Elvin's eyes were aflame with rage and despair. He said aloud what Amos—and perhaps the whole posse—was already thinking. "Those pigmen had a *plan.* Them ain't smart enough to do that on their own. Which means half our clan is fighting something cooked up by a shadower. It's another pigman swarm, and this time we're out in the middle of nowhere with our pants down. Half the clan, nearly all our fighters..." Elvin sank to one knee, grabbed two fistfuls of his thinning hair, and screamed a thunderous, desperate expletive into the ground.

"Will we make it back in time?" Amos wondered aloud.

"We'll make it in time to bury the dead if we don't grow wings and fly!" Elvin shouted.

And then, as suddenly as he'd stopped, Elvin jumped to his feet and surged forward into the brush with the crazed full-out tilt of a man seeing his house going up in flames. Amos and the rest of the Tuckers followed, haunted by the thought of everyone they had left behind in that yawning gorge.

Ralph willed his frantic shivering to settle, but the mental effort only made it worse. He looked to either side and guessed the entire camp had crammed itself into the cleft at the base of the hill where a springtime runnel had carved a mere six inches of cover in the barren soil. The hill rose up sharply in front of him, but not so sharply as to give their attackers a clean line of sight all the way to the bottom. A scabrous slope of chalky gravel separated the two forces with a natural kill-zone which neither side dared enter. Without any obvious targets, the shooting had stopped, for now.

Ralph was too busy hugging the lowest place he could find to notice when Nigel sat upright next to him, but the scream of alarm broke through.

"Pigmen! The pigmen are back! They're coming from the flank!"

Ralph looked and saw it was true. Scores of the beasts charged at them from the forest, appearing as suddenly as they had disappeared.

"They knew about the Greenbriers," Ralph muttered to himself as the Tuckers around him turned to face the onslaught. Somehow, they knew. They'd been waiting. Waiting for the Greenbriers. Ralph's hand went to the curved knife at his side.

Ella tensed in the woods at what she thought might have been the town's alarm bell. She looked back, but she was too far now to see the town wall. She reckoned she'd be nearing the Finches' farm soon. She ought to head back. Whoever had wandered out into these woods ought to have enough sense to do the same.

She picked her way through the bushes, rounded a great mossy boulder, and came face-to-face with a shadower.

Ella screamed.

She ran straight away from the unbred monster, stumbling once, throwing a look over her shoulder to see the thing following with an ambling gait, unnaturally long arms swinging down by its knobbly knees. She ran without heed to where she was going, aiming only to put as much space between her and the ghoulish creature as she could. She clambered up a short hill, eyes on the uneven footing, looking up just long enough to see—

A second shadower stood silhouetted between two trees, waiting for her.

Ella made a sharp turn to her left and burst through a screen of undergrowth before hitting her stride and racing pell-mell through the trees. "Lord Jesus, have mercy," she whimpered. She skittered to a stop when she saw a dark mass leaning at the base of a tree. Not another shadower, please, Lord...

She marked the pale, wrinkled flesh of an old hand and knew she'd found the elderfather. "Hey!" she called, running up to the unmoving form. "Hey, mister! Mister—Mr. Brody?"

But Old Man Brody wasn't there, not in the eyes rolled back in his head, not in his trembling, shaking head, barely in the murmuring nonsense that passed his parted lips.

"Devil's ... Devil's studies. Turn down. Turn it down. Brain's too bright."

Ella shook him. "Mr. Brody, snap out of it. What's going on with you?"

Brody's eyes focused to a point far beyond and above Ella. "Knew it was wrong. Knew when they came for me. Is that you, Sandy? Why'd you leave that on the stove so long?"

Ella looked up and saw a shadower not far off. She looked behind her and saw the first two gliding towards her with an uncanny stride. She looped one of Mr. Brody's arms over her shoulder and heaved him up.

"You'll fry your brain, watchin' that garbage."

She wasn't strong enough. Not strong enough to get away, and nothing to fight back with. The shadowers came together in a loose circle around her, then slowly closed the loop.

"We'll sell you life eternal. Sign here; no need to read the fine print. You're special, don't you know? Don't you know? Better than them. Special. You were made for better things. Better than them."

The old man sagged back down to the ground, his shirt hitching up and revealing his tattoo-covered torso. The space just above the heart bore the image of a twisted ladder.

Misshapen hands stretched out, blocking the sky from her sight. Ella closed her eyes and bit her lip, expecting to feel claws or teeth. Instead, a prickling feeling bloomed from behind her eyes, and then she knew no more.

Ms. Speaker, Mr. Vice President, fellow men and women of Congress, we have a decision to make today, one that may be the gravest we've ever had to make. I know we have not always agreed on everything; politics being the adversarial game it is, even members of my own party have criticized me for being too slow to act, too indecisive, too afraid to do what is necessary. Many of you have put the responsibility for all this unrest on my shoulders. I understand your concerns, and I accept the full weight of your expectations and the expectations of our kind. I ask that you do the same.

We've developed a weapon that can neutralize, in the space of a single year, every single hostile anti-genetic actor globally. It will do this without inflicting a single casualty on humans with any WHO-approved gene sequencing. It will guarantee a clean and spotless future for our children and grandchildren. But it will also mean the death of billions.

We cannot put our hand to the plow unless we know what our work must be.

We are in desperate times, and you know what they say about desperate times. The world is on fire, whole governments collapsing under the weight of a global unsequenced uprising, and everyone is looking to us for leadership. Major state actors are capitalizing on the chaos to seize strategic territory and threaten our influence abroad. We stand on the brink of a total, multi-front war in a time where global cooperation is most necessary. We cannot afford to point fingers and jockey for short-term political gain as we approach the crossroads of history.

We are here to make the hard decisions no one else can make. Lesser humans could not see this through, but history will honor us for what we do now. Hundreds of millions have entrusted their lives to us, and we must do what is necessary to protect them from a clear and present danger.

But the responsibility is too great for any one human to bear. Therefore, my fellow citizens, my fellow representatives of the people, we must share this burden together. The command staff, with my authorization, and in coordination with governments on every populated continent, have set in motion the mechanism which will save our species. Although I have been smeared as a coward and flip-flopper, I was the first to make this decision.

But now, I stand before you as an equal. Another human on the same journey toward a brighter tomorrow. We cannot go forward with anything less than absolute unanimity. I'm putting the lives of millions of our kind in your hands, to spare if you are strong enough, or to condemn to centuries of ceaseless war and suffering. But the choice is for every last one of you to make. Neither I nor anyone will stop you.

Those fucking ingrates had it coming, Brody, don't you worry. We could be living in a worldwide paradise by now, but these morons want to cling to religion and tradition and persecute us because we're different. We tried to do it the easy way. Most of them didn't even want to have kids until we told them they couldn't, and now we've got mobs of lessers roaming the streets, murdering our kind in their sleep.

You know we can't fight this the conventional way. Even stateside, the lessers outnumber us three-to-one. And if you think there's going to be any kind of peace outside of total fucking annihilation, you're wrong. Look at the news. You've got Christians and Muslims marching arm-in-arm against us. Do you know how much they have to hate us for them to decide to buddy up? You can't reason with that. You can't even hurt them bad enough to make them stop. All they know is hate. All they want is power. The only solution to that is a bullet to the head.

You're not the one who made the virus, and you're not the one who released it. All we have to do is make sure the lessers don't break anything too important before they kick off. A few months, and it will all be over. We'll have the world to ourselves. Go into retirement early and pick yourself out a nice little estate by the beach. Hang that Purple Heart above the fireplace. Or don't. Either way, it's not going to change what'll happen to the lessers. Science and reason were going to win, eventually. It's just the pressure of natural selection. And those shit-for-brains fuckers who burned scientists at the stake and threw books into the river and did everything they could to keep humanity in the darkness for every minute they could squeeze out of it? Fuck 'em. Like I said, Brody, they had it coming. The sooner I can snip their DNA out of my gametes, the better.

A dream-like vision of shuffling forms and a moving picture faded, though the sharp clarity of the voice echoed in her ears even as she woke in a new place, somehow already upright.

A ruckus lay out ahead of her, across a brief open area at the mouth of a box canyon. The sporadic pop of gunfire. The tang of burnt powder. Something moved next to her. A pigman. The monsters moved all around her. She jumped at the sight, her hand darting to her mouth to smother a scream. Except she didn't jump, she didn't scream, and her hand stayed curled in a fist on the ground. And her hand was no longer familiar to her. Instinct and surprise seized her, but she remained motionless, eyes fixed ahead, frozen not by fear but by something she did not at first comprehend.

Then her eyes twitched to the side, taking in the scenery of a new locale. Her limbs twitched into action. The spasm that wracked her body sent her bounding forward on all fours in an ape-like crouch. The familiar contours of her body were now alien to her. Her back hunched over, and her mouth bristled with what felt like shattered flint.

The low grunt of a pigman gurgled in her throat.

Before the horror and revulsion could overwhelm her, the sensations multiplied many times over, like the image in two looking glasses placed opposite one another. She was now no longer one pigman, but many, the sights and sounds and smells of all fusing into one massive overwhelming experience. Her mind shriveled up like cobwebs exposed to a flame as the convergence of many consciousnesses upon her own assaulted her with something less definite but far more profound than agony. Her awareness slipped. Her vision, or what counted as vision, blurred into hazy nothingness.

A solitary cry broke through, and Ella saw someone she knew. Becky.

She lay crouched on one knee among a host of Tuckers cowering in a narrow dell. Becky drew nearer as the pigman horde charged. She was plunging a ramrod down the muzzle of a rifle with the determination of a woman bent on fighting like a hellcat, but Ella could see the despair in her eyes as Becky looked out at the oncoming pigmen—at her.

Horror rose up, steeling Ella's nerves against the tide of oblivion threatening to crush her mind. The host of sensations buffeted her consciousness, and the cavalcade of sinewy limbs beat a frantic stampede, heedless to her will.

She hardened her focus, cooling her panic and heating a fury inside her she didn't know she had. Not my kin. Not my kin. *NOT MY KIN!*

Ralph opened his eyes again to find the pigmen scattering to the wind. The entire pigman wave beat a disorganized retreat into the woods once more, routed without a single shot fired.

Chapter 29

In Which Ralph Tests His Mettle

Ella opened her eyes to see a hook-nosed man hunching over her, a brilliant spike of light held aloft in his hand. She picked her head off the ground where she'd fallen and glimpsed a shadower retreating with hands covering its giant eyes.

"Hurry, girl. Help my father to his feet. We must hurry," the man said, and she recognized him.

"Reverend Brody?" Her voice came out as a low wail. Her hands, now under her own control again, seized her dress as she writhed on the ground. She thrashed, peeling away the disgusting remnants of whatever had encased her. She caught herself before clawing at her own face. "Wha—"

"Hurry, girl!" Reverend Brody repeated, brandishing the flare he carried like a cross to ward off evil spirits. "I can only keep them off as long as the flare burns."

Ella shuddered, then heaved Old Man Brody to his feet and helped him, still insensible, hobble along back towards town. The Reverend held out the burning flare to blind the shadowers retreating further and further into the woods.

"When I heard the alarm bell and word of shadowers in the woods, I checked on father's house. When I didn't find him there, I feared the worst," the Reverend explained, the certainty of his tone a sliver of reassurance. "I was right."

Ella looked behind her. She could still see the shadowers, but they were no longer following. Rather, they melted back into the woods they'd come from. Up ahead, the palisade came into view.

"H-how did you find us?" Ella asked. "How did you scare them off with only a flare? I didn't think shadowers were scared of fire."

Reverend Brody stooped under his father's weight, less like a vulture than a tired-out mule. "They're not."

"What's going on, Reverend?" Ella's voice quavered as her experience with the shadowers crept back into the dark recesses of her mind. "What happened to me?"

"We all have our cross to bear," the Reverend said, turning sad eyes toward Ella. "This one is mine—is ours."

I thought that was it, Ralph thought as he watched the last unbreds disperse into the tree line across the meadow once more. In considering the miracle, he nearly forgot about the host of Greenbriers taking potshots at them in defilade. A spray of shattered rocks and dirt to the back of the head reminded him.

The elders, it seemed, were less apt to waste time marveling. Job Brody stuck his head above the rest of the Tuckers long enough to shout, "Shane Bunton, get the hell over to me right the hell now!" Ralph had never heard Job swear so much.

Becky Brody crawled past Ralph. "Uncle Job, we've gotta sweep the woods up there," she said, pointing to the mouth of the dell and tracing up the arc of the hill to where the Greenbriers positioned themselves.

"You crazy, girl?" Job said. "You're lookin' at a good three hundred paces worth of open ground."

"We could climb the steep part straight up. They won't see that comin'."

Job ducked his head as movement flitted at the ridge crest. "How 'bout you watch for targets and leave the tactics up to the elders, hon?"

"Whatever you do, you'd better do it quick, 'cause I reckon it'll take those jack-rackers all of ten minutes to get shooters on the other side of the dell and turn this into a turkey sh—" Becky jerked back as a shot nicked the stock of Job's rifle, scattering chips of wood in her face. Ralph looked up the hill in time to see a silhouette duck behind the curve of the slope again.

"Dadgummit, Becky, I'm aware of the situation!" Job hollered. "Shane!"

"*WHAT*?" Mr. Bunton had wiggled in behind Job, looking none too forbearing himself.

"We've got the numbers on them, I'm guessing two-to-one, at least." Job risked a glance up the slope again.

"Won't make much difference charging uphill without cover against a score of breech-loaders. We gotta—FOOWA!" Shane rubbed debris kicked up by the fusillade out of his face. "We gotta get fire superiority first." Shane Bunton shook the bow he carried. "Arrows can hit what's up over the ridge, and we got enough bows to pincushion everything up there."

Ralph followed Shane's finger pointing up the hill, scanning the imaginary trajectory of an arrow in flight.

Mr. Brody, it seemed, agreed with Shane. "Make it happen. You look after the bows and I'll look after the rifles."

Now that the elders in charge had passed down the first hint of a plan, the huddled Tuckers worked themselves into something resembling an organized fire line. Bows in front, rifles behind, near enough to touch. Ralph nocked an arrow with still-shaking hands and watched the rim of the ravine above as the shaft of his arrow rattled against his bow.

The brief time it took for the Tucker bowmen to get into position was enough for the shooters above to get some clean shots off. Covering rifle fire made most of the shots go wide, but Ralph saw Mrs. Varner go down with a fist-sized chunk missing from her throat.

"Hold!" Shane bellowed. "You shoot on my order and not before! Mark my angle, now!" Shane raised his bow and loosed an arrow up over the crest of the hill in a high arc.

"Okay, archers," Shane instructed, "that's your angle. Volleys on my mark, fire for effect, pull, and—go!"

Ralph fired his arrow along with forty others, and a thick volley arced through the air, up the hill, over the crest, and dove back down beyond their sight.

"Next volley! Pull, and—go!"

The next swarm of arrows they lobbed over brought a few shooters into sight to return fire. An old-time rifle round cracked, and Ralph watched as a silhouette reeled and tumbled down the slope, tail-over-teakettle, coming to rest as a shattered heap in the gravel in front of the Tucker fire line. Ralph looked to his left to see a smoking cartridge leap into the air as Job Brody worked the bolt on his thirty-aught-six.

"Next volley! Pull, and—go!"

No Greenbriers showed themselves to return fire this time.

Job Brody leapt from his crouch fully upright. "They're pulling back. Hot damn, it's a-workin'. Anyone not manning a bow, up that hill, now. Come on, right the hell now, light and lively." Job slung his rifle over his shoulder, palmed a pike, and picked his way up the rocks. Becky Brody clambered up on his heels. Not wanting to be outfought by the prettiest girl in the clan, a posse of Tucker men followed her.

A hand snatched away Ralph's bow before he could nock another arrow. He turned to see Cephas Finch pass him a spear. "Go on, Ralph. Now's your chance to do your pappy proud," Cephas said, taking Ralph's position of relative safety.

I hate this I hate this I hate this, Ralph thought as he leaned into the rocky hill and shinnied up the naked cliffside.

"Keep up that fire rate, and don't poke their butts," Ralph heard Shane order behind him. The whoosh of the next volley sailed a mere ten feet over his head, near enough to make him flinch.

The hillside was steep and uneven, but the mess of rough stones supplied plenty of handholds, and if he leaned into the climb, it wasn't unlike scaling a ladder. A ringing silence enveloped the climbers, punctuated only by the cracking and scraping of stones and the panting of the toiling clansmen.

Job Brody paused long enough to whisper down to those following him, "Keep low and stay quiet until we can charge. Wanna get the drop on 'em."

Another volley soared overhead. Ralph kept up the climb as fast as his limbs would allow. His lungs chugged like blacksmith bellows, but otherwise he didn't feel tired. He figured he could run a mile at a dead sprint and not grow weary. The crest of the canyon wall dropped off away from them as the incline evened out, and Ralph spotted the feathered heads of the first few arrows sticking up like flag markers.

Job Brody signaled a halt, laid down prone, and loaded his rifle. The others did the same, dropping their profiles as low as they could and catching their breath. Ralph counted three more volleys as he wiped sweat from his eyes with grimy, bloody fingers. The arrow fire lulled for a moment.

That's when the Greenbriers noticed them.

A cry of alarm broke out from spear-throwing distance, and Ralph looked up in time to see a head and shoulders disappear from the canyon rim.

"That's it! Over the top!" Job Brody bellowed, and the Tuckers charged up the last twenty feet with a great war cry.

A scattering of Greenbriers appeared at the crest to oppose them. A rifle discharged close enough to blacken the foremost Tuckers with soot. It missed. A couple of arrows went wide as well, but Ralph saw Deek Evens twist backwards with an arrow bisecting his jaw. Deek's hands shot up to his face, and the shriek of agony he produced brought the gorge rising back up Ralph's throat.

Then Ralph was over the top, and he heaved himself to his feet on firm soil where the mountain slope leveled off enough for trees to find purchase again. Arrows had studded the first trees on the forward side like plumage on badly plucked fowl. Beyond the edge of the forest, a corpse lay feathered with black barbs.

Behind the cover of the trees, Ralph saw the remaining Greenbriers hustle to bring their rifles to bear. Ralph ran forward with his spear, squeezing his eyes shut.

A chorus of gunfire erupted all around him.

His eyes opened, and there was a Greenbrier dead ahead of him, a man not quite old enough to be his father raising a sawed-off shotgun. Ralph never saw the terror in the eyes. He only saw the gun.

Ralph lunged and rammed the spearpoint through the man's guts, putting the full force of his weight into as if he were driving a post. The shotgun fell to the side. And then it was over, as quickly as it had begun. Ralph let go of the spear and stumbled backward.

The outlines of the last Greenbriers bolted into the woods, fleeing the Tuckers' superior numbers. A few Tuckers made to give chase, but with the battle over, they lost steam much more quickly than their quarry. Job Brody called back the eager young Tucker clansfolk and took stock.

"Cleared 'em out?" he asked.

"Cleared 'em out!" his son Ricky confirmed, pumping his fist in the air. "Frackin' Tuckers, y'all! Even our ladies got bigger balls than those Greenie sons-a-bullhuskers."

"Easy, easy. We got wounded, here. Somebody go fetch Deek, we gotta get that arrow out of 'im. Gad-dang, if that don't look awful. Anyone else—" Job stopped midsentence at the sound of Ralph McDaniel hyperventilating.

"H-h-h-h-h-h-h I stabbed him! Oh God, I've stabbed him!" Ralph had pulled the spear out of the Greenbrier he'd skewered and was cramming the man's shirt into the gaping wound. The man's red-rimmed eyes stared into space, still seeing. His mouth opened and closed, but no words came forth.

The Tuckers stopped and stared. Some of them turned away and tromped back down the hill.

"I'm sorry! I'm sorry! I didn't mean it!" Ralph struggled to staunch the bleeding as he rattled out hopeless apologies.

Nigel Bunton came up behind Ralph. "It's okay, Ralph. You had to do it."

"Push on it, Nigel! Push on it!" Ralph begged.

"Ralph. He's a Greenbrier. They killed my cousin."

"We can still save him if we stop the bleeding, I think!"

"Ralph. He's suffering."

Ralph paused. His hand brushed the curved knife sheathed at his side. He let out a shuddering sigh, then pulled the knife free and leaned over. Ralph couldn't help but look in the man's eyes as he placed the blade against the side of the throat, like his father had taught him. Ralph closed his eyes, sobbed once, and sliced.

He crawled away from the man he'd killed and vomited. When he was done, a hand helped him up. Nigel Bunton gave Ralph his shoulder, and together they walked away from the bloody hilltop without a word.

There were so few clansmen left to man the wall back at the town that even with the alarm bell still ringing, Ella, the Reverend, and Old Man Brody slipped through the gate without anybody taking heed of their arrival.

Between the two of them, the Reverend and Ella walked Old Man Brody into the meeting-hall and sat him down on one of the split-plank pews in the church room. By then, Old Man Brody was starting to come around. He stared up at the ceiling above him before his eyes drifted toward the Reverend. "Oliver ... did it happen again?"

"Hush, Father," Reverend Brody said, his own eyes darting Ella's direction. "You're fine. Arnie called up the alarm on account of some shadowers. But we scared them off, I think."

"Where's the girl?" the old man asked, looking around before spotting Ella. "You saw it, didn't you?"

Ella opened her mouth to ask what, but the Reverend broke in. "Don't you think we should talk about this—"

"Talking is useless now, Oliver. She knows. You'll either have to kill her or make her a keeper."

Ella gasped at the old man's casual mention of murder, but the Reverend looked exasperated. "Father, you don't—"

"Those are your options." The old man gave a matter-of-fact shrug, but his face betrayed a deep weariness.

"I'm sorry," Ella tried to explain, "I saw somebody going off into the woods, and I thought Mr. Brody might be ... might be doing what old Mrs. Finch done, and—"

"Hush, girl," Old Man Brody said. "It weren't your fault. Might've saved many lives, actually."

"You mean what happened with the pigmen—"

The old man nodded. "It was real."

The Reverend broke in. "What do you mean? Was there an incident elsewhere? Did something happen to the war party?"

Old Man Brody waved his son off, his eyes still on Ella. "I saw what you saw. But I was too weak to intervene. Have been for many years."

"And the..." Ella struggled to explain. "The dream?"

Brody shook his head. "Not a dream. It's on account of them shadowers, dredging it all up." He heaved himself to his feet and started toward the door. "I'm a-gonna get on home and sleep this off. You can give her the rundown, give her the bad news."

"I'm afraid I'm not understanding things," Ella said, shaking her head.

"You mean you ain't figured out what I am yet?" Old Man Brody said, turning.

Ella swallowed. "But it can't be. Half the people in the clan would be ubermenschen."

"Not half. All of them. Half-breeds like the Griersons are the closest you'll ever get to seeing real humans."

Ella's mind rang as if from a hammer-blow. "What happened to all the real humans?"

"They're dead."

The second hammer-blow. And the old man beat her to the final one, though she knew it already.

"And we killed them."

Chapter 30

In Which the Tuckers Turn Tail

As night fell and large patrols of Tuckers scoured the surrounding woods for any sign of unbred or Greenbrier, Elvin McDaniel listened to the battle count, his eyes staring at the ground. Amos Taylor still stood with the other elders. He shadowed Elvin's movements as he had during their day spent beating around in the brush.

"Reckoning that the Greenbriers left too quick to take their dead with them, we can mark down seven killed for sure," Job said.

"And ours?" Elvin said, not looking up.

"Eight dead outright, three more on their way out. Another twelve wounded some way or another, and Dr. Bernhard reckons six of those will need to lose an arm or a leg 'fore it's settled."

"So we got our asses handed to us, is what you're sayin'."

Job cleared his throat and didn't answer.

"Those Greenbriers could have taken thirty of us," Shane growled, his arms crossed. "We were well led. And I ain't playin' favorites. I lost a nephew in that fight."

"How well you was led don't change the fact that this attack is done. Finished. We cut our losses and get our clansmen back to town."

The elders rose up in unified dismay.

Elvin raised a hand to silence them. "The Greenbriers are wise to our movement, and we've still got a full day of hard travelling ahead of us. With the wounded and those who need to tend them, that'll take a third of our strike force away. We have to ditch this hiding place, and without another good campsite, the strike force will have to leave behind most of the baggage train, lest we lose it to a Greenbrier flanking attack. Any folks we take on to the Greenbrier clan will make our party too big to sneak anymore, but too small to fight whatever the Greenbriers send to hassle us. The only way we come out on top going forward is by stupid luck, and I don't put stock in stupid luck."

Elvin lowered his hand to end all discussion and walked away from the group. The elders, grumbling about throwing in the towel too early, made as if to follow him with their protests before falling back to their grumbling and the wailing of bereaved clansmen.

Amos, however, did not break off. "We're not beaten," he said, running up beside Elvin.

"Go on, kidlin'. I know you got gumption, but you can't win a fight with just the want-to."

Amos stutter-stepped to keep up with Elvin's pacing. "It's not that. I was gonna say that you don't need this big war party. You never did. We have the nitrogel."

"The nitrogel's nice, but it ain't magic. Won't keep us from getting tracked and ambushed on our way south, and it won't flip the odds our way if a scrap goes sour."

"The Greenbriers won't be looking for us. They think they've got us beaten already."

Elvin stopped, slashing the air with his hand. "No, they don't. They ain't stupid. They'll keep up their patrols and watch for unusual unbred doings, and they'll likely find us again."

"But what they'll do first is send a party to check this canyon again, and when they find our whole camp packed up and gone back the way we came, they won't follow the tracks back more than half a mile. For sure not to the place where we turned around this morning to trap our tail of unbreds."

Elvin stopped in his tracks and turned to face Amos. "I'm listening."

Neat fences parceled a patch of land surrounding a Greenbrier farmhouse. Some animals grazed in a pasture here and there, and they could make out some farmhands mowing hay. An easy enough target, though the breastworks and sharpened stakes surrounding the center of the estate would make any prolonged siege difficult. The Tuckers dismounted and kneeled at the tree line, the wind still bearing up the smells of their enemies to their noses, rather than the other way round. Surprise was still on their side.

"Okay, we'll hit this, I reckon. Pull back into the woods, find us a spot to make camp real quiet-like. We'll take our rest this afternoon and come back tonight. From here on in, we don't take a shot at anyone, for any reason, without my say-so. If we get unbreds, use silent weapons only. Bows and spears. While we wait, cut me some limber young trees."

The night was as dark as sin, with no moon out to light their path or give them up to wary foes sleeping in the farmhouse scarcely a quarter-mile distant. They fumbled in the dark, just as they would fumble back to camp when their work was done. They would wait out the rest of the night without sleeping and without lighting a fire. It was a good thing many of them could see in the dark.

Elvin scanned the fresh battlefield glowing with the early light of dawn. His men waited behind him for instructions. "We're a-gonna split into two groups. Amos Taylor, you take a group out yonder and wait for my shot. Take down the men first, make for the house."

Seven of the war party followed Amos through the tall summer grass toward a stretched-out copse of trees that would provide plenty of cover until they were within sprinting distance of the main Greenbrier defenses. There were some fast-twitchers among them, and they could cover the ground in a flash if they were loaded light enough. The important thing was getting over the breastworks before the Greenbriers could react to the attack.

Elvin settled in and started tracking the movements of a burly-looking Greenbrier down yonder. Give it another minute yet, give the other Tuckers a chance to get ready, another minute or two—

The wind shifted, and the big Greenbrier halted his work, freezing long enough for Elvin to draw a bead and fire.

The forest on the Greenbrier side across from the homestead spat out a musketball that broke the shin of one of the Finches. He fell face-first on the ground, screaming in agony as the surrounding Tuckers dropped their loot and dove for cover. A couple sprightly young Greenbrier teenagers jumped out of cover and hightailed it away from the Tucker assault, one of them shouting an insult back at the Tucker strike force as she went.

Elvin McDaniel barked an order to call off the chase, wiped the sweat from his eyes, and waved to signal a retreat. A couple Tuckers heaved the wounded member of their party to his feet and bore him back the way they'd come. The Tuckers beat a straight line back with whatever loot they could carry. Elvin did a quick headcount to check to see if everyone had made it out.

Where was Bert Daly?

Elvin blew his whistle and ran back to the Greenbrier house. He stepped up onto the porch, over the dead body in the doorway, past the brilliant red bloodstain on the doorpost, and into the ransacked kitchen. He didn't have time to go chasing after stragglers, but leaving someone behind—

A muffled thumping turned his head upwards towards the ceiling. Slinging his long rifle over his shoulder and pulling out his bow, Elvin crept up the stairs. He pulled the drawstring as he hit the landing on one knee and checked the top floor for enemies. He continued on up, sweeping the point of the arrow from right to left as his feet glided up the steps. He was almost to the top when he heard a whimper and a yelp. A woman.

Elvin topped the stairs in a single light-footed bound. At the end of the hall, Bert Daly kneeled over a struggling woman with his britches around his ankles, grunting like a rutting animal.

"WHAT THE HELL DO YOU THINK YOU'RE DOIN'?" Elvin shouted loudly enough to shatter glass.

Bert jumped in surprise, spinning around. "Elvin! What the—" he cried, struggling to pull up his pants. Elvin's arrow punched a hole through Bert's exposed thigh. Elvin lowered his bow and drew a knife.

Bert gasped in pain and surprise. "Aaah! Elvin, I'm sorry! Just—stop!" Bert grabbed the shaft of the arrow with one hand.

"You're gonna die like I found you, pants around your knees, you filthy sonofabitch." Elvin took slow, purposeful strides down the hall towards him, twirling his knife in his hand.

"Elvin, wait! She's just a Greenbrier. Just banish me. I never wanted to go back anyway. I—"

Elvin lifted the knife to Bert's throat and slashed with a ripping stroke. Blood sprayed the wall and floor as Bert collapsed, his life spilling out under gaping mouth and wide, disbelieving eyes. His skinny white legs writhed on the floor in the spreading pool of blood.

When the gurgling had stopped, Elvin looked to the woman still covering herself with the tatters of her clothing.

For a moment, Elvin said nothing, muscles tensed. Then his shoulders sagged with a deflating sigh. "Are you okay?"

She nodded, eyes wide and terrified.

Elvin looked out the window of an adjacent room. He scratched the back of his head and stroked his whiskers. The lines in his cheeks and around his eyes deepened. He scratched the back of his head again, only rougher this time. He turned to walk away, but then returned, unslinging his rifle and pulling back the hammer.

"I'm sorry," Elvin said as he leveled the gun at the woman, "but a Greenbrier is a Greenbrier, and a feud is a feud."

A gunshot rang from inside the house, and a few moments later, a tired, frustrated, angry Elvin McDaniel left it.

His father would have been ashamed of him. Wasting a precious bullet on a woman when a knife would have done the trick!

The Greenbrier watchman folded his arms as the two whelps rode into town on a single horse. One of them was wounded.

"What happened?"

"It's the Tuckers, Seamus. Must've looped clear 'round to the east."

"How many?"

"A dozen, maybe?"

The watchman nodded. "Find the lieutenant. Tell him to take a posse north-east, to the vale o' rotting trucks, and cut off their getaway. I'll lead the back-attack, drive them into the vale."

"But sir, me sister's hurt."

"Then leave her. We'll send someone back to pick her up if she ain't bled to death by then."

The young runner gone and his sister still whimpering and holding her arm like a spoiled child, Seamus Maneater sounded the call for able arms.

In a trice, thirty Greenbrier warriors poured out of the clan main on horseback, racing to catch up with the advance scouts sent out just ahead of them.

The raiding party had gathered at the fallback point at the edge of the farm, their flanks watched and warded as Elvin had instructed.

"What took you so long, Elvin?" his cousin Clyde said.

"Bert Daly's dead. The fool let his guard down." Elvin spat. "Let's head out. A blind baby could spot our tracks going away from there, and we're upwind."

"We were ready ten minutes ago, Elvin. I just hope the time you wasted beatin' around for Daly didn't—" Clyde's eyes darted downhill to the west of them, back across the field. "Aw, hell."

The Greenbrier skirmisher ran back from the low field rock wall to report on the action. "Seamus! They're falling back!"

"Pull up!" Seamus called to his mounted counterattack. "Everyone pull up and stop! How many are there?"

"Half a score of 'em, I'd say. They took a couple shots and ran. Full tilt, breaking east-northeast toward open country. Fast-twitchers, the whole bunch."

The watchman shook the reins as he straightened in the saddle. "Then it's a hit-and-run. We'll run the lot of them down, saber them where they stand." He led the clansmen around him up the hill in pursuit of their prey.

He kept an eye out for stragglers as they spurred their horses to a brisk canter past the farmhouse, over the fence and permanent bulwarks. Nothing. Everything empty. The horses kicked on up to the top of the hill. They spotted their quarry fleeing on foot across a wide-open grassy plateau. Perfect for a cavalry charge.

"Not a single one gets out alive," Seamus called as he took his steed to a full gallop.

The line lurched forward into the vast clearing. And still the Tuckers ran straight forward through the middle of the meadow, not separating, not scattering, not veering off of the invisible line that seemed to guide them.

As the cavalry closed on the retreating Tuckers like a bullhusker on a lost lamb, the Greenbrier watchman felt the first niggling doubts. It was easy. Too easy, even for their own sheer overwhelming numbers, speed, and firepower. Something at the back of his head, whether a watchman's instinct or pure animal fear, told him to turn his horse around and flee, but the Tuckers were right there. He drew his machete. Time slowed as his focus drew to a needlepoint.

A few of the Greenbriers saw it before they hit it; none of them could avoid it.

A wide trench, hidden with a layer of grass and brittle sticks, swallowed up the horses' hooves. It happened so fast Seamus thought his horse had been shot as the ground hurtled up to meet him. Horse and rider alike both spilled to the ground in a pounding calamity. Horse and rider alike wailed as their bones snapped like twigs and the bodies all piled on each other in a thundering cascade.

Seamus pulled himself up from the dirt. A sharpened stake poked up from the ground a mere foot from his head. The horse next to him lay impaled on another stake, whinnying as its lifeblood greased the wood in its guts. He struggled to shaking knees and took his first real breath.

He peeked over the lip of the shallow trench to see the remaining cavalry—only a couple riders—falter in their charge, unwilling to chase the Tuckers further. They wheeled around to check on their fallen comrades, only to collapse to the ground as well-placed rifle fire felled their horses.

It was then that Seamus looked around and understood where they were: an elaborate shooting range. The wide-open plateau stretched out in all directions, without a single stone or tree, encircled on all sides by dense forest. The horses, which were all now dead, dying, or lame, had already trampled whatever grass there was to hide in.

There would be no going back.

One moment, one of his men had been rallying the clansmen into something resembling a defense. The next moment, a bullet blew out the base of his skull and his lower jaw, cutting his lifestrings like a sword cutting the strings of a puppet. The corpse fell beside Seamus.

"Taking fire!" someone called out. From all sides, it seemed. Seamus heard the whirr and buzz of bullets zipping through the air, but the reports of the distant rifles seemed so far off that the shots themselves seemed to spring from nothing but clouds and cobwebs.

"Watchman! Get under cov—," one of his men tried to warn him before his head blew open, spraying Seamus with blood, bone, and brains.

"I'm hit! Oh God, I'm hit!" someone else shrieked.

It was more a chaotic execution than a battle. The Greenbriers tried to return fire but found themselves shooting at bushes and trees, with only the brief flits of outlines and the flickers of discharging rifles to let them know that the attackers were human at all. The far-off guns went silent for a moment and then began again with a slow, steady rhythm, like the ring of a blacksmith's hammer on an anvil. Another Greenbrier reeled backwards with a gaping hole in his forehead, half his face caved in like a rotting car tire.

The Tuckers were too far away and too concealed. The Greenbriers couldn't reach them, couldn't touch them. What rifles could shoot that straight? When the third Greenbrier in a row crumpled from a headshot, a portion of the posse stopped trying to fight and lit out for the town on foot. They made it about halfway back before the Tucker sharpshooters who'd looped around to cut off their escape picked them off.

The shooting went on at a steady pace for another five minutes before the men fell into hysterics. A man with his forearm folded backwards at the elbow called for help and got none. Another started screaming that he didn't want to die over and over again, the spineless wretch. The only one who seemed to face the onslaught well sat leaned up against his downed horse, gazing boldly into the open, ignoring calls for him to take cover. The fellow took two rounds to the chest with the resolute stoicism of a man already dead. The ground turned soggy with blood. When Seamus tried to change cover, he took a bullet through his spine for it.

And in a couple more minutes it was over. The firing stopped, but the wounded kept on moaning and crying and bleeding in the silence, only a few of whom went still as time wore on. The Greenbrier watchman sat, languidly propped up against two stacked corpses, staring at the bloodbath as his own blood seeped through his clothes and into the ground. A bug bit his hand, but he found he did not have the strength to flick it away.

He heard a rustle and saw two Tuckers come up through the grass in a half crouch, their rifles trained on the downed Greenbriers. Two more Tuckers to the right, followed by a third. Swords and knives slipped from their sheaths, and the wounded choked on the blades.

Two forms stepped next to him. That Tucker watchman and a young man next to him, his son, maybe.

"It was a good plan, Amos Taylor," the Tucker watchman said, looking down at Seamus.

The Greenbrier looked to the young whelp who stared back at him with cold, hateful eyes. "You ain't beat us Greenbriers yet," Seamus said. "You done riled us up."

The kid grabbed his face and pulled him close. "Shut it, Greenbrier," the kid said. "I'm here for my brother."

"Like we'll come for you."

"Fine by me. I'm just getting warmed up."

"Amos," the Tucker watchman said, "quit dragging this out. Finish him and let's get out of here."

Without another word, Amos flashed out with his knife and buried it to the hilt in Seamus' throat.

Chapter 31

For Home and Hearth

Some of our number argue that trying to "take a lesson" out of everything that happened amounts to putting a positive spin on a holocaust. But if we take no lesson, it is sure to happen again. Our kind oppressed an entire generation of lesser humans, then stood by while our leaders murdered them outright. Only after the system collapsed and our own kind died by the millions have we realized that we, the ubermenschen, have committed an atrocity without precedent in the entire history of our species. We have killed more people in a year than had even existed two hundred years ago.

Who can bear living with that fact? No one can. How can we tell our children? We cannot. So we are left with two options: we deny the bloody legacy of the genetically enhanced super-humans and doom our descendants to repeat the sins of their fathers, or we take up the identity of an extinct race and keep the lesson.

Our numbers are small enough, and our settlement remote enough, that we can lay out a doctrine and expect no opposition. At least one of our group will have to keep a record of the truth and pass it on to a chosen keeper of the next generation. The keeper will manage the reality of the outside world whenever it enters the clan walls. Any contact with outsiders must first happen in the presence of the keeper, and all who wish to have correspondence with us must agree to abide by our doctrine, on pain of banishment or death.

Ella looked up from the yellowed document. "Who all's seen this?"

Reverend Brody stood leaning against the bookshelf of his private study, a study second only to Sam Chambers', stocked with what appeared to be mostly well-kept tomes on serious topics. He looked at her with grave eyes, his arms crossed. "My father penned it. He passed it on to me as his eldest twenty years ago. And now you've seen it. Wouldn't have been my first choice, but after everything, it's better that you know and understand than I keep trying to scare you away from it. I'm sorry to pass this burden on to you, but it looks like you're the next keeper."

"They're all dead?"

The Reverend nodded. "Totally extinct."

"How can you know for sure?"

"I can't, but our kind designed the virus to spread and kill, and folks back then were packed together like canned tomatoes. There might be a few wild men somewhere in the Saharan desert who escaped it, maybe some Mongol or Siberian somewhere, or a Tibetan monk."

Ella had barely ever heard of such places, let alone could imagine what people could live there.

"But I still doubt it." The Reverend shook his head, crossing his arms and leaning against the pew. "Our scientists first tested the virus on remote populations and spread it through modified mosquitoes."

"Ugh." Ella felt sick. "How could they do such an awful thing?"

"I don't know. I tell myself it's the depravity of man, but even so." The Reverend shook his head again. "My father knows how they mustered the venom to do it, but I don't think he's able to say. You should know, young lady, that you only find the Pandemic so horrific because of how we raised you. The other clans out there, who know what they are, take a much softer view toward the death of billions of innocents. The only way to make you care about those poor wretches was to convince you that you were one of them. That is why we have a keeper for each generation, and one only. It's enough to help parlay with foreigners and make sure they don't spill the beans."

"That's a lot of trouble just to keep our breeding a secret."

The Reverend looked down. "There's another reason."

"What's that, then?"

"What you saw when the shadowers gave you a vision. You know what it was?"

"Seemed like memories. Old Man—your father's?"

"It's unusual for someone like you, without any training, to stumble on that ability. And we absolutely do not want anyone, and I mean *anyone*, to know Tuckers have windows to their minds. Understand?"

Ella thumbed the corner of the paper, lost in thought. "No one else knows?"

"What happened with you and the shadowers," the Reverend shook his head, "is a truth I will never willingly disclose to anyone. Concerning our ubermensch heritage, I've entrusted some of the elders with the general idea, at my discretion." The Reverend paced, his hands folded in front. "The watchman knows some. That one-eyed Grierson figured it out on his own. My younger brother. None of them know the whole story, and they've got sense enough not to pry further."

"What about Mr. Chambers?"

Reverend Brody scoffed. "Of course not. Too idealistic. He's a teacher, for goodness sake. He can't stand not telling everybody the truth as he sees it."

Ella's face remained passive as she said, "A funny thing for a preacher to say."

"A good pastor understands that an idea can be a deadly thing. Even a good idea in the wrong place and time can destroy many things."

"I thought a good pastor would have understood the part where Jesus said 'the truth will set you free'."

"Don't get into a battle quoting Scripture with me, girl. You think God in His wisdom never commanded ignorance in His good book? 'It is the glory of God to conceal a matter.' Or have you considered the forbidden Tree in the Garden of Eden? The fruit of the knowledge of Good and Evil, that once eaten, kills the eater?" The Reverend's voice rose as he spoke. "If only the godless scientists had heeded Eve's hard lesson. Now you have tasted the fruit, and it dooms you with the same knowledge as me. Would you wish the same fate on your kin?

"They deserve to know the truth. The clansfolk ain't children afraid of the dark. I know the truth. Do you see me a-rendin' my clothes and howlin' at the sky?"

"Look what happened to Bert Daly. He glimpsed the truth, probably through that drifter, and did it make him into a more upstanding, truthful clansman? No. The moment he saw the truth didn't fit his picture of himself, he twisted the truth until it told him what he wanted to hear. His whole world was about how he was *special*, how his breeding was better than ours. He said he wanted the truth, but when he got his greasy little paws on it, he decided even the truth was a lie and made up his own. The only reason we didn't banish him then was that the nonsense he spouted only hid the true secret better."

"We're not all Bert Daly."

"When you're dealing with a large group of people, *everyone* is Bert Daly. A lie was inevitable. Either one we told them, or one they told themselves. No one looks at the naked truth and comes away whole.

"You know what Romans did with their cutthroats and murderers long ago? They put them in an arena and had them fight to the death for sport. They forced the bloodthirsty to drink from that bloody cup until they drowned. That is our punishment. Damned to everlasting war against our own kind. We are no more true humans than the pigmen. This thing we call humanity is the last feverish thought of a freshly severed head. God has abandoned us," the Reverend growled, his eyes rimmed red.

He caught his breath before continuing. "My ideal, my calling, my creed, is to convince this rabble, whom I happen to love, to believe that this is not Purgatory, that hope is not lost. Take it away, and they are left with mere survival. It might not happen overnight, but they will descend into madness, marauders and drifters the lot of them, as aimless and hollow as that tainted fellow we let fester here last winter."

Ella grimaced at the mention of Omar. "I'll keep your little secret, for now. And I'm awful sorry you've had to carry this by yourself for so long. But I think you're dead wrong. Dead wrong about the whole thing. If Eve and the apple were the end of the story, the Bible would be a lot shorter."

Ella took her leave.

When Elvin announced news of the dead—Bert Daly, killed by a hidden Greenbrier just as the Tuckers were making their escape, his body lost to the enemy—a solitary wail rose from the crowd of onlookers. Melissa Daly, Bert's new widow, ran from the gathering and fled to the confines of her ramshackle home, dragging young little Earnest along before finally picking the lagging child up and putting him on her hip.

It's too bad about Bert Daly, some of the townsfolk said, but this sort of thing always came along with war, and Bert was an ornery rascal if there ever was one. If it had to be a Tucker, best that it was him, Lord-a-mercy. It sounded bad to say it like that, but better to die fighting for the clan than of sickness or some tomfoolery like what Bert was apt to do off by himself in the woods.

Reverend Brody nodded to himself as he listened in on the short tittering of the gossipy men and women of the clan. The Reverend had learned from an early age to put an ear to the town gossip the same way a skilled tracker puts an ear to the ground to sound out his quarry. Safe now, or nearly so. There still remained one more complication to clear up, and this one might be a bit more difficult to manage.

Elvin had just dunked his head in the rain barrel beside his house to cool himself off and purge the cloying summer stink that had traveled with him for some days now.

"A welcome return, Mr. McDaniel," Reverend Brody said.

Elvin jumped and whirled, a hand reaching for the knife at his side. He relaxed the next moment later, but the glare in his eyes never left. Elvin swore softly. "You oughta know better than to sneak up on a watchman like that. 'Specially after he's been out hunting ubermenschen."

"My apologies. I just wanted to see how you're doing."

"Cheated the reaper for another day. Can't complain."

"I'm sorry to hear about Bert Daly."

"Oh, are you now?"

"The clansmen all believe the raid was a success and well led, in spite of our casualties."

"Well, that's just fine and dandy. Keep using that fine ear of your'n. But you better get back out there in a hurry. Who knows what you could miss while you're jawing at me?"

The Reverend hesitated. "There's something else."

"What? Got more questions to ask? Are folks wanting to know how Bert died? Do they want the juicy tidbits?"

"Take it easy, Mr. McDaniel. It's about his wife, Melissa."

"What about her?"

"Well, you know what kind of a hellion she was before we got her to settle down with Bert. Now that he's dead, I'm afraid of what she might do to scrape a living."

"You mean go back to whoring?"

The Reverend grimaced at the word but didn't rebuke Elvin for using it. "I don't need to remind you what kind of damage such an untethered woman could do to a clan this small. Some of the wives are already wondering what their husbands will be up to in the coming weeks."

"Not sure I understand all the fuss. If the clansmen can't keep it in their britches, just threaten them with banishment. I reckon that would straighten the lot of 'em out."

"It would likely mean the loss of quite a few fighting men."

Elvin shook his head. "Okay, *fine.* What do you want me to do about it?"

"She can't stay here. She either needs to leave with the first nomad clan that comes through or go off on her own."

Elvin laughed without humor. "You'd make a good watchman, with a heart like that."

"But will you give her notice?"

"I don't reckon I can go ahead with this without meeting with the elders."

"I'll worry about the elders. We'll call a meeting tomorrow to make it official."

Elvin hammered at the door of the home of Melissa Daly. He could hear the bawling of a young child inside. When the door opened, it was apparent that Melissa had done a fair amount of crying on her own. Elvin didn't say anything at first.

"You," Melissa started, then sniffed, "you here to bring me recompense for a husband lost honorably to battle?'"

"No, ma'am. Your husband did not die honorably. I'm here to give you a message."

Melissa's shoulders shook, but she managed to strike something resembling a defiant pose. "Don't you 'ma'am' me none. If you're going to treat me like a whore, have the honesty to admit it. Now tell me what you need told."

"The clan elders have met and decided you aren't handy enough to take care of yourself and your kid, and they reckon there's no reason for you not to go back to your old ways now that your husband's gone."

Melissa shook her head. "I won't do that no more, I prom—"

"You'll join up with the first nomad clan that comes through. It ain't an option."

"What about little Earnest?"

"You can take him with you, or you can leave him here. Reverend Brody's offered to take him in, seeing as how he's got no children of his own."

"Any nomad clan gonna take me is gonna want to know why you're kicking me out."

"And we'll tell them. There's plenty of nomad clans what offer the kind of work you'd be good at."

"Suppose I start naming names?"

"Then we'll just banish you and save us the trouble of waiting around for a nomad clan. The rumors have already come and gone, and most of the wives have already had it out of their husbands. The reason you've got to leave is because we can't have any more of this nonsense in the future."

"I ain't leavin' with no nomad clan."

"Then it's banishment."

"You'll have to drag me out of this house."

Elvin shrugged. "Fine by me. I'll be here in the morning."

As he left, Melissa Daly shouted back at him, "You bunch of hard-hearted cutthroats! My husband ain't even cold in the ground yet!"

Chapter 32

Sinners and Saints

The town clansmen and women had gathered at the eastern gate to witness the first full banishment from the Tucker clan in twelve years. Melissa stood in front of the gawping crowd with a few meager belongings and her young son, Earnest. She had refused to give him up to the Reverend and now stood ready to embark on what would likely be her last adventure. But she wouldn't wait in disgrace for a nomad clan to come and remove her like a festering splinter while the rest of the clan looked down their noses at her.

It was left to Elvin McDaniel to pass the sentence with neither relish nor disgust: banishment for the crime of prostitution and infidelity.

When the watchman was finished, Reverend Brody also stepped forward and addressed the flock. "We can tolerate no evil in our midst. Lust of the flesh pollutes the minds and souls of our families and threatens to corrupt the pureness of our breeding. God has cast out the harlot and her bastard child. May God in His infinite mercy find a place for them outside the walls of our clan. If not, may God have mercy on their souls."

The Hollands were there to see the spectacle, Ella among them. The town's main gate wasn't far from her pa and Bill's shops. Until now, they were part of the crowd. When Ella couldn't take it anymore, she shouldered her way out of the mass of tangled spectators and quietly walked over to Melissa Daly with her head bowed and her cheeks flushed in embarrassment.

Ella took Melissa gently by the elbow and started walking her and her son away from the gate. Melissa's face lit up in confusion, but she followed Ella's lead nonetheless. Reverend Brody stood disbelieving. As did everyone else, for that matter.

"What do you think you're doing?" Elvin demanded.

"I'm walking Mrs. Daly back home," Ella answered. "I reckon she's behind on her gardening, and those weeds ain't gonna pull themselves."

"Stop."

"I will not."

"That's an order!"

Ella turned, a mischievous smile spreading on her face. "What are you going to do? Kick me out, too? I'm not letting go of her, and we can't rightly stay here all day waiting for one of us to cave in."

"I reckon we could save time and boot you out, too." Elvin folded his arms and raised his eyebrows as the crowd gasped at the audacity.

"Mr. McDaniel!" Sam Chambers bellowed, red-faced. "You don't rule this clan, and the elders will not accept such a notion, even as a joke!"

"Oh, shut up, teach!" Elvin snapped, turning away from Ella. "She's draggin' this out in front of half the clan! Stirrin' up trouble, is what it is." Elvin turned again, grabbed Ella by the elbow, and dragged her away. "She ain't allowed to hijack the proceedin's this a-way."

Ella knew making a scene wouldn't save Melissa and her son, even with Sam Chambers on her side. She had to find leverage. She knew the real reason they were kicking her out, and if she could get *him* on her side...

"The elders are a-hidin' shameful secrets!" Ella shrieked, and she saw the Reverend jump.

Elvin's hold on her relaxed. "What you talkin' about, girl?"

Ella hesitated, her timidity catching up with her recklessness. Her moment of indecision, however, seemed to work to her advantage as she saw the Reverend turn white as a ghost. Leverage. "If y'all can't abide by a little ole' girl having a say out in the open, it must be because the elders got shameful reasons for electing to banish folks in the first place. You can haul my ornery hide outta here, but who knows what craziness will come spillin' out if you shut me up now?"

The Reverend spoke up with all the relish of a man fixing to pull a knife out of his leg. "Watchman, unhand the girl."

Elvin let go of Ella, but it didn't seem he was ready to quit yet. "What are you going to do once you've taken them back to their house?" Elvin demanded.

Ella thought a moment. "I suppose I'll say, 'Have a good day, Mrs. Daly', and leave."

"*Miss* Holland," the Reverend broke in. His eyes met Ella's, and she could see the bluster behind his schooled expression. "We've made no secret of the cause for her banishment. She is an adulteress, a freeloading harlot who sows discord."

"Well what about Earnest? He ain't done nothin' wrong."

"None can afford to adopt him. His blood is on her hands, not ours. It is *her* adultery that put him in danger. "

"I don't know much about this sort of thing, but doesn't adultery take two people? How come Melissa's the only one getting banished?"

"She's consorted with lovers all over town. She's led too many husbands astray."

Ella shook her head. "That just makes it worse, seems to me. If she did tempt a bunch of husbands that-a-way, seems they oughta have resisted. Men ain't animals; they can control themselves, can't they? Unless she *made* them do what they did, seems to me there should be a whole pack of men standing here right along with her, waiting to get banished."

The Reverend's color left his face again, but again, only Ella noticed. When she'd mentioned shameful secrets, she'd meant for most clansmen to take it one way, and the Reverend another. Seeing his color drain, she began to think she'd hit a little closer to home than she'd intended. Most of the womenfolk were shooing away their children—this confrontation was becoming a little too bawdy for young ears. For all her apparent effort to sound frank and reasonable, Ella herself was blushing, though her moon-wide eyes never wavered.

"Lose half a dozen strong fightin' men, or one good-for-nothing woman?" Elvin said. "I don't much care for all this hand-wringing myself, but everyone has to make sacrifices for the clan."

"The thing about a sacrifice is that someone gives it freely. Otherwise it's just a robbery."

No one said anything. Most of the crowd looked to the ground. Ella never raised her voice; indeed, she seemed more timid now than ever, but her words were enough. A moment passed, and Sam Chambers, one of the clan elders who had previously passed Melissa Daly's nigh-sure death sentence, spoke up. "She's right."

Elvin's eyes flared. "Your world's too simple! The clan's only survived because of its all-fired tough-as-nails gumption! She ain't gonna do anything to help the clan. She's damaged goods! You want to start sticking up for every lost cause, you'll liketa get us all killed one day."

"It's possible. But I figure survival for its own sake ain't worth much without the high-minded notions holding our clan together. Wouldn't you agree, Reverend?" Ella glanced his direction, the corners of her mouth twitching up as she locked eyes with him.

"You'd kill us all, then, for one good-for-nothing?" Elvin said.

"Better to die with my hands clean than to live with a dirty conscience."

"That ain't your choice to make! You're not a clan elder! No one has got the right to decide the fate of the entire clan like that. You'd take away the bread from the mouths of babies to feed a fat pig!"

Ella thought for a moment. Then she perked up. "If you knew she wouldn't do any more philandering, what kind of money would prove that she wouldn't be a leech on the clan?"

"Fifteen, no, twenty pigman jaws."

"Fine. I'll pay it."

"What?" Phil Holland's exclamation carried over the murmur of the crowd.

"Where are you going to get that kind of money?" Elvin asked.

"I've been saving it up for gettin' married."

"*What*?" Phil exclaimed again, this time pushing through the crowd to bring his daughter to her senses.

Elvin's brow furrowed. "Well—"

"Ella, what do you think you're doing? You give away that nest egg, you're never getting married, you hear? What do you think you're going to do, catch some feller with your charm? Come on back to the house and quit this nonsense, understand?"

Elvin continued on, ignoring her pa's protests. "I'd have to make sure she wouldn't go out foolin' around with folks."

"I'd keep watch over her to make sure she's safe," Ella said.

"If you made sure she kept to herself and that she wouldn't leech off the rest of the clan, I don't see why we'd have to go through with this."

"Elvin, that's for the elders to decide!" the Reverend objected.

"Then let's get the elders together and make a decision," Sam said.

"The elders have already decided on it!"

"The situation has changed. The elders will need to discuss the new development." Sam turned to face the rest of the crowd. "Could I have all the elders meet with me in the cafeteria real quick?"

It may not have been the official end of the matter, but the various flavors of stunned silence announced the end of the matter as clearly as a bell.

An old man cackled as the crowd dispersed. The Reverend waved to him as he passed. "Father."

Old Man Brody didn't even look at the Reverend to signal he'd heard. He only watched Ella as she walked Melissa Daly away. He chuckled, his eyes glistening in admiration. He shook his feeble head and chuckled again.

Becky and her beau were having another spat, a stale routine only freshened up by the fact that they were having it out in the open this time.

"No, Oliver, I don't have to put up with it. Stop acting all innocent about it. I can understand two-facedness in women, but Lord knows I can't abide by it in men."

"Come on," Oliver Craine said, trying to laugh it off and hoping Becky wouldn't mention Cynthia's name again in front of any prying eyes, "let me walk you home. You're causing a ruckus."

"I can walk myself home, thank you very much. And I think I have a right to cause a ruckus if I catch you macking on—"

"Shut *up*, Becky!" Oliver hissed, grabbing her elbow a bit more forcefully than was appropriate.

“Let go of me! Stop!”

A young man’s voice caught their attention from behind. “Hey.”

Oliver turned to face Amos Taylor’s deadpan stare. “Beat it,” Oliver said.

Amos’ arms were crossed in front of his chest. “I don’t think this lady wants to go home with you.”

“Mind your own business, Amos.”

“Only if you mind yours. And this lady is not your business anymore.”

“Yeah? Who says?”

Amos stepped closer. “I do. Now *bust off.*”

Oliver stood still for a moment, like a man dying to scratch a powerful itch. His right hand balled into a fist but remained at his side. Amos stood well within swinging range. A moment passed. Oliver remembered he was dealing with Amos Taylor, and he decided to let his famed discretion win out over his ornerier instincts. Becky jerked her arm away, and Oliver left them alone, kicking a passing dog as he went.

Amos said nothing and offered her only his arm. Becky thought for a second, then put her arm through his, and he walked her home.

When Becky was soundly deposited at her door, she turned to Amos and said, “This don’t change nothin’. But I’m awful sorry about what happened ... you know, to you. And thanks. For stepping in and helping me with that sorry excuse for a man.”

Amos merely bowed his head and said, “My pleasure” before leaving her standing in the open door of her home.

“Evening, Melissa,” Ella said on her second night over at the Daly house. “I brought some vegetables over for some stew. How’s little Earnest doing? Are we gonna chop off that hair of his anytime soon?”

Melissa wasn't anywhere in the house, though Earnest was busy babbling and playing with sticks in the corner.

"Melissa?"

Bert's widow stood outside, staring out over the garden at the setting sun. Melissa didn't move when Ella walked up behind her.

"You okay?"

When Melissa turned to face Ella, there were the traces of tears on her face. "Why you doin' this?"

"'Cause my friend Becky's volunteered to help watch out for any crazy Greenbriers who might want to jump us, and my other friend Sophie's been so busy with her twins that I don't have anyone to cook with no more. And I reckon you could use the company."

"Ain't you gettin' something outta this?"

"Well, if you look at it the right way, I suppose I am. I get a kick out of doing a good turn here and there, and I'm side-steppin' the shame I'd be feelin' if you were out there at the mercy of the unbreds. And I'd say that things tend to work out pretty well in the long run when you follow the good Lord's path. So I'm likely getting at least a little something out of this. You wanna set a pot a-boilin'? I don't know where all your cookery is."

"You're after something. Is it revenge? I could figure that. There bad blood between you and the reverend?"

"Just see things differently, is all."

"And how's that? Reckon we should all have bleedin' hearts? 'Cause I seen my fair share of 'em, and weren't a one stayed that way after I sucked 'em dry. The elders were right. I'm a leech. Your's ain't the first charity I've got. Sooner or later, you'll find me mighty wearisome and go the same way the reverend went. The only one who ever stuck with me was Bert. And I don't figure I even deserved him."

Ella sighed. "If we all got what we deserved, I don't reckon any of us would be here today. But the Lord saw fit to keep us around, so it seems to me there oughta be at least a little mercy goin' around."

“I’ll take your mercy,” Melissa said with what would have been a sneer if it hadn’t been so half-hearted, “but you’re wasting your time. All I can do is suck folks dry.”

“Well, it don’t have to be that way. I don’t figure you need a cartload of teeth as much as you need a pal. I’ll help you get your feet under you again. You’ll find you can make it on your own pretty soon, I’d reckon. Another year or so, Earnest will be able to start helpin’ you out with some things, keep you company and such. And I’ll help you out along the way, teach you a trade maybe.”

Melissa choked back a sob as if swallowing poison. “I’m too far gone to learn nothin’, leastways from some do-gooder who’s got it in mind to save me.”

“That’s okay, miss. You don’t have to believe in yourself yet. Just know that I ain’t any better than you is, and I’ll stick around until you get your head on straight. You done had yourself an awful blow, and I’m sorry about ... your husband ... and everything else, and ... well, all of it.” Ella coughed, scooted closer, and gave Melissa Daly a tentative pat on the back.

Melissa melted at Ella’s touch like a wax candle held against glowing steel. She buried her head in Ella’s shoulder and let out a sob fit to break the heart of a bullhusker. “God forgive me, I’m so happy he’s gone!”

The bodies lay twisted in a scattered mess. The flanking team meant to trap the Tuckers instead looked on the remains of a massacre, with only one cart on hand to take all the corpses back to town. When the shock of it had passed, they loaded the bodies as best as they could into the cart, stopping only to curse the Tuckers or kick at a cast-off cartridge box.

One of the Greenbrier foremen watched the grim work with a stormy gaze. "Damn those guns. We were over-matched. Still are. Look at that tree line. Ain't no more than a couple folks in the whole clan could pull a headshot from that range, and it looks like the Tuckers did it with thirty. Seamus was a fool to think he could outdo that smokeless gunpowder. You were right. We need someone on the inside. We need to take the edge off that powder."

The lean, dark-haired young man next to him nodded, answering only with a look from hollow eyes.

"How do you think we ought to go about it, Omar?"

The young man didn't answer right away. "I don't know. Play it by ear, like I done before. Folks will have to cough up a hundred jaws for me to manage it."

"We'll take it from the dead."

"Call a meetin', then. I can leave as soon as the headsmen give their go-ahead."

"Just promise me you'll make them pay, Omar."

"They'll pay," Omar said, looking to the cartload of bodies. "I can promise you that. The Tuckers will dearly pay."

Also by

Don't miss the rest of The Tucker Clan Saga:

For Peace and Purpose

For the Loved and Lost

Sneak Peek at For Peace and Purpose

Glistening with sweat under the naked glow of an LED light, a young man waited for a fate worse than death. The stainless-steel shackles around his hands and feet kept him rooted to the surgical chair that comprised the sole furnishment in the tiled, windowless room.

When the door latch snapped open, the young man jerked against his restraints hard enough to draw blood from his wrists. The door swung open on silent hinges to reveal a man in fatigues too clean to have ever seen any action abroad—a colonel, perhaps, but without any insignia.

"Salvador Brody," the officer said, as if he were a doctor confirming a patient's identity before administering treatment. The young man didn't give an answer, and the officer didn't press for one. Everything at this point amounted to mere formalities.

A thick silence passed between them before the military man exhaled through his nose. "The crucible for silver, and the furnace for gold, Mr. Brody. No other way around it. You've got the same odds as everyone else. My own nephew went just yesterday."

Young Mr. Brody looked at the colonel with baleful eyes.

"You're about to become part of something far greater than you or me," the officer said. "You are about to render a great service to your country."

"I've already served my country," the sacrificial lamb said with an accent that marked him as an odd transplant from what was a mostly unmodified, backwards community.

"Any grunt can do what you've done so far. This..." The colonel leaned in, putting a reassuring hand on Brody's shoulder. "This is what you were *made* for. It's your destiny."

"I didn't get any say in what I was made for."

"None of us did. Our fates were written in petri dishes and grown in labs. But our creators knew what they were doing. Trust the plan."

"From the looks of the news, it don't look like the plan's working out too well."

The lines around the colonel's eyes deepened in a grimace that looked sincere. "A lot of people have died. People higher than my pay grade knew that going in. And I'll tell you right now, a lot more people are going to die before this is over. But you—*you* are special. You've been granted something like immortality. Progress marches on, Mr. Brody, and the next age will be an age of gods. But time and circumstances are not on our side, and it's my job to make sure the first gods of the next age will be red-blooded Americans."

A moan in the darkness rose to become a wail and woke Old Man Brody from a fitful slumber. His hand went to his raw throat, and he realized the howl had been his own. *Another nightmare.* He lay back down, waiting for the relief of reality to calm his heart.

But that relief never came. A fresh rivulet of sweat ran down his temple, and he realized he had not woken from a nightmare; he'd woken into one. Something wicked had pulled him back from oblivion. Something that was still in the room with him.

Eyes straining in the dark, Old Man Brody pulled the matchet from his bedside sheath with a palsied hand and tried to murmur, "Who's there?" He couldn't seem to get the words out—not that it mattered either way. This darkness would give him no answer.

He struck a whetstone against his matchet in a shivering swipe and lit the wick of his bedside lantern on the fifth try. Wavering orange light bloomed in the narrow confines of his bedchamber. In the aged wallpaper of the wall opposite him, words were etched: *I require sacrifice.*

Old Man Brody forced himself to blink and look away, to think of loved ones long gone—either of his two wives, smiling in the light of morning. Images of their pale, lifeless faces flashed before him, and he lost the tenuous control over himself. “Goddamn you, you won’t have me or any one of mine!” he hollered. “Not a one!”

The darkness outside his room gave no answer but for the skittering of retreating claws on worn-out planks.

Acknowledgements

An acknowledgments section is essentially a space for a writer to say "Hey Mom! I wrote a book!" I'm man enough to admit it and artless enough to get on with it.

Hey, Mom. I wrote a book. Thanks to my mom, Nina Beaver, and my cousin, Joshua Lewis, for reading through very early drafts and still suffering to keep me around in spite of it. Sorry for the bad language; I promise I don't say those words normally. I'm also not a rapist. And I have yet to tamper with human germline DNA.

A big thank you to my wife, who was at ground zero for most of the writing of this novel, who convinced me to split one story into two and then into three parts, and who refused to accept "okay" as a final draft. Thanks for bearing with me through my bouts of writer's block and the whole tortured artist shtick.

Thanks to my creative writing teacher, Michael Czyzniejewski, who gave me the confidence to believe I just might pull this off.

This novel took eleven years to write, and there likely wasn't a single friend or family member who wasn't roped into listening to my ramblings somehow. Even if you didn't think we were talking about this book, we were, and it helped.

Thank you to the folks on Critique Circle. I know you about as well as I know anyone on the Internet, which is not much at all, but I learned a lot from y'uns.

Finally, a huge thanks to my sister, Emily Beaver, without whom this novel likely would never have seen the light of day. Your continual feedback and advice has always been spot-on, and your patience inexhaustible.

About the author

Ethan Warrener grew up in Southwest Missouri, which resembles West Virginia if you really squint. If he's not writing or teaching, he's spending any extra free time with his wife and kids or playing too many video games. As you might expect from a Midwesterner, he's an occasional farmer, a regular churchgoer, and a huge metalhead. For Home and Hearth is his first novel fit to see the light of day.

You can connect with Ethan Warrener on:

Website: https://www.ethanwarrenerauthor.com/

Goodreads: https://www.goodreads.com/author/show/22454806.Ethan_Warrener

Facebook: https://www.facebook.com/profile.php?id=100082438853863

www.ingramcontent.com/pod-product-compliance
Lightning Source LLC
LaVergne TN
LVHW100509110826
845146LV00002B/571

* 9 7 9 8 9 8 5 5 3 0 9 0 2 *